By J. Kenner

THE STARK TRILOGY
Release Me
Claim Me
Complete Me

STARK EVER AFTER NOVELLAS
Take Me
Have Me
Play My Game
Seduce Me
Unwrap Me
Deepest Kiss

STARK INTERNATIONAL NOVELS

THE JACKSON STEELE TRILOGY
Say My Name
On My Knees
Under My Skin

THE DIRTIEST TRILOGY
Dirtiest Secret
Hottest Mess

MOST WANTED SERIES
Wanted
Heated
Ignited

say my name

say my name

say my name

A STARK NOVEL

J. KENNER

BANTAM BOOKS NEW YORK

A Bantam Books Trade Paperback Original

Copyright © 2015 by Julie Kenner
Excerpt from *On My Knees* by J. Kenner copyright © 2015 by Julie Kenner

Published in the United States by Bantam Books, an imprint of Random House, a division of Penguin Random House LLC, New York.

BANTAM BOOKS and the HOUSE colophon are registered trademarks of Penguin Random House LLC.

This book contains an excerpt from the forthcoming book *On My Knees* by J. Kenner. This excerpt has been set for this edition only and may not reflect the final content of the forthcoming edition.

Library of Congress Cataloging-in-Publication Data
Kenner, Julie.
Say my name : a Stark novel / J. Kenner.
pages ; cm.—(Stark)
ISBN 978-0-553-39519-8
ebook ISBN 978-0-553-39520-4
1. Man-woman relationships—Fiction. 2. Sexual dominance and submission—Fiction. I. Title.
PS3611.E665S29 2015
813'.6—dc23   2014049095

Printed in the United States of America on acid-free paper

randomhousebooks.com

9 8 7 6 5

acknowledgments

For my family. Because they've gotten used to Mom walking around with stories in her head.

say my name

say my name

one

The *thwump-thwump* of the helicopter's rotors fills my head like a whisper, a secret message that I cannot escape. *Not him, not now. Not him, not now.*

But I know damn well that my plea is futile, my words flat. I can't run. I can't hide. I can only continue as I am—hurtling at over a hundred miles per hour on a collision course with a destiny I thought I had escaped five years ago. And with the man I'd left behind.

A man I tell myself I no longer want—but can't deny that I desperately need.

I clutch my fingers tighter around the copy of *Architectural Digest* in my lap. I do not need to look down to see the man on the cover. He is as vivid in my mind today as he was back then. His hair a glossy black, with just the slightest hint of copper when the sun hits it just so. His eyes so blue and deep you could drown in them.

On the magazine, he sits casually on the corner of a desk, his dark gray trousers perfectly creased. His white shirt pressed. His cuff links gleaming. Behind him, the Manhattan skyline rises, framed in a wall of glass. He exudes determination and confidence, but in my mind's eye, I see even more.

I see sensuality and sin. Power and seduction. I see a man with his shirt collar open, his tie hanging loose. A man completely at home in his own skin, who commands a room simply by entering it.

I see the man who wanted me.

I see the man who terrified me.

Jackson Steele.

I remember the way his skin felt as it brushed mine. I even remember his scent, wood and musk and a hint of something smoky.

Most of all, I remember the way his words seduced me. The way he made me feel. And now, here above the Pacific, I can't deny the current of excitement that runs through me, simply from the prospect of seeing him again.

And that, of course, is what scares me.

As if to emphasize that thought, the helicopter banks sharply, sending my stomach lurching. I reach out to steady myself, pressing my hand against the window as I look out at the deep indigo of the Pacific below me and the jagged Los Angeles coastline receding in the distance.

"We're on our approach, Ms. Brooks," the pilot says a short while later, his voice crystal clear through my headphones. "Just a few more minutes."

"Thanks, Clark."

I don't like air travel, and I especially don't like helicopters. Perhaps I have an overactive imagination, but I can't seem to shake the mental image of dozens of absolutely essential screws and wires getting wiggled loose by the persistent motion of these constantly vibrating machines.

I've come to accept that I can't avoid the occasional trip by plane or helicopter. When you work as the executive assistant to one of the world's wealthiest and most powerful men, air travel is just part of the package. But while I've resigned myself to that reality—and even managed to become somewhat Zen about the whole thing—I still get all twisted up during takeoff and landing. There's something horribly unnatural about the way the earth rises up to meet you, even while you are simultaneously careening toward the ground.

Not that I can actually see any ground. As far as I can tell, we're still entirely over water, and I am just about to point out that little fact when a slice of the island appears in my window. *My island.* Just seeing it makes me smile, and I draw in one breath and then another until I actually feel reasonably calm and somewhat put together.

Of course, the island isn't really mine. It belongs to my boss, Damien Stark. Or, more specifically, it belongs to Stark Vacation Properties, which is a division of Stark Real Estate Development, which is an arm of Stark Holdings, which is a wholly owned subsidiary of Stark International, which is one of the most profitable companies in the world, which is owned by one of the most powerful men in the world.

In my mind, though, Santa Cortez island is mine. The island, the project, and all the potential that goes with it.

Santa Cortez is one of the smaller Channel Islands that run up the coast of California. Located a little behind Catalina, it was used for many years as a naval facility, along with San Clemente Island. Unlike San Clemente, which is still operated by the military and sports an army base, barracks, and various other signs of civilization, Santa Cortez lacks any development at all; it was used for hand-to-hand combat and weapons training. At least, that's what I was told. The navy is not known for being forthright about its activities.

Several months ago, I'd noticed a small article in the *Los Angeles Times* discussing the military's presence in California. The article mentioned both islands, but noted that the military was ceasing operations on Santa Cortez. There wasn't any other information, but I'd taken the article to Stark.

"It might be up for sale, and if so, I figured we should act fast," I'd said, handing him the article. I'd just finished briefing him on his schedule for the day, and we were moving briskly down the corridor toward a conference room where no less than twelve banking executives from three different countries waited with Charles Maynard, Stark's attorney, for the commencement of a long-planned tax and investment strategy meeting.

"I know you've been looking for potential sites for a couples' resort in the Bahamas," I continued, "but since we haven't yet found a suitable island, I was thinking that in the meantime, a high-end getaway location for families with easier access to the States might have real potential as a business model."

He'd taken the paper, reading as he walked, and then stopped outside the conference room's glass doors. I'd come to know his face during the five years I'd worked for him, but right then I hadn't even an inkling what he was thinking.

He handed the article back to me, held up one finger in a silent demand for me to wait, and then stepped inside the room, addressing the men as he entered. "Gentlemen, I apologize, but something has come up. Charles, if you could take over the meeting?"

And then he was back in the corridor with me, not bothering to wait for Maynard's reply or the executives' acquiescence, but absolutely confident that things would go smoothly, and just the way he wanted them to.

"Call Nigel Galway at the Pentagon," he'd said as we moved down the hall back toward his office. "He's in my personal contacts. Tell him I'm looking to acquire the island. Then get in touch with Aiden. He's gone to the Century City site to help Trent with some problem that's come up during construction. Ask if he can get away long enough to meet us for lunch at The Ivy."

"Oh," I said, trying to find my balance. "Us?"

Aiden made sense. Aiden Ward was the vice president of Stark Real Estate Development, and was currently overseeing the construction of Stark Plaza, a trio of office buildings off Santa Monica Boulevard in Century City. What I didn't understand was why Mr. Stark would want me at the lunch, when his usual practice was to simply fill me in after the fact on any post-meeting details that I needed to track or follow up on.

"If you're spearheading this project, it makes sense for you to be at the initial meeting."

"Spearheading?" Honestly, my head was spinning.

"If you're interested in real estate development, especially for commercial projects, you couldn't ask for a better mentor than Aiden," he said. "Of course, you'll be pulling longer hours. I'll still need you on my desk, but you can delegate as much as makes sense. I think Rachel would like to pick up some more hours, anyway," he added, referring to his weekend assistant, Rachel Peters.

"Use the business plan that Trent put together for the Bahamas proposal as a model, and work up your own draft and timeline." He glanced at his watch. "You won't be able to finish before lunch, but you can take us through some talking points." He met my eyes, and I saw the humor in his. "Or am I assuming too much? I thought that real estate was one of your particular interests, but if you're not looking to shift into a managerial role—"

"No!" I practically blurt the word, my shoulders squared and my back straight. "No. I mean, yes. I mean, yes, Mr. Stark, I want to work on this project." What I really wanted was to not hyperventilate, but I wasn't entirely sure that was going to be possible.

"Good," he'd said. We'd reached my desk in the reception area outside his office. "Call Nigel. Make the lunch arrangements. And we'll go from there."

Go from there had led in a more or less straight line directly to this moment. I'm officially the project manager for The Resort at Cortez, a Stark Vacation Property. At least I am today.

Hopefully, I'll still be tomorrow. Because that's the question, isn't it? Whether the news that I received two hours ago is going to shatter the Santa Cortez project, or whether I can salvage the project along with my nascent career in real estate.

Too bad I need Jackson Steele if I'm going to pull that off.

My stomach twists unpleasantly and I tell myself not to worry. Jackson will help me. He has to, because right now everything I want is riding on him.

Considering my frayed nerves, I'm especially grateful that our landing is soft. I slide the magazine into my leather tote, then unstrap myself and wait for Clark to open the door. As soon as he does, I breathe in the fresh scent of the ocean and lift my face to the breeze. Immediately, I feel better, as if neither my worries nor my motion sickness are any match for the pure beauty of this place.

And beautiful it is. Beautiful and unspoiled, with native grasses and trees, dunes, and shell-scattered beaches.

Whatever the military had been doing here, it didn't harm the natural habitat. In fact, the only signs of civilization are right where we've landed. This area sports a tarmac sufficient for two helicopters, a boat dock, a small metal building used for equipment storage, and another small building with two chemical toilets. There's also a Bobcat, a generator, and various other bits of machinery that have been carted in so that the process of clearing the land can begin. Not to mention the two security cameras that had been mounted to satisfy both Stark International security and the insurance company.

There is a second copter beside the one that Clark set down, and beyond it is a makeshift path that leads away from this ramshackle work area to the still-wild interior of the island. And, presumably, to Damien, his wife, Nikki, and Wyatt Royce, the photographer Damien hired to take seaside portraits of his wife and also predevelopment photos of the island.

While Clark remains with the bird, I follow the path. Almost immediately, I regret not taking the time to change out of my skirt and heels before making this jaunt. The ground is rocky and uneven and my shoes are going to end up scuffed and battered. I'd planned to put on jeans and hiking boots, but I'd been in a hurry, and if I can get this project back on track, then I figure my favorite navy pair of heels are a small price to pay.

The ground slopes up gently, and as I crest a small hill I find myself looking down at a sandy inlet nestled against a cluster of rocks. Waves batter the stones, sending droplets of water up to sparkle in the air like diamonds. On the beach area, I see Damien slide his arm around his wife's waist as she leans her head upon his shoulder while they both look out at the wide expanse of the sea.

Nikki and I have become good friends, so it's not as though I've never seen the two of them together. But there is something so sweetly intimate about the moment that I feel as though I should turn back and give them time alone. But I have no time to squander, and so instead I clear my throat as I continue forward.

I know of course that they won't hear me. The sound of the ocean crashing against the shore was sufficient to drown out the helicopter's approach; it's certainly enough to cover my small noises.

As if to prove my point, Damien presses his lips to Nikki's temple. Something tight twists inside me. I think of the magazine in my tote—and the image of the man on the cover. He'd kissed me the same way, and as I remember the butterfly-soft caress of his lips against my skin, I feel my eyes sting. I tell myself it's the wind and the saltwater spray, but of course that's not true.

It's regret and loss. And, yes, it's fear.

Fear that I'm about to open the door to something I desperately want, but know that I can't handle.

Fear that I screwed up royally so many years ago.

And the cold, bitter certainty that, if I'm not very, very careful, the wall I've built around myself will come tumbling down, and my horrible secrets will spill out for all the world to see.

"Sylvia?"

I jump a little, startled, and realize that I have been standing there, staring blankly toward the sea, my mind far, far away. "Mr. Stark. Sorry. I—"

"Are you all right?" It's Nikki who speaks, her expression concerned as she hurries toward me. "You look a little shaky." She's beside me now, and she takes my arm.

"No, I'm fine," I lie. "Just a little motion sick from the helicopter. Where's Wyatt?"

"He set up down the beach," Stark says. "We thought it was best if he went ahead and got started on the shots for the brochure."

I wince, because I am over an hour late. The plan had been for me to spend the morning in Los Angeles while Nikki, Damien, and Wyatt came early to the island. I'd arrive later, once they'd had time to complete the private portrait shoot, and I'd spend the rest of the morning working with Wyatt to capture a series of shots that we could use in the resort's marketing materials.

Damien would pilot his copter back to the city, and then Wyatt, Nikki, and I would return with Clark. Nikki and I recently discovered that we share a love of photography and Wyatt has offered to give us some pointers after the work is finished.

"You didn't bring your camera," Nikki says, her forehead creasing into a frown. "Something *is* wrong."

"No," I say, then, "okay, yes. Maybe." I meet Stark's eyes. "I need to talk to you."

"I'll go check on Wyatt," Nikki says.

"No, stay. I mean if Mr. Stark—if Damien—doesn't mind." I'm still uncomfortable calling him by his first name during working hours. But as he has repeatedly pointed out, I've spent a good number of hours drinking cocktails by his pool with his wife. After so many Cosmopolitans, formality when we're alone begins to feel strained.

"Of course I don't mind," he says. "What's happened?"

I take a deep breath, and spill the news I've been hanging on to. "Martin Glau pulled out of the project this morning."

I see the change in Damien's face immediately. The quick flash of shock followed by anger, then immediately replaced with steely determination. Beside him, Nikki isn't nearly so controlled.

"Glau? But he's been nothing but enthusiastic. Why on earth would he want to quit?"

"Not want to," I clarify. "Has. Done. He's gone."

For a moment, Damien just stares at me. "Gone?"

"Apparently he's moved to Tibet."

Damien's eyes widen almost imperceptibly. "Has he?"

"He's sold his property, shut down his firm, and told his attorney to let his clients know that he's decided to spend the rest of his life in prayerful meditation."

"The son of a bitch," Damien says with the kind of contained fury I rarely see in his business dealings, though the press has made much of his temper over the years. "What the hell is he thinking?"

I understand his anger. For that matter, I share it. This is *my* project, and Glau has managed to screw us all. The Resort at Cortez might be a Stark property, but that doesn't mean that it's fully financed by Damien, or by Damien's companies. No, we've worked our tails off over the last three months pulling together a who's who of investors—and every single one of them named two reasons they were committed to the project: Glau's reputation as an architect, and Damien's reputation as a businessman.

He runs his fingers through his hair. "All right then, so we handle this. If his attorney is notifying clients today, the press will get wind of it soon, and everything is going to unravel fast."

I grimace. Just the thought makes my skin feel clammy, because this project is mine. I conceived it, I pitched it, and I've worked my ass off to get it off the ground. It's more than a resort to me; it's a stepping stone to my future.

I have to keep this project alive. And, dammit, I *will* keep it alive. Even if that means approaching the one man I swore I would never see again.

"We need a plan in place," I say. "A definitive course of action to present to the investors."

Despite the situation, I see a hint of amusement in Damien's eyes. "And you have a suggestion already. Good. Let's hear it."

I nod and tighten my grip on my tote bag. "The investors were impressed by Glau's reputation and his portfolio," I say. "But that's not something we can replicate in another architect." As the moving force behind some of the most impressive and innovative buildings in modern history, Glau was a bona fide starchitect—an architect with both the skill and celebrity status to ensure a project's success.

"So I suggest we present the one man who by all accounts is poised to meet or surpass Glau's reputation." I reach into my bag and pull out the magazine, then pass it to Damien.

"Jackson Steele."

"He has the experience, the style, the reputation. He's not just a rising star in the field—with Glau out of the picture, I think it's fair to say that he's the new crown prince. And that's not all. Because even more so than Glau, Steele has the kind of celebrity appeal that this project can use. The sort of publicity potential that will not only excite the investors, but will be a huge boon when we market the resort to the public."

"Is that so?" Stark says, his voice oddly flat. I see him catch Nikki's eyes, and can't help but wonder at the quick look that passes between the two of them.

"Read the article," I urge, determined to prove my point. "Not only is there a rumor that the story surrounding one of his projects is going to be adapted into a feature film, but they've already produced a documentary on him and that museum he did last year in Amsterdam."

"I know," Damien says. "It's premiering at the Chinese theater tonight."

"Yes," I say eagerly. "Are you going? You could talk to him there."

Damien's mouth twists with what I think is irony. "Oddly enough, I wasn't invited. It's only on my radar because Wyatt mentioned it. He's been hired to take the red carpet photos and some candids of the guests."

"But that's my point," I press. "It's a red carpet event. This guy has celebrity sparkle all the way. We need him on our team. And the article also says that he's looking to open a satellite office in Los Angeles, which suggests that he's trying to move more into the West Coast market."

"Jackson Steele isn't the only name in the pot," Damien says.

"No," I agree. "But right now he's the only one with a serious spotlight on him. More than that, I've already looked into the few others who might appeal to the investors, and none have current availability. Steele does. I didn't present Steele as a possible architect in the original development plan because he was committed for the next six months to a project in Dubai." At the time, I'd been grateful that Jackson was unavailable because I didn't want to be in exactly this position. Now, however, things have changed.

"The Dubai project fell through," I continue. "Political and financial issues, I guess. It's all outlined in the article. I did some quick research, and I don't believe Steele has another green-lit project, but it won't stay that way for long. Jackson Steele can save the Cortez resort. Please trust me when I tell you that I wouldn't suggest him if I didn't absolutely believe that."

And wasn't that the god's honest truth?

"I believe it, too," Damien says. "And I agree with your assessment of the situation. If we don't get Jackson Steele on board right away, we'll lose our investors. The only other way to keep the project alive is if I fully fund the project, either using corporate assets or my personal funds." He draws in a breath. "Sylvia," he says gently, "that's not the way I do business."

"I know. Of course I know that. That's why I'm suggesting we approach Jackson. I mean Steele," I correct, biting back a wince at my unintentional familiarity. "This is a high profile project— exactly the kind of thing that he's focusing on these days. He'll sign on. Everything about it is what he's looking for."

Once again, Damien and Nikki share a look, and worry snakes through me.

"I'm sorry," I say. "But is there something I don't know?"

"Jackson Steele has no interest in working for Stark International," Nikki says, after a brief hesitation.

"He—what?" It takes a moment for the words to sink in. "How do you know?"

"We met him when we were in the Bahamas," Nikki explains. "Damien offered to bring him in on the ground floor for the Bahamas project, pulling him in even before Stark International acquired property. Full access to every detail of the project. But he made it very clear that he doesn't want to work for Damien or any of Damien's companies. He says that Damien casts a long shadow, and he's not interested in being caught under it."

"In other words, we won't be landing Steele for this project," Damien says. He glances at his watch, then at Nikki. "I need to get back," he says, then returns his attention to me. "Call the investors personally. This isn't the kind of thing I can sit on. I'm truly sorry, Syl," Damien adds, and it's the nickname that drives home how real this is. The project is dead. *My* project is dead.

I tell myself I should be relieved not to risk the memories. That I've been a fool to think that I have the strength to tempt my nightmares. That I should just let this project go rather than walk right back into everything I once ran from.

No.

No. I've worked too hard, and this project means too much. I can't just let it go. Not like that. Not without a fight.

And, yes, perhaps there is a part of me that wants to see Jackson Steele again. To prove to myself that I can do this. That I can see him, talk to him, work so goddamn intimately with him—and somehow manage to not shatter under the weight of it all.

"Please," I say to Damien, as I squeeze my hands into fists and tell myself that the staccato beat of my heart and the clamminess of my skin stem from fear of losing the project and not the thought of seeing Jackson again. "Let me talk to him. We need to at least try."

"There will be other projects, Ms. Brooks." His voice is gentle, but firm. "This isn't your last opportunity."

"I believe you," I say. "But I've never known you to walk away from a floundering deal if there was any chance of saving it."

"Based on what I know of Mr. Steele, there isn't a chance."

"I think there is. Please, let me try. I'm just asking for the weekend," I rush to add. "Just enough time for me to meet with Mr. Steele and pitch the project to him."

For a moment, Damien says nothing. Then he nods. "I can't keep this from the investors," he finally says. "But it's already Friday, and we can make that work for us. Call them. Let them know we need to update them about the project, and schedule a conference call for Monday morning."

I nod, quick and businesslike. But inside, I am jumping with glee.

"That gives you the weekend," Damien continues. "Monday morning we'll either announce that we have Jackson Steele on board, or that the project is in trouble."

"We'll have him on board," I say, with a confidence born more of hope than reality.

Damien's head tilts ever so slightly to the left, as if considering my words. "What makes you think so?"

I lick my lips. "I—I met him. About five years ago in Atlanta. Right before I came to work for you, actually. I don't know if he'll agree, but I think he'll hear me out." At least, I thought he would before I learned that he'd already turned down a Stark project.

Now, the entire playing field has changed. Before, I'd thought I was bringing him a kick-ass project on a silver platter. Me, doing a favor for Jackson. Me, in control.

Now I know the opposite is true.

He can walk away. He can say no. He can lift his middle finger and tell me to stay the hell out of his life.

I think about the last conversation we had—a conversation that had ripped me apart.

I need you to do something for me, I'd said.

Anything.

No questions, no arguments. It's important.

Whatever you need, baby, I promise. You only have to ask.

He had kept his word then. He'd done as I asked, even though it had just about destroyed us both.

Now there is something else I need.

And I desperately hope that once again I only have to ask.

two

"Whatever time he has available today," I say, holding my phone tight to my left ear and my hand tight over my right. Even so, it's hard to hear Jackson's New York–based secretary over the noise of the helicopter powering down.

"I'm sorry, Ms. Brooks. Mr. Steele's documentary is screening in Los Angeles this evening, so I'm afraid every minute is booked."

I'm on the roof of Stark Tower downtown, and despite the sensation of literally being on top of the world, I do not feel composed or in control. I want to pull open the door to enter the elevator alcove, but I know from experience that I run the risk of losing my cell signal, and I have a feeling that if I let this woman get off the phone I won't ever get her back.

So I stand in the wind with the sun burning down on me and the asphalt all around me, feeling decidedly at the mercy of not only the elements, but of Jackson Steele, his secretary, and even the damned cellular provider.

"How about tomorrow?" I ask. "I realize that's Saturday, but if he's not going right back to New York—"

"Mr. Steele will be staying in Los Angeles for at least a week."

"Perfect," I say, going limp with relief. "When would be convenient?"

"Just a moment, please. I'll see if I can reach him on his cell."

I stand there, feeling a little foolish, as the peppy hold music plays. When the phone clicks, signaling that the woman has returned to the line, I straighten my back and shoulders as if springing to attention, then roll my eyes at my own ridiculous behavior.

"I'm afraid there is no convenient time, Ms. Brooks."

"Oh, no, really. I'm happy to make myself available anytime. And if it's more convenient I'll go to his hotel or he can come to my office. Whatever works."

I hear her sigh, long and deep, and I bite my lower lip as she says, "No, Ms. Brooks, you misunderstand. Mr. Steele has asked that I decline your request for a meeting. And to express his regrets, of course."

"His regrets?"

"He said that you would understand. He said that you two discussed this already. In Atlanta."

"He—what?"

"I'm terribly sorry, Ms. Brooks. But I can assure you that Mr. Steele's refusal is final."

My mouth has gone completely dry. Not that it matters. I may want to argue, but it is too late. The line has gone dead.

I stare at my phone for a moment, not quite believing what I've just heard.

Jackson said no.

"Shit." I run my fingers through my hair, then look up at Clark, who has secured the helicopter and is heading my direction.

"Trouble?" he asks, his brow furrowed as he peers at my face.

"Not if I have anything to say about it," I reply. Because there is no way I'm calling Damien and telling him that I blew it so badly I couldn't even get a meeting. Which means that I very badly need a Plan B. Another starchitect. A magic potion. A goddamn freaking miracle.

I start to follow Clark into the alcove, then stop short, remembering. "Have a good weekend," I say to him. "I need to make one more call."

And then I scroll through my contacts, find Wyatt's number, and call the photographer to see if he can wrangle that miracle.

"You do know how awesome this is, right?" Cass asks as she climbs into the limo and takes a seat opposite me.

She looks amazing, as usual, in a slinky black dress slit so far up her thigh it's a wonder she didn't flash the neighborhood. The dress is held up by a single, simple bow over her left shoulder, and she fills it out with the kind of curves I can only dream about. Her hair is red this week, and she is wearing it up so as to accentuate the dress. Other than a small diamond stud in her nose, she wears no jewelry, which makes the tattoo of an exotic bird on her shoulder, its tail feathers trailing down her arm in an explosion of color, all the more stunning.

As soon as she's settled, Edward shuts the door and returns to the driver's seat. We don't see him, as we are snug behind the privacy screen, but I feel the motion as the limo pulls away from the curb in front of Cass's tiny house in Venice Beach.

"Seriously, Syl. Your job perks rock."

"Definitely on the upside of awesome," I agree as I pass her a glass of wine. The limo is one of the Stark International fleet, and Edward is Damien's personal driver, on loan to me for this evening. With any luck, I'll make this worth Edward's overtime.

"I think we both need a moment of deep contemplation," Cass says. "You, in appreciation of the serious perks of your job. And me, in gratitude that you are so antisocial that there's no one else you wanted to invite tonight."

"Bitch," I say, but I'm laughing as she closes her eyes and tilts her head back.

"Ommm," she says, as if she's in a yoga class and not in the back of a stretch limo on her way to a Hollywood release party.

I'd debated whether or not to bring her, but in the end had decided that not only would Cass get a kick out of a red carpet premiere, but she'd also make a damn fine human security blanket.

Cass has been my best friend since I marched into her dad's tattoo parlor at the ripe old age of fifteen. He'd sent me packing, telling me in no uncertain terms that he wasn't about to lose his license so some Brentwood brat could get a tat in order to piss off Mommy and Daddy.

I hadn't cried—I haven't cried since I was fourteen—but I had felt my face go hot as my temper and frustration rose. I'd called him a bastard, yelled that he didn't know a thing about my parents and he sure as hell didn't know anything about me. I don't actually remember calling him a fucking prick, but Cass assures me that I did.

What I do remember is storming out, then running blindly until I reached the beach. I'd rushed across the bike path, almost knocking over a toddler, and then tripped in the sand. I'd fallen facedown and just laid there like an idiot, my forehead on my arm and my eyes squeezed together because I wanted to cry—so help me, I wanted the tears to flow—but they didn't. They couldn't.

I don't know how long I laid there, breathing shallow so I wouldn't suck up the sand. All I know is that she was there when I looked up, all long legs and tanned skin and short black hair slicked into dozens of spikes. She crouched on her haunches, her elbows on her knees and her chin in her hand as she stared at me. Just rocked back and forth and stared.

"Go away," I'd said.

"It's not his fault. My mom bailed, and he's gotta take care of me, so it's not his fault. I mean, if they yank his license, they'll close his shop and then they'll repossess the house and we'll end up living in the back of his Buick, and I'll have to turn tricks in Hollywood just to keep us in Snickers and Diet Coke."

My gut clenched at her words, and for a second I thought I would be sick. "Don't," I said. "That's not even funny."

Her eyes narrowed as she studied me, then she stood up, as gangly as a colt. She held out her hand to help me up. "He can't do it, but I can."

"Can what?"

"You want a tat, I can give you a tat." She shrugged, as if tattooing someone was the kind of thing every teenage girl knew how to do.

"Bullshit."

"Suit yourself." She started to walk away.

I pushed myself up so that I was kneeling in the sand and watched her leave, never once looking back to see if I'd changed my mind.

I had. "Wait!"

She stopped. A moment passed, then another, then she turned. She crossed her arms over her chest and waited.

"How old are you?" I asked.

"Sixteen. How old are you?"

"I just turned fifteen. You can really do it?"

She came toward me, then stuck her leg out so that there was no missing the black rose on her ankle. "I can do it."

"Will it hurt?"

She snorted. "Duh, yeah. But not any more than it would if he did it."

I assume she was right about that, but I'll never know for sure. Because Cass is the only one who has ever given me a tattoo, and she's given me several. That first day we'd hung out on the beach until her dad had locked the shop. Then we'd snuck back in, and she'd adorned my pubic bone with a beautiful golden lock, sealed tight and bound with chains.

She asked me why I wanted that design, and I hadn't told her. Not then. And even later, I didn't tell her everything. Just the surface, but not the deep-down truth. And even though she's my best friend, I don't think I ever will.

That tat—and the ones that followed—are for me alone. They are secrets and triumphs, weaknesses and strengths. They are a map, and they are memories.

Most of all, they are mine.

"So who's going to be there?" Cass asks after a while. "There's a red carpet, right?"

"That's what I hear. But don't get too excited. It's a documentary, not a blockbuster. I'm guessing a few studio execs, some agents, maybe a few C-listers."

"Doesn't change the fact that we're gonna walk down a red fucking carpet. I guess I can knock that one off my bucket list."

"I guess you can. The dress rocks, by the way. Where did you get it?"

"That Goodwill near Beverly Hills. It's my favorite hunting ground." Cass owns Totally Tattoo now and makes a good living, but it wasn't always that way, and I don't think I've ever once seen her buy retail.

"Usually I only score a ten-dollar pair of 7 For All Mankind jeans and some kick-ass tees," she continues. "But this time there was an entire rack of evening clothes. I swear, I don't get those women. Wear it once and then donate it." She shrugs philosophically. "But whatever. I'm happy to take advantage of their economic idiocy."

"And look incredibly hot in your frugality."

"Damn skippy. You look pretty amazing yourself," she adds.

"I should. I spent two hours getting a trim and having my makeup done." I've worn my hair short since I was fifteen. That's when I cut off my long, loose waves in favor of a cut that's a cross between a pixie and a bob. At the time, all I'd wanted was a change, and as dramatic a one as I thought I could get away with. Since shaving my head was a bit too radical even for my mood, I'd dialed it back.

Now, though, I genuinely like the cut. According to Kelly, the girl who does my hair, it suits my oval-shaped face and highlights my cheekbones. Honestly, I don't care about the reason. I just want to like what I see in the mirror.

"The red tips are especially awesome," Cass says.

"I know, right? Isn't it fun?" My hair is dark brown with natural golden highlights. Frankly, I like it that way, so I've never been tempted to follow Cass's lead and dye my hair temporarily pink or purple or even just plain red.

Tonight, however, I thought I'd have a little fun, and I'd asked Kelly to see about giving me some colored highlights. She went a step further, focusing on the tips of a few chunks of hair in a way that seems not only fun but elegant.

"It's awesome, yes, but what I meant was that the color matches your dress. Which is fabulous, by the way."

"It should be. It cost a freaking fortune."

I may not spend my life trolling consignment stores like Cass, but I rarely spend as much on a dress as I did on this one. It's fire-engine red, and though I decided to go with cocktail length, I think it's as elegant and sexy as Cass's floor-skimming evening gown. And, yes, as I did a turn in front of the dressing room mirror, I'd tried to see myself through Jackson's eyes. Not because I wanted to look hot—or, not entirely—but because I wanted to look success-ful. Competent.

Powerful.

"It works?" I ask Cass. "Not too slutty? Or worse, too corpo-rate?"

"It's perfect. You look like a confident, professional business-woman. And clearly you took my advice and invested in a padded push-up bra, because you even have cleavage."

"Bitch," I say, but with the utmost affection. I've got an athletic build, slim and lean. Which is great when it comes to finding clothes, but not so great when I'm trying to fill out a dress.

I expect her to shoot me a snarky comeback, but instead there is only silence. "What?" I demand, when I can't take it any longer.

"Are you sure you want to do this?"

It is the gentleness in her voice that cuts through me. Cass is loud and boisterous, and I am used to that. Softness from her can break me.

I nod. "I've put my heart and soul into this project. I'm not going to let it die if I can save it."

"Even if saving it hurts you?"

I force myself not to wince. "It won't."

"Dammit, Syl, it already has. Do you think I don't get it? There is no one who knows you better than I do, and in case you've forgotten, I'm the one who inked your back when you got back to LA from Atlanta. I know how wrecked you were, and I swear to god, if you hadn't been pumped up about the job with Stark you would have just crumbled into dust and blown away."

"Cass, don't—"

"Don't what? Don't worry about you?"

"It was five years ago. I put it behind me."

"And now it's back in front of you."

"No," I say, and then stop, because she is right. "Okay, maybe. Yes. Guilty as charged. I'm walking into the lion's den. Pouring the gasoline and striking the match. Jumping off the cliff. Pick your metaphor, because it doesn't matter. I have to do this."

"Why?"

"Are you really asking me that?"

Her shoulders droop. "No. I get it. I've watched you work this project. I know how much it means to you. It's like me and the studio. I loved working for my dad, but it's better now that the place is totally mine. I feel, I don't know, grown up. Complete."

"Yeah. It's like that."

"It's just that he already said no, right? He told Stark, and then he refused to even take a meeting with you. So do you really believe you can change his mind?"

"I have to believe it," I say. "Right now, unsupported optimism is all I've got going for me."

"Oh, man. Don't say that."

I lean forward to take her hand. "I can do this. And I'll be fine. Really. I'm not as fragile as I used to be. I can do this," I repeat, as much to convince myself as her.

"Fuck yeah, you can," she says, though the words are belied by a weak smile.

"Come on," I urge. "How can I fail when I look this hot?"

That gets a laugh. "You've got a point," she admits. "I mean, right now you look good enough to eat. And, hell, I can remember when you schlepped around looking so ratty that not even a dog would want to give you a lick."

"No kidding, right?" I'd spent my last years of high school trying very hard to be invisible. It was Cass who'd slapped some sense into me the summer before I started college at UCLA.

It's a day I remember with crystal clarity. It was a Tuesday, and we'd decided to go check out the campus that would soon become my home. A couple of upperclassmen had given us both the once-over, and my immediate reaction had been to hunch my shoulders and cross my arms over my chest.

"Are you a fucking moron?" she'd asked in that gentle Cassidy way that she has.

"Excuse me?"

"Oh, come on, Syl. You need to stop this. You're totally hot and you hide it under ugly sweatshirts and baggy jeans. And the hair—"

"I am *not* growing out my hair."

"Have ya considered maybe, I don't know, *combing* it?"

I'd shoved my hands into the pockets of my baggy jeans and stared at the sidewalk.

"Look," she'd said more gently. "I get it. I do. You wanna get all comfy on my shrink couch and I'll tell you exactly what is going on in that head of yours."

"I didn't finally tell you about what happened so you could pick me apart," I'd snapped.

"Guess what? I don't care. Because you are my best friend and I love you and you are handing that asshole power on a silver fucking platter."

"I'm not handing him anything," I'd said. "He is gone. Long gone." And thank god for that.

"The hell he is. He's the reason you walk around looking like you're trying to get typecast as Dumpy Female Neighbor. Maybe you haven't seen the prick since you turned fifteen, but he is with you every fucking day."

I'd clenched my hands into fists as my temper rose. "Do not even think about going there," I'd said, lifting my head and taking a step toward her.

"I'm already there." Cassidy is only about three inches taller than me, but she's always been larger than life, and I'd been overwhelmed by her shadow. And that had just made me angrier. I was hurting. I was lost. And even my best friend wasn't backing me.

"Just. Fucking. *Don't*."

"Don't what?" she'd asked. "Don't tell you the truth? Don't try to beat through that thick head of yours how absurd this is? Some pervert photographer preys on you because you were young and pretty, and so now you're still trying everything in your power to disappear? Fuck that shit. You were fourteen—*fourteen*. He was the asshole."

I'd shaken my head slowly, my eyes burning even though no tears came. I'd wanted to run, but it was Cass I always ran to, which meant there was nowhere left to go. "I should never have told you."

The truth is I hadn't told her all of it—not even close. But I'd told her enough.

"Dammit, Syl," she'd said, and there'd been tears streaming down her face. "Don't you get it? Some fucked up a-hole took your virginity. He took sex. But he didn't take you. You're smart and you're beautiful, and he can't touch that shit. You need to own it. Because every time you hide behind some bullshit like this," she'd said, plucking at my ugly gray sweatshirt, "you're letting him win. You want your life back, you take it back. And you look damn hot doing it."

Now, as I sit in my sexy red cocktail dress in the back of the limo, I can still feel the way my stomach twisted when she'd talked about what Bob did to me during those months when I was fourteen. More than that, though, I remember how warm and safe I'd felt just knowing that I'd had a friend who really cared.

"Thanks," I say softly.

She tilts her head, obviously not following my train of thought. "For what?"

"For this," I say, plucking at the dress. "If you hadn't bitched me out all those years ago, I'd probably be wearing sweatpants tonight."

"Not if you were going with me," she retorts, and we both laugh.

"Look, Syl," she says after a moment, "I just don't want you getting all twisted up again. You never really told me what happened with Steele, but I know you well enough to know you're kinda screwed up where guys and relationships are concerned."

"Understatement of the century," I agree. I don't need a shrink to know I still have issues.

"Have you even slept with a guy since Atlanta?"

I tense. "I've been focusing on work," I say, my words crisper than I intend. "It's not like my job is nine-to-five."

She holds up her hands in surrender. "Hey, I get it. I do. And it's not like I'm saying you should go back to the way you were before Steele, either."

I cringe, because the truth is I'd fucked a lot of guys in college. Not because I wanted them, or even because I wanted to get off. No, I was using sex as therapy, proving over and over that despite everything I knew about myself, I could keep my feelings and reactions and emotions in a nice, tight little box. That I could win over the memories and fight the nightmares. That I could keep control.

Cass knows more about that time in my life than anybody. And she also knows that it isn't a time I want to talk about. "Don't do this, Cass. Don't fuck with my head tonight. Please."

"I'm sorry. I am. But tonight's the whole point. You're still raw."

I shake my head automatically, wanting to deny even though she's right. "I haven't had a nightmare since I moved back to LA."

"And that's great. That's my point. And I don't want you to get hurt now. Again. You've already gone through too much."

"I won't," I say, though the promise is hollow. "I love you, you know."

Humor flashes in her green eyes as her mouth quirks into a half-smile. "Yeah, but will you get naked with me?"

"After all the time I took to get dressed?" I quip. Considering I really am screwed up where guys and relationships are concerned, I sometimes wish I could go there. But that's not me. And though we've had our awkward moments, for the most part, the crush she's never bothered to hide is just one more dynamic between us.

She grins wickedly, then glances at her watch. "We've still got a couple of minutes before we get to the theater. We could drop the privacy screen. Give Edward a little show." She purses her lips, then manages a boob-shaking shimmy.

I laugh out loud. "That is wrong on so many levels."

"Honestly, what's the point of going to a Hollywood shindig if sex and alcohol aren't part of the mix?"

"We have alcohol," I remind her, as I refill her wineglass. "As for the sex, I'm sure there will be plenty of prospects."

"From the C-list," she reminds me.

I consider a moment. "Actually, I wouldn't be surprised if Graham Elliott shows up." Elliott is Hollywood's latest mega-star. "Apparently he's gunning to play Steele in a feature film that's in the works, and he's A-list all the way."

"Not exactly my type, but that means Kirstie Ellen Todd is probably coming, too, right?"

"I doubt it. I saw online that they broke up."

Cass makes a face, then sighs. "Well, at least I've got a shot at her again."

"One, I'm pretty sure she's straight. And two, there's the small problem that you'll never in a million years meet her."

"Minor inconveniences, all."

I shake my head, amused. "Confidence, thy name is Cassidy."

"Damn straight. Oh, wow, check it out." She slams back her wine, then uses the empty glass as a pointer. "Spotlights."

She's right. Twin searchlights are doing the crisscross-in-the-sky routine right in front of the old Grauman's Chinese Theatre, which is now the TCL Chinese Theatre. When I was growing up, it was Mann's Chinese Theatre, and so mostly I just think of it as the Chinese theater in Hollywood with the hand- and footprints of so many movie and television stars.

Edward slides the limo into line, and we creep forward slowly until the rear door is even with the red carpet. The limo stops, the door opens, and Cass and I emerge to the flash and buzz of reporters. It slows down as soon as they realize that we aren't celebrities, though I think that Cass's killer legs probably kept them snapping a bit longer than they otherwise might.

In front of us, red velvet ropes separate the theater and its forecourt from the spectators who have gathered along this section of Hollywood Boulevard.

Cass squeezes my hand as we start to walk the red carpet toward the iconic pagoda-style entrance to the famous theater. "This is completely iced."

I really can't argue, and as we follow the path, I feel a bit like a celebrity myself. That fantasy is only accentuated as I glance around at the tuxedoed men and well-coiffed women who mingle in this open area, chatting with the press and giving tourists and celebrity watchers a chance to snap dozens and dozens of photos.

Wyatt waits at the end, and as Cass and I approach, he grins. I expect to pass by and join the mingling guests, but he ushers me in front of a banner advertising the studio that financed the documentary, and proceeds to do the full-on Red Carpet Photo Moment.

"Thanks for wrangling the extra tickets for me," I say. "I owe you big."

"No problem," Wyatt says as he aims his camera at Cass. "Just another manifestation of my subversive, artistic personality. I'm all wacky that way," he adds, making me laugh.

Cass and I link arms and follow the well-dressed crowd. We go first toward Grauman's Ballroom in the adjacent multiplex where the VIP reception is being held prior to the screening in the original theater. I lean toward Cass. "Definitely iced," I say, repeating her word. And I mean it. Right then, I feel pumped up, confident, and ready to conquer the world. Or, at least, to conquer Jackson Steele.

Uniformed staff stands at the door, offering us flutes of champagne as we enter the ballroom. "Wow," Cass says, and I silently echo the sentiment.

The room is stunning. Huge, but not overwhelming. Golden light fills the space, but is broken up by a pattern of geometric blue images projected onto the floor and ceiling. A few corners of the balcony are highlighted in red, giving the room a festive, nightclub atmosphere. Two massive columns seem to stand guard over the space, and between them, a crowd gathers around a circular bar, the stacked wineglasses twinkling like colored stars in the clever lighting.

Behind the bar, a screen displays a montage of photographs— soaring skyscrapers, angular office buildings, innovative housing complexes. I recognize each as a Jackson Steele project, and those images are interspersed with sketches, blueprints, and construction shots of the Amsterdam museum that is as much the focus of the documentary as the man himself.

Cass drains her flute of champagne and makes a beeline for the bar. "I need a refill and you need liquid courage," she says.

"I do not," I lie, but she orders a glass of cabernet for both of us anyway.

I take it, ignoring the voice of reason that tells me that I shouldn't be even slightly tipsy around Jackson Steele. That if I am going to get through this, I need to be clear-headed, professional, and ice, ice cold. Smart words, and I shoot them all to hell when I lift my glass and down a long, slow sip.

"To kicking butt and taking names," Cass says as she holds her glass out in a toast. I clink mine against hers, then take another smaller sip. What had she said? Liquid courage? Yeah, maybe that was a good thing, after all.

I glance around, scoping out the area and searching the faces. The room is comfortably elegant, with linen-covered tables mixed in with plush couches and designer chairs. Most are empty, as the guests are standing to mingle and work the room. I recognize a few of them. A reality TV star in the corner, an agent I met once at a party. I don't see Jackson, though, and I'm starting to get antsy. He must be here somewhere, and I'm afraid that if I don't find him before the screening, he'll be whisked away to some after-party before I have the chance to talk with him.

"What's he look like?"

"You don't know?"

She shrugs. "You didn't tell me until today that your Atlanta fling grew up to be a hot-shit celebrity architect. Hot shit and just plain hot, right?"

"That's about the sum of it." I stumble for a moment—because how do you describe perfection—and then I stop, because he is right in front of me. Not the man, but his image, projected on the screen behind the bar for all the world to see.

"Whoa," Cass says as she follows my gaze. "Shit, fuck. Seriously? That guy is positively gorgeous."

I nod, my eyes glued to the screen, my throat thick. I'd thought that the magazine cover did him justice, but I was wrong. On the cover, he is brushed and polished, his rough edges smoothed away by the magic of Photoshop. But this—this is raw and grainy. It's candid and stunning and awe-inspiring.

It's Jackson, standing astride two parallel iron girders at least thirty stories above a city I don't recognize. He's wearing jeans, a long-sleeve white T-shirt, and a white hard hat. He is holding on to a giant hook suspended in front of him, and seems unaware of the camera that I can only assume is taking this shot through a long lens from a safe distance.

The shadow of beard stubble is as unmistakable as the brilliant blue of his eyes, which seem to burn in the white light of the sun. His free hand rests against his forehead like a visor, blocking the sun as he surveys the structure rising all around him. Behind and beneath him, the city spreads out, but it is Jackson who is the focal point. And from this single image, there is no question that Jackson is a man with the power to grab hold of the earth and remake it as he wants it. And in that moment, I can only hope that what I can offer is something that he wants to claim.

I hug myself, then step back as the image fades and is replaced by another building site. I turn and find Cass staring at me. She sighs, then shakes her head slowly. "Christ, Syl. I can see it on your face."

I look away, but she grabs my arm.

"This job isn't worth it. He's going to rip you to pieces all over again. He half has already."

"*No.*" I take a deep breath. "No, he won't—he hasn't. And he didn't rip me to pieces in the first place. I did that all by myself. All he did was—"

"Leave?"

"All he did was what I asked him to." And with any luck, he would do exactly that again.

"Fine. Okay. But are you sure you don't want a wingman? At the very least I can hang with you until you find him."

"No. I'm good. Go mingle. Who knows. Maybe Kirstie Ellen Todd really is here."

She hesitates, then nods. "I'll tell her you said hi." She gives me a quick hug, then slides up to the bar again for another glass of wine. I do the opposite and set my half-full glass on a passing waiter's tray. Definitely better to be clearheaded.

After fifteen minutes, though, I'm regretting my forced sobriety. I've circled the room twice and seen dozens of almost famous actors and well over a hundred other faces that aren't familiar at all. I've seen Cass chatting up pretty much everybody, a waitress I recognize from my favorite restaurant who tells me she's moonlighting, and Wyatt circulating through it all with his camera and flash.

But I haven't seen Jackson.

He must be here, though, so I decide that the best approach is to go up to the second level, park myself along the balcony, and scan the guests from above. I'm heading that direction, my head slightly down as I'm taking a second to check my office email and messages on my phone, when I catch a glimpse of something familiar in my peripheral vision.

I look up, ignoring the sudden tightness in my chest, and search the surrounding faces for him. Except he's not there, and now my chest tightens even more, this time with disappointment.

I take another step as I slide my phone back into my tiny red purse.

And that's when I see him.

He's descending the stairs, his attention focused on the distinguished-looking man beside him. He is clean-shaven and elegant in a collarless black jacket over a white cotton pullover. I had expected a tux, but can't deny that this is a much better choice. He looks dark and sexy and unpredictable. More, he looks important. The kind of man who can say "fuck you" to convention, and have everyone scrambling to keep up with him.

This is the man who lives in my memories. Those crystalline blue eyes. That wide, gorgeous mouth. The thick brows and sculpted features.

He descends two more steps, then turns slightly away from his companion. As he does, I realize that he isn't entirely as I remember him. Now there is a scar that intersects his left eyebrow, then arcs across his forehead to his hairline. It wasn't there in Atlanta, but it's well-healed, and must be several years old.

The scar does nothing to mar the sensuality of this man who so undeniably commands the room. Instead, that single flaw adds to his mystique, giving him a dangerous and mysterious edge. Even so, I know that there must be pain beneath it, and my fingers itch to touch it, to trace the path of it. To hold and soothe and comfort against whatever evil had the gumption to scar that incredible face.

But that is no longer my right, and that reality is pounded home as I glance around and realize that every woman in the vicinity is looking at him, just as I am. I close my hand into a fist, feeling suddenly proprietary, even though I have no claim on this man anymore. I gave that up. Sacrificed him to save myself.

A wave of melancholy crashes over me, and I tell myself to stop it, stop it, *stop it*.

I did the right thing, I am certain of it. And it doesn't matter anyway. The past is over, goddammit. I need to just suck it up and move on, just like I've been doing for my whole screwed-up life.

I take a deep breath, then another, as I force myself to get my shit together. I'm a businesswoman with a lucrative proposition. I'm not a starry-eyed girl getting weak-kneed around the ultra-sexy man of the hour.

I can do this. I can approach him, greet him, tell him that I'm not going to accept a brush-off. That it's been five years, we're both grown-ups, and he's just going to have to listen to me.

Straightforward. Direct. To the point.

Right. I can manage. No problem at all.

I take a step toward him, then another.

I straighten my shoulders and put on the professional smile that I have honed over five years of working for the CEO of Stark International.

I keep my eyes on Jackson as I move toward the staircase, taking a path designed to intercept him as he reaches the ballroom floor.

He doesn't see me—he is completely focused on the man beside him. I cannot hear their conversation, but Jackson's hands move as he talks, and I know that they are discussing architecture. I smile with affection, remembering the way he would outline a skyscraper in the air and the way his fingers would dance as he considered facades and footprints, purpose and plan.

His companion says something, and Jackson laughs, his wide,

sensual mouth curving into a smile that freezes in place as he casually scans the crowd—and then finds me.

A wild heat burns across his expression, but is banked so quickly that I almost think I imagined it. Now when I look, I see only a blank stoicism. And yet there remains an intensity to him, the illusion of motion even though he has stopped dead still on the staircase.

His eyes are locked on mine, and I stand motionless as well, unable to move. Almost unable to breathe.

"Jackson," I say, but I am not sure if I have spoken aloud or if his name has simply filled me, as essential as oxygen.

We hold like that, time ticking by, the world around us frozen. Neither of us move, and yet I feel as though I am spinning through space and hurtling toward him. The illusion terrifies me, because right then I know two things—I want desperately to be in his arms again, and I am absolutely terrified of the collision.

And then, suddenly, the world clicks back into motion. His eyes hold mine for a split second longer, and in those few brief moments before he turns away, I see the flash of cold, hard anger. But there's something else, too. Something that looks like regret thawing under the ice.

I realize that my limbs will function again, and take a step toward him, knowing that this is my chance. For the project—and for something deeper that I do not want to think about because opening that door scares me too much.

But it doesn't matter. Not my fear, not the project.

Because Jackson doesn't look at me again.

Instead, he strides right by me, never looking back, never even slowing. And I am left to watch him pass, as anonymous as all the other women who stand there and look after him with longing.

three

What the hell had I been thinking?

The man had flatly declined a meeting with me. Had I really believed that once he saw me in person everything would change? That he would rush over, take my hands, and ask me how he could help?

I didn't believe that, no. But damn me, I'd hoped it.

It had seemed so simple in theory. Not easy—nothing about seeing Jackson again is going to be easy—but by the numbers. I could do it, especially because I *had* to do it.

But I'd choked.

Instead of taking the straightforward approach—find him, talk to him—I'd frozen. Instead of moving in, I'd let him pass me by.

Shit.

I'd miscalculated everything, and whatever slim confidence I've been clinging to has been thoroughly and dramatically shattered.

I see Cass across the room laughing with a woman in a short, tight dress and sun-streaked blond hair. She glances my way, and I see her brows lift slightly in question. *Need me?*

I shake my head and smile. Cass broke up with her longtime girlfriend five months ago, and has been pretty much off the market since. If she's connecting with this woman, no way am I going to mess up her rhythm.

Besides, it's time to bite the bullet. I came here to pitch a project, and I'm damned if I will leave without giving it a shot.

Jazzed from my mental pep talk, I start off in the direction in which he'd disappeared, only to be waylaid by the announcement that the film will begin in fifteen minutes, and guests should start making their way toward the theater.

The announcement pretty much destroys any chance of getting a spare moment with Jackson. For one thing, I'm certain he must have some sort of man-of-the-hour thing to do onstage before the film starts. For another, the crowd has become so thick that I have no choice but to be swept along with the throng.

I allow myself to become part of the surge, making peace with the realization that I am going to have to either find Jackson right after the screening or wrangle my way into the after-party—a perk that my invitation doesn't include.

Black-clad ushers who are probably USC film students direct us out of the multiplex and over to the original Chinese theater. It is one of my favorite places in Los Angeles. I used to escape here as a teenager, losing myself to another reality hidden in this exotic venue. It's been recently remodeled, but unlike the shining modernism of the ballroom we have just left, the lobby of the Chinese theater still has a bit of camp, with statues brought from Beijing and Shanghai, ornate ceiling tiles and fixtures, folding screens used as wall decorations, and lots of red walls and carpets.

Once inside the theater, though, technology rules. The IMAX screen is huge and state of the art, and I can't deny the thrill of knowing that I'm about to see both Jackson and his work splashed larger than life in front of me.

I grab an aisle seat in the very last row, figuring that I'll have the best chance of extricating myself from the crowd and finding Jackson if I can get out the door quickly once the film is over. The theater isn't completely full, and there are five or six seats between me and the next person over by the time the lights dim. I can't help but be relieved. I'm on edge and antsy, battered by memories that are butting up against me, pushing and prying and trying to break free. I'm tired of fighting them. After the film, I can be strong again. But for the next seventy minutes, I want to lose myself to the past, to Jackson, and to the soaring images of the world that he has made.

A ripple of applause fills the room as a man I recognize as Jackson's companion from the stairs takes the stage and introduces himself as Michael Prado, the documentary's director.

"As many of you may know, I serve on the board of the National Historic and Architectural Conservation Project, and in that capacity it has been my privilege to observe the growth of many talented young architects. Some display raw talent. Some, a keen business sense. Still others have an innate ability to mesh form and function, location and purpose. Only once, however, have I seen all those attributes embodied in one man. And that man is here tonight. Ladies and gentlemen, please welcome Jackson Steele."

There is considerably more applause as Jackson takes the steps two at a time, then waves at the audience before shaking Prado's hand.

"Thank you all for the warm welcome," he says as he takes the mike. "And thank you, Michael, for your incredibly generous words. As you might realize," he continues, turning so that he faces the audience without putting his back to the director, "a documentary of the nature that Michael has put together is an extremely invasive beast. And I say that with the utmost respect and affection," he adds as the audience laughs.

"He's trying to say that I got in his way," Michael jokes.

"Or that I got in his," Jackson says, handling the audience with undeniable skill. "But seriously, I owe this man a great debt. This documentary was in the works even prior to the board of the Amsterdam Contemporary Art and Science Coalition choosing my design for their museum. And while I can't say that I was prepared to have my process so fully scrutinized, I can say that the experience has been both educational and rewarding. I've had the luxury of seeing my work through another's eyes. That is a rare gift and one that should not be squandered. It taught me to respect my vision, but also to open my eyes."

I am riveted as I watch him, so personable, so comfortable in front of a crowd.

He shifts on the stage so that he seems to look at everyone in the audience. "And now I am pleased to welcome you to the US premier of *Stone and Steele,* and to offer you this glimpse into another type of joint work. Michael Prado's interpretation of the trials, tribulations, and successes that surrounded the funding, building, dedication, and opening of the celebrated—some might say infamous—Amsterdam Art and Science Museum."

He pauses as the audience applauds once more, and it strikes me how much he reminds me of Damien Stark. Not only in appearance—they both share a dark, masculine beauty—but in his ability to handle the spotlight and draw people in. If he were ending with a sales pitch, I'm entirely certain that he would rake in a million tonight.

But there is no sales pitch. Tonight is a celebration, and after a few more words about the history of the project, Jackson invites the audience to settle in and enjoy the show.

The lights dim, the curtain parts, and I lean back in my seat as the music swells and the screen fills with motion and light. The camera rises in a magnificent shot that starts at the ground, then climbs faster and faster, rising up the now-iconic smooth edge of the museum to ultimately flare out as blue sky and sun fill the frame.

The screen turns a blinding white that dissolves into a title sequence and then a close-up of Jackson, his hair ruffling in the wind and his jeans tight on well-muscled thighs as he leans over a table littered with blueprints. He is deep in conversation with another man, but their words are muffled beneath the precise, careful voice of the narrator.

I watch, mesmerized by the man on the screen. By the passion and precision of his movements. He is absorbed by his work, compelled by it. There is power in what he does. Majesty, even magic.

And the depth of emotion I see on his face makes my skin heat and my heart pound in my chest.

I have seen that same fire, that same determination. I have seen joy and rapture. I have held him close and felt his heat, and I have been burned by the intensity of this man.

My chest aches and my hands begin to hurt. I realize that I am clutching the armrests too tightly. More, I have been holding my breath.

Air, I think as I start to stand. I just need to get to the lobby. Maybe hit the ladies' room and splash some cold water on my face.

But as I start to lever myself out of the seat, someone slips into the chair beside me.

Jackson.

I haven't seen him—don't even turn to face him—and yet I have no doubt. How could I when my skin already tingles simply from his proximity? When the scent of his cologne surrounds me, all spice and musk and smoke?

I close my eyes and hold myself half in and half out of the chair, suddenly unsure of where I am going and why.

"Stay."

One simple word, and yet it compels me. I draw another breath, nod, and then settle back into the upholstered theater chair. I turn toward him and find him focused on me. Shadows dance upon his face, and I swear that I could tumble into the brilliant blue of his eyes.

I start to speak, though I'm not at all sure what I'm going to say. Then he leans toward me and places his palm on my leg, so that the heel of his hand rests on the thin material of my dress, but the tips of his fingers graze my bare skin. Every nerve ending in my body seems clustered in that one area, sparkling and sizzling.

I'm desperately, painfully aware of the contact, and I have to fight the urge to draw in a breath, to stiffen as my pulse pounds and a wild heat bursts through me. I don't want to react to him; I don't want to give anything away. And I damn sure can't let go of the tight grip I have on control.

But he is leaning closer, the pressure increasing upon my thigh as his lips come within a whisper of my ear. "What the hell do you think you're doing here?"

I consider playing it coy, but there is no profit in that. Not to mention the fact that I'm not at all sure I could pull it off. Not now, when he's touching me. When he's thrown me so off kilter. "I need to talk to you," I say simply.

"Do you?" he asks, his voice as smooth and tempting as chocolate. "I'm fairly certain you don't have an appointment."

His finger moves slowly on my skin, back and forth, the motion so idle that he might be unaware of it. Except I know that's bullshit. He knows exactly what he's doing.

"Do I need an appointment to chat at a party?"

"Is that what we're doing?" he asks as his finger strokes and teases. "Chatting?"

I feel my chest tighten and a thin panic rise. "Please, Jackson."

"Please what?"

"Outside." I hope that he cannot hear the way my voice shakes. "Can we just go talk for a minute in the lobby?"

I try to rise, but he holds me down with a gentle but firm pressure on my leg. In the process, he manages to slide my hem up, revealing just a sliver more of bare skin. It is enough, however, to make me feel even more exposed. Even more vulnerable.

To make me remember the way his hands felt when he was touching me without anger or pretense.

I swallow as a wave of longing and regret breaks over me. "Jackson—"

"You're so determined to talk, then talk here." His voice hasn't lost the velvet, but there is steel under it now.

"We'll bother everyone around us," I whisper, determined to regain my equilibrium.

His brows rise, and I see amusement dance at the corner of his mouth. "Will we?" His hand eases higher, pushing my skirt up with the motion. "I didn't think our . . . conversation . . . would be quite that loud."

"Stop." I close my hand hard over his, preventing him from gaining even another millimeter.

"Why?"

"Because I said so, dammit."

"I meant, why do you need to talk to me," he clarifies. "But the same applies." He eases his hand higher, pushing my skirt up inch by excruciating inch. "Tell me why you say I should stop. Because you don't want me to touch you? Because you don't want me to slide my hand just a little bit higher? Because you don't want my fingertips to stroke your panties and find you wet and hot?"

My mouth is dry, my body burning. And—damn me all to hell—he is right. I am desperately wet, my thighs hot and my sex throbbing.

"Or maybe it's because you do want me to keep going? Because you can imagine—can remember—the way my finger feels inside you, teasing you, stroking your clit. Are you wet now, princess?" he asks, his voice as gentle as the finger that still skims along my thigh.

"Are you hot and needy and silently begging me to touch you, to slide my finger over your slick, wet heat? Is that what you want? Come on, sweetheart, you can tell me. Don't you want me to take you there? To take you higher and higher until you tremble in my hand as the orgasm rocks you? Because I think you do. I think you want it so bad you can taste it."

I close my eyes, determined not to let him see the truth of his words on my face. "Stop it," I repeat. "You can't—"

"The hell I can't." The soft sensuality in his tone has vanished, replaced by harsh accusation. "Do you think I haven't watched you tonight? Do you think I didn't see the way you've looked at me? We both know you still want me, and we both know that pisses you off. So tell me, Sylvia. I want to hear it. I want you to say it out loud."

But there is no way in hell that I am conceding. Because while it may be true—God help me, I do want him, and that does piss me off—I don't want what comes after. The panic and wariness. The tightness and fear. That horrible sense that everything around me is spinning out of control, and that no matter how hard I try to hold it together, I'll inevitably get ripped apart.

"Tell me," he repeats, his words heavy with five years' worth of hurt and anger. "And then I'll listen to what you have to say."

I wince as something like guilt crashes over me. But I push it aside even as I shove his hand away and bolt up out of the chair. "Fuck you," I snap, ignoring the low-pitched "sssshhhh" from down the row.

I stumble up the aisle, then practically slam myself against the door, not even taking a breath until I am safely in the lobby.

I lean against the wall and tell myself to get my shit together. I haven't quite managed that task when the door opens and Jackson strides out and heads straight toward me. I think I must flinch, because I see his jaw tighten, and he comes no closer.

"Not exactly the sweet words I was looking for," he says wryly. "But good enough."

"Just leave me the hell alone," I say.

"I can do that." His tone is now all business. "Or you can tell me why you want to talk to me."

I blink, a little whiplashed by his sudden change in tone. "A job," I manage to say, even as my shoulders sag with both relief and, though I hate to admit it, a touch of disappointment. I push the latter firmly away—there is no room for anything but business between Jackson and me, and even imagining there might be more is a recipe for heartache.

His eyes stay fixed on mine, then he nods briskly. "All right. I'm listening."

I stand straighter, sliding into business-mode and relishing the sense of being back in control. "It's for Stark International," I say. "And before you tell me that you already turned down the Bahamas resort, I'd like you to hear me out."

I take his silence as acquiescence and continue, giving him the full rundown of the project from inception to the horrific news that Glau has not only melted down, but pulled out.

"Miss America got slammed on Facebook, and now the runner-up has the crown?"

"No," I say firmly. "This isn't about bringing in the runner-up. It's about making this resort the best that it can be."

"Really?" His gaze skims over me, as sensual as a slow caress. "I don't recall being approached when the project was initiated."

"You were tied up with the job in Dubai."

"Was I?" he says, as if that commission was nothing more than a figment of my imagination. "So this has nothing to do with the fact that your precious resort is in more trouble than you've let on?"

"I don't know what you're talking about."

"Problems with the FAA, Sylvia. Utility permitting. Environmental groups. Do you want me to go on?"

"Everything you've listed is being handled," I say, which is technically accurate. Apparently there is a lot of red tape to cut through in order to install even a small landing strip on a tiny island. And he's right about the environmental groups, too. As it turns out, the island is a habitat for a rare species of cave crickets, and negotiating that possible land mine was as fraught with destructive potential as disarming a nuclear bomb.

But what really concerns me is how he's heard about those problems. Because we've kept a tight lid on each and every one of them.

I fight the urge to drag my fingers through my hair out of sheer frustration, and tell myself not to worry about that right now. "Dammit, Jackson, the bottom line is that it's a great opportunity."

"I'm not saying it isn't." He holds out his hand. "Come with me."

I glance at his hand, but I don't take it. After a moment, he lowers it, and the shadow I see in his eyes comes very close to breaking me.

He says nothing else, but turns and starts walking. I follow him in silence all the way back to the ballroom and then into a hallway that I hadn't entered before. "Won't they miss you?"

"This is Hollywood. They're used to putting on a spin when the talent goes missing." He grins, the corners of his eyes crinkling in a way I find both disarming and very, very sexy. "Besides, the after-party is here. Eventually, whoever needs me will find me."

I nod, then take the opportunity to look around. The hallway is wide with white walls rising to a low ceiling. The floor is brushed concrete, and it's broken up by several geometric, flat-sided pillars spaced down the length.

Dozens of framed black and white photographs line the walls, and as we walk we pass Humphrey Bogart, Audrey Hepburn, Harrison Ford, Marlon Brando, and countless other stars of some of my favorite movies.

But it is not those images that Jackson wants me to see. Instead, he takes me to the first pillar and the full color photograph that hangs there. It is of the Winn Building in Manhattan, a glass and steel skyscraper that rises like royalty over the city, with so much retail, office, and living space that it is practically a city unto itself.

Jackson says nothing as we look at the image, and I estimate that a full minute passes before we move to the next pillar and the framed image of the new Salzburg Opera House, with its curved facade that seems to flow like music in perfect harmony with the mountains that frame it.

The last photograph is not of a commercial project, but of a house in the mountains outside of Santa Fe, New Mexico. Its burnished exterior blends with the stone and rock, and though the single-story residence is obviously both new and state of the art, it flows over the landscape with the kind of bold confidence that suggests it rose fully formed from the mountains that bore it.

"What do you know about these?"

I tell him, giving him the details that he already knows. How the Santa Fe getaway for a well-known philanthropist finally earned him the recognition he deserved and jump-started his architectural career. How the opera house thrust him into the design-build arena when he branched out from strict design work to the full spectrum of property development. And how the Winn Building was a major victory for Steele Development, as it marked his company's foray into the lucrative New York market, and resulted in the first project in which he retained an ownership interest.

I don't mention the murder and suicide that took place at the Santa Fe house not long after it was completed. It doesn't seem relevant and, frankly, I'm afraid that kind of gossip might spoil whatever progress we're making.

Nor do I mention that the rental income from the Winn Building must have at least quadrupled Jackson's net worth overnight. But we both know that I am aware. You can't work for a man like Damien Stark for all these years and not gain some understanding of the monetary potential for the kind of projects Jackson now commands.

In other words, Jackson doesn't need the income from The Resort at Cortez. And considering how fast his star is ascending with the documentary and the possibility of a feature film, he doesn't even need the publicity.

All I have to offer is the challenge. I can only hope that will be enough.

I turn so that I am facing him, my back now to the pillar. "So? How did I do?"

"Not bad. You've been watching my career."

"No," I say, the lie coming easily. "But I'm good at my job. And that means I know who I'm recruiting."

"Recruiting," he repeats. He takes a single step toward me.

"Yes." The word is firm, and I am proud of how steady I feel.

He steps closer, reducing the distance between us to mere inches. I tilt my head back. Even with me in heels, he is a head taller than me, and right now I cannot help but feel small. Vulnerable.

I push that down, though, and meet his eyes, hoping mine show ice and determination.

"Do you remember Atlanta?"

His words are like a slap, and despite all my resolve, I step backward, only to be foiled by the pillar behind me. "I—of course I do." I lick my lips. "Jackson, I'm sorry about the past. But this isn't—"

"No," he says, holding up a finger to silence me. "Do you remember before? Before you tore it all apart. Do you remember the way it felt when I touched you?"

My throat has gone completely dry, and I can feel small beads of sweat at the nape of my neck. "Jackson. Don't."

He steps closer, ignoring me. "Tell me, Sylvia. And be honest, because I swear I'll know if you're lying." His voice is low, seductive, and utterly commanding. "Do you remember?"

I shake my head, but that isn't enough to push away the truth. Of course I remember. I remember every laugh, every touch, every breath. I remember every word of every conversation, the taste of every meal. I remember the glorious sensation of his hands upon me and his cock inside me.

But I also remember when the panic set in. When I started to drown, and no matter how hard I fought to keep afloat I kept getting pulled down into the swirling waters of cold fear and harsh memories.

I'd ended it because I had to. Because the only way I could survive was to destroy everything. Because the only way I could breathe was to push him away.

For that matter, I'm having a little trouble breathing right now.

His fingertip hooks under my chin and he tilts my head up so that I am staring deep into his eyes. "Do you remember?" he repeats.

I say nothing.

"And at the end," he persists. "Do you remember what you asked me in Atlanta?"

I lick my dry lips, then nod.

"Tell me."

Whatever you need, baby, I promise. You only have to ask.

Jackson, I—I need you to leave me. I need you to walk away and to never look back.

The memory pounds like red neon inside my head.

"Tell me," he repeats.

"I asked you to leave." I say the words simply, as if every syllable isn't ripping me to shreds.

"And did I?" His voice is still even, still calm, but there is no hiding the tension that backs each and every word. "Did I not do exactly what you asked? Did I not walk away even though it just about killed me?"

It killed me, too. I want to shout the words at him, but I don't. I can't, because that would only make him suffer more, and after everything I've done to him, I can't add that burden. So all I do is nod. "Yes." My voice sounds lost. Hollow. "You did."

He leans closer, placing one hand on the pillar just over my shoulder. He is at an angle, his face so close I can smell whiskey on his breath. "So what exactly do you want from me now?" He strokes his free hand down my bare arm until he reaches my hand. He twines his fingers with mine and pulls me hard against him.

I gasp and try to ease backward, but it's not possible. He has moved his palm from the pillar to my lower back. He holds me close, so tight that I am breathless, lost in the feel of him and, yes, in the erotic sensation of his erection, unmistakable against my abdomen.

"Jackson—"

"Are you offering me a job?" he continues, ignoring my protest. "Are you offering to bring back everything you killed when you pushed me away?"

He releases my hand. "Or are you offering me this?" he asks, as he brushes his fingertip over my lower lip, so softly and gently that I have to fight not to gasp with pleasure. "Or maybe this?" he asks as his hand moves lower, his palm grazing over my breast.

My nipple tightens as my skin prickles with need. I have to focus on breathing, on not letting my knees give out.

Jackson takes no pity on me. Instead, he gently rubs circles on my breast, taunting and teasing even as his words continue to flow over me. "Surely you remember how it felt," he presses. "You in my arms. Your release. That expression of ecstasy etched on your face. The surrender I felt in your body."

"Don't." That single word is a cry. A plea.

"Don't?" His hand slides down again, his fingers twining with mine once more. "But I have to. So tell me, Sylvia. Because I need to know. What exactly are you offering me?"

My eyes sting, and I squeeze them shut, wishing for the release of tears but they simply won't come. "Just the job," I finally say. I take a deep breath and open my eyes to face him. "Nothing has changed, Jackson. We can't . . ." I shake my head, letting my words trail away.

He holds my gaze. The heat building in the space between us is so intense that I swear I can see the molecules spinning.

Slowly, he releases his grip on my hand. He steps back and I feel cold when he lifts his other hand from the small of my back. "You're right," he says. "We can't."

And that is it. Two little words, and then he turns away from me and walks down the hall. I stare after him, breathing hard, watching until he disappears into the shadows of the larger room.

He never once looks back.

four

The moment Jackson is out of sight, my legs give out. I sink to the ground, my skirt over my knees, my knees pulled to my chest. I hug them close, because I am shaking. Not tears, but the best I seem able to manage.

That is where I am when Cass finds me, my head down on my knees, my mind empty as I try to avoid my memories, this night, every goddamn thing.

"Jesus, Syl. What happened?"

I lift my head to find her crouching in front of me. The sun-streaked blonde is with her, standing a few steps behind and looking genuinely concerned. "How did you get back here?"

"Zee has after-party tickets. Someone saw you leave with Jackson, and when I couldn't find you, we thought you must have come here with him."

"I did," I say, and hold out my hand so she can help me up. "Zee?"

"Zelda," the blonde says. "My parents are F. Scott Fitzgerald fans. Are you okay?"

I shrug. "I'm not having the best night of my life."

"I'm sorry," she says, then glances quickly at Cass. "I am."

That lifts my mood considerably, and I flash a quick grin at my friend, who has gone uncharacteristically pink in the cheeks.

"I'm guessing he said no," Cass says.

"He said a lot of things," I admit. " 'No' was one of them."

"Business thing," Cass says to Zee. "Went south."

"That sucks. Wanna hang with us?"

I'm tempted. At the moment, getting lost in drink and dance seems like a truly fine idea. But I don't want to be a third wheel. Even more, I need to handle this. I need to think. I need to figure out a way to rewind this night, start over, and somehow get Jackson to agree.

"Thanks, but no." I drag my fingers through my hair. "I'm just frustrated. But I'll walk back into the party with you guys."

"You're staying?"

"Yeah. I think. I'm not sure. I need to talk to Jackson again. We didn't exactly get off on the right foot this last go-round."

Cass's eyes narrow to slits.

"It's fine," I lie. "It's going to be just fine."

I can tell she's not convinced, but she knows me well enough not to argue. As soon as we're back in the main ballroom, I split off from them and head to the bar for some wine. This time, I take a long sip, because as far as I'm concerned, forced sobriety has been no great benefit. Heat blooms through me as the wine hits my system, and I go slower with the rest of the glass, taking small sips as I circulate through the room.

The after-party is even more crowded than the pre-screening reception, which I suppose makes sense, as a lot of folks undoubtedly showed up right as the lights dimmed, planning to watch the film and then dive into party mode. Unfortunately for me, that's making it more difficult to maneuver, and I'm feeling a little trapped and a lot claustrophobic.

I consider texting Cass just to find her in the crowd, but sternly talk myself out of it. Zee is obviously interested in Cass, and I'm not going to mess that up just because I need a balm for my nerves. Instead, I double my efforts to find Jackson. That's why I'm here, after all. And I'm not leaving until he's cooled down and I have the chance to really talk to him.

I ease over to one of the light-bathed pillars and stand with my back to it, using that as a central point from which to scan the faces around me. I don't see Jackson, but I do see a familiar face and grin broadly when Evelyn Dodge notices me and makes a beeline in my direction.

"Look at you." She spreads her arms wide and gathers me into a smothering hug. "Did my favorite benevolent dictator actually give you an evening off?"

"Just a short break," I deadpan. "If I'm not back in the office by midnight, I'll turn into a pumpkin."

"Don't risk it, sweetie. With your complexion, you'll look terrible in orange. Now I, on the other hand . . ." She indicates the orange, eye-melting dress she has on which, despite the radioactive color, looks show-stoppingly perfect on her. "I knew there was a reason I liked you," she says, when I tell her just how awesome she looks.

Evelyn was the first person I met when I went to work for Damien Stark. She'd burst into the reception area on day one and announced to Damien that she was taking me to lunch "because the way to an executive's ear is through his assistant."

Not that she needed me to have Damien's ear. A former actress, Evelyn Dodge has held pretty much every job in Hollywood that it is possible to hold, and a few that I'm certain she invented herself. Recently, she's returned from semi-retirement to agenting.

She's known Damien since his tennis-star days, and represented him in endorsement deals and all the rest of the celebrity nonsense that comes with being a hot, good-looking athlete. And even more so when he became a hot, good-looking athlete surrounded by scandal.

Of course, I didn't know either of them back then, but I do know that not only is Evelyn mama-bear loyal to Damien Stark, she's also one of the funniest, brashest, most engaging women I've ever met. And I am limp with relief that she's materialized right in front of me.

"I had no idea you were coming," I say. "Do you rep someone here?"

"Not yet, but the night is young." She takes my arm and leads me toward a waiter with a tray of tiny puff pastries topped with sour cream and caviar. "No, I'm here because of Michael."

"The director?" I take the napkin and appetizer she passes me, then try to decide how I'm going to eat it since I'm still holding my wine in my other hand. "Do you know him well?"

"Not as well as I thought." She takes my wineglass and downs the last of my cabernet, then hands the empty glass to a passing waiter. "We used to be married."

"Oh."

I think of Blaine, the flamboyant younger artist who now shares Evelyn's bed. He's about as opposite to Michael Prado as it's possible to be. And despite their age difference, I have to say that I can't imagine Evelyn on anyone's arm but Blaine's.

"So where's Blaine?" I ask, then blush when she laughs because I am absolutely certain she has watched my train of thought play out across my face.

"Working in his studio." She winks. "He thinks Michael's a twit."

I laugh. "Is he?"

"A bit, but a harmless one. And he's a very good director, not to mention an excellent fund-raiser and board member. His failings are more concentrated in the domestic arena." She shrugs matter-of-factly. "Then again, maybe the failings were mine."

"Or maybe it's nobody's fault. Maybe you just didn't click."

"I like the way you think," she says, but I'm barely listening. My words have unexpectedly resonated with me. Because Jackson and I did click—fully and completely. And the reason we're not together right now is entirely my fault.

"You haven't told me why you're here," she says. "Personal or professional?"

"You know I'm working on the Santa Cortez project, right?"

"Of course."

"Yeah, well, it's hit a little snag." I tell her about Glau, and about my hope that I can convince Jackson Steele to get on board. I don't mention our past. Evelyn may be in the mood to overshare about her relationship, but I'm not feeling that chatty.

"You're here to do the business mingle," Evelyn says. "A time-honored tradition. I'm doing a bit of the same since I'm here." She glances around the room, pointing out a few of the actors and actresses she has on her radar. "Well, there's someone I didn't expect to see."

I follow her gaze and see Jeremiah Stark, Damien's father. I glance at Evelyn with a frown. "Guess it's a good thing Damien's not here," I say, then immediately regret my words, afraid I've overstepped my bounds. It's no secret that Damien and his father do not get along, but as his assistant, I really shouldn't be commenting on that. Even to a mutual friend.

Evelyn is completely unperturbed by my comment. "I've seen him at a lot of screenings lately—he's determined to get a foot in the Hollywood door. But I'm surprised he thinks a documentary is worth the drive from San Diego."

"Maybe he likes architecture." In truth, I don't really care. I like Damien. I don't like Jeremiah. And I don't want to waste more thoughts on the man.

"Actually, you're right. He's on the board with Michael. I'd forgotten." She waves the words away as if they're just a bother. "But speaking of architecture, where is the man of the hour?"

"I haven't seen him since just after the film ended."

"Do you know him personally?"

"A bit," I say. "You?"

"Only by reputation," she says.

"What reputation?"

Evelyn's smile borders on wicked. "Just that he has one. And speak of the devil." She gestures to the far corner of the room where Jackson stands in the red light from the balcony. The light meshes with the gold and the blue, giving that part of the room an even more surreal quality.

Apropos, I think, considering the entire night seems rather surreal.

Evelyn hooks her arm through mine. "Come on, kiddo. Let's go land you an architect."

He's alone when we start out, holding a highball glass and sipping leisurely as he looks around the room, as if taking stock of an empire. He looks in my direction, then stands a bit straighter. For a moment, I think that he has seen me.

But it's not me that he's seen.

He holds his hand out, gesturing for someone to come closer, and as I watch, a redhead glides up to him, her hair crackling like fire in the golden light. He kisses her lightly on the cheek, and I am overcome with two equally powerful urges. The first, to run away. The second, to slap the look of unabashed delight right off her face.

"Do you know who that is?" I tug Evelyn to a stop beside me.

"Not a clue, which means she's probably not in the business. Or if she is, she's fresh off the turnip truck."

"We should wait," I say.

"We should go," she counters. "You want the man to talk to you about business, don't you?"

I nod.

"And you told me he's already turned down your request for a meeting?"

I nod again.

"Then take a tip from Auntie Evelyn and talk to him while someone's with him. He'll either have to say yes, or risk looking like an asshole in front of his lovely young friend."

Considering she has a point, we continue on, only to stop again when their discussion shifts from casual to contentious.

"The one corollary to my rule?" Evelyn says as we pause several yards away. "Don't walk into a minefield."

To be honest, I'm curious enough to do just that. I want to know who this woman is, why he kissed her, and what they are now arguing about. I'm imagining a lovers' quarrel, and the thought is not a happy one. Not because I'm concerned about the quarrel, but about the lover.

I'm distracted from my thoughts by Wyatt's approach. "Now there's a great picture," he says, lifting his camera. "Smile, ladies."

Evelyn hooks an arm around my shoulder and we both smile for the camera.

"Want to make the rounds with me?" he asks. "You can take a few shots, I can give you a few tips."

The offer is tempting, but I regretfully shake my head. "Mission not yet accomplished," I say, hooking my thumb to indicate Jackson.

His mouth quirks up. "I knew you weren't just looking to party with me when you asked for those extra tickets."

"Funny."

He chuckles. "I'll wish you luck, then." He turns to Evelyn. "How about you? Want some company?"

"With you? Always. Especially if you'll get a shot of me with that woman." She points to a trim blonde flirting with the bartender. "That young lady is on the rise, and she's represented by Jake Osprey, a rat bastard of a competitor. He'll blow a gasket if he sees me in the trades with his nubile young client."

"You have a devious streak," I say.

"It's why I'm so damn good at what I do. Now go," she says, pointing to where Jackson was standing only moments before. "He's got to still be around here somewhere."

She gives me a quick hug, Wyatt squeezes my shoulder, and then the two of them slide into the crowd behind me. I stand a moment longer, looking at the faces moving in front of me, once again searching the crowd for Jackson and mentally rehearsing what I'm going to say to him as I glide through the light and people. He has to see the upside of doing this project, and I'm going to reason with him, pointing out all the pros and the very minimal number of cons.

And, yes, I realize that as far as he's concerned, working with me falls squarely in the "con" category. But there is no way that Jackson could have done so well in business if he didn't have the ability to compartmentalize his emotions.

We can make this work—and I'm absolutely determined to convince him of that.

The crowd parts, and I once again see Jackson. The redhead is no longer with him, but she has been replaced by a svelte brunette who looks vaguely familiar. As I hurry in that direction, Jackson looks up, and I smile in greeting, certain that he must see me. He doesn't acknowledge me, though. Instead, I watch as he slides his arm around the brunette's waist. Her face lights up, her expression suggesting that if his movement was an invitation, her smile is an acceptance.

I bite back a twinge of irritation as I continue forward, reminding myself that it's none of my business whose waist Jackson has claimed. "Jackson," I say once I've reached the two of them. "I'm sorry to interrupt, but I need to speak with you."

"Is this about the resort?" His eyes are fixed on me, but his fingers are twined in the brunette's hair.

"Yes. Of course."

His attention shifts to the girl. "Then there's nothing to talk about."

"Jackson, come on. You know—"

"I know that business hours are over, Sylvia." He traces his finger over the bitch's lower lip, and I feel my own lip tingle with longing.

"I realize that." I am uber-calm. I am the epitome of calm. No temper, no frustration. Calm, thy name is Sylvia.

I plaster on my reception desk smile. "It's just that we're kind of under the gun here, scheduling-wise."

"Are you?"

I think I hear curiosity in his voice, and since that's better than bland disinterest, I allow a little spark of hope to rise.

"Yes. I told you earlier that—"

"I remember."

I fight back irritation. "Okay, then. So can we talk?"

For a second, he says nothing. Then he lifts the brunette's hand and brushes his lips over her fingers. "I need a few minutes."

Her back stiffens, but she doesn't protest. Instead she shoots me a vitriol-filled look, spins on her heel, and stalks off toward the bar.

"You've got ten minutes to make your best pitch." He glances casually at his watch. "I suggest you start."

"What?" I say stupidly. "Here? Right now?"

From the expression on his face, I think he's going to make me do just that. Then he shakes his head. "No. I think this is a conversation best had in private." He nods toward the far side of the room. "Upstairs, at the far end past the bar there's a door that leads to a row of offices. There's a keypad for entry. The code is six-one-three-one. The last one on the corner is a small conference room. Michael's been using it this week to prep for the event. We can talk there. Be there in five minutes, or don't bother coming at all."

And then he turns from me, takes two long strides, and melts into the crowd, leaving me scrambling to remember the code and figure out where exactly I'm supposed to go.

Five minutes?

Shit.

Still, I try to put the time to good use, and as I plow through the crowd and make my way to the upstairs doorway, I keep my head down and my eyes focused on my iPhone as I try to organize some photos. Because, dammit, I don't have a projector, much less any sort of PowerPoint presentation. I'm going to have to entirely wing it—and I burst into the corner conference room with forty seconds to spare, albeit slightly out of breath and more than a little frazzled.

More so when I see Jackson. He's already in the room, seated at the far end of a polished mahogany table. He leans back as he silently studies me.

Whereas I am certain I look disheveled and out of breath, Jackson appears just the opposite. He is strength and power.

Most of all, he is completely in control. Everything from his choice of this room to his selection of a seat. Hell, even his decision not to rise when I entered was a deliberate power play.

It's a trick I've seen Damien use over and over. The idea is to intimidate. To claim control of the room and make sure that everyone who enters knows who holds the power. All in all, I have to admit that Jackson is putting that trick to pretty good use. Because right now there is no doubt that I'm the supplicant here. And pretty damned intimidated, too.

Yeah, well, to hell with that. Aren't I the one with the opportunity? Aren't I the one who can hand him the project of a lifetime?

Damn straight, and so I take a step forward, determined to make him realize that while he might have granted me this meeting, I'm now the one who is running the show. "You said ten minutes, Mr. Steele. I can convince you in five."

His expression is almost amused. "I'm listening."

"I don't blame you for rejecting the idea initially. I understand that our past factors into this, and that seeing me was a shock. But that's a knee-jerk reaction. This isn't personal. It's business. And you're about to see just what an excellent business opportunity it is."

"Not personal? Everything between you and me is personal, Sylvia, and you damn well know it."

"Because you're making it that way. You want to be pissed? Fine. Be pissed. But take me out of the equation."

"You're not the only stumbling block, I assure you."

"So I've heard. The rising star Jackson Steele doesn't want to be lost in the sweep of Damien Stark's shadow. Well, let me tell you something about Damien Stark," I say before Jackson has the chance to get a word in. "The man is brilliant at business. He's a goddamn powerhouse on the tennis court. And if the last charity event I saw him at with his wife is any indication, he's one hell of a fine dancer, too. But he can't do this."

I slide my phone across the table, open to the image of the Winn Building that is the first in a slideshow of Jackson Steele buildings.

"That's you," I say as the images scroll. "Your buildings. Your talent. What you do with form, with structure, it takes my breath away." I pause just long enough to emphasize my point. "This isn't just a Stark project. This is *my* project. And with you on board it will be a Jackson Steele project, too."

I can tell I have his attention, and I take a step toward him. "Damien Stark isn't the only one who casts a long shadow, Mr. Steele. How many men have documentaries made about their lives and work? How many men are the subject of a feature film?"

His eyes narrow. "That's not going forward. Not if I have anything to say about it."

"Oh." I stumble a bit, surprised by the vehemence in his voice. "But that's not even the point. This isn't about your reputation as a man or as an architect. It's about what you create. What you will create. Your buildings have caught the attention and sparked the imagination of the world, and yet you have never once worked on a property like this. An entire island, completely undeveloped. It's a blank slate, and I'm offering it to you."

I see what I hope is a spark of interest in his eyes and hurry on. "You don't want this to be just another Stark project? It won't be. It couldn't be. Because you and I both know that the resort you design will shine on its own. I want the best, Mr. Steele. I want you. And unless you're an idiot, you should want it, too."

I take a deep breath, and then, as if to signal that I'm finally done, I pull out a chair and sit.

For a moment, Jackson does nothing. He doesn't even move.

Then he stands and crosses to the window. The glass is tinted, so I can see his reflection superimposed upon the view, such that it is. A roof. The side of the multiplex. Some traffic on Hollywood Boulevard. Nothing spectacular. Not that it matters. Even a view as stunning as the Matterhorn wouldn't have drawn my attention from this man.

"I want to know something," he finally says.

"Of course." I expect him to ask me about the budget. Or timing. Or the construction firms we routinely work with. Anything but the words that come out of his mouth.

"I want to know why you ended it."

My chest tightens and I have to resist the urge to hug myself. I can feel the anxiety reaching for me even now, along with the nightmares and twisted memories that slink along, too. Slithering out of the night to fill my days. I shake my head, determined to keep it all banished, far and away. "It doesn't matter."

He turns from the window, his face a wild mixture of anger and hurt. "The hell it doesn't."

"My reasons are my own, Jackson." I can hear the panic creeping into my voice, and I fear that he can as well. Deliberately, I take slow, even breaths. I want to calm myself. And, damn me, I want to soothe him.

I want to ease the hurt that I caused, but that's impossible, because I can't answer his question.

"Why?" he asks again, only now there's a gentleness in his voice that unnerves me.

I stiffen in automatic defense, afraid I'll melt in the face of any tenderness from this man.

"You didn't want to end it," Jackson continues. "Even now, you want it."

"You have no idea what I want," I say sharply, though that is a lie as well.

"Don't I?" There is anger in his voice. Hurt, too. "I know you want the resort."

I've been looking at the tabletop, and now I lift my head. "Yes." The word is simple. It may be the first completely true thing I've said to him since Atlanta. "Will you take it? You and I both know it's the opportunity of a lifetime. Are you really going to let our past stand in the way of what can be a truly magnificent achievement?"

I watch his shoulders rise and fall as he takes a breath. Then he turns away from me to look out the window once again. "I want the project, Sylvia."

Relief sweeps over me, and I have to physically press my hands to the table to forestall the urge to leap to my feet and embrace him.

"But I want you, too." He turns as he speaks, and when he faces me straight on, there is no denying the truth—or the longing—in his eyes.

I swallow as what feels like a swarm of electric butterflies dances over my skin, making the tiny hairs stand up. And making me aware of everything from the solidity of the floor beneath my feet to the breath of air from a vent across the room.

I force myself to remain seated. Because damn me, my instinct is to go to him and slide into his arms. "I—I don't understand." The lie lingers in the air, and I am proud of the way I kept my voice from shaking.

"Then let me be perfectly clear." He closes the distance between us, then uses his forefinger to tilt my head up so that he is looking deep into my eyes. I shift, not only because the contact sends a jolt of electricity right through me, but because I'm afraid that if he looks too deeply into my eyes, he will see a truth I want to keep hidden.

"No," he says. "Look at me, Sylvia. Because I'm not going to say this again. I told you once that I'm a man who goes after what he wants, and I want you in my bed. I want to feel you naked and hot beneath me. I want to hear you cry out when you come, and I want to know that I am the man who took you there."

My eyes are burning, and I shake my head, as if by simply wishing it to be so, this will all go away.

"I want you, Sylvia. And I will have you."

"Jackson, please."

"And you want me, Sylvia. You can deny it, but we both know that you'd be lying."

"I do want you," I say, clinging tight to that fragment of truth as I try to turn this to my advantage. "But there is the man and there is the architect. I—I can't be with the man. But I desperately need the architect."

"Package deal, princess," he says, the endearment making me cringe. "You want me on the project, I want you in my bed."

"Dammit, Jackson," I say as anxiety creeps through me, its cold fingers banishing the heat. For once, I do not try to force it back, because right now I can use it. "You're being ridiculous. I mean, who *does* that?"

"Apparently, I do." He is level and cool and just arrogant enough to piss me off. I'm grateful—I'd much rather be pissed than unsettled. Or, worse, aroused.

"Is this about revenge?" I demand. "Because it seems like it."

His lips curve as if in consideration. "Maybe it is," he says, the confession slicing through me as cleanly and coldly as a well-honed blade. "But if so, revenge never tasted so sweet."

"Fuck you, Jackson," I snap, as much in anger as in confusion. "Fuck you and your grudge and your goddamn ultimatum." I snatch my phone off the table and bolt for the door, the world around me spinning in shades of red and gray.

I grab on to the frame, my back to him, then take a deep breath to steady myself. "I never meant to hurt you," I say, so softly I'm not even certain he can hear me.

"Maybe not," he says, his voice equally soft. "But you did. And now if you want me on this project, you're going to have to pay the price."

five

Bastard.

He's a goddamn bastard on wheels and I'll be damned if I'm going to let him use me like that.

I hurry down the stairs, my chest tight, my throat dry. By the time I burst outside into the cool October air, I'm working myself up into a full-blown panic attack.

I want to run—hell, I want to fly. I want to lose myself in the lights and noise of Hollywood Boulevard. I want to race blindly down the street, not toward anything, but away. Away from Jackson. Away from the past.

And away from this horrible sensation of being twisted up inside.

I want to, but I can't. Because if I try to, I'll no doubt trip in these damn stilettos, and I'll end up breaking my nose on Clark Gable's handprint outside the theater.

Dammit, dammit, dammit.

say my name   65

So I walk instead, wishing there was a way to turn off my thoughts, to push away my emotions.

You want me on the project, I want you in my bed.

Those words had hit me with all the force of a train, and now I've lost my grip on everything. My plans for the resort, my hopes for a bump in career.

I'd had everything all worked out, each step on the path so perfectly planned.

And then came Jackson, and the fantasy that I could keep a tight hand.

How could I have been so stupid? Because hadn't Jackson unraveled me from the first moment I'd laid eyes on him?

Five years ago, I think. Five years almost to the day from when I'd first met him. Five years and two days from the moment I'd asked him to walk away from me.

No, not two days. Two lifetimes. Two eternities. Because there is no way that I could have crammed everything I felt for him—everything I still feel for him—into so short a time.

Except I did. *We* did.

It started, I remember, with the pandas.

I'd had a truly crap day. I'd just been fired. Or sort of fired. My boss, an Atlanta real estate investor named Reggie Gale, had decided to retire and had chosen to tell me that rather disturbing news while we were driving to a private reception hosted by the Brighton Consortium, a group comprised of various real estate professionals, and of which Gale was a member.

Considering I'd moved from Los Angeles to Atlanta straight after college to work for Gale, and considering I loved both real estate and my job, I wasn't having the most awesome of days. I was twenty-one years old, I'd been employed by Gale for not quite six weeks, I still hadn't bought curtains for my apartment. And I wasn't thrilled about diving back into the job market.

The consortium was hosting the reception in the panda area of Zoo Atlanta, and the whole idea was to be festive and fun and woo additional investors.

Needless to say, I was not in a festive mood.

"Let me guess. You've seen one panda, you've seen them all."

The low voice, soft and smooth and just a little amused, seemed to wrap around me, forcing me to shift my attention from the pandas in their habitat to the man standing next to me.

"I—what?" Not the most coherent of responses, but he'd caught me off guard. I was standing on the veranda that overlooked the panda habitat. I'd come here to escape the mixing and mingling and to lose myself in both thought and worry. The pandas, though undeniably adorable, hadn't actually been on my mind.

Now, looking at him, all of my work-related frustrations fizzled away as well. Only one thing filled my head. Him. His broad shoulders. His chiseled jaw. The strong lines of his face, softened by just the slightest indentation in his chin.

He looked to be in his late twenties, and he held himself with a self-confidence that could seem arrogant on some men, but on him just struck me as sexy.

His face was angles and shadows, a warrior's face, and so exquisite it could make the gods weep. As for his eyes, they shone like cut sapphire, blue and hard. But they gleamed when he smiled, and the way the corners of his eyes crinkled humanized the brilliant sheen of those oh-so-perfect features. Like everyone at this outdoor reception, he was dressed casually. On him, however, casual was compelling, and the simple outfit of jeans and a starched white button-down—the top button left open—didn't seem simple at all.

Looking at him, I felt the earth tilt a little beneath me. I'd never reacted that way to a guy before, and I reached out a hand to grasp the railing, not sure if I entirely liked the feeling.

"Or maybe you've been overwhelmed by the cuteness," he continued, glancing down to where the two roly-poly pandas sat on their rears eating bamboo. "I'm hoping that's the case, because otherwise you're going to shoot my ego all to hell."

"How could anyone hurt your ego?" I blurted, then felt my cheeks go pink. "Sorry. That sounds—"

But I never finished my apology, because my words were drowned out by his quick laugh and the brush of his fingers against my bare arm. "Thanks," he said. "Ego saved." The corner of his mouth quirked up. "I really hate it when I'm upstaged by pandas."

I matched his smile. "Yeah, but they're such cute pandas." I glanced back at the bears as if in confirmation. *Of course, they've got nothing on you.*

He was silent for a moment, and I suddenly feared that he'd read my mind. I filled the quiet by clearing my throat. "You're here for the reception?" A foolish question, since the zoo was currently closed to the public, and the only people on the premises were staff and Brighton Consortium guests.

"I am," he said. "You're not, though."

I stood straighter. "I most certainly am."

"I mean you're not really here. Your mind's elsewhere."

"Oh." Considering I couldn't argue with that, I didn't. Instead I turned back toward the pandas, my hands resting on the railing. "Yeah, well. It's been a rather horrible day."

"Sorry to hear it." He moved next to me and took hold of the railing as well. As he did, his finger brushed mine, and I felt that shock of connection. A sizzling kind of awareness that I'd never experienced before and had believed lived only in the pages of books.

Out of reflex, I glanced toward him, then felt my chest constrict when I caught him looking right back at me, the heat in his eyes so intense I thought it would burn right through me.

I looked away.

"No." His hand gently cupped my chin and he turned my face back to him. "No," he repeated, and this time I heard a plea beneath the hard sheen of command.

I started to protest, but he shifted his hand so that a finger brushed my lip, firm and sensual, and I wanted to draw him in and taste him. I felt giddy and lightheaded, drunk on the proximity of this enigmatic man who had so easily captured me in his spell.

I didn't like it. And yet, god help me, I did.

"No argument," he said. "No protest, no excuses." He held out his hand to me. "You're coming with me."

"The hell I am." I stood a little straighter as the earth leveled out beneath me. I was not the kind of woman who jumped simply because a man told her to. Quite the opposite, in fact. I was used to being the one in charge. To using a man before he could swoop in and use me.

One brow rose slightly, and I could tell that he was not the kind of man who was used to being challenged. Then the corner of his mouth curved up in a sexy grin. "I'd be honored if you'd take a walk with me."

The world that had leveled out started to tilt again, this time knocked off kilter because he'd completely destroyed my expectations.

I caught myself taking a step toward him, and forced myself to stop as little bubbles of panic started to rise inside me, tempered by an unfamiliar current of excitement. "No," I said slowly. "I don't think that's a good idea."

"No? Why not?"

Because I shouldn't make decisions when I'm intoxicated, I wanted to say. But I'd had nothing to drink that night, and if it weren't for his nearness, I would be stone-cold sober. "Because I don't even know you," I said instead.

"Don't you?" His smile seemed to hold a thousand secrets, and I wanted to know each of them. "I'm Jackson. Jackson Steele. And I know you."

"You do?" I couldn't imagine how. I'd certainly never seen him before, because I would have remembered. And he wasn't one of Reggie's clients or contacts, because I didn't recognize his name. He must have come as someone's guest, but since I was only a lowly assistant, there was no reason for him—or for anyone at the reception—to know who I was. As if to illustrate that point, when Reggie and I had arrived, one of the Brighton group big shots had told the waitress to bring over a glass of sparkling water for "Reggie's girl."

I'd managed a tight smile and refrained from rolling my eyes. Always nice to be appreciated.

"Of course I do. You're Sylvia Brooks," Jackson said, my name sounding like ambrosia on his lips. "And though you're not the reason I came here tonight, you are the reason I've stayed."

I stood there, a little shell-shocked. Then I said, "Oh."

It wasn't my most brilliant conversational moment.

My idiocy didn't seem to bother Jackson, though. Instead he just held out his hand again and flashed that killer smile. "Walk with me, Sylvia," he said. "I promise I don't bite hard."

The flippant comment, said so seriously, made me laugh, and swept away the last of my hesitations. After all, what could be the harm in walking? I could always turn around and walk right back.

"All right, Jackson Steele," I said, putting my hand in his. "Lead the way."

I'd expected him to lead us off the veranda and into the covered pavilion where the dessert tables and complimentary bars were set up. Instead, he skirted the panda habitat, moving us away from the pavilion structure and down a path toward the interior of the zoo. We strolled beneath another covered structure where a few zoo employees were directing late arrivals up to the party.

I frowned. "I can't just leave," I said. "My boss is back there." I didn't bother mentioning that he was a lame-duck boss, and I was operating more on politeness than practicality.

"We're not leaving," Jackson said, as he guided me down the wide path to where it forked, one direction heading toward the exit, the other leading deeper into the zoo.

The latter was blocked by a red velvet rope suspended between two waist-high golden posts that acted like anchors. Jackson slipped between one post and a flowering hedge, then gave my hand a tug, indicating that I was supposed to do the same. I hesitated, brows raised.

He shrugged, his expression so disarming I had to laugh.

"I have a little problem with authority," he said, as I joined him on the forbidden side.

"Oh?"

"Only in certain circumstances."

"Like what?" Our voices were low as we moved down the asphalt path toward the gorilla habitat.

"If I'm not the one in charge, I have a problem."

I swallowed, because I knew we were no longer talking about velvet ropes. I expected a wave of panic followed by the urge to bolt, and when it didn't come, I wasn't sure what to think. And then when he drew me to a stop, I stopped thinking altogether.

"Sylvia," he said as he reached out to stroke my forehead, smoothing a few strands of hair to the side. I dragged my teeth over my lower lip, my breath ragged. The easy laughter that had been between us only a moment before had faded, replaced by something heavy and palpable. Something dangerous.

Dangerous, yes. But compelling, too.

We'd paused beneath the rustic log gate that marked the way into the wilds of darkest Africa. Appropriate, I thought, considering how wild I felt.

He cupped my face in his hands, then bent low and brushed his lips gently over mine.

The kiss was soft and sweet and altogether too fast, and when he pulled back, I saw both heat and a question in his eyes.

I didn't think. I didn't hesitate. I simply eased forward, rising on my toes to bring myself closer. To claim. And, yes, to surrender.

He didn't wait for my lips to reach his. I saw the change in his eyes—the moment when gentleness was pushed aside in favor of lust and need and the hard, demanding ache that throbbed between us. His hands shifted, one sliding into my hair and cupping the back of my head. The other snaking around my waist.

He pulled me close, his mouth open to mine, his hips hard against me. I felt his erection straining against his jeans, and my body thrummed in response, my skin prickling and my sex hot and heavy and desperate for his touch. I felt his palm cup my ass and pull me in tighter even as his mouth warred with mine, his tongue finding and tasting me, thrusting and demanding. Taking everything I had to give and more.

I'd been kissed, but never like this. Never so hard and deep and thoroughly that it felt like sex. That it swept me out of myself, making me forget my past and not care about my future. Making me want only *this* moment and *this* man.

Making me wish that I could cry, because when he finally pulled away from me, I wanted nothing more in that moment than to weep with regret.

I was completely out of my element, my mind in a sensual whirl. Instead of closing off, I'd opened up. Instead of walking away, I'd slid right into his arms.

Those weren't my normal reactions, not by a long shot, but I couldn't deny that I wanted more. That I wanted him.

All of that should terrify me, but instead it enticed me. And that simple reality had thrown me completely off center.

"Tell me," he said, as his fingers slid through my short hair. "Tell me why you look like a rabbit about to bolt."

I hesitated, but answered honestly. "You scare me."

He shook his head. "I don't think so. No, I think it's because I *don't* scare you." His eyes narrowed. "You're an enigma, Sylvia Brooks. I think that's why I want you. I saw you the moment you walked away from the crowd and headed out to the veranda. I asked your name and I've watched you all night. Polite, yet distant. You're never rude, but it's as if you've got a line drawn around you that you don't let anyone cross."

I gaped at him, because he was absolutely right. What frightened me was that he saw so quickly what I prided myself on hiding so well.

"I'm in that circle now," he continued. "And it's not because I scare you."

I licked my lips. "No? Then why?" I felt hope mixing with desire inside me, because I truly wanted to know what he was going to say. I didn't understand this thing I felt for him. This fierce, fast punch that had knocked me sideways and left me dizzy and giddy and, miraculously, wanting more.

"It's because you don't understand it, either."

I fought the urge to hug myself in defense against the goose bumps that were rising on my arms. "Don't understand what?" I asked, though I knew exactly what he was talking about.

"This," he said, gesturing between the two of us. "You don't understand it, but you feel it as palpably as I do. And so you let me in." He moved closer, and I caught the scent of him, smoke and wood, like a forest after a storm. "You may not understand it. But, sweetheart, you need to trust it."

I wanted to. So help me, in that moment, I'm not sure I'd ever wanted anything more. But . . .

I tilted my head back so I was looking right into his eyes. "What if I can't?"

"Then I'll just have to convince you." He drew me close and kissed me again, this time slow and sweet, but it still set my head to spinning. And so help me I craved more. So much more.

When he broke the kiss, he stepped back, and I felt my body move with him, unwilling to let the distance between us increase.

"I'm going to take you home now."

His words were a command, underscored by the kind of certainty that would normally make me run or rebel. I did neither. Instead I clung to the one small fact of which I was certain—that if I said no, he would let me go. He might not want to, but if I asked, he would let me turn around and go back to the party.

I didn't want to, but I held tight to the knowledge that at the core of it, the decision was mine. And right then, that was enough. I nodded. "Yes," I said. "Take me home."

He drove fast, which didn't surprise me. Neither did the car, a sleek black Porsche that maneuvered the tangle of Atlanta traffic as smoothly as butter on a griddle.

"Nice ride."

"It is," he agreed. "She's a classic. I bought her from a collector as a present to myself when I got my license a few years back."

"Your real estate license?" I asked, assuming he either worked with one of the Brighton big shots or was being courted as an investor.

"Architecture."

I sat up a little straighter. "Oh."

He took his attention off the road long enough to glance at me. "You sound surprised."

"I'm not," I said. "It suits you."

"Does it? How so?"

I hesitated, then told him the truth. "Because you're a little bit arrogant."

"Oh, really? And here I expected to be flattered."

"You should be. It's like the way you're handling this car. All confidence and zip, in and out of traffic." I shrugged. "That's how I think of architects, I guess. It goes back to the pyramids, right? I mean, some Egyptian architect had the audacity to say that his design would rise up to the sky, and that they would figure out a way to make that happen. It's like building a skyscraper to the heavens or a bridge that spans a canyon."

I looked out the window at the Atlanta skyline, shining over the city. "It takes my breath away, you know. There's such control and precision to creating something like that. It's—I don't know."

"I think you do," he said softly.

I glanced over at him, saw him looking back at me with both interest and understanding on his face.

I shrugged. "Maybe. It's just—okay, I used to skip school some-

times and take the bus downtown. I lived in Los Angeles," I added.
"My parents had no idea, but there were days when I just couldn't
deal with all the crap that was going on in my life. And so I'd stand
there, my head tilted back, and I'd look at the city rising up around
me. And it would fill me. I didn't understand it then—all I knew
was that it gave me hope."

"Do you understand it now?"

"Yes," I said softly. "I do."

"So do I."

"Really?"

"You were right about the hope," he said. "But you were only a
kid, so you didn't get the core. That understanding came later when
you realized that the clean, soaring lines of an office building are a
testament. A reminder that circumstances and the world can be
controlled, no matter how futile and lost some moments might
feel."

My throat tightened, because he knew. He truly got it. And in
that moment I was grateful I never cried, because I didn't want to
shed tears in front of him. "Yes. Exactly."

"Why didn't you pursue it? As a job, I mean?"

"I would have," I admitted. "But I don't have the skill set or the
vision. I can see a building and understand its greatness, but my
mind isn't set up to conceive of it in the first place. So I guess it's
more of a hobby with me, and why I've got a job in real estate. And
I like to walk cities and look at the buildings. Read books. Take
photographs. I take a lot of photographs," I added.

I didn't ask why he became an architect. I didn't need to. I could
tell simply by watching him that he was doing exactly what he'd
been born to do. Even something as simple as his confident precision when he handled the Porsche proved that he embodied everything I admired. He was a man who didn't shrink from the world,
but walked proudly within it, both capable and eager to reshape it
in accordance with his own unique vision.

Had I seen that quality in him from the first moment? I must have, because why else would nothing more than a look from him have brought me to my knees?

I was still wondering as we climbed the steps to my second floor apartment in Buckhead.

I broke the silence as we arrived at my door. "I don't do this. Not usually."

"Go home?"

He was teasing, of course, but I remained serious, and with my hand I gestured between the two of us. "This," I said. "I don't date. Not very much. It's not—it's not really on my radar."

"Good. I don't want you to date. But, Sylvia, you're on my radar now. And I think that's a very good thing."

My cheeks flushed as I fumbled in my purse for my keys. "So, I've only got wine inside. Do you like red?"

"I do. But I'm not coming in."

"You're—but—" I stopped talking, afraid I sounded as gob-smacked as I felt. He'd asked me if I wanted more, and so I'd been expecting everything. Wanting it. Even craving it.

Now I stood in front of my doorway, confused, off balance, and uncertain where exactly I'd gone off the rails.

"I'm not coming in tonight," he clarified, as his fingers brushed my cheek. "But make no mistake, Sylvia. This isn't over. It hasn't even begun."

"I don't want it to be over," I admitted.

"And what do you want?" he asked. "Because I will tell you right now that when I want something—or someone—I pursue it relentlessly and don't stop until I have possessed it fully. Do you want sweet words and chocolates? You'll have them. Hand-holding and gentle kisses? I welcome them. But I want so much more, Sylvia, and you need to know that I will have you in my bed."

My mouth had gone completely dry. The rest of me was hot and wet, and I had to reach out and press my hand against the doorjamb simply to keep from melting onto the floor.

I expected the dark to take hold, my fears to pull me down, and the cold, unforgiving fingers of memory to yank me back into myself and away from this man and his words that were both a seduction and a demand.

But there was no cold, and the only dark came from the night sky, and was bright with stars. That tingle I felt wasn't fear, it was excitement. And when I met his eyes, I was certain that he could see in mine how much of a miracle he was to me.

"Christ, you tempt me. My fingers itch to take you right now. To strip you bare and just look at you, naked and hot and wet for me. And I will, too. I'm going to touch you. I'm going to stroke every inch of you. I'm going to bury myself deep inside of you. And I'm going to memorize the way you look when you find release in my arms. All of that," he said as my body went limp and hot under the force of his words. "But not yet. Not tonight."

He reached out as if to stroke my face, but his fingers hesitated just millimeters from my skin. I sucked in air, well aware of the heat between us, and wishing desperately for even the lightest touch of skin upon skin.

Then he withdrew his hand and looked straight into my eyes. His were inscrutable. Mine, I'm certain, were wild and pleading and just a bit confused. Because with Jackson, everything had flipped. Instead of grabbing control, I'd surrendered it. And that really wasn't me.

I didn't understand why—and while that might scare me, what scared me more was the fear that he would go away.

"You want me, too." It was a statement, not a question, but I answered anyway.

"Yes." The word seemed too small to encompass so great a need.

"All right, then." The smile barely touched his mouth, but I saw pleasure light in his face. "I'll pick you up tomorrow morning. Ten-thirty."

"Oh." I blinked at the sudden shift from the seductive to the esoteric. "Okay." I ran through my schedule, grateful I had no conflicts. Not that it mattered; I would have blown off anything that stood between me and spending the morning with Jackson.

The corners of his eyes crinkled, as if he knew my thoughts. "You're mine tomorrow," he said as he brushed a fingertip over my lower lip, and then turned and walked away.

I went inside, so full of light and anticipation that I actually did a little twirl. And I am really not the twirling type.

I peeled off my clothes, and every brush of material against my overheated skin was like a sensual treat. I slid into bed naked, wanting nothing but the sheet between me and my memories of Jackson.

Then I closed my eyes, slid my hand between my legs, and let thoughts of this gorgeous, sexy, enigmatic man carry me off to sleep.

six

A sharp knock at my door awakened me, and I stretched in bed, enjoying the fading memories of some truly spectacular dreams.

Dreams. Not nightmares.

The thought brightened my smile even more. So far, Jackson Steele was proving to be the embodiment of the perfect man. Charming, funny, utterly gorgeous. And despite that whole take-charge vibe, he wasn't the least bit nightmare inducing.

Pleased, I hummed a little as I tossed on a robe. I didn't hurry—it wasn't yet eight on a Saturday morning. Anyone who needed me was just going to have to wait. Still, I called out, "Hang on," as I tied the sash and walked to the door.

I checked the peephole, but no one was out there. Curious, I opened the door to look back toward the street, only to find a beautifully wrapped box on my doormat. I picked it up and found a simple tag tucked in under the bow. *Wear Me.*

I laughed, feeling a bit like Alice as she stumbled into Wonderland. But I had no doubt that the package was from Jackson, and when I went inside and took the lid off, my suspicions were confirmed.

The dress I found cradled in tissue paper was sunshine yellow and absolutely darling, with a fitted bodice, a loose and breezy skirt, and big white buttons from cleavage to hem. It also came with matching low-heeled sandals that actually fit when I tried them on. But it was the last part of the present—the part hidden beneath a thin fold of tissue paper—that made my entire body tingle. Sheer silk stockings accompanied by a black garter and black thong panties that were nothing more than a tiny triangle of lace. The bra was equally tiny, with almost nonexistent cups that were designed so that a woman's breasts spilled over the top, adding fullness while keeping her nipples exposed.

I licked my lips, then put on the lingerie, careful not to run the stockings as I rolled them up each of my legs. Then I stood in front of my full-length mirror and tried to see myself from all sides.

I looked like sin.

More important, I felt like it. Hot. Wild. Daring.

And there was no denying the tingle between my legs when I imagined Jackson buying this. Watching me in it. And then watching me out of it.

Without thinking, I slid my hand down into the panties, my finger barely stroking my clit before finding my center. *Oh, holy Christ, I am wet.* And when that familiar electric tingle started to shoot through me, I yanked my hand away, as guilty as a teenager.

Not because I didn't want to get off, but because I wanted Jackson to be the one to take me there.

Both aroused and anxious, I slid into the dress, pleased to see it fit perfectly. Then I hurried through my hair and makeup routine, only to find myself dressed and impatient well before Jackson's scheduled arrival at half-past ten. I spent the time feeling the way I had when I was thirteen and waiting for Billy Tyson to take me on my first date—a movie and a burger, chauffeured to both by his parents. That was back when my life was full of anticipation and wonder. When I trusted my parents to keep me safe and whole. When I lived in a solid middle class bubble that I'd thought, foolishly, was impenetrable.

That was before my brother got sick.

That was before *him*.

Stop it.

I clenched my fists and forced the memories away. I was about to go out on a real date, a very rare occasion for me. And dammit, I liked the way I felt. I wanted to hang on to the feeling. More than that, I deserved to hang on to it.

I busied myself with making coffee, then didn't want to drink it for fear it would linger on my breath. When the quick, firm knock sounded promptly at ten-thirty, I just about sprinted to the door.

"Hey," I said, breathless as I flung it open, and even more breathless when I saw him standing there, tall and lean, his dark hair wind-tossed just enough to give him a sexy, reckless vibe. When he stepped inside, his primal, raw scent enveloped me. Earth and wood and rain, blending together in a way that was uniquely Jackson.

"Don't move," he said as he stood just inside my apartment. "I want to look at you."

"I like the dress," I said. "Thank you."

"You're welcome," he said as his gaze raked over me with such intensity that I was certain he was seeing both the dress—and what was underneath.

"I like the lingerie, too," I said boldly, and was rewarded by the heat in his eyes and the way his jaw tightened, as if he was fighting for control.

"Do you?" he said, and those two simple words seemed to hold a world of questions.

I lifted my chin slightly, and when I spoke, my voice was breathy. "Yes. Do you want me to show you?"

"Very much. But not until tonight. In the meantime, I'll think about just how I'm going to reveal it."

"Jackson—" There was no disguising the need in my voice.

He shook his head, his eyes full of passion and promise. "To-night. Right now I'm taking you to lunch."

I bit back the flurry of questions—where were we going, what were we eating, when would we be back—and forced myself to simply go with it. To let Jackson take the lead. Strangely, it wasn't hard. Though I rarely slid out of the driver's seat, with this man it just seemed natural. As if something inside me knew that no matter what happened, he wouldn't push me too hard.

But whether that impression was accurate or simply wishful thinking, I really didn't know.

Back in the Porsche, Jackson easily maneuvered the Saturday morning traffic. We ended up at Centennial Olympic Park. I'd only been in Atlanta for a few weeks, but I knew the park well. Reggie's office was only a few blocks away down Marietta Street, and I'd come to the plaza during my lunch hour once or twice. It's a big space, with grassy areas, a reflecting pool, and the famous Fountain of Rings.

"A picnic?" I asked as we got out of his car. "There's no basket."

I half-expected him to open the trunk and pull one out. Instead, he just took my hand. "Burgers," he said, and I laughed. "Is that bad?"

I shook my head, still laughing. "I went out for burgers on my very first date. And I was feeling some of those first date nerves when I was waiting for you. I guess it just struck me as funny. What?" I added, noting the intense way he was looking at me.

"You just surprise me. There are things you're holding back—no, don't worry, I'm not going to press you—but then there are times when you're disarmingly honest."

"Not usually," I admitted. I didn't say that I felt comfortable with him. Too comfortable, perhaps.

I didn't say it, but I was certain that he knew it.

"Should I point out that we're in a park?" I asked brightly, hoping to signal a change of subject. "Unless you're planning to grill, that's not the traditional location for a burger and fries."

"I thought you already realized that I'm not the traditional sort."

I narrowed my eyes, but he didn't explain further. Instead, he led me across the plaza, the Fountain of Rings shooting water high into the sky as children watched and ran and splashed in the jets. "Want to?" he said, eyeing the streams.

"Tempting," I admitted. "But I like this dress too much. And I'm starving."

"Then let's get you fed."

We turned, strolling the tree-lined plaza until we reached the grassy area and the Visitor's Center—and the funky-looking hamburger stand.

"Googie Burger," Jackson said, pointing to the angular building that reminded me of both the old Jetsons cartoon and Tomorrowland at the Disneyland Park in Anaheim. "Opened here not too long ago."

"That's really its name?" I asked, studying the walk-up hamburger stand and the tables that surrounded it.

Jackson eased us into the line. "Yup. Do you know why?"

I cocked my head. "Is this a pop quiz?"

He laughed. "Guilty as charged."

"I can hardly have grown up in Los Angeles, love architecture, and not know about Googie," I said. "It's like a subset of futuristic design. Very Atomic Age. Starbursts and roofs that slope up. And lots of boomerang shapes. The building at LAX, the iconic Las Vegas diamond-shaped sign, about a zillion car washes. It's all over the place. Do I pass?"

"Flying colors."

"But the really important question is, how are the burgers?"

"As excellent as the building," he assured me. And he was right. Soft buns, perfectly cooked meat, crisp lettuce and tomatoes, and French fries to positively die for. We chatted while we ate, talking about everything and nothing, and when I reached over to wipe a bit of mustard from the corner of his mouth, I was struck hard by the realization that though I barely knew him, being with him was so easy that it felt as though we'd been together forever.

That perceived familiarity didn't lessen the heat, though, and when he caught my finger and drew it into his mouth, I gasped aloud, as much in surprise as from the sudden explosion of sparks that originated at my fingertip and then pooled, wild and needy, between my thighs.

He kept his eyes on mine, then so slowly I thought I might just melt, he teased my finger with his tongue before dragging his teeth gently over my skin as he released me. "Tonight," he said. "I'm going to taste the rest of you tonight."

My lips parted as if to respond, but I couldn't manage words.

He smiled, a little smug and very sexy. Then he stood and held out his hand to me. I took it willingly.

"Where are we going?"

"I thought I'd show you some of my favorite places. You said you grew up in LA, right? How long have you been in Atlanta?"

"Not long. I came right after I graduated in August. I met my boss out there—he was brokering a deal for Damien Stark, so I knew that Reggie was legit. Reggie Gale," I added. "He needed an assistant, I wanted real estate development experience, and so it just worked out."

"Stark," Jackson said, his voice flat.

"You've heard of him, right? Retired from the tennis circuit not long ago, and he's exploded onto the business scene. He made a huge profit with some real estate investments before he retired, and he parlayed that into a tech company and a whole bunch of other ventures."

"I've heard of him. I'm not entirely sure what to think of him. Or of his success."

"Really?" I shrugged. From what I'd seen Stark was damn talented. "I actually applied for an assistant job with him, but when Reggie offered me this position, I took it. Closer to real estate."

"And Gale brought you to Atlanta."

"So it's only been a few weeks. And everything's been so busy with the Brighton Consortium project that I haven't had much time to get to know the city. So, yeah," I said. "This is perfect."

I didn't mention that it was especially perfect since I knew that my time in Atlanta might be short. Once Reggie had fired me, I'd sent an email to the HR department at Stark International asking them to please consider my application if the assistant position hadn't already been filled. Even if I didn't get that job, I knew I'd probably end up back in LA. I had friends there and connections. And at the end of the day, it was all about finding a job.

Right then, though, I didn't want to angst about my job prospects. Instead, I simply wanted to enjoy the time with Jackson.

It ended up being an even more wonderful day than I imagined, with Jackson taking me around the city, showing me his favorite buildings, and telling me why he liked them.

We started by having a post-lunch drink at the Marriott Marquis with its alien-looking atrium that rose up to dizzying heights. We hit the Georgia Aquarium next, which had that same futuristic Googie quality. We entered, then went to the largest tank and sat in the dark. I couldn't say what creatures lived inside that massive habitat. All I knew in that moment was Jackson. His heat, his scent, his presence. I could barely think, much less focus, and when he brushed his lips against my temple, even that sweetly innocent touch was enough to have me writhing with need and anticipation.

From under the water at the aquarium, he took me underground to a subway station. "This one is my favorite." Jackson spread his arms out to encompass the Peachtree Marta station one hundred and twenty feet below the ground. The ceiling and floor were finished, but the sides of the tunnel were rough, blasted rock.

"This is where men shaped the world the way they saw fit," Jackson said, his words echoing my earlier ones. "Seemingly simple, but now thousands of people can move through bedrock, and the design—with the exposed rocks—drives that home."

He ended our tour at the sleekly stunning High Museum of Art with its original design by a Pritzker-winning architect and subsequent enhancement by an Italian architectural maestro. We wandered its galleries, exploring it thoroughly, but spending most of our time checking out the current Cézanne exhibit and studying the prints in the permanent photographic exhibit. Our Day of Architecture finally ended at Table 1280, the fresh-to-table restaurant inside the museum.

"There's more," Jackson said, as he lifted a strawberry to my mouth. "But the more time I spend with you, the less interested I am in architecture, and the more interested I am in getting you naked."

I almost choked on the berry. "Not very subtle, are you?"

"I know what I want," he said. "I know it, and I go after it. I told you that last night. And, Sylvia, I thought we were clear that I wanted you."

"What you want? Sounds a bit one-sided."

"It's not," he assured me. "I know what you want, too." The way he smiled reminded me a bit of the wolf with Red Riding Hood. *The better to eat you with, my dear.* "Don't I?"

Oh, dear god, yes.

I ignored the wild pounding of my heart as I pushed my plate away, the slice of cheesecake uneaten. I didn't understand the intensity of my reaction to this man. All I knew was that Jackson shifted something inside me. And so help me, I liked the way that felt.

The short walk to his car seemed unbearably long, and the drive was almost painful. The thrum of the engine drove through me, and every time he shifted gears, I felt the shift in power between my legs. My nipples were hard and painfully sensitive as they rubbed the lace of my bra with each movement.

I was on edge and frenzied and just a bit out of control. I wasn't a woman who swooned around a man. Just the opposite, in fact. Usually I clenched up or went cold if a man came after me with as much intensity as Jackson had. Granted, he wasn't demanding or forcing or giving ultimatums. Hell, he'd even pulled back that very first time when he'd ordered me to take a walk with him.

But that didn't change the fact that his entire persona was control and power. Exactly the kind of thing that usually made me edgy and off center.

So why wasn't I feeling that way now?

Then again, right then, I really was on edge. But a different kind. A better kind. My skin tingling, my sex throbbing. My entire body was primed in anticipation of his touch. A touch that I wanted. Maybe even needed.

"Go ahead," Jackson said, his voice soft but with a subtle hint of authority.

I turned to look at him, not understanding.

"Touch yourself."

This time, there was no denying the command. Nor was there any denying my body's immediate and visceral response. The instant firing of my blood. The sudden ache between my thighs. The tightness in my breasts.

I swallowed and forced myself not to clench my hands at my sides as panic began to bubble up inside me, all the more unwelcome because I'd thought with Jackson I was past it. "I don't think so."

My words were firm, and I was proud of myself for hiding my anxiety.

"You want to," he said simply.

"No, I—"

"Don't discount your desires, Sylvia. Do you think I can't feel it, too, the heat you're generating? Do you really believe that I don't know damn well that if I slid my finger inside your panties I'd find you hot and wet for me?"

I pressed my lips together, both aroused and frustrated that he could so easily see what should have been hidden.

"I thought of you last night," he continued. "I sat in my living room with a glass of bourbon and I thought of you."

I shifted a little so that I was looking straight at him, but I said nothing.

"I imagined you in your apartment, in your bed. I imagined you naked, Sylvia. Your legs spread, one hand on your breast, the other sliding down until your fingers found your clit, so hot. So sensitive. Did you tease yourself, baby? Did you play with your clit, then slide your fingers down? Were you hot and wet and tight? Did you fuck yourself last night, Sylvia? Did you thrust your fingers deep inside? Did you imagine it was my cock inside you? Tell me, baby. I want to know."

"Yes," I murmured, both because it was true and because I wanted him to know.

"Then do it now. Why deny yourself a pleasure you so clearly want?"

"I—Jackson, no." I dragged my teeth over my lower lip. I expected a flood of horrible memories and clenching anxiety so intense that I'd end up closing myself off and letting the world turn gray just so I could find a space inside myself where I could breathe.

Except the flood didn't come. On the contrary, little by little the panic faded, subsumed by the power of my desire.

"Close your eyes," he said. "Nothing more. Just close your eyes."

Since that was easy, I did.

"You're beautiful." He reached over and stroked my cheek, then ran his fingers through my short-cropped hair. "So goddamn beautiful. And even more so with the sun on your skin. Can you feel it, low in the sky, bursting through that window? Touching your skin? Firing your senses? Making you soft and warm and languid?"

"Yes." My voice came out a whisper, and I hadn't even noticed how relaxed I'd become in the few short moments when his words washed over me, seducing me with as much precision and technique as the hands I knew would certainly follow.

"Put your hands on your knees, Sylvia."

I did, then drew in a calming breath. My skin felt too tight and my body too hot. I had no word to describe the way I felt other than *need*.

And what I needed was Jackson.

"Unbutton your dress, Sylvia," he demanded. "But don't open your eyes."

I swallowed, then reached down and found the last button. It slid easily through the hole. The next was about four inches higher, and I unbuttoned it as well. Then higher and higher until I reached my crotch.

"Jacks—"

"No." His fingertip pressed softly on my lips. "You don't talk. You don't think. You only do and feel. Nod if you understand."

I nodded.

"Now finish the buttons."

I complied, my hands shaking slightly as I reached my waist and then unfastened the buttons that rose up the bodice to end at my breasts.

"Now spread your legs, and open the dress as you do."

I was breathing hard by then, imagining what he saw. The yellow material thrust aside, and me in black lace and stockings, my breasts plump in the lacy bra with the minuscule cups. With my eyes closed, I was lost in a sensual cloud, attuned to the movement of the car and the sound of his voice, but I didn't expect the brush of his fingertip over my nipple, and I couldn't withhold my gasp of pleasure as his touch sent a shock of sensation through me from breast to sex.

I arched up, letting the glorious feeling rush through me, and I didn't even hide my smile when Jackson murmured, "Yes, oh, baby, the way you respond, it's fucking incredible."

Incredible.

I swallowed a sigh. If being incredible meant that I could feel that way, then I was absolutely beyond thrilled.

"Now tilt your seat back," he said. "Just a little. That's good. Now can you still reach your knees? Not quite, but that's okay. I want one hand on your thigh. Good girl. Now take the other and move it up to your breast. No," he corrected, "not like that. Trail it up," he said, placing his right hand over my left, and moving our joined hands slowly and gently up my thigh.

The sensation was amazing, and as our fingers continued their journey over hips and torso, I tilted my head back, lost in a heated and erotic assault upon my senses. Our movement stopped just under my left breast so that I could feel the soft lace against my fingertips, and as Jackson eased my index finger up higher, I dragged my teeth over my lower lip, then bit down when my hand found my nipple, hard and erect over the cup of the bra.

"That's it, baby," he said. "Play with it. Touch it. You feel it, I know. That tightness in your nipple. You want to pinch it. To feel it hard between your fingers. Do that, baby," he said, and I heard his low moan when I did as he asked, then arched up in surprised pleasure as the electricity jolted through me all the way to my sex.

"Oh, yes," he said, his voice so low and tight that I knew his arousal came close to my own. "Slide your right hand up," he said, and I was astounded by how eagerly I complied. I trailed my fingertips along the inside of my thighs, then found the edge of my now-soaked thong.

"There you go, baby. Spread your legs wider and pull the material aside. I want to see your cunt. I want to see just how wet you are. I want to watch as you slide your fingertip inside. And I want to watch your body tremble as you go right to the edge. But not over, baby. You don't go over until I'm deep inside you. I'm going to fuck you hard, baby. So deep and so hard that you're going to scream my name when you come, and I'm going to capture the sound with my mouth."

His words shocked me. Not because they were so coarse and bold and unexpected, but because instead of feeling used by the things he suggested, I felt special. Instead of feeling dirty, I felt powerful. As if I was somehow the one in control and not this man who was demanding such supplication and submission.

"Jesus, that's hot," he said, as I stroked my fingers over my own slick heat. A tremor rocked me, making me moan. I was close—so very close, and all I wanted was to explode in his arms. I wanted more, deeper, *harder*. And with the low command of his voice in my head, I did as he asked, touching my clit, thrusting my fingers deep inside myself, and fighting the urge to beg him to stop the car and just please, please, please fuck me.

"Jackson," I moaned, as I felt the tingling begin along my inner thighs. The precursor to the explosion I so desperately craved.

"Not just yet, baby," he said, then closed his hand over mine, the mere brush of his hand over my inner thigh was almost enough to make me come anyway. "Not until I tell you to."

"Please," I murmured, more wild, more needful than I'd ever felt in my life.

"Please, what?"

"Please fuck me."

"Oh, baby. Believe me, I'm very much looking forward to that. But right now, I think, it's time."

"Time?"

"To go inside," he said. "And so much more."

I opened my eyes and looked around, surprised to see that we were in the visitor parking area for my apartment building. I'd had no idea that we'd exited the freeway, much less that we'd parked.

Without another word, Jackson leaned toward me, then very slowly buttoned my dress. As he got out of the car, I stayed there, breathing hard and trying to grasp hold of reality. Every bit of reason told me I should race for my door and shut myself inside, locking out Jackson and the world.

But reason didn't seem to have any bearing on this moment. Instead, I was running on pure emotion, and for the first time in a long time, I trusted that. Craved it. Wanted to just let go and feel the moments flow over me, one after another after another, leading to some wondrous but unknown pinnacle that I'd never reached before.

"Your expression," Jackson said as he opened the passenger door and reached out his hand to help me out. "Tell me what you're thinking."

"I'm not," I said, then laughed at the giddy sound of my voice. "Isn't it wonderful? I'm not thinking at all."

"Then what are you doing?" he asked as he pulled me to him.

I hooked my arms around his neck. "I'm feeling," I said. "Please, Jackson. Make me feel more. Make me feel everything."

"Sweetheart," he said, "I'm at your service."

I laughed, delighted and surprised, when he scooped me up and carried me to my door. I clung to him, my head nestled against his shoulder, trying to figure out what the hell had happened to me.

Me, the woman who was always so careful. Who kept such a tight lock on control, and who never let a man get under her skin.

He was different, somehow, I thought. He could keep me safe. And if my demons ran free, well then maybe he was the man who could slay them.

"Stand there," he said, putting me down in front of my coffee table. He looked around, then put his foot against the table and gave it a quick shove sideways so that there was nothing between where he'd placed me and the couch. "Good," he said. "Now wait."

"Wait—for what?"

But he just shook his head and pressed a finger to his lips. "You asked me to make you feel, Sylvia. And I promise you that I will."

I almost answered, but the truth was I didn't know what to say. And he was gone anyway, disappearing into my galley-style kitchen.

I stood in my living room, shifting my weight from foot to foot, wondering what he would do if I sat down, but afraid to try it for fear that he would leave. And I really didn't want him to go.

When he returned, he held two glasses of wine. One he set on the coffee table. The other he held as he sat on the couch.

I glanced sideways at the wine on the table, then raised a brow. He took a sip from his own glass before giving me a single, one-word answer. "After."

"After what?"

"After you're naked." His voice had shifted. It was low. Commanding. And very, very sexy.

I drew in a breath, waiting to feel the icy fingers of the nightmares slither up my back. But there was no chill. There was only warmth and desire and the intensity of his eyes, so powerful it seemed that I didn't need to strip at all, because he had already seen me bare.

"I—I'm not sure," I said, but even as I spoke, I knew my words were only for form. I wasn't tense—on the contrary, I felt loose. Warm. Even eager.

The cold fear I had expected was far, far away, replaced by a burning anticipation. Because I wanted the sensation of his hands upon me and the luxury of him looking at me.

"Not sure?" he said as he stood up, holding his wine. He moved to me, then dipped his finger in the liquid before dragging the pad gently over my lower lip. "I think you are, Sylvia."

He trailed his finger gently down my neck, then traced my collarbone, making me shiver from the soft sensuality of his touch.

"I watched you in the car, remember? So bold. So wild. I told you what I wanted, and it made you hot. I told you what to do, and it made you wet."

I pressed my lips together, forcing myself not to whimper.

"You want to give yourself over to me, Sylvia. You want to put the power for your pleasure in my hands."

His words scared me. Not only because they were true, but because I didn't understand why I so badly craved exactly what he was demanding. For years, my relationships with men had been few and far between. And when I did go out—when that pounding need for release and escape finally hit me with so much force that it drove me to action—then I was the one with the power. I was the one who set the terms and called the shots.

And on those rare times, I never felt anything more than the physical release of an orgasm and the hard burn of one hell of a cardio workout.

Most important, I was the one who walked away.

That was the way it worked, the way I protected myself.

And yet here I was, open and vulnerable.

And god help me, I was desperately, wildly, incredibly turned on.

"You want this as much as I do," he said as he circled me, stopping so that he was behind me when he bent close to whisper in my ear. "I see it in the way you look at me. The way you respond to me.

What was it you said in the car about my work? That it's power and control? You were right. But that's not just what I do. It's who I am."

He slid his arms around my waist and pulled me close, so that my back was against him. I could feel his erection against me and the corresponding tingle between my thighs. And in that moment, I regretted not having already done what he said, because I wanted nothing more than to be naked with his hands upon me.

He moved his hands up to cup my breasts. "It excites me to know that I hold the leash on your pleasure. That I can take you to the edge or not. That I hold your trust and your passion in my hand." He released me then, and it was all I could do not to whimper.

"So tell me, Sylvia," he said, as he moved back to the couch. "What do you want? Do you want to surrender? Or do you want me to leave?"

I didn't answer in words. Instead, I slowly lifted my hands and once again unbuttoned my dress.

This time, however, I didn't simply spread it open. Instead, I let it slip over my arms and off my body so that I stood before him in only my brand-new lingerie and shoes.

The shoes went next, even though I lost a good two inches of height and felt all the more vulnerable for it.

I needed to do the stockings next, and started to bend over to roll them down. But I lifted my head and the heat I saw in his eyes fueled my imagination. I took a step toward him, then another. Then I lifted my leg and put the ball of my foot on the edge of the couch, right between his thighs. And then, I very slowly started to roll down the stocking. When I reached my foot, I carefully eased off the silk. I rose slowly, letting the stocking dangle, and very casually let the wisp of silk play lightly over his crotch.

"Naughty," he said, but the smile suggested that he liked naughty just fine.

At the moment, so did I.

I repeated the process with my other foot, only this time I extended my leg so that my foot wasn't on the edge of the couch but on the cushion. Now, my toes brushed against his cock, straining against his jeans. And I knew that because of the way I stood with one leg up and the other leg down, the tiny thong was doing very little to hide how incredibly wet I was—and right then Jackson had a front-row seat with a view.

And then, because I wanted to make sure he didn't miss a thing, I trailed my finger from my ankle to my sex. I moaned as I slipped a finger deep inside myself, and I kept my eyes on him, not wanting to miss even a single spark of passion that fired on his face.

"How do you taste?" he asked, and I slowly lifted my finger to my mouth, drew it in deep and let him watch as I sucked. "Sweet," I finally said. "Do you like candy?"

"Oh, yes," he said as he reached out and put his hands on my hips even as he slid off the couch to kneel in front of me. "Maybe just a little taste." He leaned forward and closed his mouth over my sex, then licked and sucked with such intensity that I think I would have collapsed right there if he hadn't been holding me up.

"Delicious," he murmured when he pulled away and I whimpered with regret.

"Please," I said.

"Trust me." His hands roamed down, finding the band for the thong, then easing it down until I could step out of it.

He stood, then made a circular motion with his finger. "Turn around."

I complied, then sucked in air when he unfastened my bra and peeled it off my body. He let it drop to the carpet, leaving me standing there completely naked and entirely aroused. "This," he said. "I like this a lot."

He reached around, then cupped his hands over my breasts. From behind, he trailed kisses over my body, tracing the outline of my tattoos, but never asking about them. Slowly, slowly down each vertebra, then a soft brush of lips over the dimples above my ass.

Then he was on his knees and his tongue was dancing gently along the soft line of flesh that marked the juncture between the back of my thigh and the curve of my ass.

He had turned my entire body into an erogenous zone, and I trembled, so unsteady that I reached up and cupped my hands over his, as if holding on to my own breasts would somehow keep me steady.

When he told me to turn again, I did so without hesitation. His mouth was even with my sex, and I saw the way his mouth quirked in a teasing smile as he tilted his head back and looked up into my eyes. "You're beautiful," he said, then slowly traced a finger down, down, over my breasts, my tats, my belly button.

"A ribbon," he said, when he reached the red ribbon tattoo that scrolled along the crease of skin between thigh and torso. "And a lock," he added, touching the first tattoo on my pubic bone that Cass had inked so long ago. "Why? What's written on the ribbon?"

"Nothing," I lied. "I just liked them in the artist's book."

He held my eyes for a moment as if in challenge, but I stayed silent. How could I share the extent of the lie? How could I explain that contrary to what I told him, those tats were far from nothing. Instead, they were everything. Marks of both shame and power. A reminder of who I was, and who I would never be again.

"Someday you'll tell me the truth," he said, as he stroked his thumb lightly over my sex. "But right now, all I want is to taste you."

And then, with no more warning, he closed his mouth over my sex, then drew his tongue so delicately over my clit that I saw the world turn gray and stars explode in front of me. "It won't stay this way," he said.

"What?"

"Gentle. Just a taste, sweetheart, and then I'm going to make you scream."

He was as good as his word, and his tongue played and teased as his hands roamed, holding on just tight enough to keep me from toppling over. But I felt the shift in him when he cupped my ass in his hands, then demanded that I spread my legs as he laved me in long, liquid strokes, then slid his tongue inside me, tasting and teasing and making me squirm against him, desperate for him to take me harder, to take me further.

I was shameless, standing there with this man on his knees in front of me, his mouth so violently tormenting me. And yet all I wanted was more. All I craved was everything.

"Please," I begged, when I was certain that I could take it no more. "Please, Jackson."

"Tell me what you want," he whispered, pulling his mouth away just long enough to murmur the words against my skin.

"You. Oh, god, please. I want you."

"At your service," he said as he stood and drew me to the couch. With casual ease, he tossed off his shirt, then took off his jeans. He wore briefs, and before he removed them I could see the hard, thick bulge of his erection. And when he did take them off, I drew in a breath, awed by the sheer perfection of this man's body. A man who'd surely been carved by the gods on a particularly good day. He'd taken a condom packet out of his pocket, and I watched, mesmerized, as he rolled the condom on.

Then he sat on the couch and held out his hand. I went eagerly, then straddled him, feeling the hard, enticing heat of him at my core. "I want to watch your face when you come," he said. "And I want you to take what you need."

I licked my lips, realizing that he wanted me to be in charge. To thrust myself down on him. To ride him. To bring us both to the peak.

And oh, dear god, I wanted that, too.

It was familiar territory, being the one in control. Except with Jackson, I knew damn well that he'd never truly relinquished his hold.

And in his arms, I really didn't care.

"That's it, baby," he said, as I moved over him. Teasing both of us with the tip of his cock.

He took my mouth then, kissing me rough and deep, and I thrust downward, so wet that it was easy to take all of him, and then to rise up on my legs and then ease my body down again. Slowly. Torturously. Letting the pleasure—and the anticipation—build.

I met his eyes and saw understanding. "You're a tease."

"No," I countered. "I just want it to last."

But neither of us could hold out, and soon he took my hips and guided my motions. "I thought I was in charge," I gasped.

"To hell with that," he said. "I want to feel you explode."

Harder and harder, deeper and deeper. I impaled myself over and over on him, taking everything, wanting everything. His touch, his passion, the explosion that was about to ricochet through both of us.

And when it did—when my whole body clenched around his cock and the world spun full of color and light—I screamed his name, just as he'd said I would.

"I don't think I'll ever move again," I whispered as I fell forward against him, my arms around his neck.

"You will." He shifted us both, then picked me up and carried me naked to the bedroom. And he was right. When he slid on top of me—when he kissed and caressed me—when he made love to me softly and sweetly, I moved again just fine.

And then I snuggled close and thought that maybe, just maybe, I'd actually won.

But that wasn't true.

I hadn't won at all.

And when the dark gray fingers came to me in dreams, I realized for the first time how much I'd truly lost, and how much my past had cost me.

seven

I stare at the gray stucco building with the gray steel door, then cringe as it pulses red.

I turn in the car to look at my father, sure that he has seen it, too. Certain that he won't make me go in there again. Because it's bad, like a horror movie. And I don't want to be the girl in the horror movie who walks right into the scary place.

"Daddy . . ."

"Go on, Elle," he says. "You're going to be late."

"It's Sylvia now." I am Eleanor Sylvia Brooks, and I've gone by Elle for all of my life. Until Bob started calling me that. Now, at fourteen, I hate my name. Now, I go by Sylvia.

"I know," my dad says. "I know everything that goes on in there. I'm the one who arranged this, after all."

"You know?" My brow creases. "You really know?"

"He told you so, didn't he?"

I think about what Bob had said last week when he had his

fingers in my panties. About how he'd made this arrangement with my dad. About how we were getting good money. A lot more than a silly picture is worth, especially when he doesn't even sell all of the pictures he takes. "You're pretty, Elle, but do you really think you'll grow up to be a model?"

I shake my head.

"So ask yourself what it is I'm paying your dad for."

"He wouldn't do that," I say, but maybe he would. Because we need this money.

Suddenly, my brother, Ethan, is in the backseat of the car. "It's okay because you love me. And if you stop and I die, it'll be all your fault."

My mother appears beside him. "What teenager wouldn't want to be a model? You're so, so lucky. And already you're in an ad!"

She holds up the back-to-school ad for a local store. I'm confused for a moment because we haven't shot that ad yet, but then I remember that this is a dream, and when I remember that, my mom and my brother disappear.

"Time to go in," my dad says, and now I'm inside the building, leaning against a wall. Across the room, I see myself.

The other me is leaning against a fake Roman column. Bob is in front of me. He's a photographer who does a lot of stock photo work that he sells to advertisers, graphic designers, and the like. His name is Cabot, but I'm supposed to call him Bob.

I have no idea how old he is, but I think probably in his early thirties. He's clean shaven with silky dark hair that brushes his shoulders, and which he ties back with a leather band sometimes when he's working. When I first met him, I thought he was cute. Now, seeing him makes me want to throw up.

I glance around the studio to see if anyone else is here. Bob has interns and a few assistants. Even a woman who comes in with a wardrobe rack. But there is no one today.

And I know why.

"Okay, Elle," he says. "That's good, but not quite there."

He moves in front of me and turns on a fan. My hair—still long, still wavy—starts to flutter in the soft wind.

"Oh, yeah. That's awesome. Seriously perfect for this shot."

My stomach clenches.

"The dress, though . . ."

He moves to me, and even though I am standing in the shadows of the far side of the room, I can feel the brush of his fingers as he adjusts the other me's dress. It's pale blue and short, with buttons down the front and a fitted waist. The material is thin enough to have been caught by the manufactured breeze, and it flutters against my thighs.

"That's better," he says after he's unfastened the top two buttons. "But your face. Come on, Elle, I'm going for a certain look. A softness. A sensuality. Can you give me that?"

I watch as my mouth tightens into a firm line. I say nothing.

"Put your arms above you," he says. "Hold on to the column."

I do.

"Good girl. And what a nice clean line that makes." He trails his finger down my arm, then over the swell of my breast. He stops there, cupping my breast. I watch as the other me closes her eyes.

"Actually," he says, "that's not bad. The young and nubile female against the Roman pillar. It's almost like a mythological theme. Almost like you're Aphrodite." He starts to unbutton my dress.

"No!" I say from my place in the shadows.

"Don't," I say at the column.

"Who's in charge here?" he asks. "What am I paying for? While you're here, you're mine, remember? You have to trust me. It's my job to make you look good, right?"

He pulls open the dress front, revealing my breasts, tight in the too-small bra.

I see myself squeeze my eyes tighter.

"Not gonna be a good shot if you don't relax. But don't worry,

Elle. That's part of my job. To make sure you look right on camera. To make sure you relax completely."

As he talks, he's undoing the rest of the buttons. I watch as he strokes me, as he touches me. I remember all the things he's done— all the things he's doing right now. Where his hands are. Where his mouth is.

I don't watch him—I can't. The world around me is turning gray and all I want to do is escape from these memories, but how can I leave when I would still be trapped here, that other me, angry and scared and so, so ashamed.

I hear Bob's words, raw and needy, and grit my teeth. I keep my eyes locked on the other me's face. That me is still standing, arms still above her head. And Bob is on his knees in front of me. He isn't talking now.

I scream for the other me to push him away. To slam her hands down and crack his head. To thrust a knee up and break his jaw.

But she doesn't. The opposite in fact, as she slowly loses control.

Her clenched jaw loosens. Her lips part. Her skin flushes. I see her body writhe. Her little gasps.

And then there is that building pressure. The sense of an impending explosion. It's filling her—me—us. And oh, fuck, it feels good. And it's getting bigger and bigger and I look down, but it's not Bob who's touching us. Using us.

It's Jackson.

And that's when it hits. A fierce orgasm rocks through me, and I realize that there is no other me. There's just Elle. Just Sylvia.

Just shame. And confusion. And the cold, deep fear that if I keep breaking like this, I'll never manage to put myself together.

The sound of my scream yanks me from both the nightmare and the memory.

I glance around, afraid that people have heard me. But I only screamed in my head.

I stand still and draw in one breath and then another, trying to shake the nightmare as I get my bearings. I'm in Los Angeles. I'm on Hollywood Boulevard. I'm standing on the sidewalk by the entrance to the Hollywood and Vine subway station, and I'm holding on tight to a signpost.

Atlanta is gone.

The past is gone.

But the dream still lingers. And Jackson—the man I could have loved, the man I brutally left—lingers as well.

I drag my fingers through my hair. I'd been so lost in my memories—so wrapped up in Jackson—that I hadn't been paying attention. I've walked several blocks—a solid fifteen minute walk—without even realizing what I was doing.

"*Shit.*"

I bite out the curse, more scared than angry, because it's been a long time since I've disappeared into myself like that. I tell myself that it's okay. I'm just edgy and unsteady. But as I stand there, fighting the memories and the fear and the horrible nausea, I know that I have to get my shit together.

I glance around once again, but more for show than to actually get my bearings. I know where I am. More than that, I know what I want. What I need.

I'm practically vibrating with pent-up energy, and I need to burn it. Need to take control, be the one in charge.

And I know exactly how to manage that.

I turn off Hollywood Boulevard and head up Vine. In front of me, the cylindrical Capitol Records Building rises into the night sky, as if lighting my way. I'm not going that far, though. Instead, I'm heading for Avalon, an iconic Hollywood hotspot that's been around in various incarnations since the twenties. Currently, it's a popular dance club with excellent DJs and pretty fine techno music on Fridays. More importantly, it's got a stellar dance floor and guaranteed crowds. I know, because this is where I used to come to lose myself in the days before Jackson.

I still come to dance or cut loose when I've had a crappy day. Sometimes alone, sometimes with friends. But that's all about the beat. Getting lost in the music.

That's not why I'm here now.

Tonight, I'm broken. And I'm willing to fix myself the only way I know how.

As usual, there's a line, but it moves fast, and soon enough I'm through the doors, trading the traffic sounds and Hollywood lights for a raucous techno-beat and the violent pop of purple, white, and blue lights shifting and changing over a dance floor full of writhing, throbbing bodies. *There,* I think, and start to edge myself through the crowd.

I scan faces as I go, searching for the right one. Because this isn't about dancing. It's about shaking off this entire fucking day. It's about erasing my memories and my nightmares.

Mostly, it's about proving that I'm no longer some weak little girl to be intimidated and frightened.

It's more than that, too, and I damn well know it. This is about Jackson. About the way he blew me off. About the way he touched me. And about the goddamn devil's bargain he tried to toss at me.

A bargain that I know damn well I can't take, because didn't I run from him once already?

I'm on the dance floor, hands in the air and my hips moving in time with the music when I see him. Not Jackson—not even close, really. But he's tall and he's dark and right then, that's good enough. He's standing by the stage, not dancing, but bouncing a little. He's holding a highball glass with what looks like watered down whiskey, and every few moments, he takes a sip. I dance my way over to him, getting up close and personal with a few other candidates in the process, then pause in front of the one I picked.

"You're doing it all wrong," I say.

He cups his hand by his ear. "What?"

I lean close so that my lips are almost brushing his temple. "I said, you're doing it all wrong."

"Doing what?"

I take the glass out of his hand and set it on a nearby speaker. "Dancing," I say, as I grab both of his hands with my own. "I'll show you how to do it right."

I lead him out onto the floor, not giving him a chance to protest. We slide in among other sweaty, pulsing couples. Touching, flirting, getting dangerously close and then pulling away. The mating dance of the young and single, and this man and I are going at it in full force. Building and building, hands to hands, hips to hips. And when I look at his face and see that he wants me, I know it's time for step two.

Breathing hard, I move in close and hook my arms around his neck. "So, what's your name?"

"Louis Dale. What's yours?"

I shake my head. "Nope, that's not the way we play this game, Louis."

"What game?"

But all I do is smile and give him my hand. "Do you have a car nearby?"

"I—oh, yeah. Yeah, I sure do."

I let him lead me out of the club, then across the street to a pay-to-park lot. He stops in front of a sporty gray Lexus. "Nice ride," I say, easing in so that his back is against the car. My palms are flat against his chest. "What else have you got for me that's nice?"

I press close, reveling in that rush of satisfaction when I feel him hard against me. I don't want him—not really—but I do want this. The control. The power. The knowing that whatever I give or take tonight is because *I'm* giving or *I'm* taking. It's been years since I've needed to feel that so tangibly, but dammit all to hell, I need it tonight.

"I think we need a hotel, Louis, don't you?"

"Hell yes," he says, then pushes me back and spins me around so that it is my back against the car and he's crushed up against me. He's breathing hard, leaning in for a kiss, but I only turn my head.

"Not just yet," I say, because I'm the one in control tonight. But then I gasp as Louis is ripped away from me, the look of shock on his face almost comic as he stumbles backward, then lands on his ass a good two yards away.

"Not just yet?" Jackson growls. "Try not ever." He grabs my hand and yanks me to him with such force that I fall against him. His arm goes immediately around my waist and despite my shock and anger—despite my embarrassment—I can't help the wash of both relief and longing that crashes over me like a wave.

But I don't want to be relieved, and so I shove violently back from him, burying the depth of my discomfort under the force of my words. "What the hell? What the hell do you think you're doing?"

He ignores me, but aims his finger at Louis. "You. Get the fuck out of here."

Louis's eyes dart sideways—not to me so much as to the car. Then he sort of crab-walks backward before stumbling to his feet and holding his hands up in supplication. "Hey, man, she—"

"Go," Jackson says.

Louis obeys, racing across to the far side of the parking lot.

As soon as he disappears into the shadows, Jackson grabs my arms. He yanks me toward him, so close we are breathing each other's air. He is vibrating with fury, and for a moment I can't tell if he wants to kiss me or hit me.

He does neither.

I see the struggle play out on his face, and then he slams me backward against Louis's car. "What the fuck are you doing?" he demands. "You want danger? Try me, Sylvia, because you have no idea how dangerous I can be." He tightens his grip on my arms. "Or maybe you want anonymous? Me again—because if you think you know me, princess, I promise you don't."

"Jackson—"

"*No.*" He releases one hand long enough to run his fingers through his hair, then pushes roughly back from me, breaking our connection completely. I press my hands against the side of the car, forcing myself to stay put, to stay still. Because goddamn me all to hell, in that moment I truly don't know if I want to slap the shit out of him or wrap myself in his arms.

"You really think you can come back after all this time and bat your lashes and have me fall backward over myself to help you out?"

"It's not like that. I—"

"And for *him*—for Damien Fucking Stark? We're done, princess," he says, lifting a finger toward my face. "You told *me* to leave, sweetheart. And five years later you fall back into my life. And pretty goddamn dramatically, too."

I lick my lips. "It's just business."

"The hell it is." I hear the sharp edge of emotion in his voice, as dangerous as a well-honed blade. The fight is obvious on his face, as well, and I press back against the car, wishing I could disappear through the metal. He's fire and fury, and I have no idea what he is going to do. All I know is that all that passion is directed toward me, and that no matter what happens, I won't leave this parking lot unscathed.

I see it in his eyes first—a quick flash of wildness before his hand lashes out and his palm slams hard against the Lexus. Then he pulls me close, and I don't even have time to think before his mouth closes over mine.

The kiss is violent. Wild and desperate. And when I gasp, he takes advantage, thrusting his tongue into my mouth as one hand holds my head and the other slides up my chest to cup my breast. He deepens the kiss, claiming me with such intensity that I know I would not be standing were it not for his hands upon me.

The thin material of my dress does little to hide the heat of his hand, and even less to hide my arousal. My breast is heavy and with every stroke of his thumb against my painfully erect nipple, I want to beg him to just pull the damn dress down and let me feel skin on skin.

He pinches my nipple even as he bites down on my lower lip, swallowing my cry of pain and longing. Then his hand slides lower and lower. He cups my sex, and I cannot help the whimper that escapes me. Jackson hears it, too, and breaks the kiss long enough to meet my eyes, his hot and hard.

Then his mouth finds mine again, and goddamn me, I don't even protest for show. I take him, welcome him. I revel in the taste of him even as his hand urges my skirt up. Even as he finds my sex, hot and wet and throbbing with need.

There is no romance. There's no tenderness. He roughly shoves my lace panties to the side, exposing my flesh to his fingers. He thrusts his fingers inside me, and I moan as my body clenches tight around him, wanting him deeper, wanting more. Wanting to get lost in this moment and cling hard to everything I am feeling, but know that I cannot have.

His fingers are slick when he teases my clit, playing and stroking, teasing me to the edge and back. My body is alive with electricity, sparks dancing over me, my lips tingling, my nipples hard and tight and so painfully aroused. I want his touch, I want him inside me.

I simply want.

"Now," he growls, making me forget both fear and reality. "Dammit, Sylvia, you come for me now."

I do. And when I shatter in his arms—when I spin out and explode into the light-splattered night—I can only wish that I could stay like this, lost in pleasure with this man. But I know better than to believe in wishes, and when reason returns to me, I lean back, once again relying on the car and not Jackson to keep me steady.

His eyes stay on me for an instant longer, but I cannot read his expression. Then he takes a single step back. "Goddamn you, Sylvia," he whispers, holding his hands up as if in shock. "Goddamn you all to hell."

I tremble, lost and light-headed and confused. "I—I thought you said we were done."

"We may be done, but we're not over. We're a hell of a long way from over." His tone is still harsh, but beneath it, I hear something more. Regret? Resignation?

I don't know, but whatever it is rips through my heart, leaving it ragged.

He drags his fingers through his hair, then exhales. He looks me up and down. He says nothing about what just happened. Nothing about our past. Nothing about the present. His expression is harsh and hard and unreadable.

But his eyes . . .

His eyes don't lie, and the tenderness I see there comes close to destroying me. Because tenderness from Jackson is something I can't handle.

"Come on," he says, then surprises me by taking my arm.

"Where are we going?"

"Unless you want to make poor Louis walk home, we should probably get away from his car. I imagine he's hiding around here somewhere."

"Right. Of course." I take a deep breath and force my thoughts back in the right direction. This isn't about me. This isn't about Jackson. And it's not about us, because there is no us.

It's about the resort, and I'd do well to remember that. "There's gotta be a coffee shop open back on the boulevard," I say. "Let's have some coffee and dessert and we can talk about the project."

"I already gave you my terms, princess."

I don't bother to answer. I tell myself he can't be serious. He's too accomplished a businessman and this is too plum a project. And once his temper cools down we can move on to serious discussion.

From his expression, however, I think that the resort is the farthest thing from his mind. Still, he starts heading toward Hollywood Boulevard, and I consider that a victory.

But we don't make it that far. Instead, he shifts right past the nightclub and leads me to the door of the Redbury Hotel, a luxury boutique hotel that Cass has raved about a few times.

"No way," I say, but I remember the way his fingers felt inside me just moments ago, and I have to forcibly plant my feet outside the main entrance. "No fucking way."

He turns around and I expect to see either frustration or irritation on his face. Instead, I watch him melt a little. "No," he says simply, almost gently.

Then he leans in and kisses me, this time so softly and gently that I think I will melt. "I'm not the man you think I am."

"You are," I say. *And that is the heart of the problem.*

He hesitates only a moment, and then continues through the doors. I consider protesting more, but I'm both confused and exhausted. I have no more fight left in me. And so I will stay beside him and see where this is going.

"Jackson Steele," he says to the clerk. "Is Jennifer working tonight?"

"Of course, Mr. Steele. One moment." A short while later, a stunning woman in a pencil skirt joins us in the lobby. She has a name tag pinned to her jacket lapel—Jennifer Trane, Night Manager.

"Jackson," she says, shaking his hand in a manner that I'm certain would have been a very deep kiss were she not on the clock. "I didn't realize you were checked in."

"I'm not. I finally bit the bullet and got my own place. But my friend needs a place for the night. Could you see about getting her a room? Sylvia Brooks," he says. "But I'll take care of the charges."

"The hell you will," I say.

"We'll get her settled," Jennifer Trane the night manager says, as if I hadn't spoken at all. If there is any jealousy lurking there, it is well hidden. Even so, I can't help but wonder how they know each other. And as I wonder, I want to swiftly kick myself in the ass. Because I really don't need to be going there.

"All set," the night clerk says, then passes Jennifer a small envelope with my card key. "Right this way, Ms. Brooks," Jennifer says, and I start to walk after her. For one moment, I consider simply bolting and getting a taxi. But my Santa Monica condo suddenly seems very far away, and the thought of a soft bed nearby is incredibly enticing.

I turn back, expecting to see Jackson behind me. Instead, he is still standing in the lobby. "Goodbye, Sylvia," he says. And for the second time that night, Jackson Steele walks away.

eight

Sylvia . . .

Sylvia . . .

Sylvia!

I sit bolt upright, breathing hard. I'm in a strange, dark room, and something is buzzing repeatedly, sounding to my tormented mind like my name being called over and over and over again.

But it's not my name. It's my phone. And as I scramble to find it, reality returns.

I'm in a hotel room. I'm by myself.

And Jackson is standing firm on his ultimatum about the resort.

Well, hell.

As for the rest of it—the memories, the zoning out, the way he touched me—I really don't want to go there.

But even though I tell myself that, I can't help the jolt of disappointment when I finally squint at my now-silent phone and see that the call wasn't from Jackson.

Damn.

I sit up, stretching as I play the voice mail from Cass.

"Hey, girl, I tried to find you last night, and then someone said they saw you leaving with Jackson right behind you. So I hope that Jackson said yes to the resort and you're home sleeping the sleep of victory. Or he said no, and you're home sleeping the sleep of defeat. Either way, I hope you didn't do something stupid. Zee and I are about to crash for a few hours, but if you get this right away, then call me. It's, um, not quite eight. And if I don't hear from you by ten, I'm going to be supremely pissed. No excuses, Syl. Call me."

The phone goes dead.

Well, I think. *All right then.*

I hesitate, because I'm not entirely sure I want to talk. But this is Cass and she loves me and even though she didn't outright say it, I also know that she's worried. So I bite the bullet and call.

"You bitch," she says without preamble. "You didn't even text me. Where were you? Were you with Jackson?"

"I'm sorry. I just didn't think. And no. I mean, yes. I mean, later. I was with Jackson later."

"So you're home now?"

I glance around the hotel and frown. "I'm at the Redbury."

The pause is so long that I pull my phone away from my ear so that I can make sure we haven't been disconnected.

"Did you fuck him?"

"No!" My tone is full of righteous indignation, which, considering Jackson had his fingers in my panties, is a little bit disingenuous. "I wasn't even with him most of the time. I—oh, shit, Cass. I went to Avalon."

"Fuck me sideways, Syl. Seriously?"

Now the worry is plain in her voice, and it's clear that she understood my meaning—I didn't go there just to dance.

I rush to reassure her. "It's okay. I'm okay."

"Am I giving you another tattoo?" Her words are controlled and evenly spaced. Not anger, I think. But fear.

"No," I say, grateful that Jackson showed up when he did. "Almost," I admit. "But no."

"I'm on my way," she says.

"No, Cass, really. I'm fine. I'm going to get cleaned up and get to the office. See if I can find another architect who will make the investors happy." I say it lightly, even though I know there's no way in hell.

"You're sure? You don't have a car, and I'm not that far away."

"I'm sure," I say. "And you don't want to leave Zee, and she doesn't want to spend the morning with me. Seriously, it's all good."

"Okay. Listen, Zee lives in Silver Lake, and my cell signal is for shit here, so if you call and I don't answer, leave a message and I'll call you back from her landline."

"I won't. I'm fine. Quit playing Mommy."

"I'm worried about you."

"Don't be," I say gently. "It's all good."

I can practically see her dissatisfied expression. "Fine. Tonight, then. I've got a one o'clock that should take a couple of hours, but after that I'm free. Meet me at the shop at three?"

And because we both need reassurance that I'm all right, I nod. "Yeah," I say into the phone. "We can grab a late lunch."

"Forget the late lunch. I'm going to want an early drink."

I laugh, and we end the call.

I briefly consider whether I should go back to sleep for a few hours or just grab a taxi and get out of here. After I hit the bathroom, though, I decide to compromise on a shower. Because this bathroom is truly fab. With black tiled walls, ultra-modern fixtures, and a walk-in rain shower.

I turn the water on and wait for the temperature to adjust, standing naked in front of the mirror as I do.

Am I giving you another tattoo?

Cass's words seem to echo in the small room, and I slide my hand down until my fingers brush the lock that Cass inked just above my line of pubic hair. The first of so many. The mirror isn't a full-length style, but if I stand back far enough I can see most of myself. And the truth is, I don't need to see anyway. I know where they all are. Every souvenir. Every mark. Every pain, and every memory.

I turn my leg out, revealing the curving red ribbon inked onto the soft skin between my torso and left thigh, the ribbon curling from my pubis to my hip. And on it, the ornately scripted initials, *TS, KC, DW*. Small and intricately designed, like the text of a medieval manuscript, so that the letters appear to be little more than a random design. Of course, they are anything but.

I remember that night with Jackson—one night that held all the force and emotion of a lifetime. He'd traced his finger on the ribbon, and asked what it meant. I'd told him that it meant nothing, but that was a lie. The initials mean everything. They are a mark of both shame and power. A reminder of who I was, and who I will never be again.

They represent men like Louis. Men I'd gone after in those years before Jackson. Men I'd taken to bed so that I could use instead of being used.

I drag my teeth over my lower lip, silently thanking Jackson for stopping me last night. Preventing me from going so far that I would have no choice but to add LD—Louis Dale—to my collection.

I haven't done that—trapped a guy in my sights and gone after him like that—since before Atlanta. But last night, I'd craved that release, that control. This morning, I would only have regretted it.

I shift sideways so that I can glimpse my back. From this angle I can tell only that something has been inked in red between the two dimples above each of my ass cheeks. But that's okay, I know the tat. Even though I have never seen it except in reflection, I know the line and the curves. An ornate J intertwined with an S, like a fancy monogram.

Jackson's initials—and they are marking me.

I sigh and reach back, pressing my palm flat over the tat. I'd gone to Cass the day I returned from Atlanta. I didn't explain, didn't say a word. It was at least a month before I told her anything about Jackson and me. But I'd needed the ink right away. I'd needed the pain that marked the memory. And I'd needed a piece of him to be with me always.

There are other tats. On my breasts, between my shoulder blades, marking my hips. A silent path winding through the pain in my life. All discreet, so that no corporate skirt and blouse would ever reveal my secrets. But all there when I need them.

Right now, I tell myself, I don't need them. I'm doing fine. I have a career in which I'm advancing, good friends, a great boss. I'm moving forward in my life; I no longer have to stand naked before a mirror and trace the path of my triumphs and tragedies to give me strength.

And for years, I've felt strong and capable and in control.

But now the world is getting gray around the edges again, and the control I've always clutched so desperately is slipping away as if I'm holding tight with buttered fingers.

Fingers of panic are creeping back in through the cracks in my veneer, and I know why. Because instead of conquering them, I hid from them. I ran as fast as I could from Jackson, and then curled up into a little ball, living an anesthetized life.

But he's back now, and I'm tingling all over, just like a numb limb coming back to life, and I honestly don't know if I can handle this.

No, that's not true. I know that I *can't* handle it. I know, because I couldn't handle it the first time.

Somehow, I need to get Jackson Steele out of my head.

Except, dear god, I want him.

There, I've said it, even if only in my head. *I want him.*

Time and distance haven't lessened the desire any more than hurt and anger have.

I want his touch. I want his hands. I want everything he has to offer.

But god help me, I don't want to lose it again. I don't want to be so overwhelmed that control is ripped away from me. I don't want to be scared of my own reaction.

I can't handle that sensation of being lost outside myself—as if someone else is feeling things. Doing things.

And I sure as hell can't handle the nightmares that come with it. Nightmares that I've mostly left behind—and that I do not want coming back. Not now. Not ever.

Even more, I don't want to be used.

I don't want to be chattel.

Just the thought of it makes me panic, and I have to close my eyes and hug myself and breathe in slowly and steadily.

Hell, maybe I should be grateful he tossed me that ultimatum. Because I was an idiot to think that I could work with him, even if that was the only way to save the resort.

No. I can't give up. Not yet. Not until I've tried everything.

Which means that my plan is to dig into the extensive array of files that the company has on every building project around the world.

And even though I already know that every potential replacement is fully booked for years, I also know I have to try.

There's a red line station at Hollywood and Vine, and since the red line lets off just a block from Stark Tower, I decide that the best plan is to wear my cocktail dress to the office, change into the spare outfit I keep there, and get busy.

I skip the shower, dress quickly, then hurry to the station. Most of the outside is a matte gray metal, but the interior glows with yellow light from the dozens of golden and yellow-green glass tiles that line the interior, providing illumination as the escalator and stairs reach down into the actual station.

I don't have my pass, but I do have a credit card, so I grab a ticket and hurry to reach the train that's just pulling into the station. I'm lost in a crowd of tourists, and I let the mass push me along. It's standing room only, but when we reach the stop at Western, a guy in a business suit gets off. I collapse gratefully into his vacant seat, and as I do, I see a familiar face in the crowd.

Jackson?

I blink, and when I look again, he is gone.

I know it must have been an illusion. Someone with his eyes, his hair. But it doesn't matter. I still feel sad and more than a little lost.

Mourning, I think. And it's true. I'm mourning my career and the resort, which will never have the chance to be. But mostly I'm mourning the promise of Jackson that died five years ago. A promise that I soundly and painfully killed when I told Jackson to leave.

I'd awakened in a cold sweat, the sheets soaked through, memories of Jackson's face merging with Bob's still filling my mind.

Beside me, Jackson slept, and I rolled out of the bed, fighting nausea as I stayed on my hands and knees on the floor just breathing in and out until I was certain that I wouldn't throw up.

Didn't work. I clapped my hand over my mouth and ran for the bathroom, making it just in time. Then I turned on the shower, made the water just shy of scalding, and got in the tub.

I didn't stand. Just sat there with my knees up to my chest and my head down so that the water sluiced over me. And even as the steam rose around me, I shivered.

This was a mistake. I'd been so overwhelmed by the man that I'd forgotten what that would do to me. I'd ignored the warnings. The little sparks of panic and fear.

I'd thought that I'd actually kept some control. But that wasn't true at all.

I'd surrendered completely. Mind. Body. I'd responded to every touch, yielded to every whim.

There'd been pleasure—oh, god, yes, there'd been pleasure—but it was tainted by his demands. And, more, by my reaction to him. By the fact that whatever control I'd thought I still clung to was nothing more than an illusion, because all he had to do was tell me to spread my legs and I did so eagerly. Shamelessly.

I asked only one thing of myself, and all it took was this one dangerous man to shatter everything.

Jackson had come into my life like a storm, fast and wild and unexpected, and I'd been so overwhelmed by his power and intensity that I forgot to consider just how dangerous he was for me. For years, I'd worked so hard to keep such a tight rein on control. To fight back all the demons that Bob had planted inside me. And I had. I'd found a way. Maybe it wasn't perfect, but it worked for me. Or it had until tonight.

Tonight, Jackson had swept all of that away. And now there I was, battered and broken.

I didn't know what to do. All I knew was that I wanted to run, but I feared that if I did, Jackson would follow.

The thought made my heart twist, but whether with longing or fear, I wasn't sure. All I knew was that I had to end it now. While it was new. While it would be easy.

Except it wouldn't be easy.

On the contrary, it would be the hardest thing ever.

The only thing harder would be to stay with him.

And though part of me begged to do just that, the rest of me knew that I wasn't that strong, and if I wanted to survive, I had to end it.

Even if ending it ripped both of us to pieces.

When the train pulls into the Civic Center station, I blink the memories away, then follow the crowd to the street, then walk down the sidewalk to Stark Tower. Joe is working the security desk, and his brows lift when he sees me. "Are you all right, Ms. Brooks?" he asks as he rises, and I realize that in my wrinkled cocktail dress and smeared makeup I must look like I'm doing the walk of shame. And I guess I sort of am.

I hold up a hand to forestall him before he gets too worked up or worried. "I'm fine, really. It's been one of those days to the nth degree. But everything is okay. I just need to get to my locker."

He doesn't look entirely convinced, but waves me through to the elevator banks.

"Clear me for the gym, please," I ask, referring to the private fitness facility on the twentieth floor. "I have a spare access key in my locker, so I'll be good to go after that."

The gym is rarely busy on Saturdays—when folks come in on weekends, it's usually to work, not to work out—so I'm able to get to the women's locker room without being noticed. As with everything Stark, the place is completely decked out, rivaling the most high end of Los Angeles fitness centers. I take a shower, put on the spare skirt and blouse I keep for wardrobe emergencies, along with the matching pumps, then take some time with my makeup. I doubt Damien is on-site—he tends to work weekends from his Malibu house these days—but if I do see my boss, I want to look professional and in control.

With any luck, my research will only take a few hours. Then I can call the house, arrange to meet with Damien there this evening or, worst case, schedule an in-office appointment for first thing in the morning.

Either way, time is running out, and I can only pray that luck is on my side.

I take the elevator to the penthouse, which houses Damien's private office on one side and his residential apartment on the other.

The elevator opens to the office side. I see Rachel at my desk, her head bent as Damien's voice filters through the intercom. "Try her at home."

"I did," Rachel says. "I got her voice mail there, too. I'm guessing she's out and the battery on her phone is dead, but I'm sure she'll check her messages once she realizes— Oh! She's here!" Rachel looks up and then sags in obvious relief. "I'll send her right in."

She disconnects the intercom as I approach, then shoves a folded newspaper section at me. "Look at it later," she says, "but you look fabulous."

"What's going on?"

"He's in there with Aiden. Go!"

"With Aiden?" As the VP of Stark Real Estate Development, he's my immediate supervisor on this project, and the fact that he's in with Damien—and that they are both looking for me—knocks me sideways. "What happened?" I'm certain she'll know. Being at this desk means being aware of pretty much everything.

"Aiden got a call from one of the island's investors."

"Aiden did? Who? When?"

"I don't know. He called Damien and they met up here. Damien's been here for about half an hour and Aiden was right behind him."

"Shit." I glance at my phone. Sure enough, it's dead. I shove it at her. "Charge, please."

"On it," she says, then thrusts her arm out toward the door again. "Go," she adds frantically.

I go.

"Good, you're here," Damien says without preamble. He stands by his wall of windows, looking out at the spread of downtown. Aiden is on the small couch in the sitting area and he acknowledges me with a nod. Originally from London, he moved with his family when he was a teen. I confess I love the way he talks, very East Coast with just a hint of British accent.

Despite his years in the States, he's got that upper crust Brit thing going for him. Bearing, class, the whole nine yards. Someone told me that he's number one hundred and something in line for the throne. Looking at him, I believe it, though I doubt he's holding his breath.

Now, he pours me a glass of water, then sets it on the table across from him. I take the chair closest to the water, then sip it gratefully. "Rachel told me the bare bones," I say. "What happened?"

"Dallas Sykes called me at home," Aiden says, referring to the CEO of one of the country's largest department store chains. "He was rather discombobulated."

I raise a brow at his choice of word. Dallas Sykes is gossip rag material—a sexy bad boy who inherited his position and spends most of his time bouncing from woman to woman. Somehow, "discombobulated" doesn't fit. And I can't imagine what could have happened to bother him anyway. I say nothing, though. I'm certain either Aiden or Damien will elaborate.

I'm proven right when Damien turns from the window to face us both. "Apparently a reporter called Dallas just after dawn this morning. Word is out the project is dead."

"What?"

Damien meets my eyes, but doesn't pause. "The reporter knew that Glau quit—which can be attributed to Glau's own people—but he also heard that our first potential alternative said a big fuck you to working for Stark International."

I feel a sharp pain in my chest, as if someone has thrust in a knife. "That's—" I start to say *ridiculous,* but it really isn't. Jackson pretty much had said that. And he'd given me only one way around it—a way I have no intention of taking.

"I don't know where the reporter could be getting his information," I say. "Steele hasn't said yes, but he also hasn't said no." I fidget with the newspaper in my lap. "And if this spreads to the rest of the investors . . ."

I stand, tossing the newspaper onto the coffee table as I do. It lands open to a picture taken at the gala. I'm standing close to Jackson, who has his arm around the exceptional brunette. Seeing them twists something up inside of me, and I bite back a curse.

"Dammit, I handled this whole thing badly," I say. "Not only did I not manage to lock Steele in last night, but I somehow managed to create a leak." I look from one man to the other. "I'm sorry."

The truth is, I don't actually know where I went wrong, but this project is my responsibility, and if something got fucked up, then I'm the one shouldering the responsibility.

"Did you tell anyone that Steele was our go-to alternative for Glau?" Stark asks.

"Cass and Wyatt," I say. "But they have no vested interest."

"And Steele?" Aiden asks.

"Well, of course. But considering I was approaching him, that would have been self-evident anyway."

One brow quirks up in a way I consider very British, and he glances toward Damien. "Wouldn't surprise me," he says.

I turn my attention from one to the other. "Wait a minute. You're suggesting that Jackson Steele leaked this to a reporter? Why on earth would he do that?"

"I did some digging after he so emphatically turned down my offer to sign on to the Bahamas project," Damien says. "Turns out that where I've had a few deals flourish, he's had a few go sour." He meets my eyes. "I knew the odds of getting him on board were slim. It didn't occur to me he'd set the rumor mill buzzing."

"I can't believe it." I'm not sure if I'm angry or flabbergasted.

I start to tell the men that I absolutely don't believe that Jackson would do such a thing, but then remember what Jackson said about revenge. If he's going to mess with me, might as well go all out.

"You gave it your best shot," Aiden adds, even as my temper is spiking. "And the work you did was first-rate. Get Damien to cut you loose and I'll give you an office on twenty-seven whenever you want it."

I manage a smile. Stark Real Estate Development takes up the entire twenty-seventh floor, with thirty-three satellite offices around the globe. But this isn't about the job, it's about the project.

A project that Jackson Steele has ripped right out of my hands. *Shit.*

I look straight at Damien. "It's really over, isn't it?"

"Unless by some miracle Steele says yes, then yeah, I'm afraid it is." He shifts his attention to Aiden. "We already have the conference call scheduled for Monday, so have the PR department respond with no comment until then. After the call we'll release a statement. Syl," he continues, "get me a draft by morning."

"I'll get on that now," I say, grateful for a reason to leave. Right now, all I want to do is get out of that room.

I excuse myself and am stepping out when Damien's intercom buzzes. Since the door is partially open, I hear Rachel's voice in stereo. "Mr. Stark, there's a Jackson Steele here to see you."

I freeze. Just freeze right there in the doorway, with my arm thrust out in front of me. Then he's there, taking hold of the door and pulling it open all the way, so I have to either unfreeze or topple over.

I manage to get my act together and stumble back into the room.

"Ms. Brooks." He takes my hand, but whether it's in greeting or to steady me, I'm not sure.

After a moment, he releases me, then strides confidently toward Damien. "Mr. Stark," he says as they shake hands. "How nice to see you again. I'm sorry to come without an appointment, but I wanted to tell you personally how excited I am to be a part of The Resort at Cortez."

nine

The rest of the meeting is blurred by my fury, though I manage to keep it in check until Jackson and I leave Damien's office so that he and Aiden can personally call Sykes and the rest of the investors in order to both dispel the rumors and announce Jackson's participation.

I manage to stay silent until I've led him into the single small conference room on this floor. "What the hell?" I snap as soon as the door snicks shut behind me. "What in the goddamn hell did you just do?"

I surge past to the control panel on the nearby credenza and hit the button to close the electronic blinds. I fully intend to scream and rage, and I damn sure don't want an audience when I do it.

Jackson, damn him, is brutally calm. "I'm just making sure that everyone has all the relevant information."

"What does that even mean?"

He moves to the window and stands beside it, so that downtown Los Angeles is spread out behind him. I'm reminded of the image from the premier—Jackson on the girder in jeans and a hard-hat, all power and control, force and motion.

Today, he wears a finely tailored suit, and looks crisp and put together.

Or mostly put together.

Because it is impossible not to notice the wound on his cheek. It's covered by an adhesive butterfly bandage, but the cut and the bruising are still somewhat exposed. And when I glance down, I see that his knuckles are raw as well.

Those injuries weren't there last night, and as I stand there, I'm absolutely certain that I am the reason for them.

I'm not entirely sure how that makes me feel.

He may be injured, but nothing about this man looks like a victim.

On the contrary, he's a man used to getting what he wants— and right now, I know that's exactly what he's doing.

"Stark's a powerful man," he says, then turns from the window to face me. "I don't want him thinking ill of me because he believes I turned down his project."

"That's a load of crap," I retort. "You turned down the Bahamas resort without even blinking."

He simply shrugs. "Maybe I was overbooked. Maybe the terms were unacceptable."

"Or maybe you told Stark you didn't want to work on a Stark International project. That he casts too long a shadow."

"True," he says. "But don't you think it's reasonable that now I want to show Mr. Stark that I spoke too hastily? Because the truth is that I cast a long shadow, too, and if I do this, it will ultimately be known as a Jackson Steele project." He meets my eyes, his expression flat, but the corner of his mouth curves up just enough so that his amusement is plain. "Don't you agree?"

Since he has just tossed my words back in my face, I can hardly disagree.

"I'm ready, willing, and able to perform," Jackson says. "Stark needed to know that. The only question is whether the specific terms of the deal are acceptable, and I believe that's what Stark told you to work out with me."

It's true. Damien had originally left it to me to put together the deal points with Glau, and now I'm supposed to do the same with Steele.

How uncanny that I already know what our sticking point will be. *Me.*

His smile is wide and smug. "If it turns out that we can't come to terms, then you can relay that to him. But at least I'll leave here knowing that Damien Stark is aware that I was, at least for a time, ready to work on his resort. Enthusiastic, even," he adds as he looks me up and down.

I feel a rush of sensual pleasure that, God help me, I do not want to feel. I don't want to surrender. All I want to do is run.

I force myself to stand taller. Straighter. To speak cleanly and crisply despite my frayed nerves. And, yes, despite my own damnable desire. "Why are you doing this?"

"You know why," he says as he strides to me. I hold my ground, resisting the urge to move backward and clutch the credenza behind me. "Because I want you, Sylvia."

He reaches out, then traces his fingertip along my collarbone as I stand stock-still, trying very hard not to shiver from the thrill of his touch.

"I want you naked," he whispers in a voice as tempting as sin. "I want you exposed. I want you open to me. And I think," he adds in the kind of voice that will broach no argument, "that you want me, too."

I exhale slowly and force myself to look at him. "Goddamn you, Jackson Steele."

"I once told you that I'm a man who goes after what he wants, and that's still true. But here's a question for you, Sylvia. Are you a woman who does the same? You say you want this project, this resort. Prove it. It's here for the taking. Right now, the only obstacle is you."

I say nothing, because if I speak, I'm afraid of what I'll say.

His eyes, like blue fire, meet mine. "Tonight. Eight o'clock. Be ready for me."

I pull open the glass door to Totally Tattoo and am immediately accosted by both loud colors and equally loud music.

"Sylvia!" Joy high-fives me as I step up to the glass case that doubles as a cash register stand and a display for the shop's various rings and bars. Cass doesn't do piercings herself, but she hired Joy just shy of a year ago, and the arrangement has worked out well for both of them. "When are you getting your tongue pierced, girl-friend?" she asks, just as she does every time I come in.

"This side of never," I reply, just as I always do.

In theory, I have nothing against tongue piercings. In practice, I lean far too much toward the wimp side of things.

"You are seriously early, but I'm just about done!" Cass calls from the back.

Joy cocks her head as she looks at me. "Cass is just about done. She says you can go on back."

"You can come on back!" Cass's voice rings out from her table near the back of the shop.

I exchange a grin with Joy and head back.

Cass is standing now, pulling off latex gloves as her client—a tall, bald man with arms the size of most men's calves—stands shirtless, admiring the huge colored dragon she's inked on his back.

"Looks great," I say.

"Fucking awesome," the guy agrees.

"Looks great so far," Cass corrects. "See you in two weeks, Gar, and you'll really see that bird pop."

"You got it, Cass," he says, then pulls on a T-shirt with a logo that I don't recognize, but assume is either a heavy metal band or a motorcycle.

"He's a sweetheart," Cass says, as soon as the guy's out the door. "Wants the tat done before he gets married in January. Guess they're going to Cozumel for the honeymoon and he wants to rock the look if he's going to be shirtless ninety percent of the time."

As she talks, she cleans up her station, and I hop onto the table and get comfortable watching her.

"Just give me ten to get everything put away and then we can head out. I don't have any more appointments today, and Tamra's here in case we get a walk-in."

I glance around, looking for the elusive Tamra. "Is she folded up under one of the stations?" I ask, which isn't entirely unreasonable. Tamra's the most petite woman I've ever seen, short, lean, and perfectly proportioned.

"Funny. No, she's in the back. At any rate," she continues, her voice rising in a way that signals she's excusing my idiotic interruption but may not be so gracious about another one, "I'm thinking late lunch with alcohol, then shopping with loose inhibitions."

"And alcohol is the only way to loosen your checkbook?"

"Absolutely. And I have to shop because I need a Halloween costume."

"Seriously?" In all the years I've known her, Cass has worn the same costume. A floral print skirt, a solid pink T-shirt, and three-inch high pink stilettos. Her straight girl costume.

"Zee's throwing a party," she says. "I need to trot out something new."

I cock my head. "Falling for someone who doesn't share your sense of humor?"

"Just being careful," she says, a little sheepishly. "I like her, okay?"

I nod. What little I'd seen of her, I'd liked, too. But Cass is a little wild, a little weird, and a whole lot out there. She pulls off feminine, grunge, sporty, and elegant with equal aplomb, and she has about as much politics attached to her sexuality as she has wheatgrass in her kitchen. Which would be exactly none.

If she's afraid that the straight girl costume won't go over with Zee, then my ears are pricking.

"Chill, Mom," she says. "I just want a change. New girl. New costume. It's not a big conspiracy."

"Fine," I say. "Then I wish you awesome shopping."

"You like her, right?"

Once again, I eye Cass sideways, because she is not the insecure type who needs reassurance about who shares her bed. Which means she's either really into this girl, or entirely unsure.

Since that makes me unsure, I go for the casual, supportive best friend vibe. "I do like her," I say, and since that's true, the words come easily. "What does she do, anyway?"

"Co-owns a restaurant. How cool is that, right? I mean, I love food."

I glance at her workspace, where she habitually keeps two jars full of snacks. One full of Jelly Bellies and the other of Tootsie Rolls. Her non-snack choices aren't much different. "So you're saying her restaurant serves frozen bagels and Cap'n Crunch?"

Cass shoots me a frown as she takes stock of her area, searching for anything she forgot to store or clean. "Cap'n Crunch is a core member of one of the basic food groups."

"Of course it is," I agree. "Just like wine is a member of the fruit group."

"Yes. Exactly."

"So, if she owns a restaurant, you should ask her about the franchise thing." Cass wants to expand Totally Tattoo throughout California, and maybe into a few other states, too. She's leaning toward franchising, and I told her I'd get one of the attorneys at Bender, Twain & McGuire, Stark's primary law firm, to sit down with her and go over her options.

Cass looks up from the counter she's tidying. "That's a really good idea. Except I don't think it's franchised."

"Can't hurt to ask," I say. "There's no such thing as too much information. Besides, if you talk to her about it at her restaurant, you might actually get a free meal." I grin to show I'm teasing. Mostly.

"Oh, hell. Now you're just making me hungry. Let's blow this Popsicle stand."

"Yeah, about that—"

I cut myself off with a grimace, and she stops cold, hands on her hips. "Okay. Spill."

"The thing is, I kind of need a tattoo."

"You bitch. You told me you didn't sleep with him."

"I didn't. I swear. This one's not about sex. It's about—" I cut myself off, then suck in a deep breath. "Okay, so here's what happened." I give her the rundown, and watch as her eyes get wider and wider.

"That fucking prick."

"I've already called him that," I admit. "And a few other choice names." I pull my feet up on the table and hug my knees to my chest. "He's trapped me, and he's using me, Cass. He's using me, and I want you to put a fucking chain on me, because I'm letting him, which is something I swore I'd never let happen to me again. But here I am, caving to him, because I can't let the resort go."

I squeeze my eyes shut, willing myself to cry. Wanting to cry. And not being able to manage even one fucking tear.

Not even that, I think. Even that one small thing—the release of tears—and I can't manage it.

"He's locked me up tight," I say, opening my eyes and meeting hers. "A chain. I want a chain."

"*No.*" Her face is as fierce as her voice. "No, don't you dare look at it that way. You *could* let it go. But the resort means a lot to you. And so you're using him. You," she repeats, pressing her fingertip against my shoulder. "*You* are using *him*. Using him to get what you want."

"The resort," I say. "I want the resort. And I'm taking steps."

"Fuck yeah, you are. Just like you took the idea to Stark in the first place. You're doing what you need to do to get the job done. *Your* job."

"Yeah," I say, liking the way she thinks. "But my job is going to keep me pretty much attached to Jackson's hip. Tonight," I say. "And then tomorrow, too."

Her brows lift. "Expecting an all-nighter, are you?"

I lick my lips. "Considering Jackson's terms, don't you think I should be?"

She winces. "Sorry."

"It's okay. And that wasn't what I meant anyway." I pause for dramatic effect. "We're having after-lunch cocktails with Nikki and Damien tomorrow afternoon. At their house. In Malibu."

"Seriously?"

"Nikki called as I was driving over. She'd already asked Jackson. Just casual food and drinks, she said. A welcome to the project thing. And it's exactly what I should have expected, because that's the nature of this job. I'm the project manager and our schedule is tight. We're going to be working together pretty intimately." I exhale, because the truth is that when I factor in Jackson's ultimatum, there aren't going to be many moments between now and the completion of the project when I'm not right there at Jackson's side.

"Attached at the hip," I repeat. "So I really want that chain."

"No way, Syl."

"Dammit, Cass," I begin, because she knows me. She knows I need this.

But before I can get on a roll, she holds up a hand. "You need to own it, babe. Like I said, you're the one using him. Your resort. Your project. So I won't give you a chain. But I will give you a flame."

"A flame?"

The smile that blooms on her face is just a little bit crooked. "Out of the frying pan, babe," she says.

I laugh. I can't help it. "And into the fire?"

"Abso-fucking-lutely."

I draw in a breath, then nod. "Yeah," I say. "I think I can live with that."

ten

In the end, Cass and I blow off both the drinks and the shopping. I can only mix so much Jackson and alcohol and still feel safe. And although I could use a costume to hide behind, right now, I figure I can always rely on the tiny but brilliant flame that now flickers at the side of my left breast.

So when Zee called Cass and invited her over to spend the evening watching television on the couch, I didn't mind the parting.

Now, it's not even six and I'm already home, and as I ride the elevator up to my third-floor condo, I'm glad of the extra time. Jackson said he'd arrive by eight. That gives me two hours to chill. And to maybe, hopefully, find some peace with my decision.

I tap my code onto the keypad, hear the familiar whirr of the locks, and then push the door open. Despite the mountains of moving boxes that mar the landscape of my living room, my mood immediately shifts for the better. The condo is tiny but it's all mine. Well, mine and the bank's.

Damien had given me a bonus along with the project manager position, and I'd taken the leap and dived head-first into the wonderful and wacky world of home ownership. Now I own seven hundred square feet above retail space on Santa Monica's Third Street Promenade. And while the access to shopping is definitely a perk, the best part is the view.

The entire back wall works like a garage door. Down, it is a wall of glass panels that provide a view. Rolled up, it provides more living space by opening onto a balcony that looks out over the streets and the ocean beyond. And, of course, a really great breeze.

I press the button beside the front door and grin like an idiot as the mechanism kicks into gear and my back wall begins to roll up.

After that, though, I just stand there, a little at loose ends.

Jackson.

He's going to be here in only two short hours. And, yes, I may be armed with my plan to use him before he can use me—to treat him just like one of the guys whose initials now mark my body—but that doesn't change the fact that in the end, he'll have his hands on me. His mouth on me.

And oh, dear God, his cock inside me.

And the sick, horrible truth?

Despite the fact that he's forced my hand and tricked his way into my bed, I cannot deny that I want him there. And I hate myself just a little for that.

My phone rings, and I'm grateful for the distraction. I'm even more grateful when I check the caller ID and see that it's Jamie.

"Hey, what's up?"

"I'm calling to tell you I sent you an Evite," she says.

"You're calling me to tell me you sent an email?" That's undeniably weird, but not entirely surprising. I met Jamie Archer through Nikki and liked her immediately. She says what she thinks and doesn't mince words and as far as friendship goes, she's as loyal as they come. She's also a lot of fun during happy hour.

"I want to make sure it didn't go to spam. It's an invitation to my Halloween party. Three weeks," she says. "That gives you tons of time to find the perfect costume."

"Sounds like fun," I say, meaning it.

"Totally. It'll be my first party in the condo. Well, since I've been back in the condo," she amends. She'd rented her place when she returned temporarily to Texas to live with her parents. But she's back now, doing the struggling-actress thing and happily dating Ryan Hunter, Stark International's security chief.

"So you're all settled back in?"

"Oh, yeah. I let my tenant have the place furnished and with all the kitchen stuff and linens. So when he moved out and I moved back, it was sort of like going on a backward vacation. Totally easy."

I glance around at my stacks of poorly labeled boxes and grimace. "I think I hate you right now."

"Need help?"

"Nope," I say. "I'll get it done."

"Good, because I'm not doing anything today except lounging in bed naked and sending Evites."

"Is Ryan with you?" I ask.

"Indeed he is."

"Then I'm betting you're doing more than lounging."

"See, this is why you work for a guy like Damien. You're so damn smart. Speaking of, I saw the pics of you from the premiere. Very cool."

"The ones in the paper?"

"You rocked your outfit," she says. "And how very stealthy of you."

"Stealthy?"

"Nikki told me about the whole architect snafu. And how you ended up going to the premiere to meet with Jackson Steele. And persuade him . . ." She adds the last with a suggestive lilt.

"Is that what Nikki told you?" I ask, all the more mortified that she'd landed scarily close to the truth.

"The persuade part," Jamie says. "I added the va-voom part myself. Makes a better story."

I roll my eyes.

"Anyway, I think this Jackson dude is a way better choice than Martin Glau."

I laugh. "Jamie, you don't know shit about architecture."

"True. But I know Glau is pushing sixty, is as round as Hitchcock, and actually has jowls. *Jowls.* And Steele's all over the internet this morning, and he is hot. But I guess Irena Kent wouldn't cozy up to someone who's a schlub."

"Who?"

"Jackson Steele."

"No, the woman. Did you say Irena Kent? The actress?"

"Yeah."

I frown. That's why the brunette on Jackson's arm had looked so familiar. I remember the way they'd looked last night, and the way seeing their picture in the paper had felt like a knife twist.

I tell myself I'm not going to ask—and then of course I do exactly that. "What do you mean she's cozying up to him?"

"Rumor is they're dating," Jamie says, and considering she's dipped her toe repeatedly in the Hollywood pool, I figure she would know.

"Like, serious dating?" I cringe the second the words leave my mouth. I am not with Jackson—our absurd arrangement notwithstanding—and I do not intend to be with Jackson in the future. So who he fucks is no business of mine.

"I don't think so," Jamie says, and I am uncomfortably but undeniably relieved. "To be honest, I think she wants the female lead in that movie they're doing about that Santa Fe house he built. You know, the one that had all the gossip after the family moved in. Sex and murder and suicide."

"I know the stories," I say. "And I knew that Hollywood's been buzzing about doing a feature film that centers on Jackson. But I didn't know it was about that house." Honestly, I wasn't sure why it would be. The whole murder-suicide stuff happened after the project was wrapped and Jackson was off to conquer the next mountain of stone and steel. "How the hell could I not have heard that?"

"Why would you?" Jamie asks, which is a good question considering she doesn't know that I have followed every bit of Jackson Steele trivia over the last five years.

"I don't think it's public knowledge," she continues. "I know a guy who knows a guy who did a rewrite on the script. I think they're keeping it pretty close to the vest. I guess Jackson's not thrilled. My friend says he's the reason the woman went ape shit."

"The woman?" Jamie has completely lost me.

"In the story. The woman who murdered her sister and then killed herself. It was because of Jackson. At least in the script, anyway. Not sure about real life."

I realize I have tightened my grip on my phone to the point that it is painful. "Oh my god," I say, because I can think of nothing else. "Is it true? I mean, what does that mean, 'because of Jackson'?"

"Not a clue. But there's another rumor that he beat the shit out of the first screenwriter. Also unconfirmed," she says, and I can't help but think about Jackson's temper. About the cut across his face and the way his knuckles looked so raw today.

"But what I can confirm," Jamie continues, "is that he doesn't want the movie made at all. *That* I know is true because one of Ollie's law school buddies represents him."

Ollie is the attorney that I'm hoping to hook Cass up with for her franchise questions. He's also a friend of Jamie's. I have no idea who Jackson uses as legal counsel, but I have no reason to doubt Jamie's intel. As far as gossip goes, Jamie is part bloodhound.

"It sounds like a huge mess," I say, because at the moment, that's the only take-away I have.

"Oh, a complete clusterfuck," Jamie says cheerily. "Anyway,

I've done my duty and delivered your daily dose of gossip. Now I've got to send out a million more Evites and make a million more follow-up calls. I have no idea how we're gonna fit all these people in my condo, but I'm going to make it work. You're coming, right?"

"Wouldn't miss it."

"Awesome. Later! Ta!"

I'm not sure how long I stand there with my head full of Jackson, my mind spinning in a freakish mix of desire and question, angst and anticipation. But there is no way I'm obsessing over this for another hour, much less another minute. Instead, I grab a knife from the kitchen, then slice open the tape on one of the boxes sitting on my coffee table.

Since I'd been in a hurry to move, I hadn't taken the time to label anything that wasn't a necessity like clothes and pantry items. That has made unpacking both frustrating and exciting, because I never know when I might be about to open a treasure trove.

In this box, I find my photographs.

Dozens and dozens of prints in every size, ranging from eight by tens all the way down to three by fives. I pull a few out and feel a little karmic tingle. Because they're images of the Winn Building in New York. The soaring testament that Jackson built in Manhattan, and that I'd made a pilgrimage to see last summer.

I'd been traveling for business, going with Damien to meet with a number of his East Coast executives. I hadn't yet seen the Winn Building, although I'd read everything I could get my hands on about it. I'd told Damien I was going to the museum one afternoon—I'm not sure why I lied—and I'd gone to the financial district instead. I'd stood across the street, my head tilted back, and I'd simply let myself go with the pleasure of those clean, perfect lines reaching up to the heavens and a sky as blue as the eyes I remembered so well.

And, yes, in some small way standing there in the shadow of what Jackson built was a bit like standing by the man himself.

I'd taken dozens of pictures, but as I look at them now, I can see that none comes close to capturing what in my memory is so raw and so vivid. I toss them back into the box, my dissatisfaction with the images reminding me that I need to reschedule with Wyatt and Nikki.

Before I can give Wyatt a call, though, my intercom buzzes. I'm not even close to ready for tonight, and I jump a little, only to sag in relief when a guy's voice announces, "Got a delivery for Sylvia Brooks."

I buzz him up, and a messenger in jeans, an oversized sweatshirt, and slanted baseball cap with the service logo bounces out of the elevator about the same time I open the door. He passes me a box wrapped in plain white paper and topped with a bright red bow.

Under the bow is a tag—and the tag says, *Wear Me*.

Despite myself, I smile. But when I open the box and peel open the tissue paper, my smile fades. The dress is red, but that doesn't matter. Because it's the dress. *My* dress. The exact same style as the yellow dress with the white buttons that he'd given me in Atlanta. I lift my hand to my mouth and make a small mewling sound as my knees go weak.

I'm standing by my kitchen table, and now I clutch the back of a chair, steadying myself, because I am certain this will shatter me.

And that, I realize, is exactly what he's trying to do. This is about revenge, after all. About Jackson getting payback for what happened in Atlanta.

I take a breath, then another, trying to calm down. He wants to play dirty? Well, screw him.

He wants to play games, then fine. We'll play games.

I stalk to my bedroom. It takes a few moments, but I find the box with my lingerie. I don't own much in the way of fancy underthings, but I do own one set. A sexy black bra, a tiny thong, a garter belt, and a pair of elegant silk stockings.

It's the set that Jackson gave me in Atlanta, and I'm relieved when I find the soft pink lingerie bag that I'd purchased in which to keep them.

I'd almost thrown them away, both the dress and the underthings. But I hadn't. And the yellow dress, in fact, is folded up beneath the lingerie bag.

I consider tossing the red one aside and putting on the yellow dress, but no. I already have a plan, and it's more subtle.

I don't know why he hasn't included lingerie with the red dress, but that means he isn't expecting anything bold. For all I know, he's forgotten, and instead of making me angry, that possibility makes me sad. Because every moment of every hour I'd spent with Jackson is burned into my mind. I've clung tight to those memories for five years, pulling them out to soothe me when I feel lost and alone.

It didn't last—how could it with me being a basket case?—but at least I can hold the memories close and know that, for one shining moment, I had something right and sweet and wonderful.

For years, I've been silently grateful to Jackson for at least giving me those memories. I've spun our time together into nighttime fantasies and daytime dreams. I've made him a hero in my mind.

A knight, a protector. A man willing to make the sacrifice to keep me safe, and he'd proven it by walking away when I told him to.

That Jackson would never want revenge and he wouldn't try to break me. He was a man worthy of my fantasies.

And he is not the man who is coming to my door tonight.

I need to remember that, I think. I need to keep it perfectly clear in my mind that the Jackson of today is playing games. And if I want to have any chance of surviving this round unscathed, I need to play, too. More than that, I need to win.

eleven

I'm in the short hallway leading to my bedroom when the intercom buzzes promptly at eight.

I've been standing there, my dress open, my body angled to put the lingerie to best effect as I look at myself in the mirror. As I do, my fingers touch my tats. Or, at least, the ones that will give me strength tonight.

The flame that Cass put on my breast, now slightly slick with the ointment I applied to soothe and protect it.

The lock that hides just under the tiny thong panties.

And the ribbon of initials marking the men I have claimed.

Each reminding me that I know how to do this.

Each a symbol that I can keep control. That I can prove to myself and to Jackson that I'm the one using him to get what I want, and not the one being used.

I start to button up the dress, expecting another buzz of the intercom. An annoyed second try, because how dare I make him wait.

But the next sound is not a buzz. Instead, it's a sharp rap at my front door, and I tense because just that tiny deviation from the plan is enough to rattle my nerves.

Get it together, Syl. Just keep it the fuck together.

"One sec," I call, and then I button the dress slowly. Not because I want to make him wait—though that is an unexpected side benefit—but because my hands are shaking just enough to make the task more difficult than it should be.

I take one deep breath followed by another. And then I go to the door.

I stand tall as I pull it open, because I want to look confident. Nonchalant. Like this is just any other date on any other day. But all of my good intentions go to hell the moment I see him.

He is leaning casually against the door frame in khaki slacks and a faded denim button-down. His hair is slicked back from his face, and his eyes are hidden behind aviator style glasses that partially cover the cut on his cheek. He hasn't shaved and I can't help the way my fingers itch to stroke the stubble that makes him look even more masculine and delicious.

Without a word, he takes off the glasses to reveal eyes that are filled with so much wicked promise it makes me aware of how very little I wear beneath this dress.

It's not the reaction I want—tonight, he is supposed to melt for me, not the other way around. And so I cock my head and keep my face blank, the kind of expression I've relied on to get me through so many of Damien's business meetings, where my role is to simply take notes and not react to the progress of negotiations.

"How did you get through the security gate?"

"I'm a man of many talents," he says, then steps past me into the foyer. As he does, our hands brush, and though I don't want to feel anything, there is no denying the sparks that this man generates in me. I tell myself that's okay. I can use that. I can let my own attraction to him fuel my performance.

And I can let his attraction to me cement his fall.

"The dress looks lovely on you," he says, examining me with a look so incendiary it's a wonder my blood doesn't boil. "But I knew it would. The memory of you looking innocent in yellow is burned in my mind. But you weren't innocent at all, were you?"

My foyer is little more than a short hallway, and now I lean against the wall beside the door, feeling a bit trapped as he stands in front of me, just close enough to be inside my personal space. Just close enough for me to catch his scent.

Just close enough that I can't help but remember.

"Don't tell me you've forgotten." His words are an eerie echo of my thoughts, and as he reaches out, I draw in a breath, unprepared for his touch. But it is not me he's reaching for, and when I realize that all he is doing is closing the door, I release a shaky breath—and curse the wave of disappointment that crashes over me.

"I haven't," he continues, apparently unconcerned that I have yet to say a word. "You in yellow, as bright as the sun shining through the car window. You unbuttoning your dress, revealing yourself to me. Touching yourself, teasing yourself. And it was me you imagined, wasn't it, princess? Me who filled your thoughts. Who made you hot. Who made you *need*. Open your eyes," he demands, and I do, surprised to realize that I had shut them in the first place.

He is right there, so close I can feel his heat. So near that all I would have to do is lean slightly forward to feel him warm and hard against me.

I do the opposite, leaning back, my palms flat against the wall behind me as I desperately wish that I could sink into the drywall and simply disappear.

"Tell me you remember, princess. Tell me you remember how it felt."

I want to stay silent—to prove to him that even though he thinks that he took control the moment he walked through my doorway, it isn't true.

Except, of course, it is. I may have hoped to keep the upper hand, but I should have known better. I know the man, don't I? And I know myself, too.

"Tell me," he repeats.

I tilt my head back. I meet his eyes. And I give him the answer he's looking for. "Yes. I remember. And I remember you wanted me, too."

"I did. I do." His smile is thin and cunning and just a little bit wicked. "Looks like I'm about to get what I want." As gently as a summer breeze, he brushes his fingertip over the swell of my breast.

I draw in a breath, determined to fight against the heat that even so simple a touch is fueling in me.

"I think you're going to get what you want too, princess."

"I want the resort, Jackson." I meet his eyes, making sure that mine show nothing but cold calculation. "*The resort*. And like you, I'm willing to do whatever it takes to get exactly what I want."

As far as I can tell, my words don't faze him at all. If anything, he seems amused. "And that's why your new dress is red. You've lost your innocence, princess."

"Stop calling me that."

He cocks his head, as if considering. "My rules," he says. "Or had you forgotten already?"

"Dammit, Jackson." I don't know why the nickname bothers me when his touch did not. There's nothing in a name, after all. And it is his touch—and my reaction to it—that reveals so much.

Even so, I don't like the endearment. And the extent of my distaste bothers me enough that I push away from the wall and then push past him, away from this corner in which he's trapped me and where my face and body reveal far too much.

I hurry through my small living area and stop by the patio door. It's down, and I place my hand on one of the glass panes as I look out at the world. That's where I want to be—out there, not trapped in here with my past and a man I cannot deny I want, but can no longer have. A man whose mere presence makes me just a little bit crazy even though I need to hang on tight to cold rationality.

I do not hear his footsteps, but I see his reflection, and I am expecting it when he places his hand on my shoulder. Even so, I close my eyes as if in defense against the powerful surge of longing that cuts through me when he bends his head and kisses the back of my neck.

"Don't," I whisper.

"Don't? I believe the terms of my offer were clear." He takes a step back as he pulls his phone out of his pocket. His eyes meet mine in the reflection. "So you tell me. Do we have a deal? Or should I call Damien and tell him I'm not your guy, after all?"

"Dammit, Jackson. Why are you doing this?"

"You know why."

I shake my head, though that is a lie. Because I do know. It's retribution. It's punishment.

I saved myself from one type of hell only to be thrust headfirst into another.

"No? Well then, let me tell you. I'm doing this because I want you to remember." His lips brush my neck again, then move up to dance lightly upon the curve of my ear, making me tremble with sensual longing.

"I'm doing this because I want you to understand what you gave up." His hands stroke my shoulders, then down over the short sleeves of the dress until he reaches the bare skin of my arms. He continues, finally finding my hands and twining his fingers with mine.

"I want you to know the future that you threw away, princess," he says, as he lifts our joined hands to cup them over my breasts.

I stiffen, my body a riot of emotions and sensations. I want to lash out against him—to tell him to go to hell, because I damn well know what I gave up. I know it as well as I know that I had to. And at the same time I want to melt into him. To let his touch take me all the places that I've imagined over the last five years. To let him have me so fully and completely that I am used up and there is no room for fear or nightmares or memories.

But that, of course, is impossible.

Most of all, I want to turn in his arms and kiss him. I want the

Jackson I once had, not the one who stands here today. Not the one who sees only the woman who hurt him, and not the woman who could have fallen in love with him.

And so I do nothing. I just stand there, trying hard to ignore the sensation of my hands upon my body—of his hands upon my own. Trying to breathe. Trying to get centered.

And trying desperately to remember that it had been my plan all along to take charge of this night, and wondering how things could have turned so horribly sideways.

Finally, I push my hands back down to my sides, then force myself to turn around even though he doesn't step back. He's so close that our bodies are brushing, and I have to tilt my head back in order to see his face.

"That really is what this is about, isn't it? You just want to punish me."

"Hell yes," he says. "And I think that's what you want, too."

"Excuse me?"

"Maybe you feel guilty about ending it the way you did. Maybe that's why you've agreed to my terms."

"I haven't agreed to anything. You ambushed me."

For a moment, I think I see compassion in his eyes. Then they go cold again. Good. I want them to be ice. I want them to freeze me. I don't want to melt for this man. I don't want to feel the heat. I don't want to succumb to the guilt that he is so damn right about.

"I see right through you, princess," he finally says. "And you can play games all you want, but you and I both know that you're fighting. Well, guess what? I am, too. And I'm not accustomed to losing."

He reaches out and ever so slowly undoes the top button of the dress.

"What are you doing?"

"What you're letting me do."

"I—"

"You can stop me, princess. Just say the word."

I lick my lips, but I do not move and I do not protest. I tell myself that I cannot back down—I cannot give up the resort.

But that isn't the only truth, and I know it as well as he does.

The truth is I want this, too. And since I can't willingly give it, then I will acquiesce to letting him take it.

"Good girl," he says, as he flips open the second button, then the third to reveal the black lace of the demi-cup bra, the swell of my breasts, and my very erect, very sensitive, nipples.

"Like I said," he murmurs, then bends close to take my nipple between his lips. He sucks, drawing it in, then grazing the tender flesh with his teeth and sending coils of red-hot desire spinning though me to throb with violent intensity between my legs. "You want this as much as I do."

"You bastard," I say, and he only laughs.

"Princess, you don't even know the half of it."

He returns his mouth to my breast, his lips skimming my cleavage as he moves to find my other nipple. "Why don't you finish those buttons?" he murmurs, his lips never leaving my skin.

"What?" His words haven't quite registered with me, at least not until he takes my hand and places it on the fourth button, then lets his own fingers trail up to tease the nipple that he'd abandoned, cool and tight and still wet from his tongue.

Oh, god.

His teeth nip me, and I arch in pleasure, understanding that this is not just a sensual tease but a silent demand.

And so help me, I comply, moving my fingers down the dress with slow, steady movements. I keep my back to the patio door, because what he is doing to my breasts is making me crazy, and I'm afraid that if I don't have that support my legs will simply give out.

When I'm almost done with the buttons, he pulls back, removing his mouth from my breast and forcing me to bite back a whimper of protest.

"Don't fight it, princess," he says. "I see it on your face, in the flush of your skin. Even in your eyes, that you're trying to keep so cool and hard. Don't you know that I see what you want? That I feel what you need?"

My traitorous body aches with the desire for him to touch me, and I can only stand there frozen, unable and unwilling to give in to his games.

"Go ahead," he says, as if reading my thoughts. "Touch yourself. Show me how you like it. Show me exactly how to put my hands on you."

I shake my head. "Jackson. No."

"My rules, princess, remember?" He reaches for the dress and eases me out of it. He tosses it backward so that it lands on the couch. And there I stand, clad only in the sexy underwear and fuck-me red heels.

"Christ, you're gorgeous," he says, and there's such honest arousal in his voice that I'm overcome with a sense of déjà vu. I've stood like this before. Dressed like this—or, rather, undressed like this. Hot and wet and wanting, and Jackson's eyes on me, so full of desire that I could drown in them.

But that night I'd wanted everything he had to give—and I hadn't been afraid. Not then. The fear had come later.

Tonight—god help me—I want it, too. And that scares me to death.

"Go ahead, princess," he says, lifting my hand and placing my palm against my stomach. "I want to watch you melt."

I meet his eyes, expecting to see heat. But all I see is the mask of a man holding tight to his emotions.

Fuck that—if he's going to force me to play, then I'm going to play to win.

"Is this what you want?" I ask, sliding my hand up to my breast and finding the nipple that he just abandoned. I close my hand over my breast, squeezing and teasing, then so slowly it is almost painful I trace my fingertip over my tight areola. "Or maybe this?" I ask as

I roll my nipple between my thumb and forefinger. I suck in air, more turned on by my performance than I'd intended to be, but I see the flicker of heat in his eyes.

Touchdown.

"Do you like to watch, Jackson?" I slide my other hand down my belly, all the way to the elastic band of the tiny thong panties and the little triangle of lace that barely covers my sex. Then lower and lower still. "Or do you want more? Is that it, Jackson? Do you want to touch me? Do you want to fuck me?"

I see the way the muscle in his jaw clenches. I watch his throat move as he swallows. And I wallow in the pleasure of my victory.

"Do you know how wet I am? How good I feel?" My words are not a lie. Despite the situation—hell, maybe because of it—my body is traitorously aroused, and as I stroke my clit, I can't deny the simple reality that I am all the more turned on because I know that he is watching me.

I tell myself that's okay. The only goal here is to keep the upper hand. If I can manage an orgasm in the process, well, I'll just call that a perk.

I keep my eyes on him, watching his face and relishing the tightness in his jaw that signals he is fighting for control. *Good,* I think as I shamelessly stroke my sex. *I want him on edge. I want him off kilter.*

I close my eyes, telling myself to go with it. To push the envelope. To push *him.*

But then his hand closes around my wrist. And when I open my eyes, he is right there—right in front of me.

"No," he says, and there is steel in his voice. "That orgasm belongs to me, baby."

And just like that, he's turned the tables on me again.

Fine. I'll turn them back. "Does it?" I say, then reach over and cup his cock. "Then this belongs to me."

He laughs as he takes a step back, breaking contact. "You think you're the one in control? Think again, princess."

I meet his eyes and see that he has known all along what I have just fully figured out. That I do not have the upper hand. That I never did. And that so long as we are playing this game, Jackson is setting the rules.

"No touching," he says. "Not unless it's me touching you. But don't worry," he adds as he strokes a finger up my bare belly and over the curve of my breast. "I intend to do a lot of touching."

His hands are like a live wire sending sparks of electricity to crackle over my tender skin, and despite myself I let my head tilt back and close my eyes to this onslaught of pleasure.

"So damn beautiful," he murmurs as his hands touch and stroke and tease and caress. "I wonder," he says, as he cups my sex. "Do you still taste as good as you look?" He drops to his knees, his hands on my hips, then very gently kisses the juncture of my thigh. I whimper, expecting his mouth on my sex, but he teases me by sliding a fingertip under the thong to find me hot and wet and so very ready. "Oh, yes," he says. "I think you like this."

He torments me with his finger, sliding it over my sensitive flesh, then thrusting inside me while my body clenches tight around him, wanting so much more than that simple, complicated, wonderful touch.

When he withdraws, he stands, then traces the finger he'd penetrated me with over my lips. "Suck," he demands, and I do eagerly, tasting my own arousal and watching the reflection of his in his eyes.

After a moment, he withdraws his finger, then takes my hand. He leads me toward the couch, only to pause by the coffee table. I'm confused at first, and then I realize that he has seen the photographs that litter the tabletop.

I wince, because those are a secret that I am not ready to share.

He releases my hand, then goes to the table. He looks down at the spray of photos that I'd left lying there, then reaches down to pick up several. "Who took this?" he asks, holding up a photograph of the Union Bank building in Las Vegas.

I consider lying, but the photo is important to me, and I do not want to deny it.

"I did." I meet his eyes, mine defiant.

"When?"

I don't bother to answer; the picture says it all.

"You were at the grand opening?"

"I was in Vegas for work." That was a lie. I was in Vegas for the grand opening.

His eyes linger on me long enough that I think he has seen the lie. Then he holds up the photo of the Winn Building. "This one?"

"I go to New York with Damien all the time. And photography is a hobby. I think I mentioned that back in Atlanta. Or had you forgotten?"

"I haven't forgotten a thing about Atlanta." His voice is low and steady and his eyes never stray from mine. "Not a single moment."

I say nothing, but my mouth has gone strangely dry.

"Why?" he asks. "There must be more than a dozen pictures of my buildings on that table. I want to know why."

"I told you why in Atlanta. I like architecture."

"I want the truth, Sylvia."

My name sounds soft on his lips, and I sag a bit, losing some of my defiance. "Maybe I misstated reality a little when I said I didn't follow your career."

He cocks his head. "You took all these pictures? Of dozens of my buildings?"

"I like architecture," I say again.

He returns to the table and pulls out a few of the photos that sit inside the open box. The first are additional shots of Jackson Steele buildings. But under that, he finds my house photos.

He pulls out one, two, eight, a dozen. After he's spread them on the table, he turns to me again. "I know you like architecture," he says with more than a little irony in his voice. "But I never saw you as going fangirl over residential buildings."

"I like to look at houses." I shrug, because there really is no more to say.

"Why?"

"Does it matter?" I snap. I go to the coffee table and gather them up—small cottages, large mansions, log cabins, adobe pueblos. Some in fancy neighborhoods, some in gangland. Some in places like Brentwood where I grew up.

I toss them all back inside the box.

"Why?" he asks again, this time more gently.

"I don't know." It's only half a lie. I have done this for years— even back when I was a child I would walk the neighborhood with a disposable camera—and I can sit for hours staring at a house, making up stories about the people who live behind the walls. In college, I took photography classes and spent almost all my time shooting houses. Now, it is both an obsession and a passion.

But I tell none of that to Jackson, and I still don't answer his question. But the truth is, I don't know why. Because I'm not sure what I expect to find when I look through the lens. All I know is that I haven't found it yet.

For a moment Jackson says nothing, he simply looks at me. Then he picks my dress up off the couch and hands it to me. "Put it on."

"But—" I'm not sure why I'm protesting, I only know that I'm confused.

"It's well after eight," he says, though his voice sounds tired enough that it could be after midnight. "I think it's time I take you to dinner."

twelve

Jackson has my skirt unbuttoned and his hand on my thigh when the waitress pushes open the sliding paper partition to enter the small, private booth.

As she does, Jackson leans over and kisses my ear, at the same time whispering, "Quiet."

At first I don't understand what he means, but then his hand slides north and his fingers find my thong. I freeze, terrified that he is going to do exactly what I know he's going to do. And yet even as I'm fervently wishing that I could slide over to the next colored cushion, some tiny treacherous part of me wants what he is offering. A forbidden touch. A secret pleasure.

Good god, what the hell am I thinking?

I start to squirm away in protest, but he catches my eye and shakes his head just slightly as the kimono-clad waitress bows, then kneels carefully on the far side of the table from us. As she places the decorative tray of sushi and sashimi in front of us, Jackson's finger slides under the lace to tease and play with me.

We are sitting on a backless bench of cushions that is directly on the floor, our feet descending into the sunken area which holds the table in this high-end, Beverly Hills sushi restaurant.

It is the kind of place where executives broker million-dollar deals. It is not the kind of place that hides lust and passion in dark corners while the rest of the world looks away.

And yet there is Jackson, gently stroking my clit as the waitress refills our sake.

And there is me, biting my lower lip, my cheeks surely burning, as I try to sit completely still as tremors of pleasure burst through my body.

Whether I should be or not, I cannot deny that I am wet—so desperately wet. And that right then I am craving more.

Jackson does not disappoint, and as he slides his finger inside me, I swallow a small sound of surprise and pleasure, then close my hands tight around the edges of the table.

The waitress's smile never wavers as she takes our empty soup bowls, stands, and leaves silently with another small bow at the door.

"Jackson!" There is something like panic in my voice as I whisper his name.

"Tell me more," he says. "What did Galway say when you told him Stark wanted to buy the island?"

When we'd arrived at the restaurant, I hadn't known what to expect. Jackson's mood had shifted in the apartment, going from heated demand to practiced politeness, as if we were a couple out on a first date, each being slightly careful around the other.

His choice of restaurant had surprised me as well. We'd never gone out for sushi in Atlanta, but I'd mentioned once that it's my favorite food. I considered asking if he'd come here on purpose, but the truth is I wanted to believe it had been intentional, and didn't want to know if coming here had been little more than a coincidence.

He'd insisted that we sit next to each other, and so we'd both taken a colored cushion on the side of the table facing the sliding door. I kept anticipating his touch, and yet there was none. Instead, he was practiced politeness, asking me about where I'd traveled with the company, what I did as Stark's assistant, even how I came to be the project manager for The Resort at Cortez.

And the entire time I was going a little bit nuts. He wasn't touching me at all. He was a perfect gentleman. This was, for all intents and purposes, a perfectly lovely date.

It was what I'd told myself I wanted—to have Jackson back off from his ridiculous game. To simply work with him and not get my head and my emotions all twisted up.

And yet . . .

And yet there I was, my body primed, my heart skittering with every movement and casual brush of his hand as I wondered if, maybe, he was finally going to touch me.

Nor did it help that I was certain that Jackson was intentionally tormenting me. And yet I had no proof whatsoever. His conversation was smooth, his manner polite.

And even so, he was slowly and methodically driving me crazy.

"So you got the idea for the resort from nothing more than a newspaper article?" he asked.

I don't remember answering, but I must have, because I remember distinctly that he put his hand on my thigh and started unbuttoning my dress while I was telling him about how Damien blew off his tax-planning meeting.

I froze, the words stumbling over my tongue. I had the ridiculous urge to scoot away, but damn me, hadn't I been craving this very thing, despite all my good sense and judgment?

So I stayed, and I talked, and I was talking still when the waitress came in, and I realized that was what Jackson had planned all along. Not simply the touch, but a forbidden one.

Not simply desire, but the need to fight it. To hide it.

And goddamn him, I couldn't deny the fact that the secret pleasure made the sensation of his finger playing with me, fucking me, that much more incredible.

"Galway," Jackson urges now as his finger strokes small circles on my clit, making my head spin and my thoughts scatter.

"Jackson, I—"

"Tell me," he repeats, and so I do. I tell him about the phone call and Galway's laughter when he thinks that Damien is joking, then his surprise when he learns that Damien really does want to acquire the island.

"Stark sounds like a man who gets what he wants," Jackson says.

"He is."

"So am I," Jackson whispers as he thrusts three fingers inside me, fucking me with his hand, and damn me, I writhe against the motion, wanting him to go deeper, trying to feel the brush of his skin against my clit as my thoughts continue to spin and my mind loses focus.

"What is it you want?" I gasp, as spirals of pleasure seem to burst around me.

"You," he says. "At my mercy."

And with those four simple words, he withdraws his hand and my pleasure. "I think," he says casually, "that it's time to eat."

I am frustrated and antsy and thoroughly pissed off during the meal. He'd taken me right to the precipice, then left me dangling, and the more I think about it, the more I realize that the meal— though it has all my favorite rolls and sashimi—holds very little appeal.

There is instead something I want much, much more, and I put down my chopsticks and slide my left hand under the table to rest upon his thigh. He glances sideways at me, but doesn't protest. Not even when I slowly ease my hand up, higher and higher until I find his cock, hard and thick beneath his slacks.

I smile, once again feeling powerful and in control as I slowly stroke him, then ease my fingers up to search for his zipper.

"Stop."

His voice is low and simple and he does not look at me.

I find the zipper pull and start to ease it down. "What if I don't want to stop?"

"Then don't." He turns now and looks straight at me. There is heat in his expression, and amusement as well. "That's what free will is all about."

"Exactly," I say, happy to have finally turned the tables.

"But if you don't stop, I will."

I halt my effort to carefully unzip him. "What do you mean?"

"I mean it's up to you. Do you want me to touch you? Stroke you, make you come?"

I do not answer, but I have also stopped moving.

"Do you want pleasure, Sylvia? Or do you want the more hollow satisfaction of thinking that somehow you've managed to best me, when we both know in the end I will have you naked and open to me, limp and sated. And the more you come in my arms, the sweeter my victory will be."

I swallow, not entirely certain I could form words right then, even if I had to.

"Surrender, princess, and you'll get the orgasm I denied you earlier. Don't stop, and I'll be the only one who gets off for a very, very long time."

I believe him. And while I wish I had the strength to follow through and make him come—to sacrifice my own pleasure for the sake of a victory—I just can't do it.

I pull my hand away.

"Good choice," he says, and there is no denying both the heat and the victory in his voice. "I promise, sweetheart, that you won't regret it."

He nods at the table and I realize that we've finished the meal. "Dessert?"

I shake my head.

"No? I want dessert. I just don't want it here." He brushes his finger over my lower lip. "A moment," he says, then stands. He goes to the door, slides it open, then signals for the check.

As he's returning to the table, the theme from *Star Wars* starts to blare from my purse.

I wince as Jackson laughs.

"Yoda calling?"

I roll my eyes as I rummage for my phone. "My brother."

I glance down at the screen and feel the blood drain from my face as I read the text message.

> Hey, Silly!
> Guess who's finally moving back to the good old USA?
> Arriving in three weeks—just in time for Halloween.
> Pick me up at LAX? Then let's shoot down to Irvine.
> Mom's all psyched about putting on a huge spread for us.
> And Dad says he doesn't see enough of you, either.
> Love you, big sis.
> Miss you.
> See you soon.

"Something wrong?"

I realize that I've been staring at the phone for a hell of a lot longer than it takes to read one text message.

"I—no. Not a thing. Just give me a sec." I manage a smile as I type out a response, but am frustrated to see that my hands are shaking.

> So psyched you're coming home! At a work thing, so more soon.
> Send flight details—I'll be there with balloons!
> Not sure can swing Irvine. Crazy busy at work.
> XXOO

I force myself to look up at him, then flash as bright a smile as I can manage. "So, check all taken care of?"

He hesitates, then nods. "We can go."

I smile, trying my best to look normal, and follow him out of the restaurant.

Origami is one of the new, hot places on Rodeo Drive in Beverly Hills, just a few doors down from the entrance to the Beverly Wilshire hotel. Jackson had parked at the hotel, and I'd anticipated dinner in one of its incredible restaurants. But he'd surprised me by leading me through the lobby and to the street.

Now, we're heading back, and Ethan's text still weighs on me, along with all the tension and fears that just the thought of seeing my parents raises.

"Do you want to talk about it?"

I turn to look at him, surprised. "I didn't think that conversation was part of tonight's program." My words come out harsher than I meant, and I immediately regret them. Despite everything, there was genuine concern in his voice, and even though this night is all about punishing me, I truly didn't mean to be a bitch.

"I'm sorry," I say. "And no. I'd rather not talk about it. Really," I add, because the expression on his face suggests that he is going to argue.

He nods reluctantly, and we continue walking in silence. But the odd thing is that I feel a bit better. The night is cool and clear, the air crisp and sweet-smelling. I'm on one of the prettiest streets in the world, with glitz and glamour lit up in the shop windows that we are passing.

And despite the fact that I hurt him so deeply, the man at my side still cares about me. At least a little.

It's enough to sweep away my anger and fear. Three weeks is a lifetime away, and tonight is not the time to open the door to more memories. And, frankly, tonight I have enough on my mind with Jackson. I don't need my family in my head, too.

I frown as we pass the valet stand. "Aren't you getting your car?"

"Not just yet," Jackson says as a liveried doorman greets us. With Jackson's hand pressing gently against the small of my back, we enter the stunning lobby. It's awash in a golden light that makes the polished marble floor glow in a way that draws out the iconic circular design that looks a bit like a target symbol. At the center of the circle stands a giant table with an enormous—and gorgeous— flower arrangement blooming bright beneath one of the most ornate chandeliers I've ever seen.

"I love this hotel," I say. "It's like stepping back in time with its mix of classical and art deco elegance."

"I'm glad you like it," Jackson says. "I thought we'd have a drink here."

"Really?" I look around for the lobby bar.

"No. Not in the bar." He heads toward the registration counter, and I follow, a little bit curious—and a little bit certain that I know exactly where this is going.

"Jackson Steele," he tells the girl. "I booked a room this afternoon."

"Of course, Mr. Steele." She hands him his key. "Is there anything else you need?"

"I spoke with the sommelier earlier as well. I'd like a bottle of the Petrus Pomerol 1998 sent up to the room. Two glasses. And caviar, please."

Her eyes have gone a little wide, and I understand why. I'd ordered five bottles of that very vintage last Christmas for Damien to send as gifts to some of his most important clients. Even with Damien's wholesale sources, the bottles sold for over a grand each.

"Of course, Mr. Steele," she says, apparently remembering herself. "I'll have that sent right up."

Up turns out to be the penthouse, and I have to admit that even after all I've seen traveling with Damien, I have never stayed in such highbrow accommodations. I know I should play it cool, but I have to confess that I goggle a bit. So much, in fact, that I'm still standing near the ornate double doors when the room service waiter knocks. I scramble out of his way as he wheels in a small table with the wine, two glasses, and a spectacular selection of caviar. Jackson lets the waiter uncork the wine, but declines his offer to pour. And as soon as the man is gone from the room, he crooks his finger at me.

"Come," he says, and I can't help but think about how many meanings that simple word has.

"You have a very strange idea of revenge," I say. "My favorite dinner. A penthouse suite. Caviar. And one of the most expensive bottles of wine in the history of the universe."

"I don't know that it's quite that pricey."

I merely look dubious.

"Like I said, princess. I want you to remember everything you gave up."

"Dammit, Jackson—" I cut off my words.

"No. I don't want to hear that you had to. I don't want to hear that you're sorry."

"No?" I hear the exasperation in my voice. "Then what the hell do you want?"

"I thought I was clear," he says as he pours a glass of wine and strides toward me. He pauses just inches away and hands me the wine. I take a sip, barely even noticing the incredible palate. I'm too intent on watching Jackson to notice something as unimportant as wine.

He is looking me up and down with the kind of intensity designed to make a woman melt, and it's clear from his expression that while he is hungry, it is not for caviar.

"I want to take you to the edge and back," he says as he unbuttons my dress. I stand perfectly still as he peels it off my body. "I want to watch you lose control," he continues, and now he unfastens my bra and slowly removes it. "I want to make you come," he says as he eases me out of my shoes and stockings, then unhooks the garter and lets it fall to the floor. "And, princess," he adds as he hooks his finger in the band of the thong and pulls so hard the elastic snaps, making me flinch, though I do not otherwise move. "I want to make you scream."

He leans in and kisses me, soft and sweet, like a man seeking sanctuary, and in sharp contrast to the brutality of his words and the way he stripped me from the last of my clothes. "But first things first."

I stand there, my mouth tingling from his kiss, not entirely certain what just happened. One moment I was standing there, facing a slow seduction with caviar and wine. The next, I'm naked and hot and more turned on than I want to be by the wildness of his words.

"With me," he says, then leads me into the gorgeously appointed bedroom. It's done in beige and brown, with some cream thrown in, and looks both comfortable and elegant.

He nods toward the bed, and I sit on the edge. He looks at me a moment, as if considering, and though I try to discern his thoughts, I cannot read his face.

He moves to the window and lays his hand flat on the glass. I see his eyes in the reflection, and I know that he is looking at me. "I need you to tell me something."

I am relieved by his words since now I will perhaps have some clue as to what is going on in his head. "Sure," I say. "Anything."

"Are you still fucking him?"

I'd been starting to stand, using my arms to help lever me off the foot of the bed. They go limp, and I fall back onto the mattress. I am more confused than angry, and my reply of "Who?" sounds lost and anemic even to my ears.

He turns his back to the window, his laser blue eyes now focused intently on me. "Stark's married now," he says, as if we were discussing the weather. "So I want to know if you're still fucking him."

Now anger launches me to my feet. "Damien? Are you insane? I never—"

"You *left* me." Gone is the calm tone, the bland expression. He's wild now, ferocious as he strides the short distance across the room to stand in front of me.

His anger is no match for mine, though, and our joined fury seems to fill the room, making the air buzz and pop. All we need is a lit match, and we'll both go up in flames. "Five years ago, you left me so you could go fuck Damien Stark."

Without thinking, I lash out, slapping him hard across his left cheek, right over the still raw cut. I hope it hurts. I hope it fucking brings him to his knees.

He grabs my upper arms, tight enough to bruise, and yanks me toward him. I can see the wildness in him, can feel the tempest building between us. For a moment I'm not sure if he's going to hit me or kiss me, and he better not goddamn do either, because I am as close to losing it right now as he is.

I do nothing, though; I know better than to poke a wounded animal. And after a moment, he pushes me away. *"Fuck."*

I back off, breathing hard. I lean against the bed as I watch him pace the room. Once, twice, until he stops at the window again. Until he lashes out once more, the force of his hand against the glass making the images in the window shimmer, as if the fury of this one man has upset the balance of the world.

Slowly, very slowly, I walk toward him. I pause behind him, close enough to reach out and touch him, though I do not. "I told you before—I left because I had to."

"You left Atlanta. You went to work for him."

"Yes. Because after Reggie fired me I contacted human resources at Stark International and asked them to put my application back in the active file. I told you I'd applied for a job with him. And I got it. The old-fashioned way—by having a solid résumé. I didn't leave you for Stark, and I swear on my life that I have never slept with that man."

He pulls me to him, the motion so unexpected that I gasp, and as I do, he closes his mouth over mine. The kiss is wild and hard and almost painful. Teeth clashing, mouths burning. It is a claiming, not a kiss. A battle, not a seduction. And when he backs away, I am breathing hard, a little bit aroused and a lot lost.

And Jackson is himself again. Cool and controlled as if the last few moments haven't even happened.

"This is the way it's going to work. You're mine. Wholly and completely. You're ready for me when I say. How I say. Do you understand?"

"Do I have a choice?"

He doesn't even bother to answer. We both know what the answer will be.

"On the bed," Jackson says, and for a moment I do not move.

This really is it, I think. I can walk away right now, and save myself the pain of my memories. The misery of being with a man who wants only to punish me for our past.

I can walk—and I can lose the resort, which is the only thing that has truly mattered to me in years.

I look at him, struck hard by the irony. Because five years ago, Jackson mattered to me. He'd bent time with me, cramming what felt like a lifetime of emotion into just a few short days.

But that's the past, and the resort is my present. And I cannot risk losing it if I have the chance to save it.

And so I do as he asks. This was the deal I made, after all. And, yes, I cannot deny that despite the memories that I fear will creep back into my dreams, I want what he has promised. I want the release. And, god help me, I want to shatter against this man again even though it is not real, and even though in the end, I know that I will get hurt.

"Good girl," he says once my head is on the pillows. "Now stretch out your arms."

I do, though I'm not sure what he's planning. I find out soon enough, though, because he steps into the bathroom, then comes back with the white cotton sashes from two hotel robes.

I shake my head, feeling panic rising. "No," I say, but he doesn't stop. He simply takes my wrist and knots one end of a sash around it. The other end he ties to a lamp that is fastened to the wall right at the side of the headboard.

"Jackson . . ."

My protest seems to echo in the room, but he does not heed it.

Instead, he moves around the bed and repeats the process with my other arm.

I lick my lips, not liking how vulnerable I feel. I squeeze my thighs together, then whimper when he shakes his head.

"No," he says. "Wide. I want to see how wet you are. I want to see how much you want me."

I swallow, but I say nothing, because what is there to say? But as he draws his fingertip along my leg and up my inner thigh, I feel my body clench with need. I see the small smile touch his lips. And I know that he has seen the extent of my arousal. That he knows what he is doing to me. That he has damn well won because no matter how much I want to keep a tight rein on myself—my body has its own response, and I'm desperately, hopelessly, completely turned on.

He touches me mercilessly, trailing his fingers over every inch of my body until I feel as though my skin is alive with need, and all the more so because I cannot move. I can only submit to this pounding of desire.

And when he goes to the living room and returns with a glass of wine and a small bowl of caviar, I cannot help but wonder what new torment he has in store for me.

And torment it is.

He slowly dribbles the thousand-dollar wine over my belly button, then uses the tip of his tongue to taste it. He lifts the glass to me and lets me have a small sip, and the tang of it on my tongue seems to match the way my entire body tingles with need for him. And when he puts a tiny spoonful of caviar on each of my breasts and then closes his mouth over me to suckle, I cannot help but arch up from the pure, overwhelming, erotic sensations.

He moves lower then, kissing his way down my belly until he reaches my sex. He looks at me, his eyes hard on mine, before kissing me oh-so-intimately.

"For a man who wants to punish me," I say on a wild breath, "you're doing a terrible job."

"I told you," he murmurs, "I want you to remember. I want you to know pleasure. And I want you to think about everything you tossed away."

"Jackson—"

But he is not listening, and when his tongue attacks my clit once more I really don't even care. He takes me to the edge, his mouth working magic on my senses, turning my body into nothing but sensual awareness, a mass of erotic energy just waiting to explode.

Waiting . . . and waiting still . . .

And when he pulls his mouth away—when he sits up on his knees to look at me—I think that I really will scream.

"Tell me what you want," he says, but there is such tension in his voice, I have no doubt that he wants exactly the same thing. And I want it badly enough that I have no shame.

"Fuck me. Please, Jackson. Just fuck me now."

He gets off the bed and comes to stand closer to me. For a moment, I fear that he is going to deny both of us. "Please tell me you have a condom," I say.

For a moment, he says nothing. Then he takes something out of his pocket and sets it on the side table before stripping off his clothes. I turn my head, managing to see that he's put a condom packet there. But there's something else beside it, and that's what he picks up now.

It takes a moment, and then I realize that it's a blindfold.

"Oh, no," I say. "No way."

"Oh, yes," he says. "My rules, remember? And right now, I own you," he says as his fingers dance over my skin, highlighted by the sensual tones of his voice. "You're mine to pleasure. To take. To fuck. And right now I want you to experience nothing but the feeling of me touching you," he adds as my body clenches with need in response to this new seduction. "Of me inside you. You're mine, remember, and tonight, I want you to know it. Fully and very, very completely."

His words seem to crash over me, echoing through my memory. *While you're here, you're mine.*

You're mine, you're mine, you're mine . . .

Familiar words that once made me sick, but right now I can't deny that I am wet. That I am on fire.

And that the goddamned flame on my breast is a symbol not that I am the one in control . . . but that if I'm not careful, Jackson will reduce me to ashes.

I do not protest when he moves forward and puts the blindfold over my eyes. The world goes dark, and as he said, it is only him that I know. The sound of his breathing. The feel of his hands upon me. The touch of his breath upon my skin.

He caresses my body with hands and kisses, a sweet seduction as he moves back onto the bed, making the mattress shift as he does. And then he is lightly caressing my sex, his fingers teasing and exploring, making me even hotter than I already am. Opening me. Readying me.

Without warning, he lifts my legs, and I feel the sensation of being stretched as he raises them onto his shoulders. I gasp at the sensation of his cock pressing hard against me, seeking entrance, and I relax, welcoming him. Wanting him.

And then, when he grabs my ass and thrusts into me, impaling me without warning, I scream just as he wanted me to, lost in the incredible sensation of being filled by this man.

He is huge, but I am so damn wet that it hurts only for a bit. Now he moves in a sensual rhythm, holding my hips with one hand as he guides my motions to work in tandem with his, and at the same time using his other hand to tease my clit so that I am overwhelmed by the sensation of both being filled and of catching fire.

I'm alive with pleasure—wild with desire. And the fact that I can see nothing only adds to the vastness of what I feel, just like Jackson had said it would.

"Come for me," he says, thrusting harder and deeper. "Christ, Sylvia, I want you to come for me now."

I cry out in surprise when I feel his own release, and then in pleasure when every bit of sparkle in my body seems to center on my sex, only to burst out again and send me spinning. I arch up, feeling as though I could fly, and then fall back down on the bed, wanting nothing more than to have Jackson beside me.

I fear for a moment that he will not come—that he will punish me by leaving me alone and bound in this bed. But he does not. Instead he unties my arms, then removes my blindfold. And then, to my surprise and delight, he brushes a tender kiss across my lips before sliding into bed beside me.

"Sleep now," Jackson says.

I lay there breathing hard, my back against his chest, my body exhausted and my mind content. And as he holds me in his arms, I sink into his warmth, entirely unprepared for the cold fingers of memory when they creep up to fill my sleep and haunt my dreams.

I watch myself in the red dress, as Bob circles the other me who stands in the soft lighting.

"Lovely," he says as his camera clicks. "Just perfect. Now let's add a little heat to these photos."

The other me shakes her head. "I don't think—"

"Hush," he says as he steps closer. "I need these photos to stand out, and how can they miss with you in them? Innocence mixed with passion. And if there's arousal . . . oh, Elle, that photo will pop." His hand brushes her nipple, and I watch as the other me gasps. But I don't feel it. Over here, away, I don't feel a thing.

His smile is slow. "There you go. You see? That beautiful flush. The camera loves it. And I'll tell you a secret, Elle. I do, too. There aren't many fourteen-year-old girls as mature as you. With such a natural heat. Do one more button for me. For the camera."

"Don't," I say to the me in the dress.

But she bites her lip and lifts her hands to the dress. And I suck in air because I know this. I've seen it.

I remember what happens. The way he finishes the rest of the buttons for her. The things he says so that it seems okay but really isn't. The way it feels when his hands are on her—when he touches her. When he's inside her.

And the shame and loathing that come after.

I remember it, and so I scream for her. I yell for her to fight it. To stop him.

But I don't hear me. Only Bob does. And when he turns to me with a victorious smile, it's Jackson's face that I see.

I sit up, gasping for air, then jump when Jackson's hand strokes my thigh.

"Syl?" His voice is sleepy, concerned.

But I don't answer. Instead, I run to the living room and throw on the dress, ignoring the ripped underwear and not bothering with the bra.

I stand for a second, unsure, then I tiptoe back into the bedroom and dig in the pocket of his khakis for his wallet. I find the valet ticket, and I clutch it tight, breathing hard.

"Syl? What's going on?"

I look up to see him blinking at me as he switches on the bedside lamp.

Fear clutches me, and I can barely breathe.

I spring to my feet and race out of the bedroom, then out of the suite. I jab my finger on the elevator button and will it to whisk me to the lobby at something close to the speed of light.

The young man at the valet stand doesn't question me when he brings me the Porsche, and I'm grateful that I remembered my purse so that I can tip him.

I slide behind the wheel, lock the doors, and peel out of the driveway.

I have no idea where I'm going. I only know that I want to escape.

But since it's my own skin I want to leave behind, it's never going to happen. And all I can hope is that somehow, someway, I can drive fast enough to leave the nightmares behind.

thirteen

I race up Coldwater Canyon, hugging the road's curves, watching as the spray of light from the headlights turns the tree-lined road into a fairy tale path of dark shadows and witches' fingers that are reaching out to claim me.

But it's not the shadows I'm running from. It's not even Jackson. Not entirely.

It's Jackson and myself and the whole fucked up situation.

Because damn me to hell, all Jackson wants is to punish me. I know that—*I know it*. And yet all he has to do is crook a finger to make me melt.

Just like Bob did all those years ago.

Fuck.

This was a mistake. Such a huge mistake. I should never have gotten in Jackson's bed, and if that meant abandoning the resort, then I should have just walked away. Because I cannot be this woman. I can't be the girl who surrenders. Who gives in. I have to hold on tight to control, because it is the only protection I have.

I hate that as well.

And so I drive, taking the curves wildly, trying desperately to lose myself in the thrill of danger, burying my fear under this rush of pure adrenal sensation and absolute concentration.

Except it doesn't work. My head is too full, my thoughts too wild, and with one violent turn of the wheel, I whip the car into a turnaround and slam on the brakes. The Porsche jolts to a stop dangerously close to the drop-off, and for a moment I wonder what that would have been like, soaring out into space and then dropping down, down, down into nothingness.

I push the thought away. That is not me; not who I am at all. And it never has been.

Even as a teen, when I so desperately wanted it to end, I never wanted to end *me*. Instead I wanted to get lost inside myself, to find that safe place and to cling to talismans that would protect me from the nightmares.

My whole life, I've managed to keep a tight hold, with only two exceptions—Atlanta and right now.

And there's Jackson Steele right in the middle, sending me battering about as if he is a storm and I am nothing more than a cork bobbing in violent waters.

I get out of the car and walk to the edge, then look down at the lights of the world. The houses where happy people sleep through dreamless nights.

I am jealous, I realize. And I am alone.

I close my eyes against a sudden, powerful longing for Jackson. To let him hold and soothe me.

You're a fool, I think. *A goddamn, messed up fool.*

The purr of an engine pulls me from my thoughts, and I turn to see a black sedan pull into the turnaround.

I frown. I'm not looking for company, and I'm not stupid. I'm a woman alone in the dark standing beside a pretty damn expensive car. All of which means that this is my cue to leave.

I get back into the Porsche, lock the doors, and back out.

The sedan is still there, its engine off, its interior dark.

But as I turn the wheel so that I can maneuver back onto the street, my headlights sweep over the sedan, and for a moment the interior is illuminated.

It's Jackson.

Somehow, he followed me.

I grip the steering wheel tighter, expecting a wave of anger.

But it doesn't come. Instead, I feel a little less lost. A little bit safe.

And because of that, I feel a little bit scared.

I don't go back to the hotel. Instead, I go home.

I feel like a sleepwalker as I stand in my front hallway and press the button to open the back patio door. It rolls up, and I move forward in time with the motion.

I have no idea what I want right now.

No, that's not true. I've known since the moment my headlights revealed him.

I want Jackson.

I want him here beside me. I want him to hold and soothe me. But I can't have what I want, not only because of this ridiculous game that we are locked in, but because there is no future there. In the end, he will have his revenge and leave. Or I will push him away, my only defense against my fears and insecurities, those horrible demons with which I cannot live, and that I do not know how to fight.

Either way, I will be alone.

And that's why I am here on my patio, my blanket wrapped tight around me, and my eyes closed in the hope that sleep might find me.

Sylvia.

I smile, letting the sound of my name on his lips slide into my dreams. I feel the press of a hand on my shoulder, gentle but firm, and I take a long, deep breath. These are not the cold fingers of a nightmare, but the warm and soothing touch of that knight I so often imagine. I shift, pulling the blanket up under my chin, wanting to go deeper into this place of safety that I so rarely find in sleep.

Sylvia. Baby, wake up.

I stir, confused, then open my eyes to find Jackson's blue ones looking back at me, full of concern.

"There you are," he says gently.

"I—" Since I have no idea what I intended to say, I stop talking. But I force myself to sit up and peer at him and convince myself that he's not a figment of my imagination. "You came after me," I say. "In the car. On the road."

"Of course I did." His voice is as gentle as a breeze.

"How?"

A tiny smile plays across his lips. "Ever heard of OnStar?"

"You tracked your car."

"I've got a Lexus, too," he says. "You ran out on me in one car, I followed you in another."

"To make sure your Porsche was safe?" I ask, unable to keep the challenge out of my voice.

"No." He brushes his thumb over my cheek. "I wasn't worried about my car."

"But you didn't get out. You just sat there."

"I thought you wanted to be alone."

"You're here now," I say.

"I thought you'd been alone long enough."

I actually smile, which feels pretty good. Then I push myself up, so that I'm sitting instead of lounging. "How did you get in?"

"You left your front door wide open," he says. "Good thing this is a security building and nobody can get through the gate."

"You're still not going to tell me how you managed that?"

"A magician never shares his secrets." He's been kneeling beside me, but now he stands up. "You're better now?" he asks, and when I nod, he steps back into the apartment.

I fight a sharp pang of panic as I shift on the lounger so that I can look inside, then sag with relief when I see that he isn't leaving but getting something out of my refrigerator.

"Corkscrew?" he asks, then immediately answers himself. "Got it. Never mind."

A moment later, he returns with two glasses of white wine. He hands one to me, then uses his free hand to pull over the metal folding chair that Cass brought out here the last time she was over.

He sits, then puts his glass on the concrete next to him. He leans forward, his elbows resting on his knees. He looks completely casual and totally in control, and every ounce of his attention is focused on me.

"We're done, Sylvia," he says, and I jolt bolt upright.

"What? No! You told Damien, and I—I agreed to—you know. Dammit, Jackson, you can't just quit. You can't—" I am starting to rise, but he takes my arm and tugs me back down.

"Not the resort," he says calmly. "I'll design a magnificent resort for you. But this," he says, gesturing between the two of us.

I shake my head, not understanding. Because surely after everything, he isn't tossing away all of his demands and ultimatums.

Is he?

He reaches for his glass, then stands and walks to the railing. He stops there, so that he is silhouetted against the now-gray sky. "You fucked me up, Sylvia, it doesn't get more basic than that. I said this was about revenge, and it is. It was. I wanted to punish you for leaving me. For leaving me for him—for Damien, I thought—and god, how I wanted to punish you."

"But I didn't. Not like that. I told you."

"And I believe you. But that wasn't all of it. Because I still wanted to make you pay for hurting me. Hell, for hurting both of us," he says, and I can't help but wince, because what he says is true.

"But it wasn't all about punishment." He takes a sip of wine, then sets the glass down. "Do you need to hear it plainly? I'll say it.

I want you, Sylvia. As intensely as I wanted you in Atlanta. And the moment I saw you in the theater, I knew that I was willing to make any deal I had to in order to get you close."

His words are punctuated by each step he takes toward me. "Did I want your submission? Did I want you naked and willing beneath me? Hell, yes. I still do. But that's not the whole of it. I want to make you feel. To make you laugh. I want to see that fire that burns in you. I want you to look at me the way you did five years ago. And, Sylvia? I want you to stay."

My chest is tight, and I am having a hard time breathing.

"But I want none of that if the cost is hurting you."

He reaches down and cups my chin in his hand, his expression so tender it makes my heart squeeze. "So there will be no deal. No game. No conditions put on my agreement to work on the resort. I will still do my best to seduce you," he adds with a tender smile. "But I can't be the one who brings you more pain."

I open my mouth to speak, but I cannot. I can only shake my head, wanting to deny what he has so obviously seen.

His takes my hand, and though it is only our fingers that are touching, it feels as though his strength is running through me. "I've seen the lock, the tattoo, and I can guess what it means. I should have guessed in Atlanta."

I look away, unable to meet his eyes.

"You shouldn't have to bear that kind of burden. And if I added to the weight of it, I am so damn sorry."

I look at him now, my throat thick and my eyes burning. "You didn't," I say. "Not really. Oh, god." I draw in a breath and raise my hand to my mouth, then bite down on the soft flesh at the base of my thumb. "I want to cry—I really, really want to cry right now. I'm full up with tears," I say, feeling almost like I'm drowning in my own emotions.

"Then let go," he says, moving to sit beside me and gathering me in his arms.

I manage a half-laugh, then press close. "I can't. I haven't cried since I was fourteen."

He pushes a lock of hair off my forehead, then slowly trails his fingers down my shoulder to my back. " 'It is some relief to weep,' " he quotes. "Ovid."

I draw in a stuttering breath, picturing the tattoo in my mind. The delicate blue tears. The precise lines of the script in which Cass had inked that quote upon the shoulder blade where his hand now rests.

"It would be relief," I say with an ironic smile. "If I could manage it."

"It's some relief, too, to talk about it," he says. He strokes my hair, and despite everything, I feel safe. "Can you tell me who?"

I close my eyes, because I don't want to think about it.

Except that's stupid, because somehow, some way, I seem to always be thinking of it.

"Was it your brother?"

"No!" The answer is fast and vehement and true. "No, Ethan doesn't even know about it." I can hear the panic in my voice. Oh, god, if Ethan ever found out the real story . . . I shiver, as determined as always to protect my baby brother.

"I saw the way you looked at dinner after you got his text."

"He's coming in a few weeks. He wants us to go visit our parents. They're in Irvine. They moved there from Brentwood when Ethan graduated from high school."

"And that's bad?"

I take a deep breath and remind myself that not only am I awake, but Jackson has handed me back control on a silver platter. I can talk about this, and I will be okay.

"Not Irvine—as far as I'm concerned distance is good. And I can't wait to see my little brother. He was really sick when he was a kid, and we were incredibly close. He—he got better."

I draw in a breath, determined not to think about the price of my brother's health. "Complete recovery," I say, hurrying on with my story. "And he's been living in London for over a year now."

"But not your parents."

I look down and realize that I've twisted my hands together so much my fingers hurt. "The man—the one who raped me—" I take a breath, realizing that I haven't said that word since I told Cass this same story. "He was a friend of my father's. I called him Bob." Just saying the name makes me shiver. "And I got a job with him when I was a freshman. My dad set it up. So I'm not very good with the family-dynamic thing. I kind of shut myself off, you know?"

He nods. "So you were fourteen?"

"Yes." I keep my voice matter-of-fact. The only way to get through this is to just say it. Like I'm summarizing business documents. "It started then."

I see the way he flinches at the word "started," and I'm grateful he doesn't ask how long it went on.

"And your parents?"

"I haven't told anybody," I say, which isn't actually an answer to his question. "I told my friend Cass, but that's it."

"No professionals? No therapy?"

"I'm not interested in spilling my troubles to strangers. No way am I handing that kind of intimacy and control to someone I don't even know."

"You need help."

"I've got my own kind of therapy. I'll be fine."

"But you're not fine," he says reasonably, and the worry is plain on his face.

I turn away. He's right, of course, but I'm not going to admit it.

"All right, then. If you won't get help from a professional, you'll get it from me."

"Jackson . . ."

"What? I'm the problem? I'm not. I'm the man who—"

My chest tightens, hearing a word that he hasn't said. "What?"

He hesitates. "I'm the man who'll fight your demons," he says, and I can't help but smile. Because in my mind, that is who he has always been. In reality, though . . .

"A nice sentiment," I say, "but I'm already fighting them."

"Are you? Because from where I'm sitting, you're not winning."

"Please," I say, and I can hear the strain in my voice. "Can we just drop it? At least for now?"

The expression on his face is so wretched it almost tears me in two. "I made it so much worse for you," he says, then kneels beside me and cups my face. "I'm sorry."

"No. You haven't. I just need it out of my head for a while."

"You need rest. Come on. I'm going to carry you to bed. Nobody should be up this early on a Sunday."

He shifts so that he can stand, and I press my hand against his thigh.

"Wait."

The muscle of his thigh is tense beneath my hand, like a spring ready to explode. His entire body seems to quiver with the struggle of restraint, and when his eyes meet mine, I see the moment when realization hits him. "No," he says, his voice as taut as a wire. "That's not what you want. Not now."

"Please," I say, because right then he is exactly what I need. "Help me fight my demons. Tuck me up in bed like a child and it will feel like he's won. Like he's taken something from me."

He cocks his head, his blue eyes as sharp as lasers and at least as penetrating. I hold his gaze, wanting him to see not only what I need, but what I want.

"Please," I repeat after another moment clicks by. "Don't you get it? I wanted you so desperately last night, but not like that. Not when it felt like revenge. Like you wanted to fuck me out of your head or something."

"Oh, baby." He cups my cheek in his palm. "I never wanted you out of my head. Just the opposite. I wanted you too damn much."

"Then stay with me." I don't have the words to tell him how much I need this. How much I need him. And I can only hope that he can hear it in my voice. "I need you. And oh, dear god, I've missed you."

"Sylvia." My name is so soft that it's little more than air upon his lips. Then he cups my head in both hands and pulls me toward him. "I'm going to make love to you, Syl. And if you don't want me to do that, you need to say something right now."

I say nothing, merely tilt my head back and part my lips in silent invitation.

And when he bends his head to mine—when he brushes his lips softly over my mouth as if testing this new reality—I cannot help the moan of acquiescence and pleasure.

I lift my arms to wrap around his neck, then pull him closer. I know what I am risking—only a few hours ago, the nightmares had sent me running, literally, for the hills.

But it is morning now, and I do not intend to sleep anytime soon.

And when the nightmares do inevitably find me ... Well, I guess it will be worth it.

fourteen

Jackson's mouth closes over mine, his lips soft, yet demanding. But right now, no demand is required, and I surrender eagerly, opening my mouth to him, welcoming him. Letting him fill me, taste me, consume me.

His hands are on the chaise, one on the back support and the other on the cushion near my waist. Our bodies touch only at our lips, and yet every inch of me is alive with awareness, as if there is not even the tiniest bit of flesh that he has not explored and brought to life with his finger, his lips, his tongue.

He breaks the kiss, then sits beside me as I gasp, trying to remember who and where I am. "I'm going to take you inside," he says, even as he moves to gather me up.

"No." I push his arms away, the plea clear in both the word and my tone. "No, I want to stay."

"You have neighbors," he says, though I don't really. My balcony is private on both sides, and though it is theoretically possible that someone is on top of the roof of one of the retail buildings across the street and looking this direction and through the glass barrier with a pair of binoculars at four in the morning, I highly doubt it.

I say nothing, just take his hand, and tug him toward me.

"That's what you want?"

"Yes."

He lifts a brow. "I suppose that's fair. In our original deal, you belonged to me. So for this morning, I'm entirely yours."

I lick my lips. "Entirely?"

His smile manages to be both devious and sensual. "Tell me what you want, Sylvia. Exactly what you want."

I meet his eyes. "Undress me," I demand.

His mouth curves up, his eyes bright. "At your service," he says as his fingers work down the buttons of my dress.

He makes a quick job of it, doing no more and no less than removing my dress, and since I had burst out of the hotel in nothing else, I am now completely naked.

But there had been nothing sensual about his movements. No seduction. No stolen caresses. And though I am frustrated at first, I soon realize what he is doing. Despite his promise, Jackson Steele is still playing games.

"Stroke me," I say. "Draw your fingers over my belly and down to my sex. But not quite there. I want to be teased. I want you to take me to the edge."

"Do you?" His brow arches up as he considers my words. "Well then, I think we can manage that."

I smile, then lay my head back and close my eyes, losing myself to his touch as he gently trails his fingers over my flesh, the touch light and enticing and full of promise. He draws small circles on my abdomen, then trails down in spirals to my pubis. His fingers trace the triangle of trimmed hair, and I gasp from the sensual, almost ticklish touch of his fingertip along the juncture of groin and thigh.

He cheats a bit when he bends low and blows a thin stream of air directly on my clit, but the sensation is too incredible for me to complain about breaking rules, and I only arch up in a silent demand for more, which, thankfully, he understands.

The cool air on my hot clit is mind-blowing, and I spread my legs, wanting his mouth, his tongue.

"No," he whispers. "I want to hear you say it."

"Lick me," I beg. "Go down on me. Please, Jackson, god, please."

Thankfully, he doesn't hesitate, and he takes my sex in his mouth, his tongue laving me, drawing me higher and higher with gentle flicks upon my clit. Thrusting his tongue into me with so much force, so much power, that I'm not sure I can stand it. But it's not his tongue that I want, because all I desire in that moment is for him to fill me, wholly and completely.

"Jackson." I close my fingers in his hair and tug his head up so that his eyes meet mine. "Kiss me," I demand. "Fuck me."

His slow smile sets my skin on fire, and he moves off the chaise to stand beside me. Slowly, he takes off his shirt, then peels off his slacks, his briefs. He stands there, naked and erect and with such longing on his face that I do not know how either of us will survive this night, because I am certain that when we come together the explosion will destroy us both.

"I don't have a condom," he says.

I reach for him. "I don't care. I want you. And if you say it's okay, then I believe you."

"It's okay," he says, then moves on top of me. He starts low, his lips on my hip, then kisses his way up my body, stopping at my breast to lick and tug and tease so much that the sensation shoots through me, all the way to my clit, and I have to stop him for fear that I will come right then.

His cock is hard between my legs. I spread my thighs, wanting him to find my center, and when he does, I toss my head back and gasp. In that moment, he captures me with a kiss, then thrusts inside me.

My body captures him, draws him in, and as his tongue thrusts inside my mouth, his cock pounds into me, harder and harder as if every moment of the last five years is hidden in each thrust.

This isn't like before. It's not revenge sex. It's not make-up sex.

It's need and demand and lust and passion. It's *us*. And it finally feels right.

His touch—our connection—sends me spiraling up faster than I wanted, and yet at the same time I have no desire to hold back. I want the explosion. I want him. I want everything that we have shared and will share.

I want the world, and with Jackson I do not think that is too much to ask.

And with that thought, I shatter, exploding like a billion pieces of colored glass as he slides against me, filling me, touching my core—and then, oh yes, finding his own release inside me.

He stays over me for a moment as the colors fall like stars around us. His arms tense as they support his weight above me. He watches me, his expression so tender that I wish once again I could cry, because it seems as if there is no other release for all the emotion I'm feeling.

"Sylvia."

It's all he says. Just my name. But it holds a world of meaning. And when he lowers himself and I curl close to him, I draw in a sigh and know that, right then at least, I am content.

I do not know how long we lay there, naked on the chaise. I haven't slept. Instead, I've simply felt Jackson's touch as I look out at the moon reflecting on the Pacific's waves in the distance, with the deep gray of the sky reaching down to touch the water. "I want a house," I say, though I don't know what made me think of it. "I want a rooftop patio and I want it in the hills. Somewhere with a lot of land, but a view of the ocean."

"Already tired of your new place, and you haven't even un-packed?"

I reach for the blanket and pull it up to ward off the nighttime chill. It is almost not necessary, though. Jackson is like a furnace, and his heat warms me as I curl against him, my cheek to his chest, so that I hear both his heartbeat and the reverberation of his voice when he speaks.

"I love this place," I say. "But I want to see the stars. I want a velvet black sky. And I want to be able to hear the sound of the ocean's waves breaking." I start to mention that I hold Damien and Nikki's Malibu house up as the gold standard, but decide that perhaps this isn't the moment to bring my boss into the conversation.

"You have a star," he says, dragging his foot up so that he can rub his toes along my ankle and the small tattoo that has been there since high school. "And a lovely crescent moon."

"Starlight Girls' Academy," I say.

"I've heard of it. Beverly Hills, right?"

"I managed to get a scholarship," I say. "I went there for my sophomore, junior, and senior years."

"Boarding school," he says, and I hear the understanding in his voice.

Starlight Girls' Academy is one of the most prestigious prep schools in Southern California, and the moment I learned that it offered full scholarships—with room and board—I'd killed myself to ace the entrance exams. My high school counselor had been astounded when I'd done well enough to be offered an interview—I'd nailed middle school, but I'd checked out my freshman year, doing only enough to get by and not making any close friends. But I'd been highly motivated, and I'd been bright and perky and social and witty during the interview.

I'd been accepted, and I'd kicked academic ass in order to maintain my GPA and stay in the program.

"I couldn't stay in my parents' house any longer," I admit, after I've told him the story. "So the tattoo was like a celebration. Me marking the transition. But the truth is I didn't fit in at Starlight, either." We wore uniforms during school hours, but had a great deal of freedom on weekends and holidays. Fashion and boys were the thing, and I wasn't interested in either. Instead, I hid behind boring clothes, never dated, and used to lie about having a skin condition so that I wouldn't have to wear makeup.

"And your parents? They didn't realize what was going on?"

"They had their hands full with my brother," I said. "I think they were a little relieved I wasn't in the house anymore. He was finally recovering and they didn't have to feel guilty about focusing all their parental attention on him." Not exactly the truth, but close enough.

"And the rape? That was over? Or did it end when you went away to school?" I hear the tight control in his voice, so taut it is like a rubber band stretched almost to the breaking point.

"Summer before my freshman year," I say. "It stopped then." I don't say why, and he doesn't ask. But I do pull the blanket tighter around my shoulders, then glance at his face only to find him looking back at me with a fierce intensity.

"What?"

"You're cold."

"I'm fine."

He shifts to a sitting position, then stands. I raise a brow. "More wine?"

"No." He bends, then slides an arm under my legs and puts the other behind my back. I gasp as he lifts me, then cradles me against his chest.

"Jackson, I'm fine. I like it out here."

"I'll find you a castle with your starlight view," he says. "Right now you're cold."

"I'm not," I say. "I have a blanket. I have you. I—" I stop, because I have tilted my head back and I see his face, and an odd mixture of ferocity and helplessness that makes my heart twist almost painfully. "Jackson?"

"Please," he says. "Let me take care of you."

I think of all that I have lived with—all that I have survived. I've had a lifetime to get used to it, and yet it still knocks me sideways. I just dumped it on him, and not even all of it. On a man who, despite everything, cares about me. And, despite my assurance to the contrary, fears that he somehow made it worse for me.

"Yes," I say as I close my eyes and lean my cheek against his chest. "I am a little cold."

He takes me back into the condo and through to the bedroom. Then very gently, he places me on the bed. "Under," he says, lifting the covers.

I look over at him. Naked. Semi-erect. And in that moment I can think only that he is perfection come to life.

I shake my head. "Nope. You wanted me warm, I think it's only fair that you warm me up, not pawn the job off on some blanket."

He chuckles. "Do you? Well, I'm all about fairness." With his eyes never leaving mine, he crawls onto the bed, straddling me, then he kisses me long and hard and deep.

"I think I like warming you up," he says as he sits up, kneeling over my waist so that his cock rests enticingly on my belly.

I glance down, then lift my brow in question. "Do you want?"

"Do I want what?"

He knows what I'm offering, I'm certain of it. He just wants to hear me say it.

"Do you want me to suck your cock?"

His brow lifts, as if in surprise at my boldness. "Desperately," he says, as he reaches down to stroke my skin in a lazy pattern. "But right now, I just want to bury myself in you."

"Oh," I say as he sweetly—so deliciously sweetly—eases inside me. I gasp in welcome and surprise, then move with him. Our movements are slow and sensual, but there is nothing gentle about my reaction. I'm rising up, buoyed by a web of dancing sparks and wild colors. He's taking me to the edge, bringing me to the pinnacle. And as my body clenches tight around him, drawing him in deeper, silently begging him to take me further, I once again find release in the arms of this man I have always wanted, and so desperately missed.

When I feel as if I can move again, I roll sideways and glance at the clock. It is almost five. "We've stayed up the entire night."

"Complaining?" He brushes a kiss over my lips, then sits up and stretches.

"Nope." I move as well, but I don't sit up. Instead I raise my arms above my head and stretch luxuriously all the way from my fingers to my toes.

"Hold that thought," he says as he trails a fingertip lightly up my leg. "I barely got started."

"Started?"

He traces a finger over the ribbon tattoo, then along the edge of the lock. And then, with the muscles of my belly tightening as he finger-walks up my torso, he bends to gently kiss the new flame that lights my breast. "I can't help but think I'm following a path. These. The moon on your ankle. All the rest."

He's right, of course. And yet I say nothing.

"Is this what you do?" he asks. "Your own kind of therapy?"

"What?"

"That's what you said," he reminds me. "I said you needed help. You said you had your own kind of therapy. Am I looking at it?"

I lick my lips. He knows—obviously he understands—so why am I still so hesitant to admit it to him? "Why do you think that?" I swing my legs off the bed, then stand. My robe is still on the floor from the last time I wore it, and I bend to pick it up. I shove my arms through the sleeves and tie the sash tight around my waist.

"I understand the concept of self-medicating," he says.

I turn as he gets off the bed and walks to me, completely naked and not the least bit self-conscious. "How?" I ask, then realize I already know the answer. I brush my fingertip lightly over his knuckles as he reaches for the sash on my robe.

"Jackson . . ."

"Yes," he says, but whether he's referring to my unspoken question or the unfastening of my robe, I do not know. He lifts his hands, then eases the robe off my shoulders so it falls to the floor and I am standing naked before him.

Slowly, almost reverently, he looks over my front. His fingertip grazes the two tattoos on the swell of my right breast. The new flame and a much older female symbol twined with a rose. Then he moves lower, gently running his fingertip along the red ribbon design that has been there since before Atlanta.

"You told me this was just a random design," Jackson says. "Now tell me the truth."

The truth.

The thought makes me shiver, and I know that I am not ready to go there yet. Not completely. And yet I don't want to run from the question or the man. On the contrary, I want to move in closer. I want to feel his arms around me, and I want to get lost, safe in the warmth that is Jackson.

And so I tell him. The core of it, at least. "They're triumphs," I say. "Reminders, anyway."

"I see." He steps closer, then slides his hand around my waist until his palm is pressed flat over the intertwined J and S that are inked on my lower back. "And this? Does this mark a triumph, too?"

"No." The word is raw, pushed out past a wall of emotion. "No," I say, "that one is a memory." I draw in a breath for courage and then meet his eyes. "It's the only part of you I could take with me, and I didn't want to ever be without it."

For a moment, he just looks at me. Then he pulls me close and kisses me hard. He scoops me up and carries me back to the bed, then gathers me close. "I found you curled up in the bathroom, and you wouldn't let me help you."

"I'm sorry." My voice is small, and I hate that I did that to him. Because he's right. I'd been freaked and scared and I'd wanted only to get out of there.

"You wouldn't tell me anything. You just said that I had to do something for you. You said it was important."

I swallow. "It was." I blink, wishing desperately that I could cry. "I had to ask you to leave. It couldn't be me who left. You would have followed me."

A muscle in his cheek twitches. "Christ, Syl. We've wasted a lot of time."

"No," I say, and I can see the surprise on his face. "I had to make you leave. I couldn't handle it." I draw in a shaky breath as I try to gather my courage. "I'm scared, Jackson. This," I say, gesturing between the two of us. "What if it is a mistake?"

"It's not."

"You don't know that. No," I say when I see that he is about to interrupt. "I let myself go with you once, and I regretted it. I lost control when I shouldn't have lost control. I was overwhelmed. There was—is—this intensity between us, and it was too much, because it just got all tied up with everything."

I'm talking fast, the words spilling out, and I'm not sure he understands because I'm not sure I understand myself. "I felt unanchored, and then I felt stupid because I knew I shouldn't have opened that door in the first place. I should have never left the pandas. And then it built and built until the nightmares came. The nightmares. The fears. All the goddamn memories, and—"

I cut myself off, biting down hard on my lower lip and looking away because I don't know how to say this. I don't know how to say that maybe this moment between us that felt so incredible is wrong. Is bad. Is a mistake that's just going to rip us apart all over again. "I couldn't handle it," I finally say. "And I'm scared I won't be able to handle it again."

"What did you regret?" His voice is soft and gentle, in sharp contrast to my tone of rising hysteria.

I shake my head. "I don't know what you mean."

"You said earlier that you let yourself go with me, and that you regretted it. So did you regret the nightmares? Or did you regret leaving?"

"I—" My breath hitches, and I look away.

"No," he says gently. "Talk to me, Syl. I can't help if you don't talk to me."

"I'm not asking for help."

"No, you're not. But you'll have it anyway."

I close my eyes and take his hand, then close my fingers tight around his. "Leaving." I take a breath, then open my eyes and look at him. "I regretted leaving every single day. And at the same time, I didn't. Because staying would have destroyed me."

"Oh, baby." He pulls me close against him and presses a kiss to the top of my head. "I don't know what's hiding in your nightmares, but I will help you fight them."

"I thought you were an architect, not a shrink."

"I know a thing or two about the lingering scars of childhood," he says. "My childhood was nothing like yours. But it still qualified as shit."

I look at him, this man I'd always seen as so strong, and the vulnerability I see makes my heart twist. "Will you tell me?"

"I'm a bastard." He shrugs. "That's pretty much the sum total of it. And I mean that in the original sense of the word. My mother had an affair with a married man. Got pregnant. Had me."

"So you never knew your dad?" As much as I often wished I'd never known my father, that still wasn't a fate I'd want for a child.

"Oh, no. I knew him. Knew my father. Knew all about his other family. I was two when my half-brother was born, and I knew every goddamn thing about him, and I wasn't allowed to say a single word."

"My god." I'm trying to imagine what that would be like and failing. "My god," I say again.

"Yeah, that pretty much sums it up. You could say it pissed me off, especially when I could see so plainly how much of my father's attention my brother was getting, and how very little of his time was spent with me. I got angry. Very angry. The kind that explodes out. The kind that's dangerous."

I can't help the way my gaze darts to the cut on his cheek.

He sees and flashes a rueful grin. "I turned anger into fights."

"Jackson . . ."

He takes my hand, then kisses my palm. "And I channeled control into sex."

I lift a brow. "Did you? I hadn't noticed."

"I guess I'll have to try to be more obvious." He gently strokes the hand he still holds. "My point is that when I realized I couldn't fight all the shit that was in my past—in my head—I embraced it instead. You need to do the same."

"I don't know what you mean."

"I think you do. Fight back. You have nightmares? Don't run from them. Battle them. You're strong, Sylvia. Strong enough not to be defeated by your own head."

"It's not my head," I say. "It's my history."

"And what is history but a memory, and usually a false one at that? What's that saying? That history is written by the victor? Write your own history, Sylvia. And when you do, make yourself the hero."

I don't answer, because I'm not sure I want to talk about it, much less think about it.

Instead, I deflect by reaching up to trace my finger across the scar that runs from his brow to his hairline. I'd noticed it at the premiere, and had yet to ask him about it. Now that he's mentioned his fights, I can't help but wonder what flash of anger translated into this injury.

"When?" I say nothing more. I know he will understand my question.

"About twelve hours after you told me to walk away."

I only nod, not trusting myself to speak as my fingers drift down to gently touch his cheek. "This one is new."

"After I met your friend Louis," he says, confirming what I already suspected.

"Does the other guy look worse?"

"I assure you, he does."

I meet his eyes. "Maybe you need help, too. You can't just go on beating people up."

The corner of his mouth quirks up. "I promise you I'm not accosting random tourists on the street. I belong to a gym. There's a boxing club. And no, I'm not talking about the kind of gym that has a smoothie bar and twenty-eight elliptical machines. Heavy bags, speed bags, free weights."

He strokes my cheek. "I'm doing just fine."

I picture the kind of dirty, grimy gym you see in so many movies, where guys are getting their faces smashed in. It's not a picture I like. I lift my hand to cover his so that I feel the warmth of his skin on my face. "I don't want you to get hurt."

"Oh, baby. They can't hurt me. Don't you know that you're the only one who's ever managed to tear me to shreds?"

fifteen

I wake with a jolt, my heart pounding in defense against the lingering clutch of fear.

I reach out, groping for Jackson, and as I do, I realize that it is not the cold fingers of a nightmare that cling to me, but the fear that Jackson has left.

"Now there's a lovely picture," he says, and his voice sends unexpected waves of relief coursing through me.

He hasn't left—and I didn't have a nightmare.

Thank god, thank god, thank god.

I realize that I've been lying stretched across the bed, my hip and thigh uncovered. I sit up, pulling the sheet over my breasts for modesty, which is ridiculous considering how thoroughly he explored every inch of me. I lean against the headboard and sigh in pleasure as I watch him move toward me, barefoot and shirtless in only his jeans, the top button open to reveal just a hint of the hair that arrows down toward a very enticing bulge.

I'm enjoying the view so much that a full second passes before I realize that he's holding out a cup of coffee. I take it gratefully, then smile when I realize there's already cream in it. "You remembered."

"I remember a lot of things." He gestures for me to slide over, then gets in beside me when I do. "For one thing, I remember that we're supposed to be at your boss's house in two hours, and it's a half-hour drive with no traffic. Which means that it's always an hour drive."

"We didn't get much sleep."

"And yet I feel surprisingly energized," he says, then brushes his hand over my hair.

I sigh and lean against him, amazed at how quickly things have shifted between us. This feels like it did in Atlanta. It feels like we fit. And even though I'm still scared, this time I don't want to run. Instead, I want to cling tighter.

"Can I ask you something?"

"Anything," he says.

"You came after me last night. When I took off for Mulholland, I mean. But you didn't come after me in Atlanta."

"That was different. You told me to leave, you didn't run out. And you made me promise."

"Yes," I say. "I did."

"Did you want me to break my word?"

"No—I couldn't have handled it."

"But?"

I shake my head, both amazed and a little irritated at how easily he reads me.

"But you wish that I had anyway, just so that you would have known that I cared?" His words hang soft and fragile between us.

"It's stupid, I know." But I cannot deny that it's true.

"I would have," he says, moving away from me to stand up. He moves to the far wall and the window that now glows with the light of morning. "The truth is that back then I would have said fuck the promise and gone after you." He turns to face me. "But you'd gone to him."

"Dammit, Jackson. I was never with Damien that way. If you don't believe me—"

"I do. You told me earlier, and I do. I believe you. But back then I thought otherwise."

I consider what he says as I slide out of the bed and walk naked to him. "Was that why you said no? To the resort here and in the Bahamas? You thought I was Damien's mistress or something?"

"Partly, but there was more to it than that."

"The land deals."

He cocks his head. "Let's just say that outside of the context of the Cortez resort, Stark and I are at cross-purposes."

"I don't understand."

"You know what? It doesn't matter." He lets his gaze drift slowly over me, so that the heat from his inspection seems to touch every part of my body, firing every molecule and making me forget just what the hell we were talking about, anyway. "I'm about to invite you into the shower with me. Which means that the last thing I want to be discussing is Damien Stark."

"Oh," I say, sliding into his arms. "You have a very good point."

He'd turned on the shower before he made the coffee, and when we go into my bathroom, it's already warm and cozy and steamy, just the way I like it.

Jackson strips off his jeans and I follow him in, then press close as his arms go around me, letting the sluice of water drench my hair and run over my face and body. I imagine it's washing away the past, leaving open the way for a future with this man.

I tilt my head back and close my eyes, and that is when I feel his lips brush mine.

"No time, remember?"

"I'll be fast," he says, then captures my mouth with his even as one of his hands slides down to stroke my sex.

I'm wet and ready, and all I can manage is a simple word, "yes."

His hands close over my breasts as he moves me back so that I am pressed against the tile. Then he lifts one of my legs so that my calf is over his hip, and I am open to him. I do not want to wait. I reach for him, then stroke my hand down the length of his erection, taking satisfaction in the way his expression goes hard, as if he's on the edge of something spectacular. Because he is—and because I am the one who is taking him there.

"Now," I say, urging him closer, demanding he fill me, then crying out in surprise and pleasure when he finds my core and thrusts inside me.

"Faster, Jackson. Harder." I am crazed with need of him, and when he holds on to my ass so that he can thrust more deeply, I hook my other leg around him, then gasp again and again as with each thrust I am slammed up against the warm tile wall.

Until finally, I feel his body tighten and he explodes inside me, and it is my name that I hear on his lips.

"Come on," I say when his eyes are no longer glassy. "We need to get going."

"Not just yet," he says, reaching for the handheld shower and turning it to a steady pulse. "I don't think you're quite ready yet."

"Jackson . . ." I'm too ready, too sensitive, and I'm not at all sure that I can handle what he has in mind. But this is not a morning for mercy, and when he pulls out of me and I settle one foot back on the shower mat, he keeps hold of my other leg, then aims the pulsating jet at my clit.

"Oh, god, oh, Christ, oh, Jackson."

I clutch his shoulders, my body shaking with a growing pleasure that is almost too much to bear.

"If we're in a hurry, I can stop." His lips are right by my ear, and he highlights the words by tracing his tongue along the edge of my ear, making me even more crazy. "Is that what you want?"

"Don't you dare," I say. "But, Jackson, oh, please, I'm so damn close."

"Then let's see what I can do." He puts the handheld back, then drops to his knees. With one of my legs over his shoulder, he closes his mouth intimately on me, and it is that combination of his tongue, his lips, his touch that pulls me that final distance. My body shatters as a million volts pour through me, ripping me apart so that I am nothing more than atoms spinning in space. Nothing more than heat and desire lost in the arms of this man.

"Wow," I say. "I don't even care if we're late."

"Convenient," he says. "Because neither do I. Still, the man is your boss. We should probably make an effort."

I nod, then reach for a towel once he has turned off the shower. Outside the glass enclosure, I drop the towel in favor of my robe. I'm about to tie it when I look down and notice the red ribbon tattoo.

Jackson is a few feet away, a towel wrapped around his hips as he runs a comb through his hair.

"Come here," I say.

He turns, but I simply crook a finger.

"At your service," he says with a small smile, but I can see the curiosity on his face.

I take his hand, then trace his index finger over the red ribbon.

"Theo Stiles. Kevin Carter. Dan Weiss." I give him the names as I brush his finger over each of the initials. "I didn't answer you earlier."

"Boyfriends?" he asks, though I can tell by his tone that he knows they were not.

"Weapons," I say. "Blunt instruments."

"Tell me."

I wrap my robe tight around me in defense of the cold. But we are still in the steamy bathroom, and there is no chill. It's Jackson I want, and I go eagerly into his arms when he pulls me in close.

"I told you how I hid at first," I say. "After it stopped. In boring clothes and no makeup."

I have my cheek pressed against his chest, and I am speaking softly. But I know from the way his body goes stiff that he has heard me just fine. "You didn't want to be seen."

"I would have become invisible if I could." I draw in air. "My friend Cass is the one who finally got through to me. She told me that the more I hid the more he won."

"I think I like your friend."

I look up at him, then smile at the warmth in his eyes. "She's great. Strong, too. Because she managed to pull me out of hell. But there were times—" I cut myself off, suddenly realizing how hard this was to talk about. I move away from him, then press my hands and forehead to the tile and simply breathe.

"It's okay," he says as his hands close over my shoulders. "You don't have to go on. I think I understand."

I shake my head. "You don't. You can't possibly."

"It was better for a while," he says. "You proved to yourself that you didn't have to hide. But it didn't stay easy. Maybe a man asked you out. Maybe he got too close. Maybe it wasn't even about sex, but something happened at work or at school. You felt out of control. Like you'd lost the reins of your own life."

I squeeze my eyes tight. "How can you know that?" I ask, then turn in his arms so that I can see his face. "How on earth can you possibly—"

"I saw it, didn't I? With Louis? I'd knocked you down," he says with so much self-loathing that I have no choice but to grab his hand and clench it tight. "I'd sent you racing right toward him. Right toward something you could get your head around. That you could control."

"And you stopped me, too."

He glances down, and I know that he is looking at the red ribbon. "Would you have gone to bed with him?" he asks.

I think of how lost I'd felt. How turned on I'd been by the way Jackson had touched me, kissed me. And how angry I'd been when he'd offered that deal. "I don't know," I whisper. I gather my courage, then lift my head and meet his eyes. "You mess me up, Jackson. No one has ever messed me up the way you do."

"Baby," he says, "I know the feeling." Gently, he pulls me against him, then holds me close. He is hard, and I feel the press of his erection against me, but this moment isn't sexual. Instead, it is tender, and I cling to him, feeling cherished for the first time in a long time.

Five years? Forever?

For me, I realize, they are the same.

"I want to make love to you right now," he says. "I want to hold you and sink deep inside you and make up for five long years without you, when you should have been in my bed," he says, as my body warms and tingles under the gentle caress of his words. "I want to touch you and please you. I want to hold you and caress you and make you laugh and come and hope and dream. I want to watch your eyes when you soar with me. And then I want to hold you while you sleep and stand guard against your nightmares. I can't change your past, but I will stand with you to fight your battles now."

"Thank you," I whisper, but I don't quite meet his eyes.

He tips my chin back so that I am forced to look at him. "What?"

I draw a shaky breath. I should have known better than to think I could keep something hidden from this man. "I don't like being weak."

"You're the strongest person I know, Sylvia. You walked away from us and managed to survive, didn't you?"

I know his words are a tease to make me feel better, but there is truth there, too, and I can't help but think that after surviving the past, this present is my reward.

"And now we need to get dressed because there's someplace I want to show you on the way, and if we don't hurry, we really will be late."

He runs the comb through his hair once more, then relinquishes the bathroom so that I can do my hair and makeup.

I hurry, but it still takes me ten minutes. My hair may be short, but I need various gels and goops to get it the way I want it to look, and then spray to ensure it stays that way. As for my makeup, I've never worn a lot, but even my minimal face routine takes time. Finally, I have to find something to wear, a decision I would normally have made last night considering that most of my hanging outfits are still wrinkled from the move or are still folded in random boxes.

I'm staring in the closet debating, when I suddenly realize that I have the perfect outfit tucked away. I go to the box from which I'd pulled the lingerie last night, take a deep breath, and then pull out the yellow dress. I'd folded it carefully, and that combined with the light material has kept it pretty much wrinkle-free.

I grab fresh underthings and skip the stockings altogether. I glance at myself in the full-length mirror I've propped next to the closet door, and I can't deny that the dress is flattering. But that's not why I'm wearing it. The day that Jackson gave me this dress stands as one of the best in my life. He'd filled every moment with heat and wonder, and though I know that he now understands why I left, I want him to realize how much Atlanta meant to me. That despite everything, I'd clung to those memories and my souvenirs of our time together.

When I'm finally dressed with shoes and jewelry, I step out into the living room to find him fully dressed in the clothes he wore last night. He smells clean, all soap and shampoo and male. And he looks positively gorgeous, tall and lean and sexy as he stands by my back wall and looks out at the bright, crisp afternoon.

"How the hell do men do that?" I ask, as he turns to look at me. "Just five lousy seconds in the bathroom and you look hot as sin."

"And just how hot is sin?"

"Very."

"In that case, thank you for the compliment. And even though you took longer than five minutes, I have to say that it was worth every second. You look incredible. And I especially like the dress," he adds, just when I think he's not going to mention it at all.

He crosses to me, and kisses me lightly. "You saved it."

"Are you surprised?"

"Friday I would have been. Today, I'm not."

My smile blooms, and I hook my arms around his neck. "Kiss me now," I say. "And take me to bed later."

He laughs. "How can I resist?" he asks, then closes his mouth over mine.

sixteen

I have driven up the Pacific Coast Highway from Santa Monica to Malibu more times than I can count, and yet in Jackson's Porsche it feels as though this is the very first time.

"It's like flying," I say, my head back in the seat and my eyes closed. "It's like being free." I open my eyes long enough to grin at him. "Or at least it is the way you drive."

"Vixen," he retorts, making me laugh.

"What did you want to show me on the way?" I ask.

"You'll just have to wait and see."

"Fair enough." I lean my head back and breathe deeply, and realize that for the first time in a very long time I feel completely content. "You know we need to talk about the resort."

"I want to see the island first. Then you can tell me your basic concept."

"And Glau's sketches."

"Not interested," he says, and I bite back a smile. I'd been expecting that answer.

"You still need to look," I say. "Aiden or Damien might want your thoughts."

I expect another protest, but then he nods. "But not before I see the island. I don't want anyone else's vision in my head when I see the raw space. Certainly not Stark's."

I shoot him an annoyed glance. "What is it that bugs you so much about him?"

"He's arrogant, for one thing," Jackson says.

"So are you."

The words are undeniably true, but he only smiles. "Maybe. But I'm also not a man who forgets or forgives easily. Especially when someone skirts the law to get what they want."

I must look confused, because he continues. "Atlanta, Sylvia. He swooped in, bought land out from under everybody, and screwed more people than just me."

I frown. "Even if that's true, I don't believe he did something underhanded. He'll grab an opportunity, sure, but illegally?"

"You may work for him, but you don't know him."

I raise my brows. "But you do?"

"I know enough." He runs his fingers through his hair. "And I didn't mean to go off on your boss. Sorry. I just don't want his ideas in my head when I do my initial walk-through of the site."

"Okay." That much I understand. "Okay. Why don't we go this afternoon? We'll have a few hours of daylight after the party. I'll call Rachel and have her notify security we'll be on the island, and then get her to send Clark and the helicopter to the Malibu house around three."

"Tell her we'll be on the island," Jackson says. "But we don't need the helicopter."

"We don't? Why not?"

"What? Don't you think I can handle transportation?"

I narrow my eyes. "Unless your secret identity is Aquaman, I sincerely doubt that this car turns into a boat. Or a plane, for that matter."

"Do you trust me?" He asks the question casually, almost teasingly, but I think I hear an undercurrent of something else. As if we have veered off the topic of transportation and onto something much more serious.

"Yes," I say, and realize that I mean it. Trust, however, is an elastic thing. And I am not entirely sure how far mine stretches.

I think that he is going to say something more, but before he gets the chance, my phone rings. I grab my purse off the floorboard, rummage around, and answer the call.

"Are you busy?" Cass asks.

"On our way to Damien and Nikki's for lunch," I say.

"*Our* way," she repeats. "So how did it go?"

"It's going just fine." I glance sideways at Jackson, who looks both curious and amused.

"Fine? Really?"

I can't help my laugh. "Yeah, really. Who would have guessed?"

"How very interesting," she says with a singsong lilt to her voice.

"Okay, moving on. What do you need, Cass?"

"I got an email from Ollie. He wants to meet on Tuesday to talk about the franchise thing."

"That's fabulous."

"I'm scared shitless. I don't know what kind of questions to ask. I'm not even sure why I'm doing this anymore. What if I screw everything up? My dad spent his whole life paying off this place—what if I fuck it all up by trying to expand? I can't—"

"Hey. Deep breaths. Nothing's going to happen on Tuesday. It's an informational meeting, right? He'll talk to you about what you want to accomplish, and you'll ask every question you can think of."

"My mind is blank," she says. "I can't even remember my own name, how am I supposed to think of intelligent questions?"

Considering Cass has more business savvy in her little finger than most people have in their entire body, I'm not particularly worried. I can tell that she is, though. Totally Tattoo is her entire life, and the fear of losing it is what has kept her shopping at Goodwill, and has filled her savings account to a point that she actually has the capital to consider expanding.

"When's the appointment?"

"Five. Oh my god, Syl. Can you come with me?"

"I'll see what I can do," I say, mentally reviewing my calendar. "But I don't know that my questions will be any more on point than yours."

"Moral support," she says. "Thank you, I love you."

"Love you, too."

"And, Syl? I'm glad it's going fine."

She clicks off before I can respond, and I tuck my phone back into my purse.

"Intelligent questions?"

"Cass wants to franchise her tattoo parlor and she's got a meeting with an attorney next Tuesday. She's incredibly nervous, which would be amusing if it weren't so important to her. Cass is about as cool and collected as they come."

"You're a good friend."

"I hooked her up with Damien's attorney, and he put one of his guys on it. It works out well because Cass has met him before a couple of times. Orlando McKee. He's a friend of Nikki's."

"I meant for going with her."

"She'd do the same for me. But I'm not sure how much help I'll be. I've never started my own business, and the stuff of Damien's I've worked on is on a much bigger scale."

"Why don't I come with you?"

I shift in my seat so that I'm looking more directly at him. "Really?"

"I've never franchised anything, but I have started my own business. I can't promise I'll be any help, but I think I can manage to come up with at least one or two intelligent questions."

I just stare at him for a second.

"Is that a problem?"

"I'd really like to kiss you right now."

"Well, that's not a problem," he says as I lean over in my seat and kiss his cheek. "And it won't be a problem for Cass, either?"

"What do you mean?"

"She's your best friend. And she just inked that lovely flame on your breast." He takes his hand off the gear shift and squeezes mine. "I don't know what you told her, but I can guess. And I doubt that I'm high up on her favorite-person list."

"True," I say. "I guess you'll just have to treat me really great to earn her respect and admiration."

I'm teasing, but there's no humor in his eyes when he meets mine. "That's my plan."

"Right," I say, licking my lips as a pleasant warmth washes over me. "Well, okay, then." I sit quietly for a moment, watching the world go by, the Pacific on my left and the hills rising up on my right. "The truth is we both screwed this whole thing up."

"And now we're trying to fix it."

"Lost years," I say, my words mirroring his from last night.

He gently strokes my hair. "Maybe we just met too soon. Maybe now we're ready."

"Do you think so?"

"You let me in last night, didn't you? You didn't do that in Atlanta."

"We didn't exactly have time in Atlanta. Two days, remember."

"Bullshit."

"Excuse me?"

"On the clock, maybe. But there was nothing short about our time together. I knew you, Syl, and you knew me. And in those two days we connected more intimately than I have ever connected with anyone else."

I don't say anything, but he is mirroring my thoughts.

"That's why it hurt. That's why you ran—and that's why you

pissed me off so goddamn much when you came back into my life. Not because you wanted me, but because you wanted what I do."

"I never didn't want you." My words are a whisper, but I know that he can hear them.

"I know. I get it."

"What I mean is that it's more than that. I haven't been with a guy. Not since Atlanta."

"I know," he says.

"You do? How?"

When he looks at me, I see infinite understanding in his eyes. "The ribbon tattoo. There are no new initials."

"Oh." I smile, just a little. "You're right."

"Can you tell me why?"

I lift a shoulder. "Before, I needed it. Something would go wrong in my life. In school or a job interview, and I'd feel so lost and out of control, and I'd have to—"

"You'd have a Louis moment," he says.

I roll my eyes, but can't deny it. "Yeah, well, that surprised me, too. Because I thought I'd battled it back. I mean, since Atlanta, whenever I felt that way, I'd—oh, fuck." I cut myself off realizing that I was getting into territory I wasn't sure I wanted to enter, exposing things I wasn't sure I wanted to expose.

"Tell me." His voice is gentle. "Tell me, Syl, and let's see if we can't get past these last five years."

I rub my palms over my face, feeling weirdly embarrassed. "It's just that when I felt that way—lost, I mean—after Atlanta, well, I'd—god, it sounds stupid. But I'd follow you."

"Follow me?"

"Well, not in person. But your buildings. Your career. Everything," I add, thinking of the bits and pieces of gossip about the women in his personal life that I'd seen over the last five years.

"Why?"

It's a good question, and one I'm not entirely sure I have an answer to. As far as I'm concerned, a dozen shrinks would give a dozen explanations. "I don't really know. Maybe guilt, like you said. But I think the real reason was that I needed a reminder that I'm strong. If I'd left you and survived, then how could I not survive whatever else life threw at me? And then when I realized that I needed you for the resort . . ."

I trail off with a shake of my head and suck in air. "It was like the gods were standing in a circle raising their middle fingers at me, you know? Because I'd survived so much, but the one thing I couldn't survive was you."

"And I went and made it worse for you. I'm sorry."

"No. Maybe. A little." I shrug. "The truth is, we made it worse for each other." I reach over and take his hand. "And now we're making it better."

"We are. Yes."

"Cass was with me at the premiere, by the way." I speak lightly, hoping to wash off some of the gloom I've cast over our drive. "She says you're hot."

"I'm flattered."

"You should be. You're not exactly her type."

"Dark hair? Blue eyes? An arrogant bastard?"

"A guy."

"Oh?"

I roll my eyes at the question in his voice. "She's just my best friend," I say. "We're not . . . involved."

He sighs. "Well, I can still have my ménage fantasies."

I laugh, but I can't deny that his words have gotten all twisted up inside me.

He must recognize my shift in mood, because he turns in his seat to frown at me. "You know I was joking, right?"

"About a three-way with me and Cass? Yeah. Besides, she'd twist your balls off if you suggested something like that. She's a little overprotective of me."

"I know the feeling. What I don't know is where your thoughts went all of a sudden."

"Just you and fantasies about women. And, you know, you and women. Forget the fantasies."

His finger taps a rhythm on the steering wheel. "I'm reasonably certain you couldn't be more vague if you tried."

"You've dated a lot of women." There. I have spit it out. "Irena Kent, for example. You were even with her at the premiere. It's all over the press that you're dating her." I'd confirmed that myself with a quick internet search after Jamie told me what she knew.

"Dating her? No. But I was sleeping with her. I'm not anymore."

"I see."

"Actually, I don't think you do. I've fucked a lot of women, Sylvia. Before and after Atlanta."

"And now you're sleeping with me." I hear both hurt and jealousy in my voice. And it pisses me off.

"No." His voice is hard. Firm. "None of them are like you."

"Why not?"

He takes my hand and lifts it to his lips for a gentle kiss. "Because you matter to me. And I didn't have anything to prove to them."

The words warm me, even though I don't entirely understand them.

"What do you have to prove to me?"

His grin is wide. "I guess you'll know once I prove it."

I shake my head, amused. "How much longer until we get to what you want to show me?"

"Not much farther."

"And no clues?"

"Not even one," he says.

"Fine. In that case I'll continue to harass you about old girl-friends."

"Oh, joy."

I smirk. "Actually, it's more about the movie, but talking about Irena Kent reminded me. My friend Jamie says she's hoping to get a starring role, and that's why she cozied up to you."

"I wouldn't be at all surprised." Jackson's voice is tight. "But considering I don't want to see the movie made at all, her plan is doomed to failure."

"Is it true you punched out the screenwriter?"

I see his hands tighten on the steering wheel. "Please tell me you didn't read that in the gossip rags."

"No, I heard it from Jamie. She heard it from a friend. Said it was very hush-hush."

"Good. I paid a lot of money to keep it hush-hush."

"So you really did punch the guy." I'm oddly fascinated by this. "I thought you were all about boxing clubs and not smacking down innocent people."

"Trust me," he says darkly. "That asshole was not innocent."

I decide not to press that point, but I can't stop thinking about the movie in general.

"What?" he says after we've driven about five miles in absolute silence.

"I didn't say anything."

"No, but your thoughts are deafening."

"I just don't get it," I admit. "That house is spectacular, and it's what put your career on the map. I know there was a tragedy there, but that was long after the house was completed and you were in Vegas working on the Union Bank building. So why does the thought of a movie bother you so much?"

"Because it's private." I hear the sharp edge to his voice and wince a bit. He notices, and I watch as his shoulders sag. "Sorry. But the whole project is surrounded by tragedy, and the damn producer who's interested in the film is sticking his nose in where it doesn't need to be. It's personal. It's private. And there are real people with real lives who are going to get hurt if the damn thing gets made."

I still don't understand, but I'm not going to push. It's clear enough to me that Jackson hasn't told me the entire story. But considering I'm hanging on tight to secrets of my own, I can hardly bitch too loudly.

I reach over and brush my hand over his shoulder. "I may not understand why, but I get that it's important to you. And I hope you get the movie shut down, too."

His smile is one of thanks and acknowledgment. "Speaking of movies, Michael is hosting a fund-raiser at his house Friday night. For the National Historic and Architectural Conservation Project. It's a good cause, and he's a good guy. Will you go with me?"

"Of course." I wriggle a little in my seat. Considering everything we've now been through together, it's probably silly. But the thought of going on a proper date with Jackson makes me undeniably happy.

It's only then that I notice that he's slowed to make a right turn. I glance around, then look to him in question. "The Palisades?"

"You'll see."

He turns, and I pay attention as he climbs the canyon road, then turns and doubles back toward the ocean until the road makes a sharp right and we follow it, essentially traveling parallel to the coast highway, but well above it in the hills.

I actually know this neighborhood, as I've spent a lot of time driving in these hills searching the facades of these beautiful homes for that unknown something that keeps eluding me.

The houses here are spaced far apart, with each lot taking up anywhere from one to three acres, most of that land allocated to the backyard. The place has a friendly, neighborhood vibe, but doesn't feel like suburbia. The houses are private and expensive, and that gives the area a quiet, exclusive feel. And because each lot on the west side of the road overlooks the coast highway, each home has a view of the ocean that is positively to die for.

"Let me guess," I say. "We're going trick-or-treating early."

"We're not," he says. "But feel free to put on a costume anytime you want."

I raise my eyebrow. "I just might do that. But not if you don't tell me what you're up to."

"Just a little farther." As he speaks, the road curves sharply. He makes a left turn into a vacant lot, then stops the car.

I glance around, confused, and am about to ask Jackson, but he's already getting out of the car. I do as well, then follow him deeper into the property, delighted to see that although it has no structure on it, some early developer terraced the hill so that there are stairs leading down to what will essentially be a private back-yard to whatever house is ultimately built on the lot above.

"This is amazing," I say, turning around and realizing that I have no line of sight to any of the houses on the street above. As for the coast highway, it is mostly camouflaged by the trees and brush that slope away from the area on which I now stand, which means that the dominant view is of sand and ocean. "I can't believe this lot hasn't been snatched up."

"It was," he says. "I bought it five years ago. Just a few months after you left Atlanta."

"You—" I turn, something in his voice halting my words. "But you were living in Georgia."

"I was staying in Georgia. I've always lived in California. And I left not long after you did. Things went downhill with Brighton pretty quickly."

I know from official biographies that he'd grown up just outside of San Diego. I didn't know that he'd ever lived in or considered living in Los Angeles. And now to find out that he'd come here—that he'd bought property even. Honestly, I'm not sure what to think about that, and I tell him as much.

"It's not a trick question and there is no hidden meaning. But I wanted to show you this place because I think it's special. And I thought of it last night when you told me about wanting the ocean and the stars."

I look around at the bright blue sky and the blazing sun.

"Not today."

"No," he says with a laugh. "Not today." He holds out his hand for me and I take it. "Will you tell me something?"

"Sure," I say, but my voice is a little too light, because I'm nervous about where this might be leading. "At least, I will if I can."

"Last night, when the nightmare came and you ran out on me, why did you go into the hills? Why not just race down Santa Monica or Sunset? Build up some speed? Or cruise down PCH? Or get on the highway and open her up? That time of night you could have gone all the way to the desert without hitting traffic. So why go up?"

"I don't know," I say honestly. "Usually when I'm upset or need to think I go to the Getty Center. I probably spent half my time in high school there."

"But not last night."

"No." I frown, because the question hadn't occurred to me. It had just seemed natural to go into the hills. To drive fast. "I was scared. I was running. I wasn't thinking."

"And yet you ran to Mulholland. Curves and hills and no guardrails. Sounds pretty scary, too."

"Your inner psychologist is showing," I say.

He laughs. "Perhaps. And perhaps I'm right. Maybe you were conquering fear with fear."

"I don't know. Maybe." I hug myself, not really in the mood to be picked apart. "Why does it matter?"

"Because I think you were being smart." He cocks his head, his blue eyes just a little devious. "Because we're going to push you, Syl. Fight fear with fear. Take control by giving control."

I shake my head. "I don't know what you're talking about."

"Then let me show you." He steps back, then looks me up and down. "Take off your clothes."

I see the heat in his eyes and hear the command in his voice and realize that he's not kidding. Prickles of excitement skitter over me, but I shake my head. "I don't think so."

"No? That's not the way this works, Sylvia. I tell you to get naked, and you do. I tell you to suck my cock, and you get on your knees."

His voice is firm, commanding, and I take a step backward, shaking my head in both denial of his words and in defense against the way my body heats in response. "What kind of game are you playing, Jackson?"

"The only kind I ever play. Mine." He crooks his finger. "Come here, baby. I want to show you something."

I hesitate, and he laughs.

"Come on," he urges. "I promise I don't bite hard."

I hear the echo from our past—the words he'd teased me with in Atlanta—and I move toward him.

"Good girl," he says, meeting me, then pulling me into his arms so that my back is pressed to his chest and one of his arms holds me tight around the waist as we look out over the ocean.

"Beautiful," he says, even as his free hand slowly tugs my skirt up.

"What are you doing?"

"Wait." He kisses my ear, sending shock waves of pleasure through me at the same time his fingers find my panties. He slides his hand down, cupping my sex, then growling low and deep when he finds me hot and wet and ready.

He slides his fingers deep inside me, and I moan with pleasure even as my knees go weak.

He bends his head to whisper in my ear. "And that, beautiful, proves my point."

"I—what?"

I turn in his arms. I have no idea what he's talking about.

"You like feeling used, Sylvia," he says, and I immediately shake my head.

"The hell I do. I—"

The press of his finger to my lips silences me.

"I told you to strip. Told you that it was my prerogative to order you to suck me off. And baby, that didn't just make you wet, you're so aroused I bet it's painful."

I say nothing; he's hit just a little too close to the truth.

"You get off on submitting. On giving up control to a man. But you remember the shit that sick fuck did to you—how he took control, how he made you do things against your will—and it makes you ashamed when you get turned on, and that's when the nightmares come."

I hug my arms tight around myself, not liking his words and not understanding how he can be so damn perceptive. But so far he's not saying a thing that I can argue with.

"But it's not the same with me, baby. Bob stole your control. I haven't. I'm calling it being used because that's how you see it, but that's not really true. It's giving yourself over in trust. He took from you, baby. You didn't give him a goddamn thing. But when you submit to me, you give me everything."

I do not move. I do not speak. I just stand there as he peels apart the layers of my life, hoping that he truly understands what he's seeing.

"So we're going to do exactly what I told you yesterday. You're mine, Sylvia. Wholly and completely. You're ready for me when I say and how I say. You're mine to pleasure. To take. To fuck. Do you understand me?"

"You said we were breaking that deal."

"And we did. The first time around I was taking. This time, I want you to give control to me. Willingly, sweetheart. Hell, even enthusiastically. Because I promise you, I will make it worthwhile."

I lick my lips. I am undeniably aroused—he's definitely nailed that much. But I'm scared, too. "What will you do?"

"All sorts of things, baby. Because the more you give, the less scared you'll be."

"You're talking kink? Bondage? Toys?"

"All of the above. But we'll start slow." He brushes my lips with his fingertip. "Is that panic in your eyes, or excitement?"

"A little of both," I admit.

"You ran from me in Atlanta because I didn't know what you

were battling. But I do now, and we're going to fight it together. And, sweetheart, I think this is one battle we're both going to enjoy."

I am breathing hard, my body tight with anticipation and wonder. Could he really be right? Can I really beat back my fears by giving in to Jackson's desires? Hell, to my own desires?

"Will you let me help you?" His voice is tight. Earnest. "Will you give yourself to me and let me fight this battle for you?"

I draw a breath, seeing him now as the knight from my fantasies. "Yes. Oh, god, Jackson. Yes."

"Good." His grin is slow and very, very wicked. "Now take off your clothes."

I want to protest that we are outside on a vacant lot, but the words won't come. I have just agreed to submit, and damn me, I do not want to take back what I have given him.

And, truth be told, the idea of standing naked on this hilltop with Jackson is undeniably exciting.

I strip, then lay my clothes on the jacket he has taken off. Once I'm naked, he steps behind me, then cups my breasts and slides his hands over me. "You're mine now," he says. "These breasts, this body. This cunt." His fingers tease me, and I tilt my head back, losing myself in the sensation of being stroked, aroused. "No touching without permission, sweetheart. I find out you got yourself off, and there will be a price to pay. Do you understand?"

I nod.

"This is how I want you always," he adds, stroking my sex and teasing me to the brink. "Wet and hot and open for me. So close to the edge that the stroke of my finger over the palm of your hand makes you explode. I want you ready for me. Wild for me. Not because I demand it, but because you want it. Not because I'm taking, but because you're giving."

He's been stroking me in time with his words, teasing my clit with tight circles that are building and building until I am quite certain that I will come so hard and so fast that I could fly all the way to the Pacific.

"Tell me you want that," he demands.

"Yes," I say as he turns me in his arms, then gasp as his mouth closes over mine. The kiss is deep and wild and deliciously intimate, and I cling to him, afraid that I will fall to the ground if I don't.

When he breaks the kiss, he breaks all contact, and I whimper, because I was so very close to breaking apart in his arms.

"Please," I say, but he only shakes his head and tells me to get dressed.

"But—"

"You don't want to be late, do you?" he asks, and I grimace, because I have entirely forgotten that we are supposed to be in Malibu.

I slip on the dress then bend for my panties, but Jackson gets them first, and tucks them in his pocket. "You don't need those."

"Are you insane?"

"Possibly," he says. "But that doesn't mean you get the panties back."

seventeen

"Mr. Steele," Nikki says, holding out her hand to greet Jackson at the bottom of the stairs. "It's such a pleasure to see you again. And, Syl, I love the dress."

"Thanks. You look amazing as usual." Nikki is blessed with the kind of girl-next-door good looks that win beauty pageants but still keep us lesser mortals from hating her. Today, she's in a flowing blue dress that pulls off both elegant and casual. Her shoulder-length blond hair frames her face, and she seems to glow with happiness.

"Let's get you both a drink," she says, moving between us so she can take both me and Jackson by the arm as we walk toward the stunning staircase that leads to the Starks' third-floor living room. "I was thrilled when Damien told me you'd agreed to do the resort. I think you'll bring something very special to the project."

"I'm happy to be on board," Jackson says, and I can't help but wonder if Nikki notices the way his eyes go to me. "Sorry we're a bit late."

"Traffic on PCH was a bitch," I add, hoping Nikki can't tell the way my cheeks are heating. Because the truth is, I don't really want to be here. Not now. Not when I've got nothing on under this dress and all I want to do is feel Jackson's hands on me.

"Not a problem," Nikki continues easily, and I'm grateful that she cannot hear my thoughts. "Like I said, we want to keep this casual." We pause at the base of the stairs. "Let me run through who's here so you'll know. It's a small list. Just you two, me and Damien, of course. Then there's Trent and Aiden—they're in the real estate division," she explains to Jackson.

"I've met Aiden," Jackson says. "He was in Damien's office when I agreed to work on the project."

"Oh, good," Nikki says.

"I feel like I should apologize for turning down the Bahamas project. I hope you didn't think me unforgivably rude."

She laughs. "Not rude, just honest. And I totally get where you were coming from. Damien's offered to help me with my own business dozens of times, and I keep saying no. Maybe when I'm more established I'll think about partnering with one of his subsidiaries, but right now, I want to prove that I can do it on my own. Unlike me, though, you've already proven yourself in spades."

"He has," I agree, feeling as proud of Jackson's accomplishments as if I had designed his buildings myself.

"I appreciate the compliment," he says as we start to climb the stairs. "What is it you do?"

"Software," she says. "Primarily for portable devices, though I do some web-based apps, too. I'm rolling out one very soon that Damien has his eye on. It's driving him crazy that I'm not willing to license it to the company just yet," she adds, aiming a grin at me.

"It's true," I say, because Damien has mentioned her software to me on more than one occasion, noting how much it could ease workflow around the office. And every time Nikki says no, I silently applaud her and their marriage. Because in all my experience as Damien's assistant, I think Nikki is the only person who's ever successfully told Damien Stark no.

Her and Jackson, I amend, thinking of the Bahamas.

"—since he designed this house," Nikki is saying.

"Sorry, I zoned out. Nathan Dean's here?"

"He is. I thought Jackson might enjoy talking to another architect. And Evelyn wraps up the guest list." She shrugs. "So that's the lineup. Just a small group of people connected to the resort or Stark Real Estate or Damien personally. I didn't want it to be overwhelming."

"Nathan's a little bit quiet, but a nice guy," I tell Jackson. I spent a great deal of time on the phone and at meetings with Damien and Nathan during the design and construction process.

"And talented," Jackson says. "At least if this house is any indication. It's stunning," he says to Nikki.

I know he found the outside impressive, because he commented on it as we drove up. The way the house seemed to belong to the hills, enhancing rather than overshadowing the view of the ocean in the distance. The entrance is equally awe inspiring, with a doorway that opens onto a formal living area backed by a wall of glass that reveals the infinity pool beyond. And the broad expanse of stairs acts as a second focal point, directing those staying inside to the third floor where guests are routinely entertained.

"Thanks," Nikki says. "It was almost complete when I met Damien. I'll take credit for the furniture and some of the paint colors. But that's pretty much it."

"The paint colors are stunning," Jackson says, making her laugh. And making me smile. I like Nikki a lot. So far, I think, she likes Jackson.

We reach the third floor landing and pause there. To be honest, it's impossible to climb these stairs and not pause at the top, because what you see upon arrival is so incredible that it takes a moment to catch your breath. The area is huge and designed for entertaining, and from where we stand we can see both the patio—the glass doors are now open to allow a stunning view of the ocean—and the stone fireplace that sits at an angle to the stairs so that it, too, faces the ocean.

That fireplace is the room's centerpiece, and on it hangs a life-sized nude portrait, the woman's face turned away to hide her identity. Now, though, thanks to press leaks, most of the world knows that the portrait is of Nikki.

I don't know the entire story, but I do know that Damien paid a million dollars in exchange for Nikki's agreement to pose nude. I have my suspicions that there were more terms to their agreement—quite possibly very sensual terms—but unless I ask Nikki outright, I'll never know for certain.

Even so, I can't help but see parallels between her relationship with Damien and mine with Jackson. It gives me hope, actually. Because despite all they've had to go through, the two of them are the strongest couple I know.

"It's lovely," Jackson says, still looking at the portrait. "You should be very proud of it."

"I am," she says. "I always was. But that doesn't mean I wasn't pissed off when the press took my secrets and ran with them."

"I understand exactly what you mean," Jackson says, and I know that he is thinking about the movie. "I'd love to meet the artist."

"That's Blaine." I look at Nikki. "Is he here with Evelyn?"

"He's not. He's up in Vancouver for a show. But I'm sure he'd love to talk to you when he gets back. Wyatt's here, though. I forgot to mention him earlier."

"Our photographer," I tell Jackson. "I've got a portfolio of images of the island to show you. I want to include them in a marketing brochure, and I thought they'd also make cool artwork for the public areas, maybe the individual rooms. I haven't chosen a designer yet. But I'd like your thoughts on that. I want to make sure that we hire someone who knows how to work with your design and not against it."

He meets my eyes. "Absolutely."

I nod, satisfied and, I realize, happy. Because it's not just our personal relationship that's come together, it's our professional one, too. And the idea of working with someone as talented as Jackson Steele thrills me even more than working with a man like Damien. Not that I don't love my job and think that Damien is freaking brilliant at what he does, but it's what Jackson does—designing buildings, changing the face of the world—that has always been my passion. And now to be able to share that core of him—well, the thought makes me a little bit giddy.

His smile widens, and I am absolutely certain he knows what I am thinking.

"Come on," I say with a smirk. "Let's go say hello to Damien."

"Actually, he asked if I'd apologize to you," Nikki said. "There's been a crisis at one of his production facilities in Malaysia. He had to take the call. In the meantime, let's get you both a drink and make the introductions. Wine or something harder?" she asks Jackson as she leads us toward the kitchen area tucked away behind a stone wall on the opposite side of the floor.

As far as this house is concerned, it's a small kitchen designed to service parties. In fact, it puts most residential kitchens to shame, and the main kitchen for this ten-thousand-square-foot Malibu dream house is on the first floor, decked out with more commercial appliances than most five-star restaurants.

What impresses me most isn't the setup or the luxury, it's that Nikki and Damien haven't hired any help for the party. Even Damien's valet, Gregory, who doubles as a sort of butler, is nowhere to be seen. Because despite Damien's billions and the helipad in the backyard, at the core these two people are pretty down-to-earth.

I know that Jackson has issues with Damien, but I don't understand them. And I hope that whatever is at the heart of them can be resolved, because I both like and respect my boss, and I truly value the friendship I've developed with Nikki.

Once Jackson and I are armed with scotch for him and wine for me, we head back into the main area to do the mingle thing. I'm a little nervous in light of our new arrangement. And for the first fifteen or so minutes I feel jittery and on edge, afraid—and, yes, *hoping*—that he'll pull me aside and slide his hand under my skirt.

He doesn't, and I'm not sure if I'm disappointed that he hasn't tried to push my boundaries here, or pleased that he's in full-on professional mode.

And he is, too. Jackson is cool and confident with everyone he meets. He greets Aiden enthusiastically and once again thanks him for the opportunity to work on such a cutting-edge project. He compliments my skill as a project manager and elicits effusive praise from Aiden on my behalf, which is a perk of having Jackson at my side that I hadn't anticipated.

"She fits right in with the team on twenty-seven. We're hoping we can steal her permanently off Damien's desk, aren't we, Trent?" Aiden glances at Trent Leiter, who nods enthusiastically.

"Absolutely," he says.

"And what's your role?" Jackson asks Trent. "International development? You're in charge of the Bahamas development, aren't you?"

"Actually, I oversee Southern California. That project was something of a one-off for me. Right now my attention is primarily on a new office and retail complex we're building in Century City."

Jackson looks between me and Trent. "So the chain I follow is Sylvia, you, Aiden, and then Mr. Stark?"

"Hopefully you won't need to go over my head at all." I laugh as I say it, hoping to lighten the moment. Jackson has no way of knowing it, but Trent was less than thrilled when Damien named me project manager for The Resort at Cortez, taking him out of the hierarchy entirely.

"And we're very laid back when we need to be," Aiden adds. "You can come to me anytime. Or Damien, for that matter."

"What are you coming to me about?" Damien asks as he approaches us from behind. He holds out his hand to Jackson, who shakes it warmly, dispelling my fear that his disdain for Damien would somehow spill out onto the polished wood flooring.

"Just to tell you how much I'm going to enjoy this job." Jackson flashes a quick smile in my direction, and I feel a rush of gratitude. I'm not sure if he picked up on Trent's envy or disdain or whatever it is, but I'm grateful for the change in subject.

"I'm very happy to hear it," Damien says. "We were all disappointed when you turned down the Bahamas resort. I didn't ask you on Saturday, but I'm curious. What changed your mind?"

Jackson shifts just enough to look at me. "As I said, Ms. Brooks is very persuasive. And perhaps the stars are just better aligned this time around."

Damien looks at him as if considering. "I hope you find that working with Stark International is a mutually beneficial arrangement. I don't bring people into my organization lightly. Your talent says a lot. And Ms. Brooks's enthusiasm weighed heavily, too."

"In that case, it looks like I have Ms. Brooks to thank for a lot of things." Jackson's smile is just for me. "The Resort at Cortez is just one of many."

When Nikki joins the group to ask who needs drink refills, I offer to take care of that so she can mingle. Mostly I just want to get away before my body heats to exploding from the undercurrent of Jackson's words.

I'm in the kitchen opening a fresh bottle of scotch when Trent enters and adds some ice to his glass. "Good thing you got him in to replace Glau. That was fucked up the way he just blew off for India."

"Tibet," I say.

"Odd either way. I wonder what his real story is."

"Glau? Honestly, I'm so annoyed with the man I don't even care."

"I'm curious," Trent admits. "But I wasn't talking about Glau. I mean Steele."

"His real story?" I've lost the thread of the conversation.

"It's just so strange. I mean, he was adamant that he wouldn't work for Stark in the Bahamas. And now suddenly he's all eager?"

"Trust me, he wasn't easy to convince."

"Which is also strange," Trent says, "since he's had his eye on the Cortez project from the beginning."

I put down the bottle of scotch. "What are you talking about?"

"I was pulling some permits last week for Century City and talking with one of my friends in the county clerk's office. She mentioned that he'd pulled some surveys for the island."

"Why on earth were you talking to her about Cortez?"

He shrugs. "She assumed it was my project."

"Last week we hadn't even offered him the job."

"That's my point," Trent says. "I think your Mr. Steele was playing hard to get. What I'm wondering is why."

Since I don't know the answer, I say nothing, and when Trent takes his drink and leaves, I take a moment to just breathe deep. What he was saying made no sense. So what the hell kind of game had Jackson been playing?

When I return to the main area, Aiden has moved on, and Damien and Jackson are talking alone, still looking perfectly civil. I realize then that I still expect to see tension between them, but it's just not there. Instead, I see two men with more in common than either of them probably realize. If Damien is arrogant, then Jackson is, too, because both possess a single-minded purpose.

There are physical similarities, too. Dark hair. Classic bone structure. Hollywood-handsome good looks.

They are both the kind of men who can bring a woman to her knees, and there is no doubt that as far as I'm concerned, Jackson has done exactly that.

"It's like looking at the cover of a damn men's magazine, isn't it?" Evelyn says, as she takes one of the glasses of scotch from my hand and downs it in a single gulp. "I spoke with your architect earlier. I think he'll do good. And I'm glad the two of you got over whatever hurdle needed to be leaped."

"Me, too." My cheeks heat as I think just how enthusiastically we topped that particular hurdle.

Evelyn laughs, and my blush burns hotter.

"Don't worry," she says. "Your secret's safe with me. But you be careful, too."

"Careful?"

"Jackson Steele is not a man with a one-woman reputation, and you've never struck me as the kind of woman to put up with a player."

"No, he's not—" But I stop. The truth is, she's right about his reputation. And though I asked him about it, I have no way of knowing what really went on with those women.

"Just be careful," Evelyn repeats. And this time, all I do is nod.

I head to the kitchen to get a replacement for the scotch Evelyn took, and when I return, Nathan Dean has joined the men.

"Sylvia!" he says, giving me an air kiss on both cheeks. "So wonderful to see you again. Now that Damien doesn't need me anymore, I miss going over the punch lists with you."

"Always a good time," I say, and make all three of the men laugh. "What are you working on now?"

"A residence in Brentwood, actually. For Trent Leiter."

"I didn't realize," I say. "That's great."

"Aiden gave him my name," Nathan says. "Which is how I met Damien, actually. I've known Aiden for years, and it's a friendship that's paid off handsomely."

"You've certainly done an amazing job here," Jackson says. "This home is stunning."

"Thanks," Nathan says. "Of course, Damien is a man with a lot of opinions. Several of the design features originated with him."

"He's saying that I'm a nightmare to work with," Damien says.

"I'm not. I appreciate the feedback. This is one of my most seamless projects."

"This floor is truly unique," Jackson says. "A man in your position must do a lot of entertaining."

"Actually, that was never my plan. Until recently, I rarely entertained in my own home, and I can't say I was that keen on going out, either."

"Must be nice when family is over, though."

I frown, not sure if he's asking questions with a purpose or just making small talk.

"To be honest, neither of us have large families. I don't get along particularly well with my father—if you read the gossip magazines that's hardly breaking news. And Nikki's family—well, her mother lives in Texas. You could say that as far as family goes, we're starting fresh."

An awkward silence hangs for a moment before Jackson speaks. "I'm sorry. I didn't mean to touch on a sore spot."

"Don't worry," Damien says. "My father is a lot of things, but not someone I spend any time worrying about."

In what I assume is an attempt to change the subject, Jackson turns back to Nathan. "I'm guessing you work exclusively on residential projects?"

"Primarily, but not exclusively." Nathan's voice is a bit higher than usual, as if he too is trying to push away any bad vibes. "I've been doing a bit of networking, trying to expand my presence in the commercial market, but I certainly haven't made the kind of inroads there that you have. You have quite a portfolio, Mr. Steele."

"Call me Jackson, please. And while I understand the desire to branch out, I have to say that you excel in what you do. I meant what I said about this house. It's a gem."

"Coming from you, that's high praise. Do you mind if I ask your opinion on a few things?"

"Not at all."

"Looks like they're going to talk shop," Damien says to me. "Do you mind if I borrow you for the same purpose for a minute?"

"Of course not."

As Jackson and Nathan head to the balcony to discuss foundations or arches or some other architectural details, I follow Damien into the kitchen where he gives me a quick update on his itinerary for the week. "There's a play on Broadway that Nikki's been wanting to see, and I need to meet with Isabel about next month's product rollout. I thought I'd kill two birds and go to Manhattan Tuesday night."

"Sounds like a plan. You'll leave for Brussels from New York?" Nikki is attending some sort of digital conference, and Damien is going as well. They'd been planning to fly from Los Angeles on Friday. "Do you still want Grayson on the flight? Or do you want to go commercial?"

"Make sure the date change doesn't screw up any plans Grayson might have. If he's free, book a suite for him, too. He can have a few days of R&R in New York before we make the trip."

I grin. "He'll love it."

"He'll spend the entire time at the airport looking at other pilots' birds," Damien says.

"Like I said—he'll love it."

"Bring Rachel up to speed, and make sure she knows everything she needs to about arranging my travel. The more you move off my desk, the more on top of things she has to be."

"Of course, Mr. Stark."

"And, Sylvia?"

"Yes, sir."

"You're doing a great job off my desk, too."

The praise makes me glow. "Thank you. Anything else?"

"Just have a good time today."

"Already done." I start to return to the party, then pause. "Actually, can I ask you something?"

"Certainly."

I hesitate, not sure how to phrase it. Since there doesn't seem to be any good way, I just dive in. "I was wondering what happened in Atlanta. With the Brighton Consortium."

"Were you?"

He says nothing else, and I feel myself shrinking a little under his steady gaze.

"It's just that you said something on Saturday. Before Jackson agreed to the project, I mean."

"About a few of my successful land deals having the opposite impact on him."

"Yes."

"Did Jackson ask you about it?"

I think about our conversation in the car. We discussed it, true. But Jackson never asked. "No," I say, secure in my literal honesty.

He leans against the island, his hands in his pockets. "It's complicated," he says, "but the bottom line is that the consortium was badly run—and that provided me the chance to step in and acquire some prime real estate. A business deal, plain and simple, at least where I was concerned."

"Where you were concerned?"

"If the deal had gone through, you and a lot of other people would have been embroiled in a huge mess simply because you'd worked closely with one of the major players."

"Reggie."

Damien tilts his head in acknowledgment.

"Okay," I say slowly, thinking it through. "How was it badly run? What kind of mess? Would Jackson have been caught up in it?"

"Yes to the latter. As for how and what kind, I think those are questions for Reggie. Do you still keep in touch?"

"A bit," I say. "He moved to Houston, but he's been to LA twice in the last five years. We had lunch."

"If you're still curious the next time you have lunch, ask him. Otherwise, just let it go, Sylvia. Let it go, and consider yourself lucky."

"Lucky?"

"If Reggie hadn't decided to pull up stakes, you might still be working for him. You wouldn't have Cortez. And I would never have hired a truly great assistant."

"Oh. Right. Thanks."

"Sometimes crappy things happen for a reason."

"I guess they do," I say. "Thanks for telling me."

"There's more, but it's not my story to tell. Call Reggie if you're curious. But it was a long time ago. My advice is to just let it go."

"I will," I say, though I'm not sure if I mean that I will call Reggie, or that I'll drop the issue altogether.

We walk back into the party to find that everyone has gathered on the patio. It's a gorgeous afternoon, and the deep blue of the Pacific spreads out in the distance.

"There you are." Wyatt takes my hand to draw me into his conversation with Nikki and Jackson. "I was just telling Nikki we need to reschedule your lesson. How about Tuesday? We can do some sunset shots in Santa Monica. That is if you don't mind coming to us," he adds to Nikki.

"Fine by me," she says. "We can grab a drink after, okay, Syl?"

I glance at Damien, because I know that Nikki will be long gone by happy hour. But he nods almost imperceptibly, and I go with the flow. Her trip is a surprise, after all, and we can always reschedule later. "Sounds good to me."

"And I'd like to schedule a time for you to come to the island," Jackson says. "I can take a few shots on my own, but depending on the terrain I may want you to put together a more extensive portfolio for me to use for planning purposes."

"Just say the word. I love it out there. Can't wait to go back."

"Damien was there this morning," Nikki says.

"Not you?" I ask.

"I took an investor," Damien explains. "Dallas Sykes. I've been looking at acquiring a piece of his operation. And I wanted to smooth over his ruffled feathers after he heard the original gossip about Glau."

"Damien took Sykes and his latest fling," Nikki says, her tone making clear that we've crossed over into gossip.

The conversation continues along those lines—bouncing from gossip to work to families to friends—until Jackson announces that he and I have plans to scout the island, too, and should probably get going.

We say our goodbyes, and I watch as Jackson and Damien shake hands, looking for all the world like two men who don't have the slightest problem with each other.

I release a slow breath, realizing at that moment how much I'd been worrying, even after I watched the two interact.

But now it looks like things are really on track, and whatever animosity Jackson might feel for Damien has either been resolved or very deeply buried.

And that, if it's true, is a damn good thing.

eighteen

"A boat?"

I'm standing on a slip near Fisherman's Village in Marina del Rey looking at a totally awesome cream-colored boat and wondering what the hell we are doing.

"We'd already be on the island if we'd had Clark or Grayson fly us in the helicopter," I say, but Jackson only shrugs and continues doing whatever it is he's doing on his phone. "It took longer to drive back here from Malibu than it would have to fly."

I expect a reply, but he says nothing. "Are you even listening to me?"

He looks up. "Checklist," he says, holding up the phone. "And I'm messaging the security team that we're taking her out."

I cross my arms over my chest and stare him down, trying to decide if I'm irritated or amused. I settle on amused. "Why exactly are we taking someone's boat to the island?"

"Not someone's boat," he says. "My boat. And because I wanted to show her to you."

"You have a boat?"

"I do." He points to the boat we're standing beside. "There she is."

"And you're a comedian, too," I say, but the truth is, I'm kind of delighted. I haven't been out on a boat in ages, and this is turning into a bit of an adventure. "How fast is she? How long will it take to get to the island?"

"About two hours."

I glance at the sky. It's four, and the sun is already making its descent. "It's October. By the time we get there, we'll barely have an hour of light."

"Good thing my bedroom's on board. We can start fresh in the morning." He grins, and looks so much like a delighted boy that I can't help but laugh.

"Fine. You win. Tell me all about her." I pause. "Wait. Bedroom? You live here?"

"It seemed prudent. And more economical than continuing to bounce from hotel to hotel whenever I was in town. Of course I considered pitching a tent on my land, but the boat has plumbing."

"You made a good decision," I deadpan.

"I thought so."

"The truth is, I've had meetings with a few clients in Santa Barbara. This way, I can bring my office to them." He points to what appears to be the second level, an enclosed space with walls of windows. "She has a huge area just behind the top deck designed for entertaining. I converted it to a workspace. Lots of natural light. Ocean breezes. And I've always loved boats."

"I didn't know that."

"I told you my dad wasn't around much, but the one thing he did right was teach me how to sail."

I let my eyes drift over this monstrosity of a vessel. "This isn't a sailboat."

"Look at you. I didn't realize you were so up-to-date on all things nautical."

I smirk, then walk the length of the boat until I'm at her end. Which may or may not be the stern. Unlike Jackson, I have no clue about boats. I do, however, know they have names. This one is *Veronica*.

"Who is she?"

"The boat," he says.

"Funny man. I mean, who is she named after?"

"Who says she's named after anyone?" He holds out his hand. "Come on. Let me show you around and let's get moving. I really do want to see our island."

I take his hand and follow him on board. I don't push about the name, mostly because it's so obvious that he doesn't want me to. But I can't help my curiosity any more than I can help the unpleasant and unwelcome flush of jealousy.

That fades quickly enough once we are on deck. It's hard to stay jealous of a name when a man's hands are all over you and his mouth is hot and demanding against yours. "Do you have any idea how hard it was not to take you into the bathroom at Stark's place and fuck you blind?" he asks, sliding his hand up under my dress.

"Do you have any idea how much I wanted you to?" I haven't gone without underwear in forever, and certainly never because a man has demanded it of me. A man whose hands I've been craving for the last several hours. So even though I'd managed to put it aside and function as a responsible corporate employee, the reality that my panties have been tucked in his pocket has been making me a little bit crazy.

"Actually, I do," he says as he cups my sex, finding me very wet and very ready. He nips at my lower lip. "It's been my pleasure tormenting you."

"Bastard."

He chuckles as he thrusts his fingers inside me, making me gasp. "You'll forgive me when I make it up to you."

"Someone might see." My protest is feeble, because now he's

slowly teasing me, thrusting deep and then stroking my clit when he withdraws, and I am sliding down into a sensual haze.

"No one is here."

"Jackson."

"No. Quiet. The only sound you get to make is when you come. Do you understand me?"

I say nothing, but nod in acquiescence just like I'm supposed to do. Then I tilt my head back to meet his eyes and find them dark with lust and need. I shift my stance, deliberately giving him better access, and watch as that evidence of my surrender reflects on his face, like a building storm ready to unleash.

He makes a low sound of pleasure, then hooks his other arm around my waist to hold me steady as he teases me with his fingers, and then slants his mouth over mine to get his tongue in on the action. I am completely at his mercy, uncaring that we might be seen, wanting only more of what he is giving. This wild sharing, this spiraling pleasure.

I've been on edge all day, and as much as I want to relish the sweet sensation of his touch, I cannot hold back, and before I am ready, the force of my orgasm surprises us both. He breaks the kiss, then pulls me close again. "Do you know what that does to me? Holding you? Feeling you respond like that to me?"

I manage an impish grin. "Believe me. It's my pleasure."

He laughs, then scoops me up and carries me across the deck as I laugh and order him to put me down.

"Sadly, I'm going to have to give in to your demands." He puts me on my feet and nods at the ladder. "Probably best not to risk maneuvering that together."

"Probably," I agree. I glance back at the dock, frowning slightly.

"Second thoughts?"

My smile is wide and very genuine. "Only about my wardrobe." I indicate the dress. "I can't go to the island like this."

"As much as I'd like to suggest that you frolic naked and barefoot there, you're probably right."

"Can you drive me back to my condo?" I think about the traffic between Marina del Rey and Santa Monica and wince. That's going to take forever.

"I have a better idea. Come with me."

He steps onto the ladder and I follow him down into the large area that is now his workspace. I have no time to look around, though, because he continues down another level to where two doors open off either side of a narrow corridor. The one on the right is open and I realize I'm looking into Jackson's bedroom. Considering it's a boat, it's a decent size, and exceptionally tidy. I start to glance around, just to get more of a feel for the space, but my eye is drawn to a photograph hanging on the wall near the door.

It's a red-haired woman holding a small, dark-haired girl. They're in a park and were caught in a candid moment smiling and laughing.

I recognize the woman—she's the redhead from the documentary screening.

I look at Jackson, feeling suddenly shaky. "You care about her," I say, unable to keep the accusation out of my voice.

He frowns. "What?"

"You said in the car that you didn't care about any of the women you've slept with. But you care about her." I hate the jealousy that laces my voice, and yet I cannot help myself.

He comes to stand beside me, then reaches out and takes the picture off the wall. "I never fucked Megan," he says. "Not like I did the others."

I turn to look at him, curious and, yes, jealous of the gentle tone in his voice.

"I slept with her, but it was a weak moment for both of us."

"Who is she?"

"A friend," he says, and though I expect him to elaborate, he doesn't. "It was a mistake. Can you understand that?"

I think of Louis and all the mistakes I've made. "It's not my business who you've slept with in the last five years."

"No, it's not," he says. "But it still matters to me that you know."

I nod, feeling a bit guilty for my own secrets. I'd told him in the car that I hadn't slept with any guy since him. And that's technically true. But I have slept with Cass. One stupid, drunken time after I got back, and we both knew it was a mistake right away. And though I feel like I should tell him, I don't want to put any sort of weird vibes between my best friend and my boyfriend, because no matter what else, right now, they are the two most important people in my life.

So I only nod. "It's okay," I say. "I understand mistakes."

"She's still a friend," he continues. "She and Ronnie mean the world to me."

"Ronnie?"

He strokes his finger over the little girl's image. "Her daughter."

"She's pretty darling."

"She's a great kid." He cocks his head and looks at me, just looks for so long that I start to feel a little bit antsy.

"What?"

"Nothing. I'm just glad you're here." He pulls me close and kisses me. "Someday I want you to meet both of them," he adds, as he hangs the photograph back on the wall. "At any rate, you're about Megan's size. I think there are some clothes in the other bedroom you can wear on the island."

He leads me back across the corridor into the closed bedroom. It's similar to his, only smaller. "This is her room?"

"This is a guest room," he says firmly. "She's often a guest."

"Right. Sorry. I'm still slightly green."

He laughs. "I think I like that you're jealous. Just not too much."

"Fair enough," I say as he pulls open a drawer and takes out a pair of yoga pants and a T-shirt.

"There are some jeans, too, if you'd prefer."

I check the size on pants and hold them up to myself. "No, I think these are okay. What about shoes?"

That turns out not to be a problem, either, as Megan has left both flip-flops and canvas skids in the closet. They're a tiny bit too big, but not enough that it'll be a problem. "I guess I'm all set," I say.

"Good. Because all I want to do right now is get the boat out of the marina, put her on autopilot, and make love to you on the deck."

"Well," I say, delighted. "I really can't argue with that."

I follow him back onto the deck, then watch, feeling slightly useless, as he unties the ropes holding the boat in the slip, then carefully maneuvers her out of the marina.

When we're in the open water, he offers the captain's chair to me. "Seriously?"

"It's just like driving a car," he says, and though that's not entirely accurate, it's close enough. For that matter, it's a little bit easier, because I only have to go forward. Staying within the lines really isn't an issue.

He stands behind me, his hands on my shoulders, his lips brushing my hair as I maneuver the yacht and try to focus on what I'm doing. "You know you're distracting me, right?"

"And yet I'm unconcerned about collisions."

"Can I ask you something?"

"Of course."

"Why was Megan mad? At the screening, I mean."

His hands halt. "Because I'd done a stupid thing."

I tilt my head so that I can see him. "And have you fixed it?"

"Yes," he says. "I think I have."

He doesn't elaborate, and I don't press. Instead, I let him put the boat on autopilot, then take me to the other side of the top deck with the huge mattress and low tables for snacks and drinks.

"Sunset's soon," he says. "I'll go get some wine."

I watch him descend, feeling the sun beat down on me. The air is cool, but the way the boat is constructed puts this deck in a small depression so that I'm not chilled by the rush of the wind as the boat moves across the water.

Still, Jackson's well prepared, because I find both blankets and say my name 237

pillows in a small wooden chest, and I pull them out and lay them over the mattress, making a small nest for us to snuggle down in.

And then, because I'm feeling just a bit wild and I want him to know it, I peel off the dress and slide under one of the blankets.

"Well, now. This is very interesting." He's returned with the wine, and is looking at me with the kind of heat that makes me very glad I've already abandoned my pesky clothes. His eyes flick up to where I've left the dress draped over a chair, and then back down to where I am propped up against some pillows, the blanket pulled just high enough to cover my breasts. "Very interesting indeed."

He leans over and flicks a switch on a trunk-sized gray box that sits a few feet away. "Deck heater," he says in response to my questioning glance. "I intend to pull that blanket down, and I'd hate for you to get a chill."

I grin. "How very thoughtful of you. And what do you intend to do once you've rid me of my blanket?"

"Many things."

I hesitate, then try to keep my voice casual as I say, "The kinds of things you talked about in the car?"

He slants a glance my way as he lowers himself on the mattress next to me. "Is that what you want?" He trails a finger over the top edge of the blanket. Just the lightest of touches, but the sparks from the contact ricochet through me, driving me a little bit crazy. "To go a little bit wild? A little bit kinky?"

His voice has gotten softer even as his tone has become more commanding. It's an intense combination, and I feel my sex clenching in response to nothing more than his words. "Are you longing to submit completely, trusting me to give you what you need? To take you where we both know you want to go?"

I nod, not sure I can handle speech at the moment. His smile is slow and sexy and victorious. He leans over and brushes a kiss over my lips. "Good. I want that, too." His finger hooks the top of the blanket and he pulls it down slowly to reveal all of me. My breasts, my waist, my hips, my sex. I hear the low noise he makes in his throat and feel the pleasure that comes with knowing he wants me. Then I shiver as he tugs the blanket the rest of the way down, exposing my legs, my feet, my toes.

"Beautiful." His voice holds wonder, as if he has just discovered treasure, and I tremble with delight knowing that it is me that has filled his senses.

He bends down, then draws my big toe into his mouth, sucking gently. I arch up at the unexpected sensation—the sensual sparks that race up my inner thighs to my already throbbing sex. "Oh, god."

"Do you like that?" he asks, stretching out beside me, still fully clothed.

"Not in the least," I say.

"There are punishments for lying."

"Really?" I drag my teeth over my lower lip. "That's very interesting information." I've never been spanked—that was not the kind of activity that fit with my previous approach to sex—but in this moment, with this man, I'm all about exploring the possibilities.

He laughs, then kisses me. "Someone's feeling naughty."

"Must be the sea air."

"Must be." He traces his fingertip over my breast, his touch gentle, though my reaction is wild. "I still don't know the stories behind all of these."

"Why don't you guess?"

He sits up and pours us each a glass of wine. "What do I get if I'm right?"

"A kiss."

"How can I turn down that challenge?" He makes a spinning motion with his finger. "Over."

I comply, and as soon as I'm on my stomach his fingers start dancing over my skin, teasing me, tracing my tats. Then he fingerwalks up my spine to land at the small symbol right between my shoulder blades. "This one."

"That's a hard one," I say.

"It's easy enough to see what it is. The arrows for rewind, fast forward, and play. The square for stop and the split square for pause. It's a control panel for a digital recorder."

"Clever boy. But the hard question is what does it mean?"

"I have no idea," he admits. "But I'm curious enough to sacrifice that kiss."

"I cut my hair," I say. "It used to hit right there. And when—" I take a deep breath and start over. "Bob liked my hair. Used to make a big deal out of it. And so when it was all over, I cut it. And that's what Cass put there."

"Control," he says in a musing tone. "You control it. How long. How short. What color."

I roll over, then prop myself up on my elbow and give him a kiss, long and deep, and when I pull away I let my teeth drag over his lower lip. "You're very good at this game."

"I think I'd like to play again," he says, and I take satisfaction from the need that fills his voice.

I start to roll back to my stomach, but he stops me. "No. This one," he says, pointing at the female symbol twined with a rose on my breast.

I have to force myself not to squirm, because that is the one for Cass, and I'm not sure I want to tell him about that. But I'm the one who started this game, and I don't think there's a graceful way out. And the truth is that I have kept enough secrets from him. I don't need to hold on to this one.

"All right," I say. "But you won't guess. A shame, since I was looking forward to administering your prize."

"You have very little faith."

"On the contrary, I'm quite certain."

"Give me a moment." He moves to straddle me. He is still fully clothed, and his jeans brush against my bare skin in a way that shouldn't be provocative, but really is. He puts his hands on my waist, then strokes up until he reaches my breasts. He cups the right one, teasing it and playing with my nipple even as his other hand dances lightly over the tattoo.

"You're just stalling." I'm a little breathless. Not only from the magic he's working on my breast, but because he's sitting right over my sex, and though I am not supporting all of his weight, I can feel his heat and the brush of denim against my sex. And, frankly, it's making me crazy.

"Maybe a little," he says. "I thought you might enjoy the delay." *He's got that right.*

I force myself to ignore the way my body is craving more than this slight touch and begin humming the theme from *Jeopardy!*

He laughs. "Fair enough." He meets my eyes. "This is the one for when you slept with Cass."

I am certain my face registers complete shock. "How did you get that simply from a tattoo?"

"Not just a tattoo. That tattoo. And I got it because I know you. And once you told me she was gay it just made sense."

I'm still a little flabbergasted. I'm also a little relieved. If my best friend were a guy, the question would naturally come up. *Have you two slept together,* and then we'd deal with it. But despite political correctness, no boyfriend ever asks a girl if she's slept with her best female friend. And despite being weirdly embarrassed about something I'm not the least bit ashamed of, I'm glad it's out. I don't want to be at the center of secrets between the people who are closest to me.

I sigh, struck suddenly by how important Jackson is to me, and how quickly he's filled my world.

Then again, considering all the wasted time, it hasn't really been quickly at all.

He is studying my face. "Are you upset I asked?"

"No. In fact, I was thinking that I'm relieved."

"So did you two date?"

"No—no, it was just once, and we were both a little drunk. And she made a pass and I guess you could say I caught it." I shrug. "We had fun. It was nice. Fine. I mean, I liked it, you know. But I'm not gay, although I guess maybe I was wishing I was. With the way I get, maybe I thought it would be easier. At any rate, she didn't have any expectations, and it really was never even weird after." I shrug again. "She's my best friend and I love her, but we're really just friends."

He's watching me, his expression intense. "You trust her."

"Of course I do."

"That's why it was fine."

He moves off me, and I take the opportunity to pull the blanket up, feeling suddenly strangely exposed.

"She was in control, Syl. She was the one who had the power. But you were fine. No nightmares. And you liked it."

I nod slowly. I'd never thought of it like that.

He takes my hand, then raises it to his lips. "You can trust me, too."

"I know I can," I say, but I see the truth in his eyes. We're not talking generically. He's talking about my past. About the things I've held back.

He's talking about Bob.

I manage a smile and reach for my wine. "I trust you," I say, my voice airy. "Although I'm not sure why. You're not keeping your promises, after all."

"No?"

"You promised me earlier today that I'd get kink," I say. "Wasn't that the plan you outlined on the way to Damien's? Instead, all I've gotten is talk, talk, talk." I let my head fall back into the pillows as if bored.

"You do have a point," he says. "But with a boat on autopilot the kinds of things I have in mind may not be on the coast guard approved list of safe activities. But as soon as we're tied up at the dock . . ."

He lets his voice trail off as he bends over me, then brushes his lips over my belly. "In the meantime, you tell me if it looks like we're going to hit a whale or an island."

His lips blaze a trail of kisses down my belly, making my muscles quiver and my body fire. When he reaches my pubis, he moves between my legs, then closes his mouth over my sex, teasing me with his tongue as his hands grip my hips to keep me steady against this onslaught of pleasure that is rising so fast because I have been so damn close all day.

Except I don't want it yet. Because I've decided what I want to tell him later. Not all of it. But most. Because I do trust him. And I want him to understand me.

And so I will hold back my release as an enticement. My reward for sharing a secret.

"Jackson," I say, as he brings me so very close. "Stop." I twine my fingers in his hair and pull him up.

He looks at me with a question in those heat-filled eyes.

"I want to stay here. On the edge. I like it. I don't want to go over yet."

"Don't you? I'll remember that."

I swallow, wondering what sort of sensual door I've just opened.

"The thing is," I continue, "you never got your kiss for tattoo number two. And since I don't think I'm qualified to keep an eye on the ship, I think you need to go sit in the captain's chair."

"Do I?"

I just smile innocently.

He laughs, but complies, and I follow him a moment later to the top deck. The chair is upholstered and reminds me of the bucket seats in luxury SUVs, with armrests that rise and descend. It's on a swivel base, and right now, it is facing forward and Jackson's hand rests on the wheel. The lights of Catalina are behind us, and I can see Santa Cortez getting bigger in the distance.

"How much longer?"

"About half an hour," he says.

"Good," I say, then shift his chair. I get on my knees and press my hand against his crotch, my face tilted up to his. I want to tell him that he makes me feel safe. That I trust him. But the words don't come.

I hope that he will understand from my actions.

I drop my gaze and concentrate on his jeans. Slowly, I unbutton his fly, then free his cock. He's hard and huge, and I want this. Want to taste him. Want to feel his excitement building. I need to give this to him, this man who has given me so much already.

I need to give him this pleasure before I give him the harsh reality of my secrets.

I use the tip of my tongue to tease him. I keep one hand on his thigh, but circle his cock with the other, and I can feel the way his muscles tighten. The way he shifts in the seat as he silently demands more. I feel it, and I like it. This sense of power. Of knowing that I'm leading him someplace sublime.

I can't take all of him, I know. But I draw him in, using my tongue and my hand to stroke and tease, keeping my mouth tight and sucking, trying to take him to the edge and growing more and more aroused with each small sound he makes. With the feel of his fingers tightening in my hair. With the way his cock tightens in my mouth and twitches as he comes close, so very close.

"Stop." His voice is a low demand, and he pulls me gently up. I release him reluctantly, but rise to kiss him, thrusting my tongue in his mouth, letting him taste his own pleasure.

"Are you sure?" I ask when I break the kiss.

"I want to be on the edge, too."

"Oh, really?"

"I have plans for you," he says.

"Isn't that interesting?"

"Come here," he says, and draws me into his lap. The armrest is down, and I'm cradled in his arms. I'm a little cold from the wind, but I don't want to move to get the blanket. Instead, I snuggle closer, then sigh when he uses the control button on the dashboard to turn up the deck heaters aimed at the captain's chair before wrapping his arms around me.

I feel warm and safe and protected, and begin speaking as if sharing this with him is the most natural thing in the world. "There's more, you know. About Bob, I mean."

His body tightens under mine, and when he speaks I can hear the precision in his voice, as if he has carefully chosen his words. "Do you want to tell me?"

"I don't know that I want to, but I think I need to." I look up at him just long enough to draw strength from the way he is looking at me. Then I snuggle against his chest, because it is easier to talk that way, when I am wrapped up warm in his arms.

"It was rape, what he did. I know that. But I don't think I gave you the right impression when I told you the story before. It wasn't— you know—he didn't force me."

"He seduced you," Jackson says, his voice full of vitriol. "If that's what you call that kind of behavior with a fourteen-year-old girl."

I nod, feeling all of fourteen again. "He would touch me when he was adjusting a costume. He'd tell me I was pretty. That he wanted to touch my hair. That he just wanted to show me off." My mouth feels full of cotton, but I press on, because I want to get it all out. For some reason, right now telling Jackson seems like the most important thing in the world. "Lots of that. Pretty words. And reasons why his staff couldn't stay. And then he'd—"

I draw a deep breath and swallow. "In the nightmares, it's never really the way it happened. I'm usually there twice. One of me is watching, and the other is with him. He usually ties me up. Or makes me stand a certain way. Or he's more forceful. Shoving his hand into my shirt. Making harsher threats. He just traps me somehow." I lick dry lips. "But it wasn't really like that. I mean, I know— knew—what he was doing was wrong. But it was all sort of clean."

I lift my head long enough to look up, and I can see on Jackson's face that he wants to slap that word right out of the air, but I don't know how to describe it otherwise. Because that's part of what I hate so much.

"That makes it worse," I say. "Because the thing is—the thing is—"

"You responded. You climaxed."

I press my face back against his chest and nod. "I hated what he did—*hated it*—but I liked the way it felt. I couldn't control it. It was intense. Overwhelming. And no matter how hard I tried to hang on, I couldn't. I didn't want to, but I—"

"He stole your control," Jackson says. His words, tight and measured, are so full of fury I fear that one wrong word from me and they will go nuclear. "He perverted your pleasure. That fucker scarred you as deeply as if he'd had a knife, Sylvia."

He gently tilts my head up so that I am looking at him. And now his voice is as soft as a kiss. "You did nothing wrong, baby, while he was a monster. And I swear to god, if I ever find him, I'll kill the son of a bitch."

nineteen

It's getting late by the time Jackson ties the boat up at the dock. I'd considered going onto the island tonight, but the only lights are at the dock and the area around the helipad, and stumbling around with flashlights seems silly.

Besides, at the moment I'm more interested in being in Jackson's arms than being on my island. And it is Sunday, after all. A girl has a right to enjoy her weekend.

I am in Jackson's cabin, wrapped up tight in his bathrobe as all those thoughts run through my head. And, frankly, the only thing I want right now is Jackson.

As if my wish conjured him, he appears in the doorway. His grin is a little crooked and his eyes a little mischievous, and all I can think is how happy I am that we have reached the island and the boat is tied off and we don't have to be concerned about the autopilot putting us in the path of a cruise liner.

In other words, time for the evening's fun.

"I like seeing you in my robe." He leans against the doorjamb. "I like it a lot."

"You might like it even better when I'm out of the robe."

"I might at that." The room is small, so he is at my side in only three long strides. "Why don't you take it off and get under the covers?"

"I could do that," I agree.

I start to undo the tie, when his words still my hands: "We should get some sleep."

I cinch the robe tight again and look up at him. "Sleep?"

He brushes my lips with a butterfly soft kiss. "After everything you told me—"

I grab his hand. "After everything I told you, I need this. Please, Jackson, don't make me sleep with those memories in my head. I want you. I want what you promised me."

He studies me for a moment, his expression unreadable. Then he points to the bed. "Take off the robe."

"Jackson—"

"No." He holds up a finger in a gesture of silence. "No argument. No objection. Are we clear?"

We are. Very. And I have to fight my smile of victory. Instead, I look up at him, my face bland, as I take the robe off and let it drop to the floor. I don't move, waiting for him to tell me what to do next.

He says nothing, though. He simply stands there, right beside me, the heat he is emitting so intense I fear it will burn us. His eyes rake over me, and I see the bulge of his erection beneath the denim of his jeans. "Christ, you're beautiful. I could spend the rest of my life looking at you and still not have my fill."

He moves closer, then traces my lip with his fingertip before ordering me to suck. I do, and with every tug I feel the heat between my legs grow more and more demanding.

"That's right, baby." He uses his free hand to take one of mine, then slides it between my legs. He guides me, so that I am touching myself, my fingers sliding over my slick heat, and that would be erotic enough, but the combination of his hand, mine, the sucking, is all building up inside of me, growing and growing until I am so close that all I want to do is thrust our joint hands inside myself as I come.

But just as I am on the verge of doing exactly that, he tugs his finger free of my mouth, then gently pulls my hand away from my sex. I breathe hard, mourning the loss, but I don't protest. I know enough to know that would be against the rules.

"On the bed. Spread your legs."

I do, albeit with more than a little shyness. But I am rewarded with a look of pure passion, and that emboldens me. I bite my lower lip and spread them even wider. And then, with my eyes on his, I reach down and slide my fingers into my sex, then arch up at the unexpected intensity of this touch, all the more powerful now that he is watching.

"Good girl," he says. "Touch yourself. Stroke yourself. I need a minute, and when I get back, I want you hot and ready for me, so don't stop. But don't come. If you do, we're done for the night, sweetheart."

Games. But I like them, and I do what he asks, stroking and teasing, and letting the pleasure build. And then, because I am determined to make him just as wild as he is making me, I bring my other hand up and play with my breast, teasing my nipple, and knowing that I cannot get too carried away because Jackson is a man who means what he says—and I am not ready for this night to be over any more than I want it to end without him inside of me.

He said nothing about being quiet, and so I call to him. He is in the small closet area just inside the bedroom, and he is on the floor in front of the open closet door. There is a trunk open in front of him, but I cannot see what is in it. Not until he stands and I see a length of rope and something black and silky. He hesitates, then drops the rope.

I don't have to ask to understand why. I'd run that first night in the hotel. He'd bound me and blindfolded me, and now Jackson fears that combination is too much.

It's not, though. I am certain of it. Even if the nightmares come, I'm not going to run again. Not unless I'm running to Jackson.

"Will you tell me what's in the trunk?"

He smiles as he comes toward me with the length of black silk. "I'll do better than that. I'll show you. But not tonight. Tonight, I don't intend to let you see anything." He motions for me to sit up. "Kneel," he says, "but keep your knees apart, your hands behind you."

"You're going easy on me," I say as he puts the blindfold around my eyes and secures it. I try to keep my tone teasing, but some accusation comes through.

"Easy?" he retorts. "Or starting slow? Giving us something to build to? But if you have complaints, be sure to tell me." As he speaks, his finger slides inside me, and I arch up, reacting to this unexpected pleasure.

He had touched me nowhere before, and the penetration surprises me, sending shocks of awareness through me, and heightening my senses. It is as if I am a spring waiting to pop, and as he withdraws his finger, I moan in protest, because now there is no contact at all, and I am left to the mercy of awareness and anticipation.

It's a state I've never been in before, and I am more aroused than I have ever been. So no. I'm definitely not complaining.

"You're so beautiful," he says. "Your breasts," he whispers as he touches my lips. "Your cunt," he murmurs as he flicks my nipple. "Your lips," he says, as he strokes my clit. Every touch is in contrast to his words, and I bite down on my lip trying to keep a grip on the sensual symphony that he is playing across my body.

"This is how I want you," he says. "Open to me. Trusting me. So aroused and beautiful. You fit me, Sylvia. We fit each other. Every time I touch you it's a gift. Every time I kiss you, I find myself just a little bit more."

"Jackson . . ." His words are melting me, squeezing tight around my heart.

"Lean forward," he orders. "Knees and forearms."

I do, and I feel the bed shift as he gets on beside me. I try to judge where he will touch me from the shift of the mattress, but it's no use. I feel his lips on the back of my neck, then traveling down my spine. Then his hands cup the curve of my rear.

"You have the most perfect ass," he says, and then kisses each cheek as if paying homage before silently urging me to spread my legs.

I hesitate, but not because I do not want to comply. On the contrary, I'm astounded by how much I want to do exactly that. By how easily and perfectly Jackson pegged me. The control I'd been grabbing with the men I'd claimed at places like Avalon was only an illusion. A bandage over pain and memory. But this—this is what I want. What makes me *feel*. And I trust Jackson enough to let go and do exactly that.

"Now," he urges, and I comply, then quiver with delight as he cups my sex, then strokes me all the way up, over my perineum, my ass, then along my spine, moving his own body in closer as he leans over me. The feeling is delicious, as if he is tracing a cord across my body, and with one quick tug he will light me up.

At some point, he stripped off his clothes, and the new sensation of skin upon skin makes sparks skitter all over me. "I should draw this out," he says. "I should tease you until you're close to breaking. But dammit, Sylvia, I've wanted you all day. Imagined you at that damn party with your cunt slick and hot and waiting for me. Had my mouth on your cunt. Held you naked in my lap on the deck. I've imagined fucking you so many times today, that I can't wait any longer."

"Then don't," I say, bending my arms so that I'm right there, open for him. Wet for him.

"Oh, Christ, Syl. You're going to destroy me."

I feel him move. Feel his hands grip my hips. And then the sweet pressure of his fingers teasing me, opening and stretching me before he takes me. His cock is thick, but I'm so ready for him, and when he thrusts into me, at first slowly, and then with increasing wildness, I cry out in welcome and abandon.

I am bent over as he pounds into me, from this position unable to match his thrusts, and so I am at his mercy, letting him hold me still and use me to find his rhythm, letting his fingers reach around to stroke my clit in time with his thrusts. I've never been fucked like this before, and I like it. It makes me feel open and wild. It makes me feel like I'm his.

And when he explodes inside me—when he continues to tease my clit and urges me to "let go, baby, just let go"—I find my release, too, and explode so violently that my body goes limp and I collapse onto the bed, still blind, but thoroughly and completely sated.

I feel him withdraw, soft now, then use a tissue to clean me up before spooning against me. He gently removes my blindfold and I roll over to face him. I start to speak, but he cuts me off with a kiss that is so wild and deep and passionate that it fills me as much as his cock had before, and is at least as sensual.

"Now," he says softly when he breaks the kiss. "This time you really do have to get under the covers and sleep."

"Only if you're with me."

"Sweetheart, you couldn't kick me out if you tried."

He pulls the covers down, but I'm so wasted and limp that he has to help me under. And then, when he gets in beside me, I curl up against him, our legs twined together, then fall asleep content in his arms.

I wake hours later to the scent of coffee and cinnamon. "I could get used to this," I say as I sit up against the pillows and accept the tray that has coffee, cream, and a warmed up cinnamon roll.

"I could, too," he says, then kisses me softly.

I take a sip of my coffee, enjoying it, but enjoying more the view of Jackson changing into a pair of khaki slacks and a casual linen shirt.

"Shall I hurry?"

"Take your time. I've got some work to do on the computer, and the island's not going anywhere."

He squeezes my hand, then heads out. I lean back against the pillows again, relishing this sense of belonging. Of being part of this space. *His* space.

Once I'm done with breakfast, I shower and change into the same yoga pants and shirt I'd borrowed last night. Then I head up top to find him in his office. He has three huge computer monitors and there is drafting software open on one, a topographical map of the island on another, and a word processor open on the third.

I glance at the map and see that it's one of the naval maps that Nigel sent over upon acquisition. "How'd you get that?"

"Aiden," he says. "I called while you were in the shower and he sent it over. He also said it should be in your area on the Stark directory, but that I would understand that he couldn't give me access to your files."

"You're very efficient," I say, squeezing in beside him so that I can access the company website and then the private, secure area. I've got my files open in under five minutes, and I transfer all the various maps and surveys and photographs of the island to a folder on Jackson's computer.

"And now you know what I know."

"This is good information," he says, opening files and sending them to the printer. "Let me just pull this stuff together and we can get going. I packed some snacks already, but if you'd grab some water bottles, that would be great."

Since that's a good idea, I do that. I consider taking a bottle of chilled wine, but decide against it. This may be a romantic, secluded island, but it's also work. And probably best if we keep the line from getting blurred.

We leave the boat and walk down the floating dock to the helipad and the section of the island that's been earmarked for storage and staging.

I point to the same path I'd followed to find Nikki and Damien just a few days before. "So I figure we can head that way and follow the island's perimeter. It's not huge, but it's not tiny. It takes about three hours to make the full circle, more if we're stopping to take notes or photos."

I wish I had my camera, but Jackson has brought a pocket-sized one that has a decent zoom lens, so at least we'll be able to document areas to accompany his notes.

I'm thinking about that—and wondering if I need to run back for an extra notepad—when Jackson takes my hand and tugs me to him, then draws me into a long, intense, bone-melting kiss. One hand is twined in my hair, the other sliding down the waistband of my pants. He cups my ass, then squeezes as his tongue teases me, and I know that I am already desperately wet.

I break away, breathing hard. "Not exactly workplace behavior, Mr. Steele."

"And there won't be a repeat performance, Ms. Brooks. But I thought a long kiss to tide us over was in order. After all, if I'm not going to get my *From Here to Eternity* moment in the cold Pacific, I at least wanted a kiss under the hot sun."

I can't help but laugh. I'd told him we need to focus on work, especially since we have to be back in the office tomorrow. Apparently he took my admonition to heart.

"Then again, I'm not sure it's worth trying to keep a professional demeanor," I say. I point to the security camera that has surely captured that moment.

"Never fear. Your reputation is safe with me." He goes to the pole, finds the control that raises and lowers the camera, then opens the weatherproof housing and pulls out a memory disk.

"Jackson!"

"Problem?" He flashes me an innocent look, and I do my best to appear stern.

"You realize that's just a backup? The feed goes live back to the security office at Stark Tower."

He just shrugs and grins and tucks the disk in his pocket. "Souvenir," he says. "I think I'll pull that image and make it my screen saver."

I laugh, but point to the pole and the camera. "You must have been a handful when you were a kid."

"You have no idea," he says. "Hang on."

And then he jogs back to the boat while I'm left waiting, and wondering what the hell he's doing.

When he doesn't come back immediately I consider following, then decide to spend the time checking the equipment stored here. I'm just about to open the shed when he returns. I cross my arms and tap my foot.

"Just following directions," he says, then pops the disk back in place before returning the camera to its original position.

"Let me guess. You have a new screen saver."

"You," he says as he taps the tip of my nose, "are a very smart woman."

"You're very playful."

"Why wouldn't I be? I had an extremely excellent night. I woke up beside a beautiful woman. And now I've been handed this exceptional canvas." He sweeps his arm out to encompass the island. "Thank you," he says, and the genuine sincerity in his voice makes my knees go a little weak.

"I always wanted you," I confess. "Glau was a very poor substitute."

"Hell yeah, he was," Jackson says, and we both laugh.

He picks his rucksack up from where he left it by the security camera, then nods toward the path. "Show me our island."

Our island.

I like the sound of that.

As it turns out, I'm right about it taking more than three hours to walk the circumference. Instead, it takes six. We spend the time discussing my vision for the resort. The section of the island carved out for couples, the area devoted to families. How the various rec-

reational activities will be woven in. The number and type of restaurants I anticipate.

"This resort will be family oriented, but there should still be
some areas that are private. I don't want someone on a honeymoon
or anniversary to feel this isn't the place for them."

We've made it back almost full circle, and now we're on a sandy
beach a few hundred yards from the dock. "Maybe one exclusive
area with upscale bungalows and private beaches. The area with
the inlet would be perfect," he says. "Let me show you."

He pulls out a notebook and sits in the sand, completely unconcerned about the way his pants are getting soaked or the water coming in to tease his feet, now bare since we tossed our shoes up by the
dunes.

I watch his face and the sketch that is coming to life on the
paper. He is completely absorbed, lost in this new world that right
now lives only in his imagination.

His intensity is compelling, and I drop down beside him, then
watch, enraptured, as he continues to put his vision on paper. Even
as a sketch, it captures everything I've told him I want and yet
makes it bolder, better.

He pauses and looks up, his eyes just a little glazed as if he has
forgotten where he is. When he focuses on me, though, his eyes
clear, and he lifts a brow in question.

"Perfect," I say. And when I press a kiss to his cheek, I hope he
understands that I mean so much more than the resort.

twenty

"I see what Glau was getting at with the consolidation of all the recreation facilities in one area," Jackson is saying as the elevator doors open and we step into the office's penthouse foyer. We'd spent the morning on the twenty-sixth floor in the previously empty space that Stark International has made available to Jackson and his team for the duration of the project.

Now, we're on our way up for a meeting with Damien, but Jackson's mind is still on the designs that he'd taped to the wall and then immediately started revising with bold blue pencil.

"It's not only a terrible use of the natural space, but it also limits the flexibility of the resort as a whole." He glances up, sees Rachel waving us over, and gives her a halfhearted wave as he flips more pages in the notebook he's holding. "I also want to discuss the construction crew. Unless you're contractually locked in, I'm more comfortable with my own team."

"If we hit a snag, we can bring Aiden in, but you and I can work it out. Is Mr. Stark ready for us?" I ask Rachel as we reach her desk.

I glance down and can see by the light on the phone that he's not. I glance at my watch and then frown. Damien is exceptionally prompt, and I can't help but wonder why he's still on a call when we're scheduled to meet with him right now.

Not my problem.

The reminder isn't easy to swallow. I've sat at this desk for so long that it's strange not to be behind it on a weekday, even if the reason I'm not behind it is management.

"How's the desk?" I ask Rachel, my curiosity getting the better of me.

"Busier than on the weekends," she says. "Thanks for letting me pick up Monday and today."

"Don't thank me. I'm thrilled, too. Gives me more time on real estate."

"Speaking of, guess who I had drinks with last night."

"Aiden?" Rachel's pretty and fun, and I've always thought they would make a cute couple. But she just shakes her head and says, "I wish! No, Trent." From her smile, I can see that she does not consider Trent to be sloppy seconds.

And while I would be less than enthusiastic about him myself, I have to agree that Trent is both nice and competent, if rather dull. I keep my mouth closed about that last part.

"So?" I say. "Details, please."

"No big deal, really," she says, but her blush suggests otherwise. "But he was up here last night. I was, too, because Damien had one of his international conference calls from his house, and I was here in case he needed me to pull files or something."

"Why was Trent here? Was the call about the Century City or Bahamas projects?" Those may not be my projects, but I'm hoping to be officially in that department soon, and if there's something cooking, I want to know about it.

"Oh, no. He didn't say why he was here, but since he asked me out, I think that was the real reason. And he hung out for the whole call. Even watched my desk when I had to run into the apartment to get some files that Damien left in the kitchen," she adds, referring to the private residence that covers half of this floor. "After that, we split an entire bottle of wine down at the Biltmore's bar. And I think that if we both hadn't needed to get up early, I might still be on a date."

My smile is genuine. "Good for you."

"I know, right? It's been forever since I've had s-e-x." She glances at Jackson as she spells, as if that's going to somehow keep him from picking up the thread of our conversation.

I'm about to ask her what happened with the last guy she was dating when the intercom buzzes.

"Are they here?"

I frown. Damien's voice is rarely that tight, and I wonder what morning crisis he's had to handle with Rachel at the desk rather than me.

"I was just about to send them in," Rachel says.

As Jackson levers himself off the reception couch, I give Rachel a quick nod, and she pushes the button to open the door.

Damien is standing by the window when we enter, and as the door shuts behind us, he hits a button on the remote he is holding. Immediately, the automatic blinds that cover the wall of windows start to close, shifting the room into dark.

The projection screen begins to descend and a tabloid-style headline splashes onto it:

Sex, Sand & Starkalicious Scandal!

"Would one of you care to tell me what the hell this is?" Damien's voice is taut to the breaking point.

I look at Jackson, who does not look at me. Instead, he studies the screen where an article is now scrolling beneath the headline, complete with hyperlinks to other *LA Scandal* website articles.

Damien Stark—whose place in the scandal firmament was assured by both his recent murder trial (the charges of which were dismissed—the scandalous Stark was *not* acquitted!)

and the sexilicious deal he made with his now-wife Nikki Fairchild (more here)—just might be at it again!

Has he opened up his problem-plagued, not-yet-operational resort on the recently purchased Santa Cortez island to investors for use as their own private playground? A secret hideaway for illicit affairs? Take a look at this footage of scandal-magnet Dallas Sykes and "friend" Melissa Baronne and draw your own conclusions. We can guess what Ms. Baronne's husband is thinking!

"Oh my god," I say, as a looped image of Sykes in a lip-lock with a twenty-something bombshell starts to play. "How—"

"A very good question," Damien says, his dual-colored eyes reflecting the tight grip he is keeping on control. His attention is laser-locked on Jackson. "We don't even have plans from you, Mr. Steele, and we already have scandal. Not only does this play against the family resort atmosphere we're aiming for, but this company now has a part in putting out gossip about one of our key investors. Not to mention a man with whom I'm currently in other negotiations."

"Is that an accusation, Stark?" Jackson asks.

"There were a limited number of people at my house on Sunday when Nikki mentioned Sykes and his girlfriend."

"Unless those cameras were designed during the Dark Ages, the images are sent digitally from the source to your security department. Probably also simultaneously copied to your server and backup server." Jackson's voice is as sharp and precise as a scalpel. As for me, I'm feeling rather sick.

"You have an oversight division that surely goes over incoming footage," he continues. "And I'd bet money that reviewing the incoming feed from the island is the responsibility of at least one desk security guard. If you're not going to monitor activity around all that expensive equipment, then why have the system in place at all?"

He looks around the room as if searching for something. "I wasn't the only one at your party, Mr. Stark. And there've been a lot of eyes on that image," he says. "And yet I'm the only one in here getting my ass bitten off."

"And if I learn that any of those folks are displeased about a past business arrangement, I'll be sure to call them in," Damien says as he aims the remote and continues to scroll through the article.

I read the words that pop up and feel even more queasy.

Perhaps conflict with starchitect—or should we say "Stark-itect"—Jackson Steele is adding some stress to the mix over at Stark International. Our scandal scouts say that Steele is the newest addition to The Resort at Cortez team, but that Steele is no fan of Damien Stark. Just a few months ago, Steele announced that he had no interest in working on a Stark International project. So what could have un-hardened a heart made of Steele? We smell scandal!

"Care to explain?"

"I said that to your wife several months ago," Jackson says mildly. "And repeated it to you. What someone who overheard us prints or tells a reporter isn't something I can control."

"Are you unhappy about what happened in Atlanta, Mr. Steele?"

"What?" Jackson asks, his eyes darting immediately to me.

"With the Brighton Consortium," Damien continues smoothly. "I've come to learn that if the project had gone forward, you would have been awarded the contract to design and build the complex on the full four hundred acres."

I look between the two men. I hadn't realized how much Jackson lost when the Brighton deal exploded.

"I wasn't the only one hurt when you swooped in, Stark. The consortium had investors, and yet you pulled strings and got your hands on enough of the earmarked land that there was no way the complex could be completed. Everyone involved took a loss. Everyone but you."

"Business is about opportunities, Mr. Steele. Not coddling."

"I see. I must have been confused by the references to racketeering and fraud being tossed around at the time."

I have my hand on the edge of Damien's desk, using that to keep my balance. I may not know the details of what happened in Atlanta, but I do know that the vitriol in this room is beyond toxic.

"So you've been holding on to a grudge based on your skewed version of the facts for five years, and when the opportunity arose to shove a few barbs my way you jumped on it—and injured Ms. Brooks and the real estate department in the process."

"Are you actually suggesting that I would harm a project that now bears my name simply to get back at you?"

Damien takes a single step toward Jackson. "I know my own mind. I know my own code, and I know how I value my work and what I have built over the years. But I know very little about you, Mr. Steele. I'll give you the benefit of the doubt for now. But if it turns out that you're behind this, I promise I will bury you."

"Understood," Jackson says.

He turns to leave, and I move to follow. Because right then, I want to know what's inside Jackson's head.

"Stay," Damien says.

Jackson catches my eye, nods a brief acknowledgment, then strides out the door with the cool and calm demeanor of a man who doesn't have a care in the world.

"What did you notice?" Damien asks me the moment the door shuts.

I force myself to stand up straight and not panic. "He never denied it."

"No," Damien says as he takes a seat behind his desk. "He didn't."

"What does that mean?" I ask, afraid that I already know.

Damien surprises me by shaking his head just slightly. "Might mean nothing." He meets my eyes. "If I'd been in his position I wouldn't admit or deny anything, either. Why give some fucker who's put you on the spot the satisfaction?"

I exhale, then sag a bit in relief. "I see." My relief is short-lived, however, when I remember the one thing that Damien still does not know—the memory card that Jackson took from the island. I think of it—and feel anger and betrayal boil in my gut.

"But I'll keep my eye on him and the project. He's in a unique position to cause some real hurt. You should keep an eye out, too," he adds, and something in his voice suggests that it's not hurt to the company he means, but to me.

I conjure a generic smile. "I will. Of course." I take a half-step toward the door, eager to get out, but Damien halts me with his next words. "There's something else you need to see."

Something in his voice fills me with dread, and I turn back to him slowly. "What's wrong?"

He nods toward the screen. The *LA Scandal* article disappears, replaced by a single photograph.

I swallow as my cheeks heat with mortification. It's an image of me and Jackson locked in an embrace. And not a sweet end-of-a-movie-type kiss, either. No, this was when Jackson had grabbed me, pulling me close, practically fucking my mouth with his tongue. One hand is in my hair, the other starting to slide under the waistband of the yoga pants to tease my ass.

Just looking at the image makes me squirm—in embarrassment, yes, but also from the memory.

"Mr. Stark," I say, then have to clear my throat because that came out way too high and squeaky. "I'm—"

I give up, not sure if I should start by apologizing for being caught on tape or for being unprofessional. And not entirely sure how to phrase either.

"Sit down."

I sit. Legs together, hands in my lap, eyes down.

"Look at me."

I draw in a breath and lift my head, prepared for whatever lashing he's about to dole out. But where I expect to see retribution on his face, I see only concern. "You're not in trouble, Syl," he says gently. "But I am worried."

I feel myself relax immediately. "I didn't think about the security cameras. And then when I remembered—well, I never thought that you—that anyone—would see that." Not entirely true. I knew the guys in security would, but none of them would have sent the picture to Damien without telling me first.

"I doubt I would have had it not been for the *Scandal* story. I pulled the feed myself."

"So this isn't wide?" I realize only as I say the word that I'd been half-worried that this was fodder for some second *LA Scandal* story.

"As far as I know, no one's seen it except me and Nikki. I found it at home. She was with me. I'm sorry about that."

"No, it's okay." I run my fingers through my hair, not really sure how I feel about any of this other than horribly embarrassed and incredibly unprofessional. "You should know that—"

Once again I cut myself off. I'd been about to deny, but deny what? That Jackson and I are involved? We are. That it has nothing to do with the resort? It does.

Finally, I settle on the generic. "You should know that although I'm incredibly embarrassed that you've seen that, it doesn't negatively impact the resort. Not my dedication to the project or Jackson's."

"I'm going to say this only once—I believe you. But if it turns out I'm wrong, I'll take you off the resort and put Trent on it so fast your head will spin."

I squeeze my fingers together. "I understand."

"That's not my primary concern, though."

"There's no policy against intra-office dating, and—"

"Dammit, Sylvia."

I freeze. "Sir?"

"This isn't about policy. This is about you."

I wait, not sure where this is going.

"You're a good employee, but you're also a good friend. I understand men like Steele, and I don't want to see you hurt."

"I—oh." I draw in a breath.

"I don't trust him. I've given him the benefit of the doubt about the Sykes footage, but the key word there is *doubt*."

"I understand. But I believe him." The latter is not entirely true. Because right now I'm not sure. I want to believe that Jackson wouldn't do that—wouldn't use our time on the island to gain some leverage against the project. Against Stark.

I want to believe it—but there's the damn memory card filling my head.

That, however, is not something Damien needs to know, and I feel a little sick. Both from my rising anger and worry, and from the simple fact that I'm keeping secrets from my boss.

Damien's smile is thin. "I know you trust him. And now we've circled back to why I'm worried about you."

He moves his hand in a dismissive gesture. "We'll drop it now. But, Syl, I'm going to pay attention. And if I think that he's using you as a way to get to the project—or if he's doing anything to hurt you—I will destroy him. I protect my employees, Ms. Brooks. And I also watch out for my friends."

I nod, moved by the words, even though the concern behind them scares me. Because between my knowledge of the memory card and the doubt that Damien has planted, my thoughts are spinning. I rise, ready to get out and get my head clear.

"One more thing before you go. It's possible my father is part of this."

"Your father?"

"He's meddled in my business before, pulled in the gossip rags, manipulated things for his own benefit."

I nod. I know well enough that what Damien says is true.

"And he's the type of man who would pull strings from behind the scenes."

"You think he's getting information from someone here?" I frown, remembering that Jeremiah Stark had been at the documentary screening. Evelyn said he was on the National Historic and Architectural Conservation Project's board, just like Michael Prado. Did that mean he knew Jackson? And even if he did, so what?

I start to mention the connection to Damien, but decide against it. The truth is there is no connection—just my mind turning in conspiratorial circles. And until I ask Jackson, there's no reason to mention a thing—although those damn doubts of mine are now buzzing around like gnats.

"I think it's something to think about," he says, "but don't think too hard. Focus on the work, not the scandal. That's just noise, Sylvia."

I nod. From his perspective, he's right. From mine, I need to ask Jackson about the scandal—and about that goddamn memory disk. And even about Jeremiah Fucking Stark.

"I leave in just a few hours. I don't like going away when someone is fucking with my company."

"I know how to reach you if anything else happens," I say. "Or if we learn anything concrete."

I manage to remain calm and professional throughout the rest of our meeting, going over travel arrangements with Damien, things that I need to handle for his desk or pass off to Rachel.

By the time I leave, though, I've pent up so much worry and fear that I'm about to explode.

"What's the matter?" Rachel asks, but I wave the question away. I need to update her on a lot of things, but that is just going to have to wait. Right now, I need to talk to Jackson.

I find him on twenty-six, in the corner office which is the only fully finished area on this floor. The rest will be built out over the next few weeks to provide additional workspace for any draftsmen or other staff that Jackson needs to bring in on the project.

There is also a reception desk just outside the office for Jackson's overprotective secretary. Right now, she's still in New York, but Jackson has already said that he may bring her out and keep his New York office temporarily dark while he's on the West Coast.

I remember the way she kept him from me when I tried to make an appointment. This time, there is no dragon to get past, and I shove Jackson's door open and burst into his office.

He's standing at a drafting table, and looks up, surprised, when I blow in.

The room is a mess. Papers scattered everywhere, boxes tilted on their side, and I cannot tell if this is the chaos of moving or if Jackson has done a number on the room himself.

I suspect the latter, and that only rekindles my temper and fears about that memory card.

"I should have known." My voice is harsh yet controlled. Too controlled. "You told me. You told me this was about revenge. I thought you meant me. But all this time, you're trying to get back at Damien?"

He lifts a finger, and holds it toward me, his face so tight that I know he is fighting not to explode. Frankly, I know the feeling.

"Do not start with me," he says. "Don't you burst in here and tell me that you believe what that son of a bitch is saying."

"Goddammit, I trusted you. Desperately. Intimately. You can't fuck with trust like that, Jackson. You just can't."

For a moment, I think I see hurt flash in his eyes. Then there is only cold calculation. "What exactly do you think you know?"

"The memory disk? That bullshit about a screen saver. You used me." I feel my eyes burn, and for the first time in my life I'm grateful that I cannot burst into tears. "You fucking used me. And why? So you can make Damien look bad?"

"You have no idea what you're talking about," Jackson says very slowly. "And as for trust, I'm not seeing a lot of it from you, either."

I take a deep breath and try to calm my temper. "Fine. Okay. Fine." I drag my fingers through my hair and try to regroup. "Do you know Jeremiah Stark?"

"Stark's father?"

"Damien thinks that his father may be behind some sabotage at the company."

I try to read Jackson's face, searching for knowledge, but I see nothing but confusion, and I'm relieved.

"Why?"

"It's happened before. I can't get into the details, but I've seen a lot, and I've seen that man do some pretty reprehensible things, and the fact that Damien's his son only makes it worse. I mean, fathers should protect their kids, not use them."

Jackson takes a step toward me, but right then, I do not want his compassion. I've let my own shit slide into this conversation, and that is not somewhere I need to go.

I lift my head, steeling my resolve, and ask him point-blank, "Are you working with Jeremiah Stark?"

He stops cold, and the gentleness I saw in him a moment ago vanishes. "Are you fucking kidding me?"

"Stark was at your documentary," I say. "I saw him. And now I want an answer. Do you know him? Are you working with him?"

"I am absolutely not working with Jeremiah Stark," he says, and I believe him.

I still don't know what to think, though. I know what I saw with the memory disk. I remember what Trent told me about Jackson researching the island before he was even offered the project.

I think about all that—and I don't know what it means.

"So what's going on here?" Jackson says. "Is your boss firing me?"

I shake my head. "No. There's no proof." I meet his eyes. "Damien doesn't know you took the memory disk."

"I took the disk because I wanted a picture of us. I already told you that."

"Yeah," I say. "That's what you said. You also said you wanted revenge." I draw in a breath. "The truth is, I don't know what's going on, Jackson. But the bottom line is that I'm not letting you fuck up my resort because of some vendetta you have against Damien for some land deal that happened five years ago."

"I guess you know what you know," he says coldly.

"I know I need to be careful," I say. "I know I need to be smart." I'm afraid, so very afraid, that I've opened myself too much to this man. That I know better than to let myself trust. And that now I am paying the price.

"Then *be* smart," he says. "Because if you use your head, you know that I would never, ever put this project in jeopardy. My reputation means too much to me. *You* mean too much to me. Everything you've told me? Every part of yourself that you've given me? Do you really believe I would violate that trust?"

"I don't know," I admit, and feel as though my heart is breaking. "I just don't know."

"No? Well, you should."

"Jackson."

"Go," he says.

"Jackson, dammit, we need to—"

"Right now, Sylvia, I need you to leave."

twenty-one

Right now, Sylvia, I need you to leave.

The words cut through me, hot and horrible. They're my words, the ones I said to him so many years ago. And for over an hour they fill my head as I shower and redo my makeup in the women's locker room.

When I can't use that as an excuse for hiding anymore, I go up to my desk on twenty-seven and try to get some work done on the resort, hoping that poring over details will leave no room for my thoughts of Jackson.

But considering the project for the day is dealing with the FAA about the small landing strip, my mood has not improved much by the time I push my work aside so that I can walk down the hill to the offices of Bender, Twain & McGuire, where Cass is meeting Ollie for her franchise planning meeting.

I've been to this office dozens of times with Damien, so I'm not surprised when Cyndee, the receptionist, tells me to just go on back to the small conference room. The blinds are closed, and I feel a stab of guilt as I realize that I'm running five minutes late, and the meeting has started without me.

I tap on the door, then let myself in, my apology dying on my lips when I see Jackson sitting next to Cass.

Across the table from them, Ollie looks up. "Sylvia, we're just getting started. Help yourself to a cookie," he adds, pointing to the familiar tray of cookies and Danish, which is my favorite part of coming to meetings at this office. The snacks are awesome.

I grab an oatmeal-raisin cookie and take the seat next to Cass so that she is a buffer between Jackson and me. I feel his eyes on me, but I don't look his way. I can't look at him and be certain that I can keep my shit together. And this meeting is too important to Cass to allow my personal problems to mess with my head or her deal.

Despite her nerves and her fears, the questions that Cass fires at Ollie are good ones. I'm impressed with Ollie, too. I've never worked directly with him, but I do know that he was in the litigation department for a while, and I'd been a little concerned that he wasn't going to be up to speed on the ins and outs of franchising. But he knows his stuff, and he not only runs Cass through all the moving parts that need to happen to get her set up, but he's also incredibly patient with her questions and doesn't fall back into legalese.

Jackson's no doormat, either, and he interjects a number of points to clarify what Ollie has said or to ask for further explanation. He's so helpful, that despite my still raw nerves, I'm grateful that he's come.

"So I've given you a lot to consider," Ollie says as the meeting draws to a close. "Your homework is to think about bringing in investors. It will reduce your risk substantially, but also reduces your overall equity position. It all boils down to risk and reward. And control," he adds. "Right now, you're the only face of Totally Tattoo, and you have been for a while. Think about whether that's something you're willing to give up."

"I will," she promises.

We say our goodbyes, then head for the lobby while Ollie goes in the opposite direction to his office.

"Thanks so much for coming, you guys," Cass says, giving me a hug. Then she turns to Jackson and gives him a hug as well. "You're as awesome as Syl said you were."

"Am I?" Jackson says, looking over her head to me.

I bite my lip, realizing that this is the first time they've actually met. And also realizing that I haven't yet had the chance to bring Cass up to speed on the most recent drama.

"Zee was totally irritated that I couldn't meet her right after work, so I'm going to go try to catch up with her for drinks. You guys want to come?"

I shake my head. "I'm meeting Wyatt for a photography session. And I need to run home and change and get my camera first." I'd thought about canceling when Nikki left a voice mail, excited to learn that Damien was taking her to New York tonight. But the truth is, I haven't spent enough time behind the lens lately. And right now I'm messed up enough that the idea of forgetting everything else except form and light and composition is pretty damned appealing.

"Have fun," Cass says. She gestures to the elevator. "Y'all going down?"

I start to say yes, but Jackson touches my elbow. "Go ahead," he says. "I want Sylvia to myself for a minute."

Cass grins. "Of course you do." She nods toward the reception desk, where Cyndee talks on her headset to a caller. "Just be discreet."

She winks, then pushes through the door to the elevator bank.

"Thanks," I say when she's gone. "It was nice of you to come."

"I told you I would."

"You did." I shift my weight, hating how awkward I feel around him. "I didn't think that you would."

"You should have more faith in me," he says, and I know he's not talking about Cass.

Maybe he's right. Maybe I should. But I say none of that out loud. I just shrug and repeat myself. "Anyway, I am glad you came. It means a lot to her."

"And to you."

"Yes. And to me."

He looks at me for a minute, his gaze so steady that it feels as though he's memorizing my face. "You know what you know, Sylvia. Don't second-guess yourself."

I look away, unwilling to meet his eyes. I don't like the way his words sting, the way they bring out everything that I'm afraid of.

But mostly I'm afraid that I've screwed up. And that I've lost him again.

I'm back on Damien's desk on Wednesday, and the day is so crazy with him out of the office and the various fires that I need to put out that I have very little time to think about Jackson.

I'm grateful for that small blessing.

I'm even more grateful that I don't see him all day, but when seven o'clock rolls around and the building starts to empty out, I find myself thinking more and more about him. It's stupid, because I'm not ready to see him again. I don't know what I want to say or how I want to say it.

But that doesn't change the fact that I'm craving him, and the fact that he hasn't come up to see me—that he doesn't crave me, too—is bothering me more than I like to admit.

And so even though it makes me feel like I'm in high school all over again, I call down to building security and ask Joe if Jackson is in the building.

"No, ma'am, Ms. Brooks. He hasn't been in today at all."

I hang up the phone and feel like a fool. Because the truth is, I could have gone home an hour ago, but I'd been hanging out hoping to see Jackson, when Jackson wasn't even here to be seen.

I'm a mess and I know it, and as I drive home, I call Cass, who sounds about as stressed as I feel.

"What's wrong?" Pathetic, perhaps, but I'm happy to know that I'm not the only one having a truly fucked up day.

"Nothing. I'm just freaking out about the franchise thing. Zee thinks it's a mistake."

"Why?"

"I don't know." Cass sounds both exhausted and exasperated. "She says it's too much of a commitment. That it'll take too much of my time. She says it already has, because I've spent most of today reading all the material Ollie gave me, and then some. Plus she was pissy that I didn't get to see much of her last night."

I frown. "She wants to be with you," I say, hoping that I am right. "You two just started dating, so she's jealous of everyone who has your time. That includes your job."

"I guess. Listen, I have a raging headache and we're open late tonight and I'm booked back-to-back. I'm going to go pop some ibuprofen and get ready for my next client. Hey," she adds, almost like an afterthought. "Why'd you call anyway? Are you okay?"

"I'm great," I lie, then let her go.

I tell myself that I should believe my own press, and as I let myself into my condo I repeat the words like a mantra. *I'm great. I'm awesome. I'm doing just fine.*

The mantra is not working very well, so I decide to take a page from Cass's book and self-medicate.

Ibuprofen, however, is not my drug of choice. That would be Kahlua over vanilla ice cream and as many reruns of *Friends* as I can stand.

I know that I have fallen asleep when Ross steps out of the screen and turns into Bob.

"You're not real," I say. "Not anymore. You're just a dream."

"I'm as real as it gets, and we both know it." He takes a step toward me, his camera aimed at my face. "What did you think? That he would save you? He fucked you up as much as I did."

I shake my head. "No."

"He can't help you. But I can give you what you want. We both know you liked it."

"No."

He reaches for me, his fingers cold as they slip over my skin. He tries to close his hand around my wrist, but I jerk free and run, racing down dark corridors, through half-constructed sky rises, and then out onto long steel girders that are suspended across the sky.

"He can't save you. You can't even save yourself."

He's coming closer, but I can't let him get me. I look around frantically, not sure what I am searching for but knowing that I have to find it.

And then I see him.

Jackson.

He is on the ground, at least thirty stories below.

He holds out his arms. "Make the jump, Sylvia. Make the jump and I'll catch you."

I turn to see Bob coming closer. "Nobody can catch you," he says. "You're just going to crash and burn."

"Dammit, Sylvia, trust me." Jackson's voice is crystal clear despite the distance between us.

And though it scares me to make the leap—though I am about to go flying out into the abyss with nothing but his arms to save me—I throw myself off the building and hurtle through the wild blue sky to the man waiting on the ground to save me.

twenty-two

I got Rachel to cover my desk Thursday afternoon because I just couldn't be in the office any longer. Because I needed to apologize to Jackson, and because I knew exactly how I was going to do that.

But now that I'm here at the marina, all I've done for the last twenty minutes is stand on the dock looking at the *Veronica*.

Jackson's in there—I'm sure of it. I saw his shadow pass through his office right as I arrived. And yet even though he's the reason I came, I can't quite make myself go in. I'm afraid that he'll push me away—and I don't think that I could stand that.

No. He won't. He's your knight. He's the one who's going to save you.

I nod, bolstered by my thoughts. Then I hitch my tote bag up more securely onto my shoulder and make my way onto the boat.

Nothing is locked. Not the gate to the boat nor any of the doors once I'm on board.

It's not exactly safe, but I can't deny that he's made it easy.

I go first to his work area, but he's not there, so I head down to the bedroom.

The shower is running, and I hesitate outside the bathroom door, tempted to join him. Then I glance back at the bed and decide that I have a better plan.

At least, it's better if he doesn't kick me out. But I'm running that risk either way, so best to just not worry about it.

I set my tote bag on the floor, then take out the things I've brought. I made a quick shopping stop on the way over, and I place each item on the bed, then bite my lip, afraid that maybe I've gone a little too far.

Then again, what's that saying? Go big or go home? As far as I'm concerned, those are words to live by.

I hear the shower cut off, and know that he will be back here soon. I debate, but then make a last second decision. I peel myself out of my skirt and blouse, bra and panties. I leave on the black stilettos, though. And I grab a starched white button-down from Jackson's closet and slide into it, buttoning all but the top three buttons.

It hangs to mid-thigh and from the small image in the mirror over the built-in dresser I think I look cute and sexy—and hopefully desirable and forgivable.

At any rate, it's too late now, because the door is opening and Jackson is entering, and I suck in a breath when he steps fully into the room and I see him, lean and tan and perfect, with nothing but a thin towel slung low around his hips.

"Sylvia."

I can't read his reaction in his tone, and so I just clear my throat and manage a weak smile. "You should lock your boat if you're going to be in the shower. You never know who might let themselves in."

"I don't usually shower during the afternoon. For some reason, I've been distracted." His eyes skim over me, and though his voice is still flat, the towel does little to hide his arousal. And though I know that doesn't necessarily mean he will forgive me, I am more than willing to be optimistic and take that as a good sign.

I'm about to launch into an apology, but Jackson speaks first.

"What's all this?" he asks with a nod to the bed. And this time, there is no doubt that there is heat in his voice.

I clear my throat as he picks up a coil of nylon rope. "I, um, I stopped by Come Again," I say, referring to a local sex toy shop. "I was trying to figure out how to say I'm sorry that I doubted you. That I didn't trust you."

He puts down the rope and picks up a vibrator. He cocks his head when he looks at me, and though my face heats so much that I'm afraid of burning the boat, I'm grateful that he looks not only amused but intrigued. "And you trust me now?"

"Yes." The word is simple and entirely true.

He moves on to the small leather paddle, then whaps it lightly against his palm before looking at me with such wild and dangerous lust I am tempted to forgo my apology and beg him to just fuck me.

"What made you change your mind?"

I lick my lips. "I didn't. I realized that I always trusted you. I just got caught up in the noise and the doubt. It's a vile thing. It seeps into the cracks. It can destroy things." I draw a deep breath. "Jackson, I'm so sorry."

He doesn't respond in kind, instead he glances at the selection of sex toys. "And this is how you intend to prove it?"

"It seemed like a good idea at the time."

There is no reading his expression, and I'm both nervous and frustrated. I want his forgiveness. I want his touch.

I want him, plain and simple.

And right now I have no idea how I will survive if he tells me to get off his boat.

"You don't need all of this."

"Are you saying you want me to leave?"

Something like pain slashes across his face. "God, no."

"Then this is what I need, Jackson. You said so yourself."

"Sylvia—"

"Dammit, I'm not breakable. I need you to know how much I trust you. This is what I want." I pick up the paddle. "I fucked up, Jackson. Don't you want to spank me?"

I close the distance between us, then breathe in the scent of him, all soap and shampoo as I watch the fire flare in his eyes. He takes the paddle from me and tosses it onto the bed, then grabs my wrist and pulls me close. "Don't you get it? I pushed you in Atlanta and you ran."

"We talked about this on the way to Malibu. About why I ran. About what I was running from. You're the one who said it. Bondage. Kink. Toys. That's what you promised me. And you were right."

"That was before—"

"Before I told you the full story?"

I see the affirmation in his eyes. "I don't want to push too hard," he says.

"I want you to push," I counter. "I want you to push harder and farther. I want you to take me as far as you want, as far as you need. You're holding back because you think I need you to. Reining in what you want. Who you are. Control and power, remember? That's what you told me you are."

He says nothing, so I rush on.

"You said you could anchor me. That I get off on being used, but only by someone I trust. That you like control. That it makes you hot and hard." I take a breath and try to slow down. "You told me you wanted me to submit to you. Do you still want that?"

"Desperately." The word sounds as though it's been ripped from him. "But I'll tell you again what I said before. Not if the price is breaking you."

"You won't. You can't." I slide my arms around his waist and tilt my head back so that I can look at him. At this man who is strong enough to hold back so that he doesn't hurt me. "You're my glue, Jackson. My glue, my knight, my hero."

"That's a lot of responsibility."

I narrow my eyes and grin, because I've finally heard the acquiescence in his voice. "Can you handle it?"

"I think I can struggle through."

"Then we start slow," I say. "But we go large."

He takes a step back so that he can see all of me with just a flick of his gaze, from my heels all the way up to my eyes. "What do you have on under my shirt?"

"Nothing."

His eyes darken with the kind of passionate promise that makes my sex clench in anticipation. He walks around me slowly, and though I don't move, I can feel his eyes upon me, and every inch of my body tingles with awareness.

He moves to the bed and retrieves the paddle he'd thrown there only moments before. "You have been naughty. But I don't want this."

I'm surprised by the wave of disappointment that crashes over me. I'm not sure how I can miss something I haven't yet experienced, but I cannot deny that I want it. Like a tattoo, I want Jackson to mark me, and I am about to confess that to him when he steps up behind me and bends his mouth to my ear. "When I spank you, sweetheart, it will be my palm on your ass. Not leather. Not a tool. Nothing at all between you and me. Do you understand?"

"Yes, sir."

"Have you been bad?"

"Yes."

"How?"

"I should have trusted you."

"Do you trust me now?"

I turn, because I need to see him. "Completely."

My answer seems to spark something in him, because he grabs

my shoulders and pulls me close, as if he is going to kiss me. He doesn't, though, and the anticipation leaves me breathless. When he backs away to sit on the storage bench at the foot of the bed, I am left gasping from the force of my rising desire.

"Here," he says. "Over my knee."

I do as he says, positioning myself across his lap so that my rear end is right there for him. And, I realize with interest, I can feel his erection beneath the towel as it presses against me—and right now he is fully aroused, as turned on by this as I am.

Gently, he pushes up the shirt to reveal my ass. He keeps one hand on my back, but with the other, he strokes the curve of my rear, and just that simple motion makes me squirm.

"Still," he says, and I obey immediately. Or I try to, because his movements have changed. They're slower. More sensual. And when he slides his finger down to find how wet I am, I can't help but wiggle with pleasure. "You like this," he says. "Let's see if we can't make you like it more."

He lifts his hand, then brings his palm down on me. The sting is local at first, then seems to spread, a million tiny sparks that start out hot and then fade to a pleasurable glow. He repeats it, and this time a moan of pure pleasure is wrenched from me.

"That's it, baby," he says as he dips his finger lower to explore my drenched and ready sex. "Oh, yes, you definitely like that."

He lands another spank, then another, then soothes my ass with gentle strokes as fire seems to fill me, making me burn with a wild need.

Once again, he slides his hand down, but this time instead of simply teasing my sex, he thrusts in hard and I rise up on my toes, lifting my ass and giving him better access, because right then all I want is this. This feeling of spiraling off as Jackson pours pleasure through me. Of knowing that I can go as far as he can send me, but that he is my anchor and will bring me back.

He finger-fucks me, moving in and out in a rhythm that makes my pleasure rise, and as his cock twitches beneath me, I imagine that he is over me, pounding inside me, and I moan from the overwhelming pleasure of it all.

"Do you feel that?"

"Yes."

"That's me, baby. My cock. My hand. My skin. You brought the vibrator, and that's fine. I promise I'll make good use of it with you one day, but not now. Today, nothing gives you pleasure other than me. Do you understand?"

"Yes," I say as my muscles clench tight around his fingers, wanting to draw him in deeper. I'm close and so wet and my head is spinning and all I want right then is for Jackson to take me over, hard and fast and very thoroughly.

And then, because this is all about punishing me, he withdraws his finger.

I whimper, and he responds with a chuckle. "Patience, sweetheart." He gives my rear a very light swat, but even that simple contact sends sparks through me. "Bed," he says, and I know that I'm going to have to wait a bit longer for the sweet pleasure of release.

Then again, I'm on fire from what he's doing to me, dancing along a precipice, with my body primed and ready to fly. And oh, dear god, I want to know what he will make me feel next.

I get on the bed as ordered, then watch as he stands, negligently letting the towel drop. He is fully erect, his body lean and tight, his face so full of passion that he looks like need personified. More than that, he looks like a god, and I am awestruck by the fact that someone like Jackson—so brilliant, strong, and sexy—can look at me with such undiluted desire. But he does, and I am weak from the force of it.

He holds up the rope, then crooks his finger.

I crawl to him, then pause in front of him. I'm aware of every part of my body. Of every slight wisp of air from the vent above.

"Turn around," he says, and I comply.

"Now arms behind your back, elbows at ninety degrees. Hands to elbows so you're making a square."

Once again, I comply, and he uses the rope to tie my arms and wrists so that I have no use of them at all. It's an odd feeling, trapped and vulnerable, and yet at the same time arousing. But only because I am with Jackson, and I crave his touch and trust him to take care of me.

"Now kneel, then turn on your side with your calf and thigh still together."

It's an odd position, but I manage it, and he uses a knife from the side table to cut a length of the cord so that he can bind my left thigh to my left calf.

"Your arms are in a box tie," he says. "I'm putting your legs in a frogtie."

I take his word for that. And I bite back the desire to ask him how he knows all of this. Then again, I know damn well that Jackson hasn't been a monk. Far from it. I tell myself that's good. That I'm getting the benefit of his experience. And I try very hard to banish jealous thoughts.

Considering the attention Jackson is paying to me, that's really not hard. With every loop of rope, he caresses me. With every new knot he strokes me. He has been busily tying me—first the left side, and then the right—and even as he is doing that he has been touching and teasing me, so subtly that I only now realize just how aroused I am. How ready for him—and for whatever it is that comes next.

When he is finished, my legs are bound such that I am forced to kneel with my arms behind me, almost like a penitent.

"You look amazing." His eyes echo the words, as does his erection. "Next time, we'll do more. A cord around your breasts to heighten their sensitivity. Or between your legs so that every movement teases your clit. So many sweet possibilities."

I lick my lips, already intrigued, and close to an orgasm simply from being positioned like this, my legs wide and my sex exposed.

"Do you know why I want to bind you?"

I shake my head, wanting only to hear his answer.

"Because I want you to fully feel everything I give you. No struggling against sensation. No pulling away from pleasure because it is so heightened that it borders on pain. Bound, you have no choice but to take it in. Bound, you have no choice but to feel."

He slides his hand between my legs and slowly strokes me. I tremble, lost in the overwhelming awareness of every brush of skin against skin. "And do you know why this position is so popular?"

Again, I simply shake my head.

"Because you are completely open. I can take you any way. Your cunt. Your ass. Your mouth." He brushes his finger over me with each word, and I shiver at the thought of being so thoroughly fucked. "I will, too, one day. I want all of you, Sylvia. But right now, I want to feel you on me. I want you close. I want to hold you and control every movement. And I want to be close enough to see your eyes and claim your mouth when you come."

"Yes," I whisper, so wet I can feel the slickness on my thighs. "Please, yes."

He spreads my legs, then kneels between them, lifting my hips as he uses one hand to ease me onto my back before thrusting into me with one quick, powerful stroke. I am wet—so desperately wet—and there is no hesitation, no need for gentle coaxing, and I cry out with the pleasure of being so thoroughly and deliciously filled.

I'm on my back, and the sensation of arching up as he fucks me is wonderful. My skin feels tight and awake, my breasts teased by even the motion of the air. But he soon changes that. He reaches down and slides his hands under me, then lifts me up so that I am straddling him.

I have no hands to use, and no legs for balance, so though I am on top of him, he is doing all the work. He holds me at the waist, lifting me up and down so that I am pumping him, and he is filling me.

It is insanely erotic, this sensation of fucking and being fucked at the same time, and I do the only thing I can do and that is squeeze my muscles tight around him with each thrust, trying to milk him so that he comes hard and fast, even though I do not want this glorious sensation to end.

"Yes," he says, urging me on. "That's it, baby." With each word, he moves me harder. Faster. And I can feel the pressure building in him, the explosion coming.

Mine as well, because in this position he is so deep that with each thrust he pushes me closer, and at the same time the rocking motion against my clit is making me spiral up, reaching for climax.

"Please," I moan as we get close, so close, and he's moving me tighter and faster until finally his hands grab my back so that I sit straighter upon him and I meet his eyes and see that we are both on this same collision course.

And when it comes, it is almost nuclear, and the only thing that keeps me grounded is Jackson's mouth, hard and deep against mine, his tongue seeking and claiming, as if this kiss holds a secret that only the two of us can share.

We stay like that until our bodies quit shaking and then he pulls me limp against him.

He strokes me, and the feel of his hands against my skin is like warm comfort.

Slowly, he unties me, then gently rubs my arms where the cord has cut into my skin. "How do you feel?"

I grin up at him, tired and wrung out and absolutely thoroughly satisfied. "Amazing," I say sleepily. Then murmur, "Can we do it again?"

I feel his chuckle reverberate through me as he pulls me close. "I think that can be arranged. Sleep now, sweetheart."

His words seem to float over me, and by the time I realize that I am already half there, the world goes dark and I lose myself in the safety of Jackson's arms.

It turns out that Jackson is a typical bachelor in that he has absolutely nothing in his refrigerator except cheese, and nothing to drink other than wine, scotch, and beer.

Since I'm not keen on defrosting frozen pastries or waiting an hour for a delivery, we decide to go with popcorn and a movie, and just call it a date night.

Now, I am stretched out on the sofa in Jackson's office space, my feet on his lap and my computer balanced on my stomach. Across the room, the television plays *The Big Sleep,* an old Humphrey Bogart movie that Jackson found when he was doing that annoying thing that guys do with the remote, and said we absolutely had to watch.

Since I like Bogie and anything is better than sports, I'm happy about his choice.

Technically, I'm supposed to be working, since it's still early and I got nothing accomplished in the afternoon. So I've got my laptop open and I'm reviewing Aiden's notes on my revised marketing plan and budget. I'm alternating that task with filing and responding to a variety of pending emails from both my account and Damien's.

In other words, I'm truly multitasking. The real estate life. The assistant life.

And the good life, I think, as I look at Jackson and grin.

I'd changed into a pair of Megan's shorts and a tank top, and Jackson keeps looking up from the sketch pad he has balanced on the side of the couch to grin lasciviously at me.

"You are so transparent," I say.

"Am I? Maybe you're just extremely intuitive. Let's test that theory. What am I thinking about?"

"Sex."

"Lucky guess," he says with a grin. "Slow, lazy, easy sex? Or hot, nasty, kinky sex?"

I raise a brow. "Totally transparent," I say, then bend my knee so that my foot slides over his jeans to stop right over his crotch. "Hot," I say as I move my foot back and forth. "Nasty. Kinky sex."

"How right you are." He closes his hand over my foot, so that the arch is pressed now against his growing erection. "More," he says, and suddenly this lazy autumn evening has turned mid-summer hot.

And then, of course, my phone rings.

"Ignore it," he orders, but we've both already seen the display from where the phone sits on the coffee table. *Cass.* "All right, answer it. But tell her she's not scoring points."

I laugh and promise to make it up to him later, then I take the call and am immediately flooded by a diatribe of stress. "It's just everything," she concludes. "The franchise stuff. Zee. I know we're in that be-together-all-the-time phase, but I'm starting to feel claustrophobic."

"You need to chill," I say. "Do you want me to meet you for a drink?" I shoot Jackson an apologetic smile.

"That would be great, actually. Jackson won't mind?"

"Hang on."

I relay the situation to Jackson, who says he's fine with me going, but suggests I invite her over instead.

"Seriously?"

"She's your best friend. You can drink without driving. I can get to know her a little better—though I promise to go to my office and leave you two alone, too. And she can stay the night. For that matter, invite her to the fund-raiser tomorrow night, too. We can pick her up in the limo on the way."

I just stare at him until he shifts a bit, clearly uncomfortable with my inspection.

"What?"

"You're amazing."

"Remember that the next time we fight."

I grin. "I'll make a note of it." I take my phone off mute and relay the conversation to Cass, who actually claps when I tell her about the party.

"Seriously, Syl, I think he's a keeper."

"I'm not going to disagree. So get over here, already."

Unfortunately, Cass doesn't live far enough away to allow Jackson and me to follow through on our original plan for hot, nasty, kinky sex.

"Tomorrow night," he says, pulling me in for a kiss before I head down to make sure there are sheets on the guest room bed. "After the party. Be ready."

"I'm always ready for you."

His smile suggests he knows perfectly well that I'm not even exaggerating.

When Cass arrives, Jackson shows her around the boat, then joins us on the top deck for a drink. It's easy and casual, and I'm grateful when he asks her what's going on with the franchise, and then even answers her questions.

"I just need to talk it out, you know?" she says. "Zee doesn't even want to entertain the idea I might do this."

"Anytime," Jackson says, and I bask in the way my best friend glows at his very obviously genuine offer.

We talk a little bit about the resort, but then Jackson segues that conversation into an excuse to leave. "I should be working on that resort," he says with a glance toward me. "The woman who hired me is a tough taskmaster."

"I think stone-cold executive bitch is the phrase you're going for."

"Hey!" I protest. "I'm an *aspiring* stone-cold executive bitch."

"And you're doing just fine," Cass says with a maternal pat to my hand.

Jackson laughs at our silliness, kisses me hard, then heads down to his array of computer screens.

"I like him," Cass says once we're alone.

I smile. "Yeah. Me, too." I take a deep breath, then tuck my feet under me and stare out at the marina. "I told him, Cass. I told him what happened with Bob."

"Good for you," she says.

My stomach twists a little. "I told him all of it. I mean, I told him even more than I've told you."

She frowns, and for a moment I think she's mad. Which fits, because I'm feeling guilty. "Oh, man, don't you think I knew that?"

I blink, momentarily confused. "Wait. Knew what?"

"That there was more to tell. Duh."

"You did?"

"Sure. And I'm glad you told Jackson the rest of it."

I sit back, a little bit pleased and a little bit befuddled.

"It's not a contest, Syl. What you tell him, what you tell me. I'm here if you need me, and I always will be."

I close my eyes tight and hug my knees against my chest. "Thank you."

"Not the kind of thing you say thank you for, but you're welcome anyway. Seriously, Syl. Talk to me, don't talk to me. I love you, and nothing's going to change that. And I mean that in a fully clothed, platonic sort of way."

A bubble of laughter bursts out of me. "Okay. Thanks." I swallow. Then I draw a breath and I tell her the thing I haven't quite been able to say yet, not even to myself. "I think I'm falling in love with him."

She makes a dismissive noise. "I don't."

"Really?" I'm not sure if I'm hurt or surprised or disappointed.

"Falling? No way, babe. I think you've been in love with him since Atlanta." She squeezes my hand. "Congrats on finally realizing it."

My best friend, I realize, is a very smart woman. "I love you, too, you know."

"Hell yeah, you do. I'm extremely lovable."

We spend the rest of the night talking about nothing and everything, but it's nice to spend time on the boat with the water lapping in the background and an open bottle—or two—of wine in front of us.

When I see Cass yawn and realize that the light is off in Jackson's study, I call time-out and we both head down.

I give her a hug outside the guest room, tell her she can sleep as late as she wants, but I'll be leaving insanely early to get to the office, and that I'll text her with the time the limo will come for her.

Then I quietly open the bedroom door to go see the man I love.

He's asleep in bed, his laptop open beside him. I take it away, then slide in next to him. He pulls me close in sleep, and I snuggle against him, as moved by that simple, unconscious gesture as anything else he's done or said.

I'm content, I realize.

Content. Happy. And, yes, in love.

twenty-three

"I'm so glad the three of you could make it," Michael Prado says as he greets me, Jackson, and Cass in the foyer of his astounding Beverly Hills home.

"We're glad to be here," Jackson says, shaking his friend's hand. "I'd like you to meet my girlfriend, Sylvia Brooks, and her friend Cassidy Cunningham."

Girlfriend.

It's the first time that Jackson has used that title, and I am so astounded that I almost don't notice the hand that Michael extends for me to shake.

"Don't look so surprised," Jackson whispers after the introductions have been completed and we've joined the crowd in the ballroom. "It's true, isn't it?"

"Yes." The word bubbles through me like champagne, and I catch Cass's eye. "Yes, it is."

"It's not easy to shock her," Cass says to Jackson. "I think the only way you'll manage again is to strip her naked."

He chuckles and swings an arm around her shoulder. "Nice try, but I'm not indulging your prurient fantasies."

"Had to give it a shot."

I roll my eyes at both of them, but it's only for show. Not only am I still flying from the girlfriend label, but my best friend and my boyfriend have crossed that invisible line from friendly acquaintances to actual friends.

All things considered, life is pretty damn spiffy.

I lean against Jackson as I take in the surroundings. I've seen what an obscene amount of money can buy, but even I have to force myself not to stare. Freestanding architectural relics representing different periods in history are placed artfully throughout the space, and bits and pieces of Hollywood memorabilia are mixed among the antiquities. Movie posters, candid photographs of celebrities, pages from scripts, and even three Oscars cover the walls or fill display cases.

"It's like a museum," I say, then blush when I realize that Michael has joined our little trio.

"It's meant to be," he says. "I keep my memories here. It seemed easier than a scrapbook, and it makes the room uniquely appealing for events like this. As Jackson knows, the National Historic and Architectural Conservation Project is one of my pet causes, and when they asked me to host a cocktail party and silent auction, I was happy to do it."

"It's a wonderful cause," I say genuinely. "And I thought *Stone and Steele* was brilliant," I add, though the truth is I still haven't seen more than the first few minutes.

"It really was," Cass chimes in. She's blond tonight, and so elegant that she looks as though she belongs among Prado's treasures.

"You're both very kind," Prado says, then winks at Jackson. "Of course, I had excellent material. But first things first. Before you check out the silent auction, we need to get you drinks. I've done enough of these events to know that there's a direct upward correlation between the amount of alcohol that goes into a person and the amount of their bid. And I really do want this event to be a success."

"Well, if drinking your alcohol will help," Cass says, "then I'm happy to oblige."

Prado calls over a waiter with a tray of drinks, then selects an Amsterdam Art and Science for me, a Sydney Opera House for Cass, and a Guggenheim for Jackson. "A Cosmopolitan, an Old-Fashioned, and a vodka martini with a twist," he says. "But we needed to keep with the theme."

He points to the area beneath a massive curving staircase that sweeps across the far wall. "The auction items are set up on tables against that wall. You can't see from here, but they extend back under the stairs, and we have quite a few goodies to bid on. I've invited a number of people with more money than time, so that means that not only do I anticipate a significant number of bids, but there are also some incredible prizes. You've donated thirty hours toward the design of a single-family home, haven't you, Jackson?"

"You did?" I ask.

"A weak moment," he says, and we all laugh.

"I like him," I say to Jackson when Prado leaves us to go mingle with other guests.

"As do I. My one decent experience in Hollywood so far."

"I don't know about decent," Cass says, "but there's another Hollywood experience trying to get your attention." She nods to the stairs, where Irena Kent is descending with a fortysomething bald man with a goatee and the kind of dark frame glasses people wear when they're trying to look hip and artsy. There's something familiar about him, but I can't place him. Irena Kent, however, draws my attention completely. She's got an arm hooked through the bald man's, and with the other she's waving to Jackson.

"Well, hell," he says.

"You could ignore her." I believe him that there is nothing going on with him and Irena Kent anymore, but that doesn't mean I want to invite her over into our little circle. And, because I'm just that petty, the fact that he's slept with her still stings.

"I could. But she's with Robert Reed."

Cass and I exchange shrugs.

"The asshole producer," he explains.

"The one who wants to make the movie about the Santa Fe house?"

"The very one," Jackson says. "And because of that, I'm going to go talk to them."

"Why?" Cass asks. "I mean, if you don't want them to make the movie."

"Two reasons. One, I firmly believe in killing with kindness where appropriate. My attorneys can be the bad guys. I'll be polite and charming and quietly toxic if it comes to that."

"I like the way he thinks," Cass says.

"And second," he continues, "I want information. If they're moving forward on the project, I want to know. I might learn something my lawyers can use."

"Your boyfriend has a devious streak," Cass teases. "I'd keep an eye on that."

"You're both welcome to join me. Syl?"

"You go ahead. I think Cass and I are going to go see if there's any auction item we can actually afford to bid on."

He meets my eyes before he kisses me, and I think I see understanding there. Cass is not quite as intuitive. "Why aren't you going with him? He used to date her."

"And there you have it," I say. "Her, tall and statuesque and movie-star gorgeous. Me, utterly plain by comparison."

"Hardly. You're fabulous and you know it. And Jackson adores you."

"And if I were standing right next to her, I might turn an unattractive shade of green. Besides," I add, "we need alone time. What's the deal with Zee?"

"I'm not sure. She was irritated you and Jackson met with me and Ollie."

"Really? Why?"

"Not sure. I told her I would have loved her insight, too. But she wasn't mad because she wanted to be there. She just didn't want you guys there."

"Did you tell her about tonight?"

Cass wrinkles her nose. "No."

"Cass . . ."

"Hey, we've barely started dating. The rules for evening outings have not kicked in yet."

She has a point. I forget how fast things have been moving with Jackson. Primarily because it feels like I've been with him forever. Or at least for five years.

We look at each of the silent auction items, and I even bid on a couple's weekend at a boutique hotel in Laguna Beach. If I win, I'll surprise Jackson. And if I don't win, I may surprise him anyway.

"I expected Evelyn to be here." We've finished the auction review, and now we're standing near a glass case with pages from the shooting script for *The Wizard of Oz*. I look out over the crowd, but don't see her. For that matter, I don't see Jackson. I do see Irena Kent, though, and take a petty amount of satisfaction from the fact that she is not with my boyfriend.

"Isn't that her?" Cass asks, pointing to the far side of the room where Robert Reed stands chatting with Evelyn and a few other people I don't know.

"Good eye," I say. "Let's go say hi."

As we head that direction, I'm struck again by the feeling that I've met Reed before. I don't think too much about it, though. It's hard to grow up in LA and not run across celebrities here and there, especially now that I work for Stark.

But as we draw closer, I can overhear their conversation. His voice is also familiar, and I press my fingers to my temples, trying to place it. Then he extends a hand to one of the pretty young women.

"It's so nice to meet you. I'm Robert Cabot Reed. But you can call me Bob."

I go completely cold.

"Syl?"

"It's him." My tongue feels thick, and I'm not entirely sure I've spoken.

"Him? I don't—"

"I need to find Jackson."

"I—"

"*Jackson.*"

"Oh god." I hear understanding and panic in Cass's voice. "Oh, holy fucking god."

But I'm not listening. I'm stumbling blind through the house, my hands clenched tight at my sides because I *will not, will not, will not* lose it.

I manage to keep my shit together all the way to the foyer where Prado is still greeting latecomers.

"Have you seen Jackson?" The urgency in Cass's voice makes me realize how scared she must be.

"Cassidy? Why, yes. He said he was going out front to take a phone call." Prado steps toward us. "Are you all right?"

I don't know what she tells him. All I know is that I am pure motion. That somehow I have gotten through the doors and out into the world, and now I am spinning, looking for him. By the valet stand. In the shadows by the street. Under the streetlight.

There.

I run to him, then stop dead when I see that he is not alone.

"Goddammit," he says to his companion. "What the fuck are you doing here? I told you to stay away from me."

I cannot hear the man's reply, but Jackson's retort is crystal clear.

"That's bullshit," he says. "Aren't you the one who always says we can't be seen together? Goddamn you, Jeremiah."

"Syl!" Cass's frantic voice cuts through the night, and both men turn toward me, their faces now lit by the soft golden light of the streetlamp.

Jackson Steele.

And Jeremiah Stark.

I make a sound like a whimper.

"Sylvia!" I hear the urgency in Jackson's voice, and I see both shock and guilt on his face.

I turn—and I run.

"Sylvia, wait!"

But I don't, I am running blind, at least until I stumble, then cry out at the sharp pain in my knee.

I've broken a heel and fallen on the curb.

I see a red-clad valet hurrying toward me from one direction. Behind me, I see Jackson sprinting toward me in the dark.

I scramble to my knees, because I can't talk to him. Not now. Maybe not ever.

He lied to me. Oh, dear god, he lied to me.

"Sylvia," he calls, and I stumble to my feet and reach out for the valet. "Dammit, Sylvia, stop!"

"Leave her alone!" Cass cries, and I look over my shoulder to see her tugging on Jackson's sleeve. "Dammit, Jackson, just let her go."

I clutch the valet's hand. "Please. I need a taxi."

"Of course." The boy looks about seventeen and completely freaked out. "Are you okay? Do you need help?"

"Just the taxi. Please. Hurry."

There is one already in the pickup line, and he hurries me in. I collapse gratefully into the backseat, and as the car leaves the curved driveway for the street, the last thing I see before I fall inside myself is Jackson standing beside Cass, his body angled as if in motion, held in place only by her firm grip on his arm.

I sink back into the seat and try to decide where to go from here. Not home. Jackson will look for me there.

Not to the office, because I will be found.

In the end, I go to a motel. A boring little chain that charges way too much for its boring little rooms.

But I don't care about the money or the decor. I don't even care about the bed, because I do not intend to sleep.

I can't, not tonight. Because tonight will be the worst.

Tonight, the nightmares will come, dark dragons with sharp teeth and fiery claws.

They will come and I'll see Bob in my mind—*Cabot Reed*—and he'll touch me and seduce me and I'll come for him, and I'll hate myself.

Then I'll look him in the eyes and see Jackson, and hate myself that much more.

I'll be helpless.

Lost and alone, with no one to slay the dragon.

A burst of fury whips through me and I grab the ice bucket off the dresser and hurl it across the room. It makes an unsatisfying thud against the thin drywall and cheap paint.

"Goddamn you, Jackson Steele," I shout. "God *fucking* damn you."

He'd lied to me, by omission if not outright. Acted like he didn't even know Jeremiah Stark when I asked him about it after the *LA Scandal* website fiasco. And maybe I could believe that tonight was just one of those first-meet coincidences if I hadn't seen his face and overheard their conversation. But I had, and Jackson's is a face I know—they've known each other for a long time. And they are obviously more than just casual acquaintances.

God, how could I have been so stupid? I put my trust—*all* of my trust—in that man.

And so help me, I actually believed I was falling in love with him.

No. Damn me, I did fall in love with him, and that's why this hurts so much.

I love him, or at least I loved the man I thought I knew.

And now, somehow, I have to manage to survive losing him all over again. Because I know now that the man I have fallen in love with is not the man who exists.

"*Shit.*"

The word sounds hollow, and I grab my phone to dial Cass, then end the call before it connects. It's not her company I crave, but the ink.

Except how would I mark myself? What I feel is too big, too personal. Too damn much. And unless she can rip my body open and tattoo my heart, I don't think there is any mark she could put on me that would help even out the pain that I'm feeling.

Fuck, fuck, fuck.

I throw myself on the bed and I squeeze my eyes shut and will myself to cry. And yet still the tears won't come.

I can't even have that small relief to ease my pain.

Instead, I lay in the bed, lethargic and numb, and watch television as I fight the sleep that is determined to drag me under. Infomercials. Sitcoms. Bad animation.

Hour after hour until the dark, grimy window turns light.

Then I stumble from the room, my skin tight and my eyes grainy, and walk to the lobby for the complimentary breakfast of cold pastries and lukewarm coffee.

I sit at the cheap plastic table and sip coffee for over an hour. There is a newspaper at the place setting across from me, but I do not read it. There is a television playing one of LA's inane morning programs, but I do not watch it. I just sit and stare and slide into myself, losing myself in my head in a way I haven't done since Jackson laid out his proposition at the premiere.

Since then, I haven't wanted to fade away.

Now, I can't think of anything I want more.

Unless it's to have back the Jackson I thought I knew.

God, I'm being maudlin.

Disgusted with myself, I shove to my feet. If I'm going to be depressed—and I think I have every right to be—I'm going somewhere more pleasant than this ugly motel lobby.

I go ahead and shower in my room, then change into a pair of sweatpants and a City of Angels T-shirt. I'd bought both from the small gift and snack area behind the reception counter. Not overly fashionable, but it blends better than my cocktail dress.

I get the clerk to call me a taxi, and once again I avoid home. Instead, I have the driver take me to the one place I have always gone when things go sideways for me in this city. The place where I would go to walk or sit or read on the weekends after my "sessions" with Bob, and where in high school I would go to escape the mean girl taunts. Where I sometimes even came just because I wanted to see something beautiful. The Getty Center.

The taxi drops me at the bottom of the hill and I get on the tram with a flood of tourists. I'm grateful it's a Saturday. I want to be lost in the crowd, and camouflaged among the T-shirts, jeans, and ball caps that mark the out-of-town visitors.

The entire center is amazing, from the museum to the research facility to the tram that whisks people all around the complex. I have probably walked every square inch of this place at some point in my life.

Today, I choose the plaza and sit beside the fountain facing the rotunda.

I don't think too much about why, but part of me knows that it is because the perfection and flow of this incredible building reminds me of Jackson. The center is a masterpiece of architectural beauty, a work of art in and of itself, and I am not sure if I came to bask or to torture myself.

I have no idea how long I sit there, the familiar numbness sliding back into my bones. All I know is that I've tuned out the world. And so when I hear him, it's through a tunnel, and from a very long distance.

"Sylvia?" His fingertips brush my shoulder. "Sweetheart, I'm here."

Jackson.

His voice, his touch, his scent.

I shift in my seat and look up at him. He looks raw and more ragged than I feel. I have at least showered. Jackson still wears the suit he'd put on last night, though his collar is now open and the tie has been shoved into a pocket where it peeks out in a small splash of red.

"I don't want you here." It's a lie. It's the absolute worst of lies, because I do want him. But not like this. Not with the games and the deceit and everything he kept hidden.

"What you think you know," he says, "you don't."

"You fucking liar," I say, my words low and measured. "I needed something real to hold on to, and you were an illusion the whole goddamn time."

"Sylvia—"

"Was this always about Damien? About Stark International?"

He shakes his head. "Damien is the reason I said no to the Bahamas project. You're the reason I said yes to Santa Cortez."

I say nothing. Because what the hell is there for me to say?

"When this started," he continues, "I wanted to hurt you. You'd left me. And to make it worse, I thought you'd gone to Damien. And so help me, I wanted payback. I wanted to make you weak. To make you wild. That first night? I planned to make you need me so badly that I was like air to you. So fucking essential that losing me would destroy you."

I clench my jaw and hug myself, forcing myself not to spit out the acknowledgment that he has damn well achieved what he set out to do.

"And then, when I was your whole goddamn world, I was going to leave you. To have my revenge in the knowledge that you were burning in anger and loss."

I lift my head so that I can see his eyes. I expect to see triumph. Instead, I see regret. I see tenderness, too, and because of that, I stay despite the almost overpowering urge to spring to my feet and run.

"But all of that changed, Sylvia. I would rather die than hurt you. I thought I was strong; I'm not. I thought I was brave; I'm not.

Because where you are concerned, I have no strength to leave, and even the thought of losing you breaks me completely."

"I guess you're going to have to get used to it," I say. "Because you've already lost me."

"Sweetheart—" His hand closes over my wrist and I rip it away.

"You *lied* to me. After everything I've told you. After all of myself that I've given to you. You fucking *lied* to me."

"I didn't."

I push up to my feet. "Oh, Christ, Jackson."

"Listen to me. No," he says, grabbing my hand as I start to walk away. "*Listen.*"

I turn to face him, but I don't sit down. Instead, I stand with my arms crossed over my chest and my jaw tight.

He stands as well, then shoves his hands into his pockets. "I kept things from you, I did. Maybe more than I should."

"Gee. You think? Like maybe you should have mentioned you were scheming with Jeremiah Stark?"

"I wasn't. But I do know him. I've known him for a very long time." He draws a breath and drags his fingers through his hair. "Dammit, Syl. Jeremiah Stark is my father."

I stumble. I actually take a step backward, as if he's shoved at me with the palm of his hand.

"What?" I finally say, even though I'm absolutely certain that I've heard him correctly.

"Damien's my half-brother." The words are flat, and it's very obvious that he's not particularly thrilled with his family tree.

I'm not really sure how to process that, and so I sit down on the edge of the fountain again. After a moment, Jackson sits beside me.

"Does Damien know?" I ask.

"No. I told you the truth about my dad. My family. I just didn't tell you who."

"You should have." I try to organize my thoughts, but this news is out of left field. "All those times I asked you what your problem with Damien was, and you didn't say a word."

"I'm sorry. Maybe I should have. I don't know." I can see the anguish on his face, but I don't try to comfort him. I'm too hurt. Too numb. "Don't you get it? It's a secret I've lived with my entire life. It wasn't something I could just shout out."

"No," I say tightly. "I wouldn't know a thing about difficult secrets."

"Is that what this is? Tit for tat? You told me about Bob and because I didn't immediately toss my emotional garbage into the mix you're punishing me?"

"Bob?" I repeat. "That's all you have to say? Just some half-assed mention before we get back to your daddy issues?" His words are like a stiletto through my heart, because goddammit, *Bob* is what started all of this. Robert Cabot Reed, the asshole producer who wants to make the movie about Jackson's Santa Fe house. *Bob,* the guy who has his claws in both of our lives, and all Jackson can think about is how I'm pissed that he didn't tell me about Damien right then?

I say none of that, but the force of my emotions drives me to my feet again, and I'm about to lay it all out for him in harsh, clipped tones.

But he's looking at me with such genuine confusion that I hold my tongue.

And that's when I realize—Jackson has no idea about Robert Cabot Reed. He only knows that I was looking for him outside. He has no idea why. No idea that my mood, my fears, my entire meltdown wasn't entirely driven by his little confab with Jeremiah Stark.

Suddenly, I feel very tired.

"I need to go home." Right then, I need my condo. My patio. I need to curl up on my lounger and sleep. And with any luck, I'm exhausted enough that the dreams won't come.

"Come back to the boat with me. Please, Syl. We need to talk more. I don't want this to be the thing that breaks us. My father's taken too much from me already."

"He wasn't the one who kept secrets from me," I whisper. "That was you."

I see the way my words make him flinch, and I almost take them back. But they are true, and so I simply shake my head. "I'm sorry," I say. "Maybe we do need to talk. But right now, I need to be alone."

I don't give him time to answer. Instead, I just walk away, even though doing so leaves a hole in my heart.

twenty-four

Exhaustion pulls me under, and I sleep through the rest of Saturday, and a good chunk of Sunday morning. The sun is high in the sky when I finally wake on the patio lounger, twisted up in the blanket that I'd pulled over myself.

I remember that there were nightmares, but I do not remember what they were. I only remember one, and in it I ran. Faster and faster, farther and farther. But I never escaped what was chasing me.

I don't even know what I was running from. I can only assume it was everything.

I wrap the blanket around myself and stumble inside. I feel achy and old, as if my body doesn't want to function anymore.

And I really don't want to be alone.

I take a hot shower, and that relieves some of my aches, but not the one inside me.

The truth is that it's Jackson I want, but I'm not ready for that.

And so I call the only other person I can.

"Can I stay with you?" I ask the moment Cass answers her phone.

"God, Syl, I should come over there and strangle you. Do you know how worried I've been? Why the hell didn't you answer your phone?"

"I'm sorry. I had it on silent. I just needed time."

I hear her sigh. "Sorry. I know. I get it. *Shit*. Listen, are you okay?"

"Yeah. I'll survive. But I really don't want to be alone."

"I'll be there in fifteen."

"I can drive."

"Are you a complete emotional wreck?"

I actually laugh, which feels nice. "Duh."

"Then you don't need to be driving. Stay there. I'll be right over to get you."

True to her word, she's at my door by the time I've tossed some clothes into a duffel bag.

"And you broke how many traffic laws?" I ask as I pull open the door.

She doesn't answer. Instead she tosses her arms around me and locks me in a hug.

"Come on. I'll take good care of you."

"You sure it's okay?" I ask as we head down to the street. "Zee doesn't mind?"

Cass waves her hand. "Oh, please. Of course not."

But I see a shadow on her face, and it worries me.

I don't get the chance to ask her about it, though, because we've reached the parking area, and she is standing beside her bike.

I blink at her. "Seriously?"

"What? Traffic is a bitch this time of day on a Sunday, and I needed to get here fast. And you've only got a duffel."

My smile is watery as I hug her. "I love you."

"Well, yeah." She grins. "I'm very lovable." She unstraps the spare helmet she's brought for me and hands it over. "Get on."

I climb on the back of her ten-year-old Ducati, put on the helmet, and hook my arms around her waist.

"You should go to him," she says as she starts the bike, but then she pulls out and takes off into traffic. If she says any more, I don't hear it, because my face is buried in the back of her jacket, and I'm lost in the thoughts she has sparked.

Sixteen minutes later we pull up in front of her house. "Because he's really kind of a wreck," she says, as if the conversation hadn't been interrupted at all.

"I'm kind of a wreck," I correct. "And how do you know about Jackson, anyway?"

"I talked to him," she says as she tugs off her helmet.

I freeze on her sidewalk. "When?"

"Yesterday. He came by the studio after you left the Getty Center."

"He did?"

"He wanted my help."

"To find me?"

She shoots me a quick glance. "To figure out what to do."

"I—really?"

She unlocks the door and we step inside. The place is small—only six hundred square feet—but cute. Cass believes clutter is the devil, so the place is as tidy as the stations at Totally Tattoo. Because I know her quirks, I put my duffel in the small coat closet before heading to the convertible sofa—currently closed—and taking a seat.

"Why are you so surprised?" Cass asks from the kitchen just a few feet away. She's uncorking some wine, and she brings it over along with two glasses.

"I don't know," I say honestly. "I guess because he's so self-sufficient."

She lifts a shoulder. "But he's not," she says. "From where I'm standing, I'd say he needs you."

My heart twists a little, then a little bit more when Cass reaches out and grabs my hand. "He loves you, you know."

"Did he tell you that?"

"Nope. But I've got eyes."

The truth is, so do I. And before all of this, I would have said he loved me, too.

Now, knowing what he kept from me, I don't know what to think.

"He's Damien's half-brother," I blurt, surprising myself with my words.

"I know," she says, and that surprises me even more. "He told me."

She hands me my glass of wine. "He screwed up, Syl, I'll grant you that. With all the stuff that happened between you two, he should have told you about his dad when you asked if he knew him."

"He really did tell you everything."

"Yeah, well. Like I said, he's gone on you." She plops down on the couch. "And since I happen to know it's mutual, I figured I should be a good little intermediary."

Mutual.

She's right, of course. It is.

"He hurt me," I say. "He should have told me. Should have trusted me." But even as I say the words, I think about the things I've yet to tell him, and I know that I'm not being fair. True, he hasn't asked me point-blank, but that's just my own stupid justification.

The secret was his to keep, and it was huge. And how arrogant is it of me to believe that just because I ask, he has to shift his entire life around and spill everything to me?

"I need to see him," I say softly. "I do need to talk to him." I look at Cass. "He hurt me, and he pissed me off, but you're right. I love him. And I want to fix this."

Even as I say it, I know that there are things that may not be fix-able. This isn't a secret that I can keep—and that, of course, is an-other reason Jackson kept it to himself. Because this secret affects my boss, and their father is a man who just may be screwing with Stark International.

Damien has to know the truth—and when he does, I'm not sure if Jackson will still have the project.

For that matter, when I think about the breadth and scope of Damien's temper, I'm not sure that I will, either.

But I can deal with that. So long as I've got Jackson, we can figure out the rest together.

"Is he on the boat? Did he say?"

An odd expression flits across Cass's face. "Um, listen. I should tell you something first."

I say nothing, but my stomach is twisting. Because Cass is nervous—and that's just not typical Cassidy behavior.

She clears her throat. "Right. So, when we talked, I realized you hadn't told him about Robert Cabot Reed. And I thought he needed to understand why you were so freaked out in the first place. I mean, it wasn't really the best time for you to learn about a secret."

"So he knows?" I feel anger spiking, and I want to make sure I'm absolutely clear on my facts this time. "He knows that I came face-to-face with the man who repeatedly raped me for over a year and yet he didn't come to me? Call me? Do any goddamn thing other than nurse his wounds because I walked away from him at the Getty Center?"

I'd seen confusion bloom on Cass's face when I'd raised my voice. Now I watch it clear, only to be replaced with something I can only describe as trepidation.

"What?" I demand. "What the hell is going on?"

She reaches for the section of newspaper that sits on the coffee table, then flips it over, revealing an image of a handcuffed Jackson standing beside a uniformed officer.

I pace the length of my condo, from patio to door, then back again, waiting for Jackson to show up, or Charles to call, or anything at all to happen so that I know what is going on.

I'd called the police station as soon as Cass had told me about the arrest, but since it's Sunday I was told that bail wasn't an option.

I've worked for Damien Stark long enough to realize that there are times when "not an option" means "not an option without money or power," and so I gave Charles Maynard a call and begged his help.

Fortunately, he was home.

Also fortunately, I've gotten to know him well enough over the years that he was willing to give up a few hours on a Sunday.

Charles told me to go home, and that, assuming he was able to get Jackson released on bail today, he would drop him by my place rather than the boat.

So far, no Jackson.

I pull out my phone, pull up Charles's number, and for the eight millionth time that day, force myself not to dial. He will call when he has news. That is my new mantra.

I hate my new mantra.

I pace three more lengths, and am about to just say "fuck it" and go to the station myself, when I hear the knock at my door.

I practically fall over myself getting there, and when I yank open the door and see Jackson standing there, his hair mussed, his beard scruffy, and his face battered and bruised, I am certain that I have never seen anything more beautiful.

I practically yank him into my apartment, then wrap my arms around him and we both sink to the floor.

"Sylvia. Oh, god, Sylvia." He repeats my name over and over, and I am lost in the sound of it, holding him tight, rocking him. "I'm so sorry. I should have told you who I was."

"No." I stroke his hair. "I was being bitchy and selfish. I don't have a right to your secrets, Jackson. And I did more than just get my feelings hurt. I threw a tantrum, and I'm so, so sorry."

He lifts his head and kisses me. "I'm the one that's sorry. You were confused and hurting and I didn't even see it. I had to find out from Cass, and all this time that son of a bitch has been the man who's been crawling up my ass, too."

"You shouldn't have gone after him," I say softly. "But, Jackson, I'm really glad you did."

He meets my eyes, and I see relief in his.

"Did you think I would be angry?"

"Not exactly the civilized approach to problem-solving," he says with a wry grin.

"No. Not at all. Why did you do it?"

"You know why."

"Tell me."

"Because of what that bastard did to you. Because he stole from you. Because he used you and he hurt you. And because I will always protect you."

I blink to clear my vision, then manage a watery smile. "That's why I'm not angry."

He brushes my cheek with his thumb. "I thought you didn't cry."

"What?" I am certain I haven't heard him right, but when I lift my hand to my cheek, it is wet. My breath hitches, and my throat fills with tears. I barely remember the sensation it's been so long. "I guess—I guess you matter to me." And those are all the words I can get out before the sobs come in earnest and I shake with the force of them.

Jackson picks me up and carries me to the couch, then holds me as I cry for the past, for him, for the future that I'm suddenly afraid of. Mostly, though, they are tears of relief and joy, because Jackson is back in my arms, and somehow, someway, we'll figure out the rest of it.

When the tears finally subside and I have emptied an entire box of tissues, I curl up against him, exhausted but happy.

Happy, but also afraid.

"I'm not angry," I say, my voice raw. "I'd go so far as to say I'm glad. But you shouldn't have done it. He'll press charges. That's the kind of guy he is."

"I'll protect your secret, baby. You don't have to worry."

"I'm not. I didn't even think of that." I truly hadn't. I know with absolute certainty that Jackson will take my secret to the grave if I ask him to, and that sure knowledge warms me. "I was thinking of you."

He cocks his head, looking at me sharply. "The movie."

I nod. "If no one knows about me, they're going to assume you attacked him because of the movie, and everyone is going to start poking into it. And all those secrets are going to be harder to keep. I've seen the way the press vultures work with Nikki and Damien. So far you've only had good press. Bad press can sting."

He runs his fingers through his hair, and I can see that the thought troubles him. "I'll do what I have to do," he says. "But whatever happens, my promise to you stands."

"I know. Really." I draw a breath, because there's more. And although I hate to be the bearer of bad tidings, I have to say it, just in case he hasn't thought of it already. "This may screw up the resort project, too. When Damien gets back, I promise you he won't be happy that his architect is now in the gossip rags. Especially when he already isn't sure he trusts you."

He says nothing, and so I decide to soldier on. "And you have to tell him the rest of it, too. Or I do. And he may not be too happy about the fact that you didn't say who you were up front. I'm sorry," I add. "But that's not the kind of thing I can keep from him. Not if I expect to keep my job. Or the resort, for that matter."

"I would never ask you to lie for me," he says. "And I know the risks. But I will make you a promise—no matter what it takes, you won't lose the resort. If I have to, I'll go head-to-head with Damien."

He looks like he'd enjoy the prospect.

"Do you understand?"

I nod, though I don't really. Because in a contest between Jackson and Damien over whether or not I keep my job, I can't imagine a scenario where Damien doesn't have the final word. He's the one giving the job, after all.

The rather unpleasant thought that Jackson is Jeremiah Stark's son slides into my mind. And I am quite certain that Jeremiah knows many things that Damien would want to keep secret. Which means that Jackson may know those things, too.

But the thought that Jackson would blackmail Damien on my behalf is so disagreeable that I shove it aside. He hasn't said that, and my mind is simply spinning tales. And the truth is that Jackson doesn't really know Damien at all.

"Your brother's not such a bad person, you know."

"Maybe he is, and maybe he isn't. At the moment I don't care about Damien or the resort. The only thing I care about is you. The only thing I want is you. Tell me I didn't fuck this up. Tell me I didn't lose you."

"How could you lose me when we just found each other again?"

His eyes stay on mine for a moment, and then he pulls me close and kisses me gently. "I'm going to make love to you now," he says, then lifts me in his arms and takes me to the bedroom.

He undresses me, tending to me and stroking me as he removes each piece of clothing until I am naked and on fire, wanting nothing more than the feel of this man upon me and inside me.

He doesn't wait, and we make love slowly and sweetly, but with no less passion than when he has taken me wildly. There's a tenderness to his movements. A precision in the way he thrusts inside me. And never once do his eyes leave mine.

When I see the tempest rising in that vibrant blue, I arch up, seeking more contact, wanting to go over with him, wanting to spin off into time and space with this man who has made me feel awake and alive and found. And when the explosion does come, I shatter with him, every piece of us coming together in a perfect union before we drift back down, gasping as we return to reality.

"Sylvia," he murmurs, and my name on his lips is as sweet as honey, and as potent as making love.

I kiss him, then stretch with satisfaction, content when he pulls me close and I cradle my head upon his chest.

I feel safe and warm. And though he has never spoken the words, I feel loved.

I tilt my head up so that I can look at the face of this man who fills my heart and head. Who stands like a warrior to protect me from the demons of my past.

He looks back at me with such tenderness that I fear I will cry again, and when he bends to kiss my forehead a small tear of happiness really does trickle down my cheek.

I smile, satisfied.

I may not know all his secrets. And I cannot know the future.

But I do see the now.

And for me, for Jackson, right now is enough. . . .

epilogue

Jackson stood beside the bed and looked down at her. At the woman who made his heart beat faster and his blood burn.

She calmed him. Centered him. She filled his heart and his world.

She made him a better man—he knew that. Believed it. Hell, he cherished it.

And god help him, he cherished her, too. He'd been dead those five years without her, and he hadn't even realized it. But he was alive again, and it was because of her.

Careful not to wake her, he slid into bed. His heart twisted as she moved in sleep to seek him out, then nuzzled against him, skin to skin.

Christ, what she did to him.

He brushed his hand over her hair, then played his fingertips over her shoulder. She'd pushed the sheet down in sleep, and he could see the tattoos that marked her breasts, just a few of many. Remnants of past pain, and some for which he bore responsibility.

The thought twisted inside him, dark and unpleasant, and not for the first time he wished that he could carry her burdens.

She'd put her trust in him, shared her deepest secrets with him. And he knew that he had to do the same. But damned if the thought didn't rip him to shreds.

He wanted to stay like this forever, lost in the dark, in the place between dusk and dawn, where reality felt like a dream, and he could believe that everything was possible, and that all stories had happy endings.

But there were things he had to do. Dark places he needed to visit. Battles that he must fight.

Secrets he had to protect.

He sighed and held her close, letting himself slide down into the soft comfort of sleep. There was nothing else to be done. Not really, not then.

Instead, all he could do was hold her close and hope that, in fighting to be the man he must, that he wouldn't lose the one person who had finally made him whole.

Jackson Steele and Sylvia Brooks continue to thrill in
the second book of *New York Times* bestselling author
J. Kenner's scintillating, emotionally charged new erotic
trilogy set in the Stark world.

on my knees

Continue reading for a sneak peek
Available from Bantam Books

one

Jackson Steele tossed back the last of his scotch, slammed the glass down on the polished granite bar, and considered ordering another.

He could use it—that was damn sure—but probably better to have a clear head before he went to answer his brother's summons.

His brother.

That was something he didn't say every day. Hell, he'd spent his entire life avoiding saying it. Been told he wasn't allowed to say it.

"Sometimes families have secrets," his father had said.

Wasn't that the fucking truth?

The great and glorious Damien Stark—one of the world's wealthiest and most powerful men—had no idea that he and Jackson shared a father.

But in about fifteen minutes he'd know. Because Jackson was going to tell him. *Had* to tell him.

Fuck.

He held up his hand to get the bartender's attention because, screw it, right now he really could use another drink.

The bartender nodded, poured two fingers of Glenmorangie, neat, then slid the glass back to Jackson. He hesitated, bar rag in hand, until Jackson finally looked up and met his eyes. "Something else?" Jackson asked.

"Sorry. No." It was a lie, of course, and as Jackson watched, the bartender's cheeks turned pink.

The bartender, whose name tag identified him as Phil, was in his early twenties, and with his hair slicked back and his perfectly tailored dark suit, he looked as essential to the Gallery Bar—which epitomized the glamour and excitement of the 1920s—as the polished wood, glittering chandeliers, and ornate carvings that filled and completed this space.

The historic Millennium Biltmore Hotel had always been one of Jackson's favorite places in Los Angeles. As a teenager, when he'd only dreamed of becoming an architect, he would come as often as he could, usually begging a friend with a car to bring him up from San Diego and drop him downtown. He would wander the hotel, soaking up the exquisite Spanish-Italian-Renaissance-style architecture that blended so well with the California location. The architects, Schultze and Weaver, were among Jackson's idols, and he would spend hours examining the fine detail in all of the elements, from the exquisite columns and doorways, to the exposed wood-framed roofs, to the intricate cast iron railings and ornate wooden carvings.

As with any exceptional building, each room had its own personality despite being tied together by common elements. The Gallery Bar had long been Jackson's favorite space, the live music, intimate lighting, exceptional wine list, and extensive menu adding value to an already priceless space.

Now, Phil stood behind the long granite bar that served as one of the room's focal points. Behind him, a menagerie of fine whiskeys danced in the glow of the room's dim lighting. He was framed on either side by carved wooden angels, and in Jackson's mind, it seemed as if all three—angels and man—were standing in judgment over him.

Phil cleared his throat, apparently realizing that he hadn't moved. "Apologies," he said as he started to exuberantly wipe the bar. "I just thought you looked familiar."

"I must have one of those faces," Jackson said dryly, knowing damn well that Phil knew who he was. Jackson Steele, celebrity architect. Jackson Steele, subject of the recent documentary *Stone and Steele,* which had screened just over a week ago at the Chinese theater. Jackson Steele, newest addition to the team for The Resort at Cortez, a Stark Vacation Property.

Jackson Steele, released yesterday on bail after assaulting Robert Cabot Reed, producer, director, and overall vile human being.

The latter, of course, is what would have put Jackson on Phil's radar. This was Los Angeles, after all, and in Los Angeles, anything entertainment related passed as hard news. Forget the economy or strife overseas. In the City of Angels, Hollywood trumps everything else. And that meant that Jackson's picture had been plastered all over the newspapers, local television, and social media.

He didn't regret it. Not the fight. Not the arrest. He didn't even regret the press, although he knew that they would dig. And if they dug deep, they'd find a whole cornucopia of reasons why Jackson might want to destroy the pathetic Mr. Reed.

Still, he had no regrets.

Hell, if anything he wished he could do it again, because the few punches he'd managed to land on Reed had only been satisfying in the moment. But every time he thought about it—every moment he let his mind picture what the son of a bitch had done to Sylvia—he knew he hadn't gone far enough.

He should have killed the bastard.

For the way he'd hurt the woman he loved, Robert Cabot Reed deserved to die.

She'd been only fourteen at the time. A child. An innocent. And Reed had used her. Raped her. Humiliated her.

He'd been a photographer then, and she his model. A position of power and of trust, and he'd twisted that around, making it vile and dirty.

He'd hurt the girl, and he'd damaged the woman.

And Jackson couldn't think of anything bad enough that could happen to the man.

He closed his eyes and thought of Sylvia. Her small, slim body that felt so right in his arms. The gold that highlighted her dark brown hair, making her face seem luminous. Christ, he wanted her beside him now. Wanted to twine his finger through hers and hold her close. He wanted her strength, though she didn't even realize how strong she was.

But this was something he had to do alone. And he needed to do it now.

He slid off the stool, then dropped a fifty on the bar. "Keep the change," he said, then watched as Phil's eyes went wide.

He left the bar, then moved quickly through the hotel's elegant lobby to the main entrance that opened on South Grand Street. Stark Tower was just up the hill to the east. It was a cool October night, and the building glowed against the coal black sky. Right now, Damien Stark was in the penthouse apartment with his wife, Nikki, probably unpacking after returning from a long weekend in Manhattan.

Stark's second assistant, Rachel Peters, had called Jackson that morning. "He'll be back from New York this evening," she'd said. "And he wants to see you tomorrow at eight sharp before the regular Tuesday briefing. It's about the arrest," she added, her voice dropping to a stage whisper. "And all the press coverage."

He shook his head at the memory, half irritated and half amused. *Fucking summoned.*

If this was only about work, he would have waited until morning and gone at the appointed time. But this was personal, and he needed to do it now.

He'd already called security, and he knew that Stark's helicopter had landed over an hour ago. He also knew that Damien was staying in the Tower apartment overnight, not bothering to make the drive to his Malibu house.

It was eight o'clock on a Monday night, and it was time for Damien to know the truth.

As he trudged up the hill, Jackson thought about how quickly things had changed. A month ago, he would have rather eaten nails than work for Damien. But then just over a week ago, Sylvia had approached him with the kind of project that was any architect's wet dream. To design a resort from the ground up. And not just any resort, but one that is located on its own private island. And she was handing him a blank slate.

The overture had surprised him for a number of reasons, not the least of which being that five years ago she'd ripped a hole in his heart, brutally and permanently ended things between them.

The loss had devastated him, and he'd eased his anger in the ring and in his work. Winning—and losing—fight after fight. Burying himself in his commissions, his reputation growing as his projects became more and more ambitious.

Work may have been his savior, but working for her—hell, working for Damien—was not something he was prepared to do. He knew damn well he couldn't bear the pain of being around her. And as for Damien, Jackson had plenty of reasons not to work for or trust the man, not the least of which was that Jackson didn't want to see his work shadowed by the Stark name and logo.

But revenge is a powerful motivator.

So he'd said yes, fully intending to take her to the edge of pleasure. To reclaim her. To bind her so close to him that she could see no one else, feel no one else, dream of no one else. And then, when she was stuck fast in his web, he would clip the strands and walk away, leaving the resort to flounder, and leaving Sylvia as she'd left him, drowning in pain and loss and misery.

Dear god, he'd been a fool.

He'd accepted the offer to design The Resort at Cortez for the worst of reasons. To hurt the woman who'd hurt him. To screw with the brother who had been the focal point of so much shit in his life. Who'd tugged hard and unraveled the threads of his life. Pulling his father away. Ripping his family apart.

Now, the woman meant the world to him, and he would enthusiastically destroy anyone who hurt her.

Now, the job was his passion, a project that was already fully formed in his mind, and that he would fight to keep, because no one else in the world could bring to life the resort that lived now only in his imagination and sketches.

And as for the brother, nothing much had changed. Once again, it was Damien Stark who had the power. Who could, in one quick violent motion, tear the world out from under Jackson's feet.

All because he wanted a job.

All because he loved a woman.

All because in addition to controlling so much of the known fucking universe, Damien Stark controlled Jackson's world as well.

And what Jackson feared tonight was that when Damien knew the truth that had been kept from him for over thirty years, that Damien would wield his power like a blunt instrument.

But Jackson was a fighter, and if it came down to brother against brother, he'd do whatever was necessary to be the man left standing.

J. KENNER (aka Julie Kenner) is the *New York Times, USA Today, Publishers Weekly, Wall Street Journal,* and #1 international bestselling author of over seventy novels, novellas, and short stories in a variety of genres.

Though known primarily for her award-winning and international bestselling erotic romances (including the Stark and Most Wanted series) that have reached as high as #2 on the *New York Times* bestseller list, Kenner has been writing full-time for over a decade in a variety of genres including paranormal and contemporary romance, "chicklit" suspense, urban fantasy, and paranormal mommy lit.

Kenner has been praised by *Publishers Weekly* as an author with a "flair for dialogue and eccentric characterizations" and by *RT Book Reviews* for having "cornered the market on sinfully attractive, dominant antiheroes and the women who swoon for him." A four-time finalist for Romance Writers of America's prestigious RITA award, Kenner took home the first RITA trophy awarded in the category of erotic romance in 2014 for her novel, *Claim Me* (book 2 of her Stark Trilogy).

Her books have sold well over a million copies and are published in over twenty countries.

jkenner.com

Facebook.com/jkennerbooks

@juliekenner.com.